the Secrets
of the Tea
Garden

ALSO BY JANET MACLEOD TROTTER

The India Tea Series

HISTORICAL

In the Far Pashmina Mountains

The Jarrow Trilogy

The Jarrow Lass

Child of Jarrow

Return to Jarrow

The Durham Trilogy

The Hungry Hills

The Darkening Skies

Never Stand Alone

The Tyneside Sagas

A Handful of Stars

Chasing the Dream

For Love & Glory

The Great War Sagas

No Greater Love (formerly *The Suffragette*)

A Crimson Dawn

Scottish Historical Romance

The Jacobite Lass

The Beltane Fires

Highlander in Muscovy

MYSTERY/CRIME

The Vanishing of Ruth

The Haunting of Kulah

TEENAGE

Love Games

NON-FICTION

Beatles & Chiefs

the Secrets
of the Tea
Garden

JANET MACLEOD TROTTER

LAKE UNION
PUBLISHING

Published by Lake Union, Seattle

www.apub.com

Amazon, the Amazon logo, and Lake Union are trademarks of Amazon.com, Inc., or its affiliates.

ISBN-13: 9781503903135
ISBN-10: 1503903133

Cover design by Lisa Horton

Cover photography by Richard Jenkins Photography

Printed in the United States of America

This novel is dedicated to the people of the Indian Subcontinent who lived through the events of 1947. As a descendent of the British in India, I wish to say a heartfelt sorry that India was partitioned.

Also in memory of my grandfather, Robert Maclagan Gorrie.

PROLOGUE

Oxford Tea Gardens, Assam, 1899

Through the open office door, James Robson saw the *chaprassy* running barefoot up the dusty path. James's heart sank. It would no doubt be another summons to Dunsapie Cottage to see his boss, Logan.

'From Logan sahib,' said the perspiring messenger, holding out a chit.

Cursing under his breath, James took it. The *chaprassy* stood, panting after a run in the heat, waiting to carry back a reply.

'Tell the burra sahib I'll come now,' James told him with a wave of his hand. The messenger bowed and ran off.

Sighing, James turned to the bespectacled young clerk. 'We'll have to finish going over these figures later. Have them ready for me in an hour.'

Anant Ram nodded. James took a deep breath, jammed on his sola topee over his dark wiry hair and strode out of the garden office. The late afternoon heat hit him and he was momentarily dazzled by the whitewashed walls of the adjacent factory buildings. Beyond the neat lawns in front of the office, shimmering emerald-green tea bushes rolled away to a hazy horizon. He dismissed the idea of heading off to check on the withering of the latest batch of tea leaves. This was Logan's third demand for him to appear at his bungalow that week. His senior manager was not a patient man, and James had been avoiding him since Logan's return from leave a week ago.

How pleasant the past six months had been without the hard-drinking, womanising Scot. James had enjoyed his fourth cold season in Assam, with hunting trips and fishing, as well as the Christmas week of horse racing and socialising at the club, without Logan's sarcastic comments and boorish behaviour. James was not a big drinker but liked to talk sport with his fellow trainee managers on the Oxford tea planta-tion, especially the amiable Reggie Percy-Barratt. Reggie was equally passionate about dogs and hunting, and although they lived an hour's ride apart, he was James's nearest neighbour.

James's stomach clenched as he rode the few minutes to Logan's home. Now the ribald comments would start again: Logan would bait James, challenging him to take advantage of the female tea pickers and join in drinking games at the club. Well, he would not be bullied into doing anything he did not want to do. He might be barely twenty-two but he was a Robson and he'd stand up to anyone.

Yet, as he dismounted at the steps of Dunsapie Cottage – a modest bungalow for such a senior manager, with a deep veranda and a red tin roof – James's heart hammered. His shirt stuck to his back with sweat. Taking a deep breath, he pulled back his broad shoulders, stuck out his chest and mounted the steps.

'Ah, Robson, at last!' a voice called out from the shadowed veranda. Bill Logan, a lean, good-looking man in his early forties, was sprawled in a long cane chair. He didn't stand up.

'Sir,' James answered with a nod. 'Welcome back.'

'Sit down,' Logan ordered. He snapped his fingers at a hovering servant. 'Whisky and soda for the sahib.'

'I have work still to do,' James said. 'Perhaps just a *nimbu pani*—'

'Nonsense.' Logan cut him off. 'This is a celebration. Your father would be ashamed at your lack of stamina. Work hard, play harder. That's what James Robson Senior always told me.'

James masked his irritation. For all of his young life James had been in awe of his father and he knew he would never be as good a tea planter or businessman. But he resented Logan continually pointing out how he failed to be as formidable a character as his father.

'Just a small one then,' James said, forcing a smile.

What was there to celebrate? he wondered. He was bracing himself for a barrage of criticism but perhaps Logan had returned in better humour after his furlough in Scotland. Was his boss about to promote him? Word must have got back to him about how hard James was applying himself to his duties around the vast tea garden.

The Oxford Estates was one of the biggest tea plantations south of the Brahmaputra River, with a board of directors in Newcastle, England, and a reputation for full-bodied teas in the auction houses of London and Calcutta. James was ambitious and impatient; it was high time he was made an assistant manager. He put in twice the time and effort of the other trainees and his health was more robust. Reggie was far more prone to fever than he was and young Bradley had to take days off at a time because of his splitting headaches.

James sat gripping his glass and waited for the good news.

'I'm engaged to be married,' Logan announced, his thin moustachioed face breaking into a smug smile.

James gaped. This he had not expected. Logan was a confirmed bachelor who satisfied his sexual urges by helping himself to the young women from the tea pickers' 'lines' – the native compound. As far as James knew Logan had never courted any woman from the European community in India. In fact, he was the subject of gossip among women at the club for siring a bastard son by his favourite native mistress and shamelessly allowing them to live in his compound. James, embarrassed by the treatment of the young tea picker, tried to avoid being drawn into such scandalous conversations.

'C-congratulations, sir,' James stuttered. 'That's marvellous news.'

'Aye, isn't it? She's quite a beauty – fair looks, of course – and only twenty-one.'

Logan snapped his fingers again and told the servant to hurry and bring a photograph from the sitting room.

'She's very excited at the thought of being Mrs Logan and coming out to India.' Logan's smile turned into a grin of self-satisfaction. 'And who can blame her?' He gave an expansive wave of his hand. 'She will be mistress of all this, with a houseful of servants and a life of leisure away from the strictures of her overbearing sister in Edinburgh. Her only duties will be to me.'

James took a swig of his drink, buying a little time to control his reaction. This was hardly a palace Logan offered his poor bride: the furniture was basic and the roof leaked in the monsoon. But as far as James was concerned, the one big advantage of Logan being married was that he would stop causing trouble among the tea pickers. With a Mrs Logan at Dunsapie Cottage the bullying manager would no longer be able to order women from the lines into his bed.

As if reading his mind, Logan gave a short laugh. 'Aye, Robson, my days of "plucking" the tea workers are numbered. By December I shall be married to the delightful Jessie Anderson.' He handed James the photograph in the ivory frame the servant had fetched. 'Look at her.'

James hid his surprise. The young woman *was* beautiful. Shapely in a summer dress and with pale hair pinned up in loose coils, she stared back at him with a steady, half-amused gaze. James felt his heartbeat quicken. He swiftly handed back the photograph with a nod of appreciation. Privately he felt pity for her, marrying such an odious man.

'Miss Anderson wants to be married in the Himalayas – she loves the snow – so I've suggested Murree in the Punjab.'

'Would Darjeeling not be closer?' James suggested.

'Aye, it would, but Jessie's wretched older sister is insisting on travelling out with her and seeing her wed. I'm not letting the witch anywhere near the Oxford. Amy Anderson is one of these unnatural women who talk about politics and think lassies should earn their own keep. A bad influence on Jessie. No, Murree will suit us well. Besides, they have some church connection there. A week or so in the hills and then I'll despatch Amy Anderson back to Bombay and bring Jessie here to the Oxford.'

'I'm very pleased for you, sir.' James knocked back his drink, keen to be gone. 'Is there any business you wish to discuss before I go?'

Logan seemed nonplussed by the sudden change of subject. 'Business?'

'I must get back to the factory . . .'

'Ah yes, there is a matter of business I want you to attend to.'

Logan drained off his large whisky, went to the balustrade and bawled out, 'Come here, Brat!'

Moments later, a squeal from the direction of the servants' compound was followed by the scamper of feet and a small boy came bowling round the corner pursued by a native woman who was trying to catch him.

Logan's mistress and child. The boy scrambled up the steps and reached Logan before his mother could scoop him to her. He flung himself at the manager's knees with a giggle of delight. Logan ruffled his pale-brown hair.

'Little scamp!'

James slid the tea picker an embarrassed glance but the girl had pulled her shawl over her head and was staring at the floor.

'Go to your mother,' Logan told the boy, pushing him off his legs. 'Aruna, take the Brat.'

Aruna snatched at her son. The three-year-old squealed in protest but she held on firmly and soothed him with quiet words.

Logan turned to James. 'Do you like children, Robson?'

James shrugged. 'Not particularly.'

'Pity,' said Logan. 'I was hoping you would take on the Brat.'

James gaped at him in disbelief.

'Well, I can hardly keep him,' said his boss, 'when I'm to be a married man. How on earth would I explain him to Miss Anderson?' He flicked a look at the girl and child. 'I'll make you a gift of Aruna, though. Someone to keep your bed warm up at Cheviot View. She is very biddable.' He clapped his hands. 'Aruna, show your face to Robson sahib!'

James watched, appalled, as Logan stepped forward and pulled the veil from her head. James had never taken much notice of her looks – she had the round, rosy-cheeked face of a hillswoman – and she stared up at him now with fierce, tear-filled brown eyes. James felt a wave of revulsion at his superior's suggestion that he should take this hapless woman as his own plaything.

'I'm sure you are joking, sir,' James said, keen to defuse the situation as quickly as possible and spare this woman's dignity. 'I couldn't possibly take this woman or her boy into my household. She's a tea worker. It would cause resentment among my own servants.'

'What a prig you are, Robson,' Logan scoffed. 'Your father was far more full-blooded.'

James kept his temper. 'I'm sure she would be much happier going back to live in the lines with her own kind.'

James did not know if the girl understood his words; she looked at each of them anxiously. The grey-eyed boy watched with interest, his thumb jammed in his mouth. James squirmed. He wished to be anywhere but here. Why had his boss chosen him and not Reggie or Bradley? Then it struck James that Logan disliked him more because he was the son of the great James Robson Senior, whom everyone on the Oxford plantations and beyond admired. Even though James's father was now back in England, Logan could not contain his jealousy and spitefulness.

James waited tensely while the older man considered his words.

'Well, if you won't have her, Robson,' Logan said, 'Aruna must go back to the lines.'

James was overcome with unexpected relief. Aruna would be safer back in the workers' compound and away from his boss.

'You will take her there at once,' ordered Logan.

'Now, sir?' James asked in surprise.

'Yes, now.' Logan gave him a steely look, the bonhomie of moments before vanished. 'And then you will get rid of the Brat.'

James thought he must have misheard. 'G-get rid of?'

'Aye, you heard me,' snapped Logan. 'I can't have a bastard half-half growing up under my nose or that of my young wife.'

James winced. 'Miss Anderson is hardly going to know—'

'You know fine well how tongues wag at the club,' Logan interrupted. 'Some busybody will tell her. Besides, I don't want him growing up here. If you won't have him up at Cheviot View, then you must take him to an orphanage or some such place where they look after his kind.'

'But he's not an orphan,' James gasped. 'He has a mother and—'

'That's an order!' Logan barked. 'If you defy me on this, I can make your life hell at the Oxford.'

James was shaken. His callous boss was threatening his very future at the Oxford tea gardens – and all because of a wretched tea picker and her half-breed son. He felt suddenly furious. If Logan had shown some restraint – gone horse riding more often like the rest of the bachelors did instead of indulging base passions – then this situation would never have arisen. Logan was quick to condemn others for transgressing; he had made sure a tea planter from a small garden in the hills at Belgooree, Jock Belhaven, and his half-Indian wife along with their Eurasian daughters had been ostracised at the club.

James was on the point of refusing when Logan part-relented.

'Listen, Robson. I'm thinking only of Miss Anderson's sensibilities. You're a decent young man; you wouldn't want to see the burra memsahib embarrassed or put in an intolerable situation, would you? You can see what a sweet, innocent thing she is even from her photo.'

He held James's look. 'Do this for me, and I'll make sure that you're recommended as assistant manager at the next board meeting.'

James bit back his mutinous retort. With his stomach curdling with disgust, he nodded and turned away. Chivvying the perplexed Aruna, who still clutched her child, James led them away from Dunsapie Cottage.

Aruna appeared to accept her fate without complaint; she moved back to the lines and continued with her work in the tea gardens. Sunil Ram, the old *punkah-wallah* from Dunsapie Cottage, visited with titbits of food for her and the boy. James knew this because he found him there one morning when he came to take the boy away. Above the rows of crude huts, the air was thick with the smoke from open fires and the smell of cooking.

'Brat' was squatting next to Sunil Ram, laughing as the old man shared out a chapatti. Seeing the young manager, Aruna scrambled towards the child and held him close. James flinched at the defiance in her dark eyes, the fierceness of a mother's love. His resolve failed and he walked on.

James put off doing anything about the boy, hoping that Logan would drop the matter and allow his son to grow up among the tea pickers. But one day, the boy found his way back to Dunsapie Cottage in search of his father. Logan summoned James.

'This mustn't happen again, Robson. Take a couple of days' leave immediately and go to Shillong. The orphanage will be the best thing for the Brat. He'll have an education and a Christian upbringing. A better life than here. That's what I want for him. Do I make myself clear?'

James thought the man contemptible. Logan was now trying to justify his decision to cast out his son by pretending to have Christian sensibilities. The hypocrite! James looked around for the boy. He was sitting on the veranda beside Sunil Ram, helping the old man pull on the rope that worked the *punkah*. James called to him.

'Come, boy, *jaldi*! Would you like a ride on a horse?' James made horse noises and riding gestures.

'Brat' came willingly, with a toothy grin.

Word must have spread quickly around the tea workers, for James had barely had time to arrange a horse and trap and his bearer, Aslam, to arrive with provisions for the journey, when Aruna tore into the factory compound. At the sight of her son perched up beside Aslam, she flung herself forward and tried to grab the boy. 'Brat' laughed, thinking it a game. But Aruna yelled and clutched at his leg. He started to whimper.

'He must come with me,' James said in Hindustani. She didn't appear to understand. James had no idea what tribal language she spoke. He flicked the reins.

'Out of the way!' James ordered. 'Get her out of the way before she gets trampled.'

Men from the factory swiftly intervened to pull Aruna back. Her wails of distress pierced the air and sent a flock of parrots screeching out of the trees.

'I'm sorry,' James called over his shoulder. But his words were drowned out by Aruna's screams and the boy's crying. Aslam held tightly to the bewildered child, trying to calm him.

James quickened the pace of his horse. They picked up speed, dust rising in a choking cloud around them. The boy kept calling out for his mother till James shouted at him to be quiet. 'Brat' burst into floods of tears as Aslam cuddled the distraught boy. James ground his teeth. He could still hear the mother's weeping from miles away. But he knew it could only be in his head.

James had not been to Shillong since the earthquake two years previously. A whole hillside of buildings appeared to have vanished; the native bazaar was reduced to a patchwork of makeshift stalls and huts cobbled together out of salvaged wood and tarpaulin. The government and military buildings had fared better – or had been rebuilt more swiftly.

He had to ask the way to the orphanage, only to discover there were two: one run by Catholic nuns and the other by Baptist Missionaries. On a whim he chose the nuns. They would be kind to the boy, surely?

The young sister who came to the gateway looked Eurasian. She eyed James with suspicion as he stammered out his flimsy story. Her look told him she thought the child was his.

'D-dead, I'm afraid. Both parents,' James lied. 'They would have wanted him to come to a good Christian home like this, Sister.'

She took a look at the boy sucking hard on his thumb standing before her. Aslam held on to his other hand. Even to James's eyes the child looked exhausted and miserable. After a moment's hesitation, she ushered them inside the compound.

'We can't stay,' James said in a panic. 'We just wish to leave the boy in good hands and go.'

The look of rebuke on the nun's face made James squirm with shame. 'We can't send you away without any refreshment,' she replied. 'Your servant too. I'm Sister Placid.'

Reluctantly, James followed the nun indoors, beckoning Aslam to follow with the boy. Sister Placid showed them into a gloomy hallway. She left James with the boy and took Aslam with her to the kitchen. The wait seemed interminable. 'Brat' was uncharacteristically silent. James wanted to say something encouraging but was stuck for words too. He couldn't rid his mind of Aruna's distraught weeping and cursed himself for allowing Logan to manipulate him into helping in his sordid affair.

Sister Placid returned with Aslam, carrying two glasses of mango juice on a tray. James took one. She beckoned to the boy to sit on a stool beside her while she helped him sip his drink.

'What is your name, little one?' she asked, her voice kind.

He sat staring warily up at her. She turned back to James.

'What is his name and what native language does he speak?' she asked.

James did not know the answer to either question. He could hardly admit he was known derogatorily as 'Brat'. He searched for a suitable Catholic name to please her. A local saint from his home county in Britain sprang to mind: St Aidan of Lindisfarne.

'Aidan,' he said. 'The boy is called Aidan and he understands English. That's all I know about him. He was brought to our plantation.'

'He is a Britisher.' She said it more as a statement than a question.

'I-I believe his father was Scots,' James admitted, then cursed himself for saying so. Before she could ask him anything more, he drained off his drink and put down the glass. 'I really must be off.'

'But you must speak to Mother Superior about leaving the boy.'

'I'm sorry, I can't delay.' James searched his pockets and pulled out all the cash that he had and handed it over. 'This is a donation to the convent.'

'Thank you, Mr Robson,' said the nun, her look steely.

James flushed at her use of his name. The wretched woman must have been questioning Aslam. What else had his bearer let slip? He put his hand briefly on the boy's head.

'Now, Aidan. Be a good chap and do whatever Sister asks.'

Aslam said something encouraging in another language, perhaps Assamese. The boy's eyes filled with tears but he stayed mute.

James turned quickly away. 'Come on,' he hissed at Aslam and strode back through the convent entrance. They marched through the gate, and the *chowkidar* locked it behind them.

Climbing once again into the trap, James glanced back at the orphanage but the steps were empty. Nun and boy had not come to the door to watch them go. James's insides were leaden as he whipped the pony into a trot. He waited for the surge of relief to come, but it never did.

CHAPTER 1

Herbert's Café, Newcastle, England, August 1946

Libby Robson, hearing a man call out her name, turned around. She nearly dropped her tray of dirty tea cups in astonishment. George Brewis!

'Well, well, Miss Robson,' George said with a whistle of appreciation, 'you've grown into a beauty.'

Libby laughed, her fair face turning puce at his admiring look. 'And you are still a shameless flatterer, George Brewis!'

'Not a word of a lie.' He grinned. 'You look grand.'

Libby knew she must look sweaty and dishevelled. It was late afternoon on a hot Saturday and the tearoom was airless even though it was now empty and they were about to close for the day. The tray felt slippery in her hands. If she'd known he was going to appear out of the blue she would have worn a frock instead of slacks under the old-fashioned apron, put on some lipstick and brushed out her dark-red hair instead of tying it back with a rubber band.

George was looking in rude good health, his fair face ruddy – perhaps a little wrinkled around the eyes – and his blond hair and moustache well trimmed. She remembered her girlish crush on him; it engulfed her anew.

Libby found her voice again. 'I thought you were in Calcutta these days, working for Strachan's?'

He raised an eyebrow. 'You're well informed.'

'Cousin Adela writes regularly.'

'Aye, well, she's the one told me you were helping out here. Family are really grateful at you lending Lexy a hand on your days off.'

'I don't mind; there isn't much else to do on a Saturday.'

'Well, the lads round here must be slow off the mark,' he said with a wink.

Libby's insides fluttered. Surely he hadn't come deliberately to see her? She felt ridiculously pleased. She had idolised George for years.

'Are you back from India for long?' she asked, trying to sound nonchalant though her heart was racing.

'No, just long enough to settle some family business.'

Libby felt a kick of disappointment. She hadn't seen George for three years – since he'd been in the Fleet Air Arm – but she'd thought of him often. Libby had been smitten with George ever since she had met him at a Christmas party at Herbert's Café during the War and he had showered her with attention and compliments. She had been a gauche fifteen-year-old, and George had been twelve years her senior, but he had lifted everyone's spirits with his boisterous singing and happy-go-lucky nature. The tea salesman had been kind to Libby and encouraged her to sing along with him. At eighteen, Libby had been heartbroken when he had enlisted, then swiftly married a barmaid called Joan and fathered a child.

Yet Libby had heard his marriage was in difficulty. Before she could stop herself, she was asking, 'Is Joan going to join you in India this time?'

'No.' He gave her a direct look. 'My wife's got another lad on the go. I'm back home to finalise a divorce.'

'Oh, I see. I'm sorry.'

'Don't be. We've never really had a married life – with me being away east in the Fleet Air Arm and she . . . Well, let's say we both want different lives now.'

Just then, Lexy, the manageress, came lumbering out of the kitchen, wheezing. She gave a breathless shriek. 'If it isn't my favourite lad! How are you, George, hinny?'

'Couldn't leave Newcastle without a visit to Herbert's and all my favourite lasses,' said George, giving her a peck on the cheek.

Lexy's puffy, heavily made-up face cracked into a smile of delight. 'You'll stay for a piece of cake?' she panted. 'I want to hear all your news.' She put a hand on her chest.

'Sit down, Lexy,' Libby ordered. 'I'll get George some tea while you have a chat.'

Lexy sank gratefully into a chair, waving at George to join her. Libby left them talking and hurried into the kitchen, plonking down the tray and wiping her brow with her long frilly apron. She had no idea why Lexy insisted they still wore the cumbersome things. Perhaps it reminded her of the café's heyday when she was young and in good health, not a woman in her sixties with a bad chest who struggled to walk.

Doreen, Lexy's rosy-cheeked, curly-haired grand-niece, was washing up. 'You look in a fluster. Clark Gable walked in, has he?'

Libby laughed. 'Next best thing: George Brewis in a white linen suit and smelling of cologne.'

'Brewis? He related to the lass Jane who used to work here?'

'Yes, they're brother and sister. It's their Aunt Clarrie who started the café.'

'Oh, aye, the one that's been in India for years. Auntie Lexy talks about Clarrie Robson like she's royalty. Pity she's never come back – this place might not be going to rack and ruin if she'd stayed.'

'That's not really Clarrie's fault,' said Libby, unloading the cups for Doreen to wash. 'She's got her hands full running the tea garden at Belgooree. Her sister, Olive Brewis – she's George's mother – was supposed to take on running the café but she's never been interested.'

'Aye,' said Doreen, 'Mrs Brewis is that queer fish that never gans out her house, isn't she?'

'Apparently not.' Libby started to re-set the tray, glancing in at the tearoom. George was making Lexy laugh so much she was coughing.

'Libby, are you ganin' to give me another typing lesson this weekend?' Doreen asked, clattering the dishes in the sink.

Libby hesitated. What would George be doing? He'd implied to Lexy that he was about to leave Newcastle but perhaps there might be a chance to see him again before he did? She longed for a bit of excitement in her life. The past year had been so dull, living back at home with her mother. Was it wrong to miss the War? She had never had so much fun as when she'd worked as a Land Girl.

'Can we leave it till next week?' Libby suggested. 'I'll come after I've finished at the bank. Maybe Tuesday?'

'Grand.' Doreen's hot, round face beamed. 'I'm ganin' to work in a typing pool like you one day. I'm not settling for a life o' washing dishes.'

'Good for you,' Libby said with a smile. 'You can do anything if you want it enough.'

Libby thought how she couldn't wait to get out of the typing pool; at twenty-one, she wanted more from life than being at the beck and call of male managers with less brains than she had.

Pushing strands of escaping hair behind her ears and licking her plump, dry lips, Libby picked up the tea tray and sauntered back into the tearoom.

Libby could hardly get a word in edgeways with Lexy holding forth, reminiscing about the old days before the Great War when Clarrie had made Herbert's into the best tearoom in Newcastle, despite it being in an industrial working-class area close to the riverside.

'And Olive did them bonny paintings to hang on the walls and made it all look Egyptian-like. Eeh, they were canny days. Your mam not doing any painting now, George?'

'I've never seen her pick up a paintbrush since I was a bairn,' said George ruefully.

'Libby here is a canny artist,' said Lexy.

'I draw cartoons.' Libby blushed. 'I'm not an artist.'

'Look at that one, George,' Lexy said, pointing to an ink drawing on the wall next to them. 'That's me and the waitresses at the Victory Tea – dressed up like royalty with crowns on our heads – makes me laugh, it does.'

George grinned. 'Queen Lexy – caught your image perfectly. What a talented lass you are, Libby.'

Libby flushed with pleasure at the compliment and the warmth of his look. George winked at her then turned back to Lexy. 'I wish Mam still showed an interest in art or in anything outside the house. The only thing that brings a smile to her face is my daughter Bonnie.'

'Aye,' Lexy answered wheezily, 'at least she has a grandbairn. Will you be taking the lass with you to India?'

George shook his head. 'She'll be staying with her mam, Joan.' He drained his tea and stood up.

Libby felt frustrated at not having more time with him. She cursed herself for being so bashful in his presence. She felt like that fifteen-year-old all over again. As George fixed on his hat, Libby took courage and blurted out, 'Would you like to come round and see Mother? And my younger brother, Mungo, is at home for the summer. Do you remember playing the spoons with him one Christmas?'

'The spoons?' George laughed. 'Did we?'

Libby remembered the occasion so vividly that she was amazed George didn't. Perhaps he saw the disappointment in her look because on the spur of the moment he said, 'Would you like to go for a drink after work?'

Libby's dark-blue eyes widened. 'Yes, I would.'

'Good.' He grinned.

'Why don't you get yourself off now, hinny?' Lexy said. 'Me and Doreen can finish the dishes. There's no one else coming in.'

Libby hesitated, seeing how exhausted Lexy looked in the heat. The woman was too old and ill to be running the café. Libby would have to write to her cousin Adela about her. Even though they were far away in India, Adela or her mother Clarrie would have to take things in hand or the café would close.

'No, you get yourself upstairs for a lie-down, Lexy. It won't take me long to help Doreen,' said Libby. She turned to George. 'Fancy rolling up your sleeves too? Then we'll get out for that drink quicker.'

For a moment he seemed taken aback. Then he threw back his head and laughed – how she loved his infectious laughter – and started taking off his jacket.

'Just cos it's you, Libby Robson,' said George. 'This would never happen in Calcutta.'

Lexy rolled her eyes. 'She's a true Robson through and through,' she chuckled. 'That lass can get anyone to do anything.'

'I bet she can,' George agreed, gazing intently at Libby.

※

Doreen lent Libby a dress to wear to save her having to go home to South Gosforth to change. In the flat above the café which Doreen shared with Lexy, Libby squeezed into the flowery frock. The short sleeves pinched her fleshier arms and Doreen pinned the front folds of the dress together with a brooch.

'Stop your bosom falling out,' the girl giggled. 'Your hips fill the skirt nicely, mind. Wish I had a figure like yours.'

'Thanks, Doreen,' Libby said. 'You're much more diplomatic than Mother; she calls me "hefty". Says I eat too many of Lexy's pies.'

'Well, I wish I was your shape. Always turning the lads' heads, you are.'

'Don't be daft!' Libby laughed, incredulous.

'It's true. That George Brewis can't keep his eyes off you.'

'Stop it,' Libby spluttered. 'He's just being polite to an old family friend, that's all.'

But Libby's hand trembled as she brushed out her wavy hair and applied red lipstick that accentuated the fullness of her mouth. As she descended to the café and the waiting George, she tried to calm her rapid breathing and hoped the thumping of her heart didn't show.

George and Libby strolled through the park, walking close without touching, while they caught up on each other's lives. Libby talked animatedly about her time with the Land Army on a farm in Northumberland; how her older brother, Jamie, was now a qualified doctor and younger brother, Mungo, was at university in Durham.

'My brothers are happy – and Mother's happy being near them – but this isn't the life I want.'

'What do you want?' George asked, taking her elbow to steer her towards a bench.

Libby gave a sigh of frustration. 'The War's been over for a year. I thought by now we'd have gone back out to Assam to be with Dad. Or at the very least he'd take some leave and come to see us. But nothing's happening. I want us to be a family again. But Mother keeps making excuses not to go. It's as if she doesn't want to see Dad at all.'

'It must be hard for you not seeing your father all this time,' George said in sympathy. 'How long has it been?'

Libby's eyes smarted with emotion. 'Eleven years.' Every time she thought of her father she felt an ache of longing. He was larger than life; a big man with a booming voice and laugh, whom she had adored as a child. 'I miss him so much.' She looked at George. 'Have you seen him since you've been in India?'

George shook his head. 'I haven't been to Assam yet, but I'm hoping to get up there soon.' He slipped his hand over hers and gave it a squeeze, making her pulse quicken. 'And if I do, I'll be sure to tell James Robson that the prettiest lass in Newcastle is longing to see him.'

'Thanks.' Libby smiled, looking into his blue eyes. 'I'm sorry, I've been talking ten to the dozen and not letting you say a word about yourself.'

The way George was regarding her made her tingle. Abruptly, he pulled her to her feet and linked her arm through his. 'Come on, bonny lass; let's go for that drink, eh?'

***

Later, after two cocktails, George began to talk about his infant daughter, Bonnie.

'She's not mine, you know.'

Libby felt a jolt of shock. She had known the marriage to blonde Joan had been hasty and the baby had followed shortly afterwards, but during wartime such transgressions had been commonplace.

'Oh?' Libby didn't know how to answer.

'Joan had an affair with a naval officer while I was away. I only married her out of pity – didn't seem fair on the kiddie to be left without a father, did it?'

'That was very gallant of you.'

George shrugged and gave his disarming smile. 'I'm a soft touch when it comes to the lasses.'

'Won't you miss her?' Libby had asked.

20

'What, Joan?'

'No, your daughter, Bonnie.'

Fleetingly, George looked regretful. 'I've never really got to know the lass – and I'm just a stranger to her. Anyway,' he said, regaining his bravado, 'Joan's planning to marry the man she's courting now so Bonnie will have a new dad. He seems a canny lad. He's head groom at some posh house up the Tyne valley. I wish them luck.'

After that, they made no more mention of Joan or Bonnie. They talked about trivial matters and swapped anecdotes about the War. He had her helpless with laughter describing his fellow crewmen and their escapades, and he seemed equally amused by her stories of being a Land Girl. He made her feel as if no one else in the room mattered. George took her on to a dance hall and they moved among the crush of dancers, Libby thrilling at George holding her close and intoxicated by the musky scent on his smooth chin. She could hardly believe her luck that George had come back into her life so unexpectedly. It had been too long since she had had such fun or been treated like a grown woman.

Living back at home, her mother Tilly made her feel juvenile, constantly fussing and criticising. It was as if the two years in the Land Army – living independently and working hard – had never been. Earlier that evening, she had rung to let her mother know she would be late home and luckily her brother Mungo had answered the telephone. She knew her mother would interrogate her with endless questions about where she had been and what George's marital status was, but she didn't care. This evening was worth it and she didn't want it to end.

Just before midnight, George walked her home, arm in arm.

On the doorstep he disengaged and said, 'I wish you well, lass.'

Libby's insides tightened. She felt sudden panic that this magical evening was over. 'Will I see you before you go?'

He hesitated. 'I'll call round if I can.' He gave her a broad smile and touched her hot cheek. 'Maybe we could meet up in Calcutta – if you get back to Assam one day.'

'Yes, I'd like that.' Libby brightened.

'Then promise me, you will look me up.' George fished out a calling card with his details on. 'I'll show you a good time.' Leaning forward, he planted a kiss on her cheek.

Libby, heady from dancing and unaccustomed alcohol, gave a gurgle of laughter. 'George, I'm not your sister.'

Grinning in surprise, George pulled her towards him and kissed her firmly on the lips. Libby's heart thudded with excitement. She slipped her hands around his neck and kissed him back with enthusiasm. Too quickly he pulled away.

'Come to Calcutta, bonny lass,' he said, stepping back. 'We'll have some more fun.' Then he was strolling off into the night, whistling and leaving Libby craving another embrace.

Libby hardly slept that night. It was hot in the small back bedroom but she preferred sleeping there than having to share a larger bedroom with their lodger and friend, Josey, who chain-smoked and snored. Her thoughts whirled round and round.

What had the evening with George meant? Had he really come to seek her out or had it just been good luck that she had been in the café that day? Maybe he had just asked her out on the spur of the moment, but he seemed to enjoy being with her. It had been his suggestion that they extend the evening by going to the dance hall. Just being with him made her feel fully alive and desired. But George was known for being a ladies' man so she should be cautious. He was just being friendly. Yet that kiss . . . How she wished it could have gone on longer. It was like licking delicious ice cream and then having it snatched away. He must have meant something by that kiss. It made her insides melt to think of it.

Libby threw off the bed covers and lay naked and perspiring in the stuffy room. She remembered India being as hot as this. But in her childhood bedroom at Cheviot View an electric fan on the high ceiling had stirred the soupy air. She remembered how her mother had insisted on the fans being installed.

'James, the punkah-wallahs *are useless, they fall asleep on the job. We'll all die in this heat.'* As the long-ago words came back to Libby, she felt a rush of homesickness for Assam. She had never fully felt at home anywhere else – boarding school, Newcastle, the farm at Walton – none of them had been anything but temporary in her mind. So often, in her icy school dormitory, Libby had lulled herself to sleep with the memory of riding with her father through the jungle while he sang lustily about British Grenadiers, barking encouragement at her to keep her heels down. Everything about India had been more vivid and exciting than anything she had experienced since. She must redouble her efforts to persuade her mother to return there.

Libby resented the way her mother kept blaming her father for not taking leave and coming to England to see them. As Libby continually pointed out, it was much more difficult for her father to leave his job on the tea plantation than it was for Tilly to give up her charity work. Yet Libby was also secretly disappointed that her father hadn't taken any leave; surely he wanted to see her again as keenly as she wanted to see him? He had worked so hard during the War to keep the Oxford Estates going, he was more than due a break. It was so typical of her father not to do so but to carry on working and shouldering his responsibilities.

Libby flung out her arms with a sigh of frustration. She was just as bad as they were at coming up with excuses. She knew that the main reason stopping her defying her mother and rushing off to India on her own was her concern over Lexy and the café. Warm-hearted Lexy had been a surrogate grandmother to her; Libby had never known any of her grandparents. But more than that, Lexy had been a good friend and confidante to her during her awkward years of growing up. She could tell things to the down-to-earth Tynesider that she would never tell her mother in a million years. She couldn't leave the poor woman to run the tearoom with just Doreen and a couple of part-time waitresses.

Libby not only helped out in her spare time but she did the book-keeping and ordering of supplies, trying to make their rations stretch further. Lexy had told her how Jane Brewis, George's sister, had been a competent manager before war-work had meant her moving to Yorkshire. Jane had never come back, settling and marrying there. Joan, George's estranged wife, had briefly helped out in the last year of the War but Lexy said that Joan had been too unreliable. *'Got her head in the clouds, that one. Thinks she's a cut above the rest of us but she's just a lazy lass.'*

On Libby's return to Newcastle, Lexy had been pathetically grate-ful at her offer of help. Libby knew she would be stuck there unless she forced her cousin Adela and her family to take things in hand. After all, it wasn't Libby's branch of the Robson family who owned the business, it was Adela's. She would definitely write to her cousin and tell her she would have to return to sort out Herbert's. Perhaps it would be best if the café closed, as long as they took care of Lexy's future.

But what if Adela and her husband Sam Jackman were happy in India and making a new life for themselves? Libby would feel guilty at forcing them to return to Newcastle against their wishes. Britain was a drab, war-weary country these days, with rationing worse than ever and families still living in prefabricated temporary huts because of a hous-ing shortage. The situation for the British in India might be growing uncertain with the move towards greater independence for Indians but it was still a country full of opportunities and a good lifestyle – George was proof of that. However, Adela and her mother Clarrie needed to be aware of how run-down their business had become. Lexy shouldn't have to carry the burden alone.

Libby closed her eyes and imagined meeting up with George in Calcutta. They would play tennis at his club and go dancing at one of the big hotels and he would take her in his arms and kiss her again, this time more lingeringly. Libby felt desire flood through her.

Libby's determination returned: she would write to Adela and tell her she must decide whether to come back and save Herbert's or to close it for good. Either way, Libby would then be free to make up her own mind. If her mother refused to go back to Assam and her father refused to come to England, should she, Libby, return on her own to the land of her birth, India?

CHAPTER 2

Newcastle, late January 1947

L ibby banged on the front door of the terraced house in South Gosforth, stamping her boots and shaking snow from the old army jacket a one-time boyfriend had given her. Outside, the air was raw and the pavements still hazardous with frozen piles of blackened snow that wouldn't melt. She was chilled to the bone. Suddenly, she spotted the battered cases filling the narrow hallway. Voices and laughter spilled through the open sitting-room door. Libby's heart skipped a beat. Had Adela and Sam finally come?

'*Koi hai!*' she called, a grin spreading across her pink-cheeked face.

'Speak English, darling!' Tilly, her mother called back. 'We have visitors.'

She could hear the excitement in her mother's voice. Pulling off her woollen hat to release a cascade of dark-red hair, Libby rushed into the sitting room. Her mother and friend Josey were sitting in their usual well-worn armchairs, while sitting close together on the sofa were a pretty, dark-haired young woman and a tanned, thin-faced man.

'Cousin Adela!' Libby screeched and flung herself at the petite woman as she rose to greet her. They hugged and laughed. 'Why didn't you say you were arriving today? I'd have come to the station. How long have you been here? We thought you weren't reaching England for another week, didn't we, Mother?'

'Let the poor girl speak,' Tilly chided.

'Sorry,' Libby said with a deep-throated laugh. 'I'm just so excited to see you.'

'And so are we.' Adela smiled, pushing back her wavy dark hair. 'We took the train from Marseilles to save a few days' sailing.' She turned and beckoned to the man who had stood up the minute Libby had entered the room. He was so tall that his receding fair hair brushed the ceiling lampshade. 'This is my husband, Sam.'

Sam leant across and took Libby's hand in a crushing handshake.

'Very pleased to meet you at last, Libby. You're even prettier than Adela described you.'

Libby laughed with pleasure. 'And I'm honoured to meet the war hero of the Indian Air Force. According to Mother, you chased the Japs out of Burma more or less single-handedly.'

'Oh, you do exaggerate,' Tilly protested. 'I said no such thing. But we are very proud of you, Sam.'

Sam laughed. 'I merely dropped a few supplies behind enemy lines. Others were taking far greater risks.'

'Not true,' said Adela, slipping her arm around his waist and hugging him. 'You risked your life every day for months. I'm just thankful the War's over and I got you back safely.'

Sam kissed the top of her head. 'Me too.'

Libby felt a pang of emotion at their loving gestures. It was obvious how much they adored each other. She couldn't remember a time when her parents had been like that.

'What news of Dad?' Libby asked eagerly. 'Did you see him before you left India? He hasn't written since Christmas. Is he planning on coming over?'

'Stop badgering poor Adela,' Tilly said. 'Your father is fine.'

'How would you know?' Libby said pointedly. 'You haven't seen him since you came back to visit us just before the War – that's over seven years ago.'

Tilly sighed. 'Don't start.'

Adela gave an encouraging smile and said, 'We saw your dad at Christmas. We spent it together at Belgooree with Mother and my brother. James was a bit tired – he still works very hard at the Oxford – but he was in good heart. The fresh hill air was just the tonic he needed.'

Tilly sighed impatiently. 'James has always put work and the Oxford tea plantation before family – even in the early days. He's nearly seventy but he thinks he can do the workload of a forty-year-old.'

Libby felt her insides knot at the mention of her father's age. She didn't want him to grow old. She still imagined him as the vigorous, robust man with the ruddy face and boisterous hugs who had won her devotion in childhood. But she hadn't seen him since she was eleven years old when her parents had last been on leave together in England. She'd been granted an extra week's holiday from boarding school so that the family could go to St Abbs for a chilly winter seaside break. Then world war had come and the family had been forced apart from her father for years on end, with him out in India and them stuck in Britain.

Now she was nearly twenty-two, would her father even recognise her? He had missed her growing up and she had missed his taking her side against the rest of the family. Her two brothers had always ganged up against her with their teasing ways, while her mother was endlessly critical and always favouring the boys. But Libby was sure that she and her father would rekindle their former closeness in no time.

Tilly waved at her guests to sit down again. 'My husband should admit he's an old man. It's time he retired and came back home,' she said bluntly.

'To this?' Libby said in derision, squeezing on to the sofa next to Adela. 'Can you imagine Dad living in a house with no garden and no room for his horses and dogs? He's just not the city type.'

'We could afford to get somewhere larger,' said Tilly, 'if he wasn't running two households thousands of miles apart. I'd love a house in Jesmond – I grew up in that part of the city.'

'But Assam is his home,' Libby insisted. 'It's still *our* home.'

'Nonsense,' said her mother. 'You haven't lived there since you were eight. And your brothers don't miss it.'

'Well, *I* still think of Cheviot View and India as home,' Libby said defiantly.

Tilly tutted with impatience. 'Your father will have to come back sooner or later – now that the British are finally handing over India to the Indians. Isn't that right, Adela?'

Adela sighed. 'The tea planters are talking of nothing else at the moment. Mother is undecided. She'd really like to keep the Belgooree tea garden going so that she can hand it on to my brother Harry in a few years' time. And your husband doesn't see why the British can't stay on indefinitely.'

'James said that?' Tilly exclaimed.

Adela nodded. 'Not the civil servants or the army, of course, but he thinks the Indians will still want the British box-wallahs to help run the plantations and invest money in tea.'

'And full independence might still be several years away,' added Sam.

'See, Mother,' Libby cried. 'Our life in India doesn't need to be over.'

Her mother's plump face looked anxious. 'But, Adela, you and Sam have decided to leave,' Tilly pointed out.

Libby noticed a look pass between Adela and Sam. She felt a sudden stab of guilt that she had forced them to return because of her complaints about the running of Herbert's. Sam put an arm around his wife's shoulders.

'We want to start afresh,' he said. 'The mission I worked for before the War has folded and Adela didn't want to live at Belgooree full-time.'

'I love it on the tea garden,' Adela explained, 'but I'm not like Mother. She lives and breathes tea. I need the bright lights.'

'My sentiment exactly,' said Tilly. 'Clarrie is the most remarkable woman I know. I don't know how she runs Belgooree all by herself.'

'She has good staff and my little brother is turning into quite a useful tea planter for all he's only thirteen,' Adela said. 'And James still comes over quite a lot from the Oxford to help out.'

There was an awkward pause. Libby felt a jolt of alarm and watched her mother for signs of jealousy. Did it not worry Tilly that her husband spent so much time over in the hills at Belgooree with Clarrie Robson? Adela's mother had been cruelly widowed when her husband Wesley had been gored to death in a hunting accident before the outbreak of war. Libby knew from Adela how devoted Clarrie and Wesley had been to each other.

But Clarrie had been on her own now for over eight years and, judging by a recent photograph Adela had sent, Clarrie was still an attractive woman in middle age. Besides, Clarrie was nearer James in age than Tilly was; Libby's mother had been half the age of Libby's father when she'd married him and first gone to India. Libby was uncomfortable with the thought that her father was spending all his free time with the capable Clarrie and not just the Christmas holidays. Libby felt a familiar twist of frustration at Tilly. It was all her mother's fault for delaying her return to India and her husband.

Sam filled the silence. 'I'm hoping to start a photography business here.'

'How interesting!' Josey said quickly. She had been keeping quiet behind a gauze of cigarette smoke. Tilly's friend had a smoker's grey pallor and nicotine-stained fingers but, Libby had to admit, the thirty-eight-year-old still carried off a certain bohemian style with her multi-coloured jumper and hair bound up in a silk scarf. 'I have a contact on one of the local newspapers who might give you some work.'

'Thank you,' Sam said with a wide smile.

'That would be so kind,' said Adela. 'And I promised Mother I'd sort out Herbert's Café. Thank you, Libby, for alerting us that Lexy can't cope any more.'

'I didn't want to worry you but something needs to be done,' Libby said. 'Poor Lexy can hardly walk five steps without having to sit down. Her chest is that wheezy. I've been helping out as much as I can but I've got my boring office job too.'

'Lucky to have a job at all, sweetie,' Josey said, stubbing out her cigarette in a brass ashtray.

'It just takes a bit of effort, Josey,' Libby said with a flash of annoyance in her dark-blue eyes. To her mind, their lodger had made no attempt since the end of the War to get paid employment or contribute to the housekeeping. She lived with them for free and it was she, Libby, who brought in enough to pay for Josey's whisky and cigarettes.

'You're so much better at humdrum office work than me,' said Josey, lighting up a fresh cigarette.

'At any work,' muttered Libby.

'Now you two,' laughed Tilly, 'let's not bicker in front of our guests.'

'Are you still acting at The People's Theatre, Josey?' Adela asked.

'I'm doing more directing these days,' said the older woman.

'We'd love to come and see one of your productions, wouldn't we, Sam?'

'Very much,' Sam agreed. 'I've heard so much about the theatre and I've been looking forward to meeting all the family and Adela's friends.'

'And of course you've got your own mother in Cullercoats, Sam,' said Tilly. 'You'll be longing to see her again after all this time.'

Libby thought she saw Sam wince but he forced a smile. 'My adoptive mother,' he corrected. 'Yes, I intend to visit Mrs Jackman.'

Adela squeezed her husband's hand. 'Sam will do that in his own time. It's so kind of you to let us stay here, Tilly. We're very grateful and we won't overstay our welcome. As soon as we find a place of our own—'

Tilly cut her off. 'You'll stay as long as you want. Libby's already moved up into the attic so you can have the double bed.'

Adela protested. 'We mustn't turf Libby out of her own room!'

'She doesn't mind,' said Tilly. 'And you love birds need it more than she does.'

Libby rolled her eyes at Adela. 'Sorry about Mother. And I'm more than happy for you to have the back bedroom. It's just wonderful to see you again.'

Adela laughed, her green eyes full of merriment. 'It's so good to see you all too. I've missed the Robson banter.'

'And we've missed you more than we can say, dear girl,' said Tilly, her deep-set hazel eyes glistening with sudden tears. 'You've always been like another daughter to me.'

Libby's heart squeezed. Her mother had never hidden her preference for Adela, even though she was not even a blood relation of Tilly's. It was through their Robson fathers – James and Wesley were first cousins – that Libby and Adela were cousins. But Libby had always adored her older cousin; she was not only a glamorous entertainer who had performed for the troops during the War but was warm-hearted and good fun. Libby could never resent Adela, yet it pained her that nothing she, Libby, did had ever seemed to please her mother. Long ago, she had given up trying to win Tilly's approval.

'So did you bring any messages from India?' Libby asked in hope. She squirmed at the look of pity that flitted across Adela's pretty face.

'Your father sends his love,' she said.

'But no letter?'

'He sent tea,' Sam said. 'Didn't he, darling?'

'Yes, of course.' Adela got up.

'Don't worry about that now,' said Tilly. 'I want to hear all about your passage home. Did you throw your sola topees into the sea after Suez?'

Adela laughed, fondly touching Libby's tangled hair before making for the door. 'We did. The sea was littered with them. The boat was jam-packed. We were lucky to get a billet.'

'Everyone bailing out of India,' said Tilly, with a glance at Libby. 'I'm not surprised with all the violence going on.'

Adela dashed into the hallway and came back carrying a large lacquered box which she placed on a low inlaid Indian table.

'I remember that!' Libby grinned. 'Auntie Clarrie kept her letters in it so they didn't go mouldy in the monsoon.'

'Fancy you remembering,' said Adela.

'Of course I do.'

'Darling, you were only a small child when you were last there,' reminded Tilly.

'All my memories of Belgooree are as clear as photographs,' Libby insisted.

'Mother said I could have the box,' said Adela. 'I wanted something to remind me of h-home.'

Libby heard the catch in Adela's throat. She caught Adela's hand, squeezed it in her own and said, 'It's a lovely thing to have.'

Adela's eyes brimmed with tears and Libby realised how difficult leaving India must have been for her cousin, despite Sam's assertion they wanted to start anew in Britain.

Sam stood up swiftly and unlatched the box. 'I'll make us some tea.'

Tilly shrieked. 'Certainly not! You're our guest and a man. Sit down, Sam.'

'I'll make it with him,' said Libby, aware that Sam needed something to do. She could sense the pent-up energy in his lanky frame. He must be approaching forty but, from what she'd heard, he was a man who still relished the outdoors. Before being a pilot, he'd once been a river captain and then become an itinerant missionary, planting orchards in the Himalayan foothills.

While the other women chatted, Libby led Sam to the kitchen at the back of the house. Their cook had left ready a large tray loaded with a tea set and a plate of ginger biscuits. Libby started unloading it.

'This calls for the best china.' She nodded towards a wooden dresser. 'Can you reach up to the top shelf please, Sam?'

While he did so, Libby set about warming the silver teapot and opening up one of the packages. She scooped out black-and-green strands of dried tea.

'This looks nothing like the stuff we're used to drinking,' she said with a wry smile. 'You better get used to rationing.'

'Still?' queried Sam.

'Gosh, yes,' said Libby. 'It's worse than during the War. The Americans are sending us food parcels. I hope for Dad's sake that he can stay on in India. He'd hate it here.'

Sam didn't contradict her. Instead he asked her about herself and her job.

'I did a typing course at the end of the War and now I'm in a typing pool at a bank. I'm better at figures than the bank manager but they'll never have a manageress. It's archaic. So I do my hours and no more. I spend my spare time helping out at Herbert's Café – but you know all about the tearoom Adela's mother used to run?'

Sam nodded. 'So what job would you really like?' he asked.

Libby shrugged. 'I have no idea. I suppose I miss being a Land Girl. It was very hard work but we had a lot of laughs.'

Sam smiled. 'It was like that in the Air Force. You're thrown together with people you might never otherwise meet and you grow close because you're depending on each other. And no one else can ever quite know what you've been through together. It was like that for Adela in ENSA too.' Libby saw his expression soften. 'I know her entertainments troop went through great hardship and danger but she would never admit it. She only ever told me about the funny moments on tour.'

'Yes, that's it,' agreed Libby. 'Life was so important and intense during the War. My friends meant everything at the time. Now it's all a bit dull.'

They finished preparing the tea and Sam insisted on carrying the tray. As they walked back through the hallway, Sam asked, 'Where are your Land Army friends now?'

'Two are married and living down south. One went to America with a G.I. and I haven't heard from her since. And my best friend is a cook in a castle in the Highlands. I can't imagine how she got the job – her cooking was terrible.'

Sam gave a delighted chuckle.

'What are you two laughing about?' Tilly demanded as they re-entered the sitting room. 'Goodness me – the Watsons' best china! My mother loved it but I find the dainty cups so fiddly to handle.'

'Dad's tea will taste better out of them,' said Libby.

'Just pop the tray down here next to me, Sam,' said Tilly. 'I'll do the pouring. Libby, hand round the biscuits. Watch your lovely teeth on them, Adela; Cook tries her best but they're usually as hard as rock.'

Tilly began pouring milk into the cups.

'I'll have mine black please, Mother,' said Libby.

'You never have it black,' said Tilly.

'This is special tea,' she replied. 'I want to savour it just how I remember it.'

Libby watched the golden liquid being poured into the china cups which she helped hand around. She picked up hers and inhaled the steamy scent. The tea smelled of mango and papaya. Libby closed her eyes and sipped. Instantly, the heat and vivid colours of the tea garden were conjured up – not the oppressive monsoon humidity of the Oxford plantation, but the dappled sunshine and flowery creepers of Clarrie's house at Belgooree.

She could hear the raucous birdsong and see the glimmering tea bushes under a canopy of teak trees. In her mind, Clarrie was leaning over the veranda, her skin biscuit-coloured against a white dress, laughing with Libby's mother. So Tilly *had* been happy in India once. Libby tried to hold on to the memory but it evaporated as swiftly as it had been recalled, like the wisp of wood smoke from the plantation bungalow chimney.

'This tastes of Belgooree,' said Libby, opening her eyes and smiling at Adela.

'It does, doesn't it?' Adela agreed, smiling back.

'Sam,' said Josey in a stage whisper, 'do you go all mystical over tea?'

Sam laughed. 'Not really. I must confess I prefer to drink coffee.'

'So do I!' Josey said in delight.

'Do you mind if I smoke?' Sam asked Tilly, even though the air was thick with Josey's smoking.

'Go ahead,' Tilly replied.

Josey offered him a cigarette but Sam fished out a battered packet of Indian bidis. 'Have one of mine.'

'They look illegal,' said Josey.

'Oh, not those horrid things!' cried Tilly. 'They smell awful and you won't like them.'

Josey winked at Sam and took one. A moment later the room was filling with the pungent aroma of their small brown cheroots.

'It reminds me of Cheviot View,' said Libby, inhaling deeply. 'The servants sitting on the veranda after dark, smoking together.'

'Would you like one?' asked Sam.

'Oh, darling, don't!' Tilly exclaimed. 'It's not at all ladylike.'

Libby rolled her eyes and reached towards the proffered cigarette. Sam hesitated, not wanting to cause further friction between mother and daughter.

'What would your father say?' Tilly said in reproof.

Libby's patience snapped. 'I have no idea – and neither do you – seeing as we haven't seen him in years.'

'He wouldn't approve.' Tilly was adamant.

'Perhaps not,' said Libby, 'but you can't speak for him any more. I'm tired of you telling me what Dad would or wouldn't like, as if you even cared.'

'Don't speak to me in that tone,' said Tilly, flushing.

'And don't speak to me as if I'm still a child!'

'Keep your hat on, sweetie,' warned Josey.

'Don't patronise me, Josey,' said Libby, 'this has nothing to do with you.'

'It does if you upset your mother, yet again. And you're embarrassing our guests.'

'Not your guests,' Libby said, eyes flashing, 'they're my family. And Adela's quite used to seeing me being belittled by my mother.'

'Stop making a spectacle of yourself,' Tilly hissed.

Libby stood up, her heart pounding with emotion. 'Adela, Sam: I'm sorry if I've caused a scene. I can't tell you how much I've been looking forward to your coming. But I wish with all my heart that Dad had come with you. I can't pretend otherwise. I miss him so very much.'

Adela thrust out a hand and grabbed at Libby's, pulling her back down next to her. 'I understand, I really do. I still miss my dad every single day. But yours is still alive and you *will* see him again.'

Libby clutched Adela's hand. Her cousin was so courageous. She had been younger than Libby when she'd lost her father – she had even witnessed the appalling tiger attack and cradled him in her arms when Wesley had died. How had she ever recovered from that? But Adela exuded an inner strength and a passion for life. Adela had always made Libby feel stronger and braver when she was around. At that moment, Libby was filled with a sudden purpose. It was quite clear what she should do – would have done months ago if she hadn't felt duty-bound to help Lexy.

'There's only one way I can be certain of seeing Dad again.' She turned to face her mother. 'And that's go to India.'

Tilly's expression was a mixture of irritation and panic. 'Darling, it's far too dangerous now. The riots and killing. Your father won't agree to it.'

'He will,' said Libby. 'His Christmas card said he was longing to see me.'

Tilly turned to Adela for support. 'Dear girl, tell her it's a ridiculous idea. Things are far too unsettled in India, aren't they? It's just not safe.'

Libby saw pain on her cousin's face; she didn't want to take sides.

'It's not unsafe for the British,' Libby insisted.

'How can you possibly know that?' Tilly was disbelieving.

'I read the newspapers too, Mother.'

'The wrong sort,' Tilly exclaimed.

'I admit,' said Libby, 'that there have been some terrible atrocities – but the violence has been communal – Hindus fighting Muslims. We British may have caused all the divisions but it's not our blood that's being spilt.'

Unexpectedly, Sam spoke up. 'It's true there have been some awful incidents – Calcutta last summer saw horrendous violence – but Libby's right, the atrocities have been communal. The different communities are vying for power in a future India and sadly this is stoking up fear of each other.'

'That's my point,' Tilly said, flustered. 'The papers say the country's becoming lawless.'

'But,' said Sam, 'the hatred is no longer aimed at us British. They know we are going.'

'So what are you saying?' Tilly asked.

'That I don't think it would be too dangerous for Libby – or any of you – to visit India. The British are not being harmed.'

Libby felt a kick of triumph. She wanted to throw her arms around Adela's kind husband for sticking up for her.

'Listen to Sam, Mother!' she cried. 'We should both go.' She gave Tilly a beseeching look. 'Come with me, *please*. Dad needs you.'

Tilly's round face sagged. Libby couldn't read the expression in her eyes; was it annoyance or guilt?

Her mother glanced away. 'I'm needed more here – the boys still need me—'

'Jamie's a fully qualified doctor now and only comes home for the odd weekend,' Libby protested.

'But Mungo's still so young,' said Tilly. 'Perhaps when he's finished with university . . .'

Libby swallowed down her disappointment. Tilly was always going to put the boys first. She dug her fingernails into her palms to stop herself showing her emotion.

'Well, whatever you decide,' said Libby, 'I'm going back out to India – and to Dad.'

CHAPTER 3

L ying on the camp bed in the chilly attic room under a pile of blankets and coats, Libby could hear the murmur of Adela's and Sam's voices in the room below. Their indistinct conversation was punctuated with Sam's deep chuckle and Adela's suppressed giggles.

Libby felt bad about causing the argument earlier that evening. Why had she allowed her mother and Josey to upset her? Normally she shrugged off Tilly's chiding remarks and teased Josey back. Their household functioned well enough with Libby largely out at work, Josey at the theatre and Tilly busy with voluntary work for the Women's Voluntary Service and the church. They had a part-time cook and a maid who came in daily to do the cleaning, washing and ironing. When Mungo was back from university in Durham, Tilly was at her happiest. The days after he went away, Josey would try and cheer Tilly up with trips to the theatre or reading aloud from one of Tilly's favourite novels, while Libby kept out of the way by staying late at Herbert's Café doing the bookkeeping.

But this evening, something inside Libby had snapped. Seeing Adela again after more than three years' absence had reignited all her longing for India and her father. It had shaken her with the force and suddenness of a monsoon storm. Just one whiff and sip of the scented tea had made her realise that she still yearned as strongly to return to Assam as she had when she was a child. Torn from her family home at Cheviot View on the Oxford Estates and packed off to a spartan boarding school in Northumberland, eight-year-old Libby had cauterised her emotions – and lashed out at her mother for being the one who had abandoned her there.

Libby had never quite got over the shock of finding herself in the austere red-brick institution with its rigid rules and freezing dormitories. She had been constantly in trouble for exploring beyond the school bounds and answering back in class. She had written plaintive letters home asking for her father to come and fetch her and when he hadn't she had taken comfort in eating as much of the stodgy school food as she was allowed and spending all her pocket money on sweets and fizzy drinks at the tuck shop.

Her mother, on receiving Libby's first school photo, had worried that her daughter was growing fat and asked the school to ban her from the tuck shop. Libby had found other ways to satisfy her sweet tooth, by finishing other girls' schoolwork and letting them copy her sums in exchange for toffees and sticks of liquorice.

Luckily for Libby, a young enthusiastic teacher had joined the school and had seen the potential in the unhappy, rebellious girl. Miss MacGregor had been in the suffrage movement as a schoolgirl and enthralled Libby and her friends with tales of protest marches and run-ins with police. She had taught them history – with a liberal dose of anti-imperialist politics – and Libby had grown to adore her.

It was Miss MacGregor who had persuaded Libby to stay on at school until she was seventeen and gain certificates that would equip her for employment. She had instilled in Libby a righteous anger at injustice and an ambition to make the world a better place. Tilly had complained Miss MacGregor had made Libby impossible to live with, and her brothers had teased her mercilessly about her having a 'crush' on the charismatic teacher.

Libby wriggled under the bedcovers, trying to warm up. The talking in the room below had stopped. Then she heard it: the tell-tale squeaking of the iron-framed bed and its old springs. Adela and Sam were making love. Libby felt a hot wave of embarrassment and envy. She had lost her virginity on that very bed to a Polish refugee who had been billeted with them during the War. She'd been seventeen and Stefan hadn't been much older. They had both been inexperienced but enthusiastic, and took the opportunity to experiment while Tilly was out volunteering at the WVS rest centre.

Blue-eyed Stefan had left to train as an army mechanic and had sent her occasional postcards from North Africa. By the time she had joined the Land Army at eighteen their sporadic correspondence had petered out.

Libby burrowed down under the blankets trying not to hear the sounds of love-making coming from below. Lucky Adela and Sam! Libby had never been in love with Stefan but he had left her with an appetite for sex. Her mother would have been aghast at Libby's brief fiery affair with a handsome, dark-eyed Italian POW who had come to help with the harvest at the Northumbrian farm where nineteen-year-old Libby was working in 1944. Tilly would have called it fraternising with the enemy, but Libby had made sure that Lorenzo was no fascist sympathiser. At the end of the harvest party, they had toasted the communists and the Socialist International before sneaking off to the hay barn where she had allowed him to seduce her.

She had been briefly, passionately in love with Lorenzo but he had hurried home to Italy – and, she discovered, to a waiting wife – at the end of the War.

Libby was now fully awake. She rubbed her cold toes and pondered her new determination to go back to India. Be brutally honest, she told herself. It wasn't just eagerness at seeing her father again and revisiting the tea plantations; Calcutta drew her too. Or more specifically: handsome, fair-haired, fun-loving George Brewis. She had relived their doorstep kiss a thousand times.

Lying sleepless in the attic, Libby wondered who George Brewis had kissed since. She hadn't heard from him again. Ridiculous to hold out hope of a romance with George; he was a man of the world and she must have seemed immature and provincial to his eyes. He could have had no idea how passionately she had adored him from afar as a girl in her early teens – or how much his recent kiss had meant to her.

Restlessly, Libby turned over. The noises from below had stopped. No doubt the loving couple were now falling asleep contentedly in each other's arms. Libby let go a sigh. She sat up, turned on the bedside light and reached for her sketching pad. Whenever she was agitated about something, she found that doodling in a sketch book and creating funny figures calmed her anxious thoughts. It was a strategy she had discovered at boarding school.

Despite her numb fingers, Libby did a quick cartoon of her and George dancing, exaggerating his shoulders and flop of fair hair, and giving herself large feet and lips that were more like a duck's beak. She chuckled, discarded the pad and turned out the light.

CHAPTER 4

Newcastle, February 1947

What if your father can't come immediately to Calcutta to meet you?' fretted Tilly.

'I'll be staying with Uncle Johnny and Aunt Helena,' Libby pointed out. 'Adela says they live in a very safe part of the city – Alipore. There's been no trouble there at all.'

'I suppose I can rely on my brother Johnny to keep an eye on you,' Tilly said, 'and Helena's always seemed the sensible type.'

Libby turned and winked at Adela. It had been Adela's inspired suggestion that Libby spend the last few weeks of the cold season in Calcutta with Tilly's older brother Johnny, a retired Indian Army doctor, and his wife Helena. Tilly had always looked up to her big brother, so once he had written enthusiastically inviting Libby to stay with them, then Tilly's opposition to her daughter's 'India escapade' had begun to weaken.

Tilly still had reservations. 'You promise me you won't go gallivanting around the city on your own or getting involved in any politics?'

'Of course I won't,' said Libby.

'Or upsetting Helena with your anti-colonial views. She's from a pukka army family, you know – they've been in India for several generations. I can just hear you spouting off—'

'I won't upset Helena, I promise. I'll be a proper little memsahib.'

'And don't say things like that,' Tilly warned, 'with that naughty grin of yours. People will think you're making fun of them.'

Libby pulled a face of mock-shock. 'Stuffy colonial memsahibs in imperial capitalist Calcutta – what's there to make fun of?'

'Adela, speak to her,' Tilly pleaded.

'It's no good asking me,' said Adela. 'Our branch of the Robsons has never been pukka as far as the British are concerned.'

Tilly gave her an awkward glance. 'That's ancient history.'

Adela gave a dry laugh. 'I'm afraid not. Some people at the planters' club still cut me and mother dead at the Christmas race week.'

'Just "hen-house" spitefulness,' Tilly said, trying to explain it away. 'Some of the wives have always been jealous of Clarrie for being more beautiful and clever than them.'

Libby was indignant. 'You know that's not the reason, Mother. It's pure racial snobbery. They don't like Clarrie because she's quarter Indian. They're petty and mean minded – the worst kind of Britisher.'

'All right, all right,' Tilly said, turning pink and flustered. 'Adela doesn't want to hear it spelled out. And it won't do any good to antagonise people who hold those views – however repugnant – they're too old to change their ways now. And don't use that word Britisher – it smacks of the Quit India brigade – you'll upset your father and uncle.'

'Okay then, not Britisher,' said Libby, 'just the worst kind of imperialist, bigoted memsahib.'

Tilly rolled her eyes at Libby and Adela started laughing.

It was decided that Libby would fly to India so that she would arrive before the hot season and not have to contend with arriving in Bombay and a long, hazardous train journey across the Indian plains to Bengal. Tilly imagined all manner of dangers – blown-up tracks, robberies at knife-point, being caught in a riot, contracting typhoid, getting bitten by a rabid station dog – and insisted on her daughter flying into Dum Dum airport in Calcutta.

Once Tilly had accepted Libby was not going to change her mind about going, she had busied herself with arrangements.

'You must have new dresses,' she insisted. 'You can't possibly be seen around the clubs of Calcutta in that old utility frock or – heaven forbid – trousers.'

Josey took her up to the theatre and got the wardrobe mistress to help adapt some pre-war dresses.

'Green's your colour, sweetie,' said Josey. 'You'll look knockout in this.' She held up a satin evening dress. 'Can you believe I used to wear this?'

'Yes, I remember you in it,' said Libby. 'You looked so glamorous.'

Josey gave a throaty laugh. 'You used to like me when you were younger, didn't you?'

'I still do,' Libby replied.

'Liar,' smirked Josey.

'I would never lie. I just used to like you more then than now,' Libby said, giving Josey a playful nudge. 'You were kind to me. I remember wanting to go and live in your digs with all those eccentric women. I loved the way you did what you wanted and said what you thought. I never understood why you came to live with us instead. We were all so dull.'

Josey lit up a cigarette. 'I lost my digs when I joined ENSA. Your mother was kind enough to take me in whenever I was in the area. After a while it just became home.'

Libby took Josey's cigarette, drew on it, blew out smoke and handed it back. 'You're very fond of Mother, aren't you?'

'Of course.' Josey eyed her through smoke. 'Why do you ask?'

'You could persuade her to come back out to India.'

'You haven't been able to.'

'No, but she'd listen to you, Josey. She has to face Dad sooner or later.'

Josey picked a fleck of tobacco from her tongue. 'I've told her much the same thing. I'm not standing in her way, if that's what you mean.'

'Really?'

'Yes, really,' Josey insisted. 'Tilly's frightened to go back. She once described the Oxford plantation as a green prison. She's terrified that if she returns she'll never get away again.'

Libby felt her stomach clench. 'That's ridiculous. You make it sound like Dad is a gaoler. They just need to spend some time together. It's the years of separation that's bad for their marriage – not India.'

Josey ground out her cigarette. 'Well, maybe that's a conversation you better have with your father.'

Libby took that to be a criticism of James for not returning to see Tilly at the end of the War. But he still had a job to do, whereas Tilly had no such excuse. As far as Libby was concerned, it was her mother who was in the wrong.

Josey touched her arm lightly. 'Come on, sweetie. Let's get you pinned into this gown. It's going to show off your lovely curves. Calcutta ballrooms won't know what's hit them.'

A few days before her departure, Libby and Adela went round to the flat above Herbert's Café to spend the evening with Lexy. Doreen had gone out to the pictures with a friend. She had been mollified by Libby's abrupt plans to leave by Adela promising to pay for Doreen to continue typing lessons.

'Oh, Lexy, how it takes me back, to sit here with you,' said Adela with a wistful smile. 'Everything's the same – even the brown sofa and the green-and-gold curtains.'

'Do you remember when we all bedded down on the floor one Christmas?' Libby joined in the reminiscing. 'When you and Lexy said it was too dangerous for Mother to walk us back home in the blackout. I loved that night. It was so cosy camping beside the fire.'

'Aye,' chuckled Lexy, 'and you looked so bonny and happy singing along with George. I could see then you were ganin' to grow into a beauty.'

Libby put hands to her burning cheeks. 'Don't be daft.'

'It's true,' Adela agreed. 'Will you get in touch with George once you're in Calcutta?'

Libby felt a kick of excitement and said, 'I'd like to.'

'Make sure he's not courting some other lass,' Lexy warned. 'I love that lad but I know he's got a wandering eye.'

'Not as wandering as his wife's,' Libby retorted. 'George said Bonnie wasn't his baby – that Joan had an affair even before they were married.' Libby saw a look pass between the older women. 'Did you know?' she asked in surprise. 'You did, didn't you?'

'Yes,' admitted Adela. 'I admired George for taking on the baby as his own – despite what Joan had done. She couldn't have stood the shame of not being married.'

'She trapped him,' Libby said.

'At least she got to keep her baby,' said Adela.

'Why didn't she marry the real father?' asked Libby. 'Instead of taking advantage of George's good nature.'

'Maybe's the lad couldn't or wouldn't,' suggested Lexy. 'Or maybe's he died in action. There was a war on, remember – and she needed a ring on her finger.'

'Why?' Libby demanded. 'If I was her, I'd have gone ahead and had the baby alone and not bothered what the wagging tongues said. Rather than forcing a man that didn't love me to marry.'

Adela and Lexy fell silent. Libby saw that look of understanding pass between them again. She wondered what it meant and hoped she hadn't been too outspoken.

When Adela spoke, her voice was oddly shaky. 'Can I have one of your cigarettes, Lexy?'

Lexy passed her the packet and matchbox. Libby watched Adela light up the cigarette and inhale deeply. She thought her cousin had given up smoking.

'Have I said something to upset you?' Libby asked. 'I wasn't blaming George – far from it.'

'No, you haven't,' Adela said, immediately stubbing out the cigarette.

To Libby's alarm, Adela's eyes flooded with sudden tears. Libby leapt out of her chair and rushed to put an arm around her cousin.

'I'm sorry; tell me what I've said. I'm always putting my foot in it.'

At this, Adela dissolved into tears. Shocked, Libby wrapped her arms tighter around her. Adela's shoulders felt fragile and bony, shaking under Libby's hold. Libby let her cry against her hair, not minding. Yet it upset her to see Adela in such a state, and she felt terrible that it was obviously something she had said that had reduced Adela to tears. On so many occasions it had been the older cousin who had comforted Libby, never this way round.

Adela made an effort to stop weeping. Pulling back from Libby and fumbling in her skirt pocket to produce a man's large handkerchief – no doubt Sam's – she blew her nose.

'I'm sorry,' said Adela tearfully. 'I don't know what came over me. I'm still a bit emotional about leaving India and Mother.'

Lexy gave a bronchial cough. 'Tell her, hinny,' she said gently. 'Libby's not a bairn any more – she's a woman of the world. She knows about men who promise the earth and then leave you in the lurch.'

Libby blushed deeply. She remembered how eighteen months ago, sore-hearted over Lorenzo, she had poured out her troubles to a sympathetic Lexy. She sat on the floor at Adela's feet, watching the dark-haired woman struggle with her emotions. Her slim, pretty face was full of anguish. Libby realised her upset was nothing to do with George or Joan but something much more personal.

'You know you can trust me,' said Libby. 'I won't say anything you don't want repeated. But only tell me if you want to.'

'Gan on,' Lexy encouraged. 'A burden shared is a burden halved. Libby's broad-minded and won't judge you.'

Adela wiped her nose again. She sat clutching the handkerchief as if it gave her strength. Libby thought she was never going to speak.

Abruptly, Adela said, 'When I was eighteen, I had an affair with a man in India and got pregnant. He never knew about the pregnancy. By the time I knew, I was back in Britain and had to deal with it alone. Except, thanks to Lexy, I wasn't on my own for long.'

Libby reeled from the revelation. Adela *pregnant*? What man in India?

'Oh, Adela, you poor thing,' Libby gasped. 'How on earth did you cope?'

Adela swallowed hard before continuing. 'It was a few months before war broke out. I was living with Aunt Olive but she found out and said I had to go.'

'She threw you out?' Libby exclaimed. 'How awful!'

'It was Lexy who got me somewhere to live until the baby came.'

Libby gaped at her, searching back in her mind. It must have been when she was fourteen and railing against boarding school.

'That Christmas term,' said Libby, 'I remember being disappointed you never came to visit. The boys and I had to go to Auntie Mona's in Dunbar for the Christmas holidays. All that time I was feeling sorry for myself, you were having to deal with that terrible situation. I wish I'd known. Everyone said you were in panto in Edinburgh.'

Adela nodded, her eyes welling with tears again. 'But I wasn't. I was living with friends of Lexy's in Cullercoats, keeping out of the way so no one would know my shameful secret. The women were so kind and looked after me well – it was a little haven – I can't imagine what I would have done without them.'

Libby's insides twisted. She hardly dared ask. 'And did the baby . . . ? What happened to it?'

Adela's chin wobbled as she answered. 'I had a son. A beautiful boy. I gave him away – for adoption – just wanted it all over and forgotten. I was so young. I had no idea. But I've thought of him every day since.'

Fresh tears trickled down Adela's cheeks and she balled the handkerchief in her fist. Libby reached up quickly and put a comforting hand over hers.

'So you never told the father?' Libby asked.

Adela shook her head, too overcome to say more.

Lexy answered for her. 'It wouldn't have made any difference – the lad led her on with talk of getting wed but he was never in a position to marry her.'

Libby wanted to ask who the father was but didn't want to upset Adela any more than she already had.

'And Sam?' Libby asked. 'Have you told—?'

'Sam knows everything,' Lexy cut in. 'He knows about the bairn and all the carry-on Adela's been through.'

Libby realised how crass her remarks about having a baby out of wedlock and brazening it out must have sounded. Before the War it would have been unthinkable for a middle-class girl like Adela to have lived as an unmarried mother and kept her baby.

'I'm sorry for my stupid remarks earlier about Joan and all that.'

'You weren't to know, hinny,' said Lexy, her look kindly.

'Who else knows?' asked Libby.

Adela found her voice again. 'Mother knows – and just a couple of people here apart from Aunt Olive. I confided in Josey before I went back out to India – and Joan Brewis found out.'

'George's wife?' Libby was surprised.

'Yes – she saw me at the coast just before I had the baby. But as far as I know she's never told anyone. Neither has Josey.' Adela gave Libby an anxious look. 'I've never told your mother and I'd rather she didn't know.'

'That must be hard for Josey,' said Libby, 'keeping such a secret from Mother all this time. They're the best of friends.'

'Perhaps it's wrong of me,' said Adela, 'but Tilly would be shocked by it all and there's no point in upsetting her.'

'That's true,' said Libby. 'She's the last person I would tell about my affairs of the heart. That's why I always come running to Lexy.' She looked at the older woman with a fond smile.

'I don't know what I'd have done without Lexy either,' Adela said. 'She's one in a million.'

'Stop it, you two,' Lexy protested, 'or I'll not get me big head out the door tomorro'.'

'It's true.' Adela gave a sad smile. 'And you don't know how comforting it is for me to be here with you – being with someone who knew and cared for my baby.'

Libby felt awkward. She had forced Adela to come back to Newcastle, a place that must conjure up so many unhappy memories of being pregnant and having to hide an illegitimate birth.

'I'm sorry I upset you,' said Libby. 'And if I'd known about this terrible situation I would never have suggested that you return for the café. And dragging Sam here too.'

'No, you did the right thing,' Adela said. 'We would have come back sooner but Sam's sister Sophie was so upset at the thought of us going so far away from her. She and Sam are very close.'

'But it must be difficult being in Newcastle, surely?' said Libby. 'Being reminded of such an unhappy time. Doesn't it bring it all back?'

Adela looked at her with puzzled green eyes. 'It's not a matter of bringing back memories – I've never stopped thinking of my boy – ever! That's why we've come back – to try and find him. I live in hope that

John Wesley might still be in an institution in the area so that I can claim him as mine.'

Libby was flabbergasted. Was Adela really serious in wanting to track down an illegitimate baby she'd given up years ago?

'And Sam agrees?'

'Of course,' said Adela. 'I couldn't do this if he didn't want it too.'

'You have an amazing husband,' Libby said in admiration.

'I know I do.' Adela smiled broadly for the first time since her confession. 'Sam is my rock. I've never loved anyone so much – apart from my baby.'

'But you said you'd given John . . . ?'

'John Wesley.'

'Given him up for adoption,' Libby pointed out. 'Won't he be living with another family now?'

She saw the wince of pain on Adela's face and felt bad for mentioning the adoption. 'Even to know that would be better than not knowing what happened to him. But the problem is I don't know. And it's possible he was never chosen for adoption.'

'Why wouldn't he be?' Libby asked gently. 'You said he was a beautiful boy.'

Adela glanced away. It was Lexy who spoke. 'The bairn might not have been so easy to place.'

'Why not?' Libby was baffled.

''Cos he's coloured,' said Lexy. 'Not much; but he wasn't as white as you or me. And you know how some folk are prejudiced that way.'

Libby flushed. It hadn't occurred to her that the father wasn't British.

Adela met her look with a glint of defiance. 'John Wesley's father was Indian. He was from Gulgat, near Belgooree.'

'Where Sophie and Rafi live?' Libby asked in astonishment.

Adela nodded.

Lexy said, 'And not just any Indian. The bairn's father was an Indian prince – Sanjay, they called him.'

Libby gaped at her cousin. It sounded like something out of a Hollywood film: ill-starred lovers in exotic India. But this was real life. She could see from the deep pain in Adela's eyes how ashamed and hurt she still was. While Libby had been fretting over petty school restrictions at the age of fourteen, life for her cousin had been one traumatic incident after another. She recalled how Adela had only just lost her father a few weeks before she returned to Newcastle in 1938. It made Libby feel immature in comparison and she doubted she could have coped with so much at such a young age.

Something nagged in Libby's mind: Gulgat? Then it hit her. Adela's father Wesley had been killed in a hunting accident in Gulgat. Had Adela been carrying on her affair with this Sanjay at the same time? Had Wesley known? Her cousin had come back on the ship with Tilly later that summer. At the time, Libby had been told not to mention Adela's father in case it upset her cousin, though everyone knew Adela had come to Newcastle to get over her grief for her parent. Libby had been delighted to have Adela around – more pleased to see her than she was her own mother. Perhaps it hadn't just been the loss of her father that had brought Adela to Newcastle but the desire to escape an unhappy affair.

Whatever the truth, Libby felt deeply sorry for Adela. She would never judge her. It could just as easily be she, Libby, who had fallen pregnant from her affair with Lorenzo. She knew what it was like to be passionately in love with a handsome man and to believe all his seductive words and false promises.

Libby sat holding on to Adela's hand. With her free hand, Adela began stroking Libby's unruly hair. No one spoke. Lexy heaved herself out of her chair and went to refresh the teapot. There was an intimacy between the three women – a strong atmosphere of togetherness – which no one wanted to dispel with trivial words. Libby was touched that Adela had confided her secret in her and that both women trusted her like an equal.

Libby wondered if she would ever find friends as dear to her as these two women when she returned to India. She had a momentary pang of misgiving at what she was embarking on, but it was fleeting. She had been fending for herself since she was eight years old. Libby was used to making new friends to fill the aching void left by her absent family.

Somewhere in India, new friends awaited – as well as her beloved, dearly missed father.

The day of leave-taking came on a dank grey day in mid-February. Libby's brothers, Jamie and Mungo, had come to see her off at the cavernous Central Station, along with Tilly, Josey, Adela and Sam. Libby had already had a tearful goodbye with Lexy earlier that morning, neither knowing if or when they would see the other again.

'I'm not ready for me grave yet,' Lexy had wheezed. 'You'll be back before then, hinny. You take good care and don't go falling for the first bonny lad who pays you compliments. You deserve a canny man who treats you right, hinny.'

Now Libby was bracing herself for more hasty goodbyes on the crowded platform. Jamie busied himself supervising the luggage on to the London train while Tilly fussed around Libby, brushing imaginary specks of soot from her coat and readjusting the jaunty angle of her black hat.

'You would think I was going back to school,' teased Libby with a roll of her eyes. She tried to answer her mother's anxious questions without showing her irritation.

'Yes, I'll get a taxi to the airport. No, I won't speak to strange men.'

'And you'll send a telegram as soon as you reach Calcutta,' Tilly ordered. 'And give my love to Johnny and Helena, won't you?'

'Shall I tell them you'll be joining us soon?' Libby challenged. 'Then you can give them your message in person.'

'Darling, do try and behave,' Tilly said, ignoring the question.

Then her brothers were pushing their way in and giving her bashful kisses on the cheek. The others followed. Adela gave her a fierce hug.

'Give my love to Mother when you get to Belgooree,' she said. 'And be happy.'

They exchanged knowing looks. 'And good luck to you in all you do here,' Libby said with meaning. She dropped her voice and added, 'I hope you find what you're looking for.' She felt her eyes sting with sudden emotion.

'Hurry up and get on the train,' Tilly cried, 'or you'll miss it.'

For a moment Libby and Tilly looked at each other, hesitating. Libby was overcome with a sensation she hadn't felt since she was a bewildered eight-year-old, the enormity of being parted from her mother. For a brief instant she remembered what a gut-wrenching moment that had been. One minute she'd been sobbing and clinging to her mother, and the next, Tilly's plump, warm, lavender-smelling arms had been pushing her away.

Libby fought to control her voice. 'Goodbye, Mother.'

She wanted to fling her arms around her mother's neck in a hug. But she knew Tilly would only be embarrassed. Instead, Libby leant forward and pecked her mother's cheek. Tilly gave a distracted smile and a light pat on Libby's shoulder.

'Go on, darling. Be good.'

Libby swallowed down tears, annoyed at herself for minding that her mother appeared to feel no sadness at her departure. She turned away and mounted the steps into the train. The guard slammed the door closed. Libby pulled down the window and leant out as the train shunted out of the station.

There was a chorus of good luck and bon voyage. She grinned and waved back. Sam, the tallest, was raising his hat in farewell. It was the last thing she could see clearly before they were enveloped in a blast of smoke from the engine.

Libby waited till she had closed the window and could no longer be seen, before succumbing to tears. She felt the familiar wrench of being parted from her family. Yet seeing them standing there together, she had been struck by the feeling that they were incomplete without her father. He was the vital heartbeat of the family.

Libby comforted herself with the thought that she was finally on her way to being reunited with him. It was the first step in putting the family back together again.

Adela stood on the platform gazing after the train. She felt such a clash of emotions: excitement for Libby embarking on a new adventure and fear that she might not find in India what she desperately wanted – a father's love that was as strong as in childhood. Adela worried that Libby's nostalgic memories of India were a little rose-tinted. She tried to hide her upset at Libby's going. She had no right to keep her here. But in the few short weeks they had spent together again, Adela had been impressed with her young cousin.

Libby was mature beyond her years: capable, caring, still as outspoken as ever but with a deep intuition and empathy for others. She had grown up so much in the war years. And she was guileless; Libby seemed unaware of how attractive she was with her dark-blue eyes, lustrous hair and sensual body. She wished Tilly could see Libby's good qualities, but both mother and daughter seemed to bring out the worst in each other.

Sam slipped his arm around her shoulder and gave it a squeeze.

'She'll be fine,' he said in reassurance. 'Libby has twice the common sense of any of us – and courage in spadefuls.'

Adela smiled up at him and nodded. She looked round to give Tilly a sympathetic smile too. But she was already turning away.

'Of course you must stay the night, darling,' Tilly was telling Mungo. 'Jamie can run you back to Durham tomorrow . . .'

Adela had a sudden pang of loss. It wasn't just about Libby. For a moment she stood and wondered. If she had been able to keep John Wesley with her, would she have been just as single-mindedly besotted about her son as Tilly was about both of hers?

CHAPTER 5

Calcutta, India, February 1947

As the Dakota aeroplane descended over the swampy Bengali delta, Libby was mesmerised by the view. Tropical green fields and jungle were pockmarked by lakes and canals that shimmered in the setting sun. Settlements clung to the riverbanks and thatched huts peeked through groves of mangoes and palms.

On the last leg of her three-day journey, Libby's plane had taken off from Karachi by the Arabian Sea and flown over brown barren plains. Looking down now, her senses were assaulted by the lushness of this watery province. She could make out a black bullock being chivvied home alongside a dyke and a white church spire piercing the green canopy.

Then the plane banked and she saw in the distance the dense clutter of rooftops half obscured in a haze of smoke: Calcutta. Libby's stomach somersaulted. She had never seen it like this before, spread out like a child's miniature model, with flat-roofed houses and a railway line cutting through fields. Fourteen years ago, she had left by train to Bombay for the long voyage into exile. Now she had a bird's-eye view of the wide brown Hooghly River, shaped like a dog-leg and studded with ships at anchor. Beyond lay a forest of cranes and factory chimneys.

She held her breath in wonder as the drabness of the river delta was suddenly flooded with golden evening light and the hulks of ships began to sparkle. The sun hovered over the horizon – a throbbing disc the colour of blood orange – and then abruptly sank. As the plane landed, the sky was already a deep mauve and pinpricks of lamplight began to stud the deepening darkness.

Her uncle, Dr Johnny Watson, and his wife Helena were there to meet her. She recognised her uncle at once. He had the same lanky gait and broad smile as her brother Jamie and deep-set hazel eyes like her mother. She remembered him as being kind and good fun on a long-ago camping trip near Belgooree. Then, he had been dark-haired; now his hair was peppered with grey. Helena – who had been absent from that trip – was buxomly solid in a lilac pleated skirt and matching twin-set. Permed greying hair was arranged neatly beneath a stiff raffia hat.

'My dear, you look exhausted!' Helena greeted her with a gloved handshake. 'The car's waiting and dinner will be ready as soon as we get home. You must be hungry.'

'I'm too excited to be hungry,' Libby said, smiling. 'But now you mention it . . .'

'Good,' said her aunt. 'You look like a girl who enjoys her food. I approve of that.' She turned away to summon a porter to carry her cases.

Johnny kissed Libby on the cheek. 'Flights go all right?' he asked.

As they followed Helena, Libby gabbled about her journey – the stop-overs in Malta, Cairo and Basra – and the excitement of seeing Calcutta from the air. Johnny answered with a deep amused chuckle that also reminded her of Jamie.

As soon as they emerged from the airport building, Libby felt the balmy evening air envelop her like a soft shawl.

A Sikh driver in a crimson turban held the back passenger door open for Helena and Libby, while Johnny climbed in the front. Libby tried to catch the driver's eye to thank him but he stared resolutely over her head.

'Quickest way home!' Helena ordered. She leant towards Libby. 'We don't want to risk driving through central Calcutta after dark – there's still unrest – constant stabbings. Quite appalling.'

'No need to alarm Libby,' Johnny said, craning round with a reassuring smile. 'Things aren't so bad.'

'Still, it's best to be careful,' said Helena. 'Never go out without a chaperone whatever time of the day. But I'm sure your mother has warned you.'

'Not as such,' said Libby.

'How is Tilly?' asked Johnny.

'She's well, thank you. Sends her love to you both.'

'Such a pity she hasn't come out with you,' said Helena. 'Poor James. It doesn't do to be without a wife for such a long time in India. Especially stuck on a tea plantation. Not good for a marriage.'

'Hardly Tilly's fault, darling,' said Johnny, 'that the War broke out while she was home.'

'If it had been me,' said Helena, 'I'd have been on a ship back to India in a jiffy – bringing the children too.'

Libby felt her stomach knot. 'I wish she had.'

Helena reached out and patted her arm. 'I'm sure you do. But you're here now. I bet your father is absolutely thrilled.'

Libby grinned. 'I got a lovely letter from him before I left Newcastle saying how pleased he is that I'm coming.'

'Good,' said Helena. 'Just as long as we're given time to spoil you here first. Your uncle sees so little of his family.'

'Dad hopes to be here in time for my birthday next month and then he'll take me up to Assam. I'm so excited by it all.'

'Bravo,' said Johnny. 'That means we can give you a party.'

'Oh, yes, let's!' agreed Helena. 'We've never had a daughter of our own to make a fuss of. We're going to spoil you rotten.'

'That's very kind of you,' said Libby, quite overwhelmed. She knew that her uncle and aunt had never had their own family but her mother had always said that Helena seemed more devoted to horses than children.

Libby turned to look out of the window as they passed rows of ramshackle huts and swerved around water buffalo. She wound down the window and breathed in deeply. The smell of India that she had almost forgotten – dung fires, kerosene, the buttery smell of cooking, animals – was suddenly dearly familiar. She felt her eyes prickle.

As they reached the outskirts of the city and the streets became busier, Helena said, 'Best to wind up the window, dear.'

Libby didn't know if her aunt was objecting to the smell or whether she feared someone might attack the car.

They skirted the city, Johnny pointing out places of interest which were too dark to see clearly: Park Street cemetery, the spire of St Paul's Cathedral and the Presidency General Hospital. Libby craned for a look.

'My Cousin Adela's school friend works there as a nurse,' she said. 'She's told me to look her up.'

'That's nice,' said Johnny. 'You must do that.'

'What's her name?' asked Helena. 'We might know her family.'

'Flowers Dunlop.'

'Ah,' said Helena. 'Railway people, are they?'

Libby was surprised. 'Yes, I think her father was a stationmaster. Retired early due to ill health. How amazing that you know them.'

'Oh, no, we don't,' said Helena at once. 'It's the girl's name – sounds like a half-half.'

'Half-half?'

'Your aunt means Adela's friend is probably Anglo-Indian,' explained Johnny.

'A lot of their type become nurses,' said Helena. 'The girls are usually hard-working; some of the boys are less good at applying themselves – enjoy the good life too much.'

Libby bristled. 'Perhaps they've never had the opportunities that the British take for granted? My teacher, Miss MacGregor, said that Anglo-Indians were prohibited for years from entering the civil service or rising above lower management posts.'

'Well, I don't know about that,' Helena said, pursing her lips.

Johnny said quickly, 'They were marvellous during the War – showed great loyalty to the Empire.'

'True,' Helena admitted. 'They've always thought themselves more British than the British. But most would be like fish out of water if they actually went to Britain. They wouldn't fit in at all.'

Libby asked, 'But wouldn't it be the same for you, Aunt Helena? Mother says your family have been in India since before the Mutiny – so aren't you Anglo-Indian too?'

'Certainly not,' she retorted. 'We're British through and through. There's a world of difference between my family and Eurasians who have – well, you know – have Indian blood in their veins.'

Libby knew exactly the difference but annoyance at her aunt's attitude had provoked her into challenging the woman. She wondered what the Indian driver made of the casually racial remark. She would have to curb her tongue if she was to remain on speaking terms with her aunt for the next four weeks.

Better not to mention that Adela and Sam had also urged her to contact their other good friend, Dr Fatima Khan. Not only was she Indian but she had a notorious brother who had been imprisoned for terrorism. Another brother, Rafi, had married Sam's sister Sophie. Libby wasn't sure if Helena approved of Sophie, even though she was also a distant relation of Johnny's. She would bide her time before mentioning Dr Khan.

'There's a family friend from home that I'd also like to meet up with,' said Libby. 'He's working for Strachan's.'

'Oh,' said Helena, brightening, 'we know people in Strachan's.'

'George Brewis. I have his card,' said Libby. 'He stays on Harrington Street when he's in town.'

'Ah yes, he'll be in a chummery there with other young bachelors,' Helena said. 'Close to the Saturday Club for their sport and the bright lights of Chowringhee for their entertainment. How do you know him?'

'He's a cousin of Adela's on her mother's side – Clarrie's nephew.' Then Libby wondered if Helena disapproved of Clarrie Robson because she was also Anglo-Indian. She didn't want Helena taking against George before she'd even met him. Best not to correct Helena's assumption that George was a bachelor either; she might disapprove of her seeing a married man, even though he was soon to be divorced.

'He was in the Fleet Air Arm during the War,' said Libby. 'Saw action over Burma. That's when he fell in love with India and decided to make a career out here.'

'Good show,' said Johnny. 'Is he Olive's son?'

'That's right,' Libby answered. 'Do you know George?'

'No,' said Johnny, 'but I met Olive. She was the shy nervous type. Not at all like her older sister Clarrie. Clarrie was always such good fun. She was a marvellous step-mother to my best friend Will . . .'

Libby saw the sadness etched on her uncle's face. Her mother had often spoken of the lively Will Stock who had been killed in the Kaiser's War. Will and Johnny had been boyhood friends and all Johnny's sisters had adored him too.

'Well,' Helena said, 'enough talk about Clarrie Robson. Libby dear, you must invite your young man round to New House so we can meet him.'

Libby felt excitement curdle inside to hear George referred to as her young man. Would he be pleased or aghast to be cast in that role? She was impatient to see him again.

'You can invite any of the friends you make in Calcutta,' said Johnny. 'Just treat our home as yours.'

'Thank you,' said Libby with a grateful smile, remembering how fond she and her brothers had been of their genial uncle in those long-ago days of childhood.

Libby woke to the screeching of birds. It was dark in the shuttered room and for a moment she wondered in which hotel room she lay. Then with a flood of joy she realised she was no longer in transit but back on Indian soil. Getting quickly out of bed, she unlatched the shutters and opened the casement window. Cool sweet air embraced her.

The garden was largely in shadow and she could tell from the pearly sunrise that it must still be very early. Giant crows were making a racket in the adjacent trees and a flock of green parrots rushed overhead and disappeared into dark foliage.

Libby hurried to pull on clothes and tiptoe into the gloomy hallway of the downstairs flat just as the large grandfather clock was chiming the half-hour. It was five-thirty.

A sleepy *chowkidar* scrambled to his feet and let her out of the front door. The neat lawns and flowerbeds were glistening with dew as the dawn light crept across them. Libby took off her shoes and walked barefoot down the steps and over the grass, enjoying the cool damp on her skin. Beyond the garden wall she could hear the sounds of Calcutta stirring: the soft tinkle of a rickshaw's bell, the creak of a bullock cart and the crack of a driver's whip. From far off came the blare of a ship's hooter; two unseen men passed by chattering in Bengali.

She breathed in deeply. Turning at the far end of the garden she surveyed the Watsons' house. Despite its name, New House, the square, two-storied building looked Victorian, with its pillared frontage, balconies and crumbling stucco. Johnny had explained that Helena's family had renamed it New House when they'd moved from their former home in Ballyganj a generation ago, simply because it was new to them.

Too large now for a retired couple and Helena's elderly father to be living in, the upstairs floor was rented out to a jute mill company. She sat for a while on a damp bench enjoying the chorus of birds in the tree over her head. Was it a peepal tree or a banyan? Libby couldn't remember. After a while she smelt cooking coming from the servants' compound behind the house. She skirted the building, curious to see what they were cooking. As she passed close to the veranda she heard strange grunting sounds. Libby was stopped in her tracks by a startling sight: in the shadows, a scrawny, almost naked old man was doing press-ups.

She stifled a gasp but he seemed quite oblivious to her presence. He was bald apart from a few wisps of white hair and his withered skin was almost yellow. Thinking him one of the servants, Libby backed away. Then he hauled himself into a sitting position and called out in a reedy upper-class voice, 'Ranjan, bring me my towel!'

With shock, Libby realised this must be Helena's octogenarian father, Colonel Swinson. She hung back in the shadow of a tree for a couple of minutes until a servant had wrapped the Colonel from the waist down in a white towel and then she reappeared.

'Good morning,' Libby called. 'Colonel Swinson is it?'

He peered over the veranda. 'Yes, and who the devil are you?'

'Libby Robson, Dr Watson's niece.' She smiled up at him.

He stared at her, baffled. 'Never heard of you. Should I have?'

Libby smiled in amusement. 'I suppose not. I only arrived last night. I'm here for a month.'

'Why did nobody tell me?'

Libby imagined that Helena had told him repeatedly that they were having a guest from England but her aunt had warned her that the Colonel was very forgetful.

'Perhaps I was to be a surprise,' Libby answered.

He grunted and turned away. Libby was on the point of carrying on her way when the old man called to her. 'Do you like kedgeree?'

'Love it,' said Libby.

'Come and have breakfast with me on the veranda at six-thirty,' he ordered. 'Give me time for my cold bath.'

'Thank you,' said Libby, 'I will.'

Half an hour later, Libby was back on the veranda sitting at a small table opposite Helena's father, eating a rather dry kedgeree of rice, fish and boiled eggs. The garden was dappled in morning sunshine and a servant stood over them with a palm frond to bat away any scavenging birds.

Colonel Swinson ate slowly, his worn-down teeth chewing determinedly at the over-cooked fish. But Libby didn't mind his slowness; she was enjoying his rambling conversation in between mouthfuls.

'Born just after the Mutiny, you know. Father was in the Bengal Lancers. Mama was the most beautiful woman in Calcutta. That's what Papa said. This fish is bhekti – comes from the estuary. Cook doesn't like it – thinks it's polluted from the salt water. Prefers river fish. Can't bloody cook it properly, that's for sure.' He paused to pull out a bone that had stuck in his teeth.

'Are you here to find a husband?' he suddenly asked.

'No,' Libby said, spluttering over her tea.

'Why not?'

'I'm here to see my father. We've been apart since before the War.'

'Ah, well, he'll find you a husband. What's his regiment?'

'He's not in the Army,' said Libby. 'He's a tea planter.'

'Tea, eh?' The Colonel ruminated over this. 'Don't let him marry you off to some box-wallah up-country. You'll have a dog's life. Army chap is what you need. My daughter Helena married a doctor in the Gurkhas. She has a grand life.'

'Yes, she's married to my Uncle Johnny.'

The Colonel looked at her in surprise. Libby wondered if he'd already forgotten who she was.

'Um, yes, army officer will suit you – you're the outdoor, athletic type by the look of you. Helena will find you someone suitable.'

'Doesn't seem much point,' said Libby. 'In a year or so the British officers will have to leave, won't they? That sort of life will be over.'

He frowned, his fork halfway to his mouth. 'Leave? Why ever should we leave? The British have made the Indian Army the envy of the world. We have the most loyal of men and the cream of the officer corps.' He shook his head as if she had said something outlandish. 'Leave indeed.'

Libby decided not to argue. Instead she asked him, 'Have you ever been to Assam?'

'Ah, Assam! Hunted there as a young man. Wonderful for big game. Shot a bear once – and tigers of course.'

As he enthused about long-ago days, Libby's mind wandered to her childhood there. Why did the Colonel think it would be such a dog's life to be married to a tea planter? She suspected it was just the usual British prejudice towards men in trade compared to those in uniform. Yet she felt a twinge of discomfort. Her own mother would probably agree with Colonel Swinson.

'Bhekti – it's a kind of perch,' said the Colonel. 'Can't cook it. Comes from Goa.'

'The fish comes from Goa?' Libby asked in confusion.

He scrutinised her with rheumy blue eyes, then barked with laughter. 'Not the fish – the cook!'

Libby giggled at her misunderstanding. 'That makes more sense.'

'Helena likes him 'cause he's Christian,' explained the Colonel, 'and he'll handle pork. Bloody useless cook though.'

An hour later, as the old man was still chewing his way through a piece of cold toast, Johnny discovered them.

'So you've met my delightful niece?' he said, bellowing in his father-in-law's ear.

'Your niece, eh? Pretty young thing.' He nodded. 'Won't have any trouble finding a suitable officer to marry.'

Johnny and Libby exchanged wry glances.

'Well, I don't know about a husband,' said Johnny, 'but your Aunt Helena has a busy day of sight-seeing planned for you. And you may have to eat a second breakfast.' He gave her an apologetic look. 'My wife is waiting in the dining room at a table groaning with bacon and eggs.'

Libby wiped her mouth on her napkin and stood up, grinning. 'After seven years of rationing, two breakfasts sounds like heaven on earth.'

The next few days were a hectic round of sight-seeing and shopping with Helena and socialising with the Watsons' friends. At first, Libby revelled in being taken around Calcutta. Helena, who insisted that they were driven everywhere, enjoyed showing off the imposing colonial buildings arrayed around Dalhousie Square and which fringed the vast park known as the Maidan. As they drove along Old Court House Street, her aunt pointed out Government House and the old mansions on the Esplanade, and continued down Red Road to the huge dazzlingly white Victoria Memorial at the other end of the Maidan.

When Libby pleaded for them to get out and see round the art gallery housed in the memorial building, Helena reluctantly agreed. Her aunt thought most artists were overrated and only allowed Libby a cursory look around.

Helena was more enthusiastic about showing her around St Paul's Cathedral with its military flags and then the imposing tombs and catafalques of the British cemetery in Park Street. In the ancient graveyard,

Helen said, with a sweep of her hands, 'All the history of British India is here. Look at the names and dates. So much endeavour and sacrifice.'

Libby found the tightly packed jumble of gravestones and obelisks claustrophobic, and she winced at this very visual reminder of Britain's imperial past.

'I think it's rather a depressing place,' she said. 'I'm more interested in the living.'

Helena took that to mean that Libby would like to go shopping.

'You'll need some decent summer clothes,' her aunt said. 'I can't believe your mother sent you out with so little. And it really isn't done to wear trousers.'

Helena got her driver to deposit them on Chowringhee Street, a wide thoroughfare of shops, hotels and restaurants, its arcaded pavements busy with street vendors. Crowded trams swayed up the centre of the road, clanking and sounding their bells. Libby had a frisson of remembrance: she had been here before. Her mother had relished the rare trip to the big city to buy clothes and visit the theatre. Libby remembered being fascinated by two boys on the wide pavement doing a levitation trick under a grubby sheet.

Before she could work out where that could have been, her aunt was marching Libby into a grand department store where saluting doormen were dressed in immaculate white uniforms.

Despite Libby's protests, Helena insisted on buying and paying for three old-fashioned summer frocks with matching gloves, two sensible buttoned-up blouses that didn't show any cleavage, a parasol, a white handbag and two pairs of court shoes with heels.

'I'm not very good in heels,' Libby said.

'You can't slop around in those terrible old gym shoes, dear,' said Helena. 'Keep them for tennis.'

As they emerged again into the bright sunshine to their waiting driver, Libby gave a longing glance up the street to where Chowringhee disappeared into the melee of central Calcutta. How she yearned to explore the lanes and bazaars that led off into the teeming city.

'Perhaps we could visit Hogg's Market tomorrow?' she suggested.

'Goodness me, no,' replied Helena with a shocked expression. 'I never go there.'

'But they sell everything, don't they? Surely you must buy some things there?'

'I send the servants with a shopping list.' Helena bustled her towards the car. 'Tomorrow your calling cards will be ready. We'll spend the morning delivering them, then you'll be able to do some visiting.'

Immediately, Libby's spirits lifted; tomorrow she could get in touch with George.

❧ ❧

After a few days, Libby was tiring of Helena's constant commentary on the laziness of Bengalis, the corruption of the city corporation and the tittle-tattle of Calcutta's European society. But she bore it with good grace, remembering Tilly's words of warning not to upset her aunt. Her favourite activity was being taken for a ride across the Maidan.

'Why didn't you tell me you liked riding?' Helena had exclaimed on Libby's second day in Calcutta.

'I'm not very expert,' Libby had admitted, 'but some of my fondest memories are of early morning rides with Dad around the tea gardens – just the two of us. And I used to love exercising the old horses on the farm where I worked during the War.'

One afternoon Johnny took them to Eden Gardens – another beauti-fully laid-out central park – to watch a cricket match. Libby wore one of the matronly dresses that Helena had bought for her. She tried to make it more shapely by wearing it with a wide belt. Libby kept a look-out for George, hoping to see him. But frustratingly, since leaving her calling card at his digs in Harrington Street, there had been no reply.

'Not very polite of your young man,' Helena had said.

'I imagine George is away from the city on business,' Johnny had suggested, with a smile of reassurance.

'Yes, that's more than likely,' Libby had agreed. Only to herself did she admit the wave of disappointment that so far George had failed to get in touch.

Each day, Helena organised Libby into attending tea parties or dinners, either at New House or at the homes of their friends. They were mostly ex-army or in business, nearly all were middle-aged and none of the women appeared to have ever done a job, apart from running their households or volunteering during the War. Libby found herself comparing them to her mother; at least Tilly thought her work outside the home more important than housekeeping. Helena and one of the other women were active in the Guides but the rest of Helena's friends appeared to fill their days with socialising and playing bridge or tennis at their clubs, and reminiscing about their army days in cantonments across India.

One retired couple, the Percy-Barratts, Libby remembered from Assam; Reggie had worked with her father on the Oxford Estates and thin-faced Muriel had been the burra memsahib of the tea-planters' club. Libby recalled her as being a bit of a dragon with a permanently sour expression of whom all the children had been wary. But on meeting them again, Libby encouraged them to talk of the old days, interested to hear their memories of her parents. Muriel, now white-haired, still had a mouth which pulled down at the corners when something displeased her.

'I took your mother under my wing when she first came out to India,' Muriel Percy-Barratt said. 'She was such a town girl, not suited for life in the *mofussil* at all. I had to give her quite a talking-to, I can tell you. I always had a soft spot for your father – a lifelong friend – ever since Reggie and James joined the company as young men.'

'Lifelong friend,' her husband echoed. 'Could tell you a few tales.'

But to Libby's frustration he didn't. Muriel dominated the conversation.

'So when is your mother coming back out?' Muriel asked.

'Soon, I hope,' Libby answered.

'Your father is terribly lonely at Cheviot View. I think the War years have taken their toll on his health – he looked ghastly the last time we saw him.' Muriel's glum look filled Libby with sudden alarm. 'Of course he should never have been left alone for so long. Poor James. Still, if Tilly is really intending on coming out then that is good news.'

'Good news indeed,' Reggie said.

Libby bridled at the criticism of her mother, even though she mainly agreed with it.

'Mother spent the War looking after me and my brothers,' she replied, unable to hold her tongue. 'I think she probably had a harder time of it in Britain than any of you in India – even the tea planters.'

After that, Muriel ignored her and talked to Helena about the possibility of sharing a cottage in Darjeeling for the hot season. Libby was left worrying about her father's health but decided that the waspish Muriel had been exaggerating.

❦

On Sunday, Libby elected to go to the Presbyterian Church on Wellesley Square with her Uncle Johnny rather than with Helena to St Paul's Cathedral.

'Don't linger,' Helena warned. 'We always take Papa out to the club for Sunday lunch after church. He hates to be late.'

Libby, who had enjoyed sharing early breakfasts on the veranda all week with the absent-minded Colonel, was doubtful that the old man would know if his lunch were late or not. But to keep her aunt happy, she promised they would be prompt.

Libby relished having an hour or so with just her kind uncle for company. Johnny liked to give their driver, Kiran, the day off on Sundays and drove the car himself. At the Duff Scottish Church, Libby was surprised to find that the Europeans in the congregation were outnumbered by Indians and Anglo-Indians. Many of the women were smartly dressed in European-style clothing and the men were turned out in lightweight suits or dark-blue blazers.

'I prefer it here to the grand St Andrew's on Dalhousie Square,' whispered Johnny. 'I'm more likely to bump into one of my old Gurkhas.'

Once the service was over, her uncle took little persuasion to detour around the streets of central Calcutta.

At the square outside Hogg's Market, Libby exclaimed, 'I've been here before! I recognise the clock tower. Dad brought me here, I'm sure of it. I think he was trying to find someone to mend his pocket watch.'

'The clock is a famous landmark,' said Johnny, 'and a place of rendezvous.'

'Can we stop and have a milky tea, Uncle Johnny?'

'From a chai stall?' he asked in surprise.

'Yes. Dad and I always drank it when we were out in town together. Mother wouldn't let me drink or eat anything from street stalls, so it was always a treat and a secret that I shared with Dad.'

At once, her uncle pulled over to the curb. 'Well, it'll be our little secret from your Aunt Helena too.'

Libby was fascinated by the scene. Even though the indoor market was closed, the surrounding streets were busy with rickshaws carrying elderly men or women in bright saris. Men in white lungis or checked sarongs milled around the pavements, side-stepping the squatting vendors who were crying out for business: 'Paan, bidis, chai!'

The chai-wallah grinned toothlessly as he poured out steaming tea from a great height into small earthenware cups. Libby sipped at the hot sweet drink, which had been boiled up with milk and something spicy, possibly ginger. For a moment she was a small girl again, standing in the protective shadow of her tall, vigorous father, enjoying an illicit taste of Indian street life. Her eyes prickled with tears. Would she ever be able to recapture that close bond she had once shared with her beloved father? She was impatient for their reunion but also nervous in case they had grown too far apart in the intervening years – half her lifetime.

She was also troubled by Muriel's words. Could her father's health really be failing? Libby refused to believe that a man so vital and strong couldn't cope with plantation life. It was a healthy outdoor life and her father thrived on hard work. She mustn't let Muriel's gloomy conversation upset her; the woman had said such things merely in criticism of Tilly.

'I've always liked your father,' said Johnny, as if somehow reading her mind. 'I credit myself with his marrying your mother.'

'Really?' Libby was amazed.

'I first met James Robson in Shillong – when I was stationed there in the twenties. Extracted a tooth for him.' Johnny grinned. 'And he took me hunting as payment. I had a hunch that he would get on well with Tilly – so I asked him to deliver some of my wedding photographs to my family as he was due some leave. Next thing I heard, my sister was marrying him and coming out to India. Imagine how pleased I was!'

'Was Mother happy in those days?' asked Libby.

Johnny nodded. 'Oh, I think so. No doubt India was a bit of a shock after life in Newcastle but she soon had Jamie and they both seemed besotted parents, judging by her letters at least.'

'The fact that they had three children together must have meant they were happy, mustn't it?' Libby mused.

'Of course. On the few times we got together, you all seemed the ideal family – boisterous and full of fun – especially you, Libby.'

Libby smiled. 'Was I?'

'Yes. Helena and I were always a little envious of Tilly and James,' admitted Johnny. 'We would have liked children.'

Libby saw the regret flit across her uncle's face.

'I'm sorry you didn't,' she said.

Johnny drained off his tea. 'Still,' he said, 'we've had a very good life in India. I wouldn't swap that for anything.'

'Will you stay?' Libby asked. 'I mean stay on in India once Independence comes?'

Her uncle glanced around as if fearing he might be overheard.

'It's still not certain when that will be,' he answered. 'We might have a few years left.'

'The talk in Britain,' said Libby, 'is that it will come sooner rather than later.'

Her uncle spoke more briskly. 'I will leave that decision up to your aunt. I would quite happily retire to Northumberland or the Borders and spend my days fishing but it's different for Helena and her father. I'm not sure they could stand the climate, for one thing.'

'I think the weather would be the least of it,' Libby said forthrightly. 'I can't imagine Aunt Helena enjoying retirement in a country cottage without servants or the club. And all her friends are here.'

Johnny sighed. 'There has been talk among some of them about whether to move home.'

'But it isn't home, is it?' Libby persisted. 'Not for people who have never lived there. I can't tell you what a shock it was for me to land up in England at the age of eight. Imagine what it would be like for someone the age of Colonel Swinson!'

'We'd look after him well,' said Johnny a little defensively.

'I know you would, Uncle Johnny,' said Libby, 'but his home is here. Besides, colonial attitudes like his don't go down well in Britain these days – and I agree with that.'

'Tilly warned me you were a bit of a socialist,' he said with a wry look. 'So what would you do with an old *koi hai* like my father-in-law?'

Libby didn't hesitate. 'Let him stay here and live out his life on his veranda, overseeing his tropical garden.'

'So have you come back to India to stay?' asked Johnny. 'Despite all the uncertainty.'

'Yes, I hope so,' said Libby. 'This is my country and I love it.'

Her uncle placed a hand on her shoulder. 'You sound like James,' he said, smiling. 'Just as strong-willed and just as brave.'

They dropped their empty pottery cups on to the pile by the chai-wallah's stall and walked back to the car. On the way down Free School Street, Libby asked her uncle, 'Can we find Hamilton Road? I think it's off Park Street. I have a card I'd like to deliver there.'

'Of course,' said Johnny. 'Did you forget to go there with your aunt the other day?'

'Not exactly,' said Libby. 'I didn't think she'd approve.'

'Oh, so who lives there?'

'Dr Fatima Khan. She's a good friend of Adela's and Sam's from their Simla days. Now she works at the Eden Hospital.'

Johnny nodded. 'Ah, the women's hospital.' He glanced at her as he negotiated the traffic. 'I think you are being a bit unfair on Helena. She isn't as prejudiced against Indians as you think – especially educated ones.'

'But she might be,' said Libby, 'if she knew that Dr Khan's brother lives there too – and that he has been to prison for anti-British actions. According to Adela, Ghulam Khan blew up the Governor of Punjab's car when he was only eighteen.'

'Good Lord!' Johnny exclaimed.

'Sam says he's calmed down a lot, but I think he's still a bit of a communist,' said Libby.

'So you'd quite like to meet him?' Johnny guessed.

Libby blushed. 'He does sound interesting, but it's Dr Khan I'd like to make friends with. Both Adela and Sam really admire and like her. And Sam's sister is married to Rafi Khan, one of Fatima's other brothers.'

'Oh, that family!' said Johnny as realisation dawned. 'The one Cousin Sophie married into?'

'Yes.' Libby saw her uncle frowning. 'So I'm right: Aunt Helena wouldn't approve?'

'Well, she doesn't have a very high opinion of Sophie since she married Rafi,' Johnny admitted. 'Helena had a soft spot for Sophie's first husband, Tam Telfer, a forester. She thought Sophie behaved badly – leaving Tam and becoming a Muslim to marry Rafi.'

'I think she was very brave to do so,' Libby replied. 'And Mother always said that Tam didn't treat Sophie at all well.'

'That could be true,' sighed Johnny. 'I never warmed to Telfer the way that Helena did. Rather outspoken and arrogant type, if you ask me.'

As he drove down wide Park Street with its shops and offices, they both looked out for the turning into Hamilton Road. The further east they travelled, the prestigious mansion blocks gave way to more down-at-heel housing.

'I think this is it,' said Johnny, turning into a narrow street on the north side. Tall blocks of flats with crumbling façades and bleached shutters faced each other over a dusty uneven lane. The car bumped up the side street.

'Amelia Buildings,' said Libby, pointing, 'that's where the Khans live.'

Johnny parked the car. 'I'll come with you,' he insisted, climbing out.

They pushed at a heavy wooden door and went inside. Sitting at a small table in the dark hallway, a skinny man in a lungi and a faded military jacket stood to attention and asked if he could help. Behind him Libby could see a row of pigeonholes holding letters for the various flats.

'I'd like to leave this for Dr Khan, please.' She handed over the envelope with her letter and calling card.

Johnny handed him a few annas. 'Make sure the doctor gets it promptly.'

The man took it and bowed, assuring them that he would.

'Thank you,' said Libby as she turned and went back out into the bright sunshine.

'What took you so long?' Helena wanted to know. 'Too much chatting on the church steps, I bet.'

'We've had a lovely morning,' said Libby, determined to be more patient with her aunt. 'Will there be a chance of tennis later? I'll go and get my whites and shoes just in case.'

Johnny drove them out to the Tollygunge Club, a substantial colonial building set in lush grounds. It was busy with British families tucking into lunch at tables in the open air, waited on by an army of smartly dressed servants.

To Libby's dismay, the Percy-Barratts waved them over.

'Come and join us!' called Muriel, already ordering a waiter to set more places at their table.

They spent the next hour ploughing through a huge meal of lentil soup, fish in white sauce, mild chicken curry and chocolate sponge pudding with custard. Libby only half listened to the women gossiping about people she didn't know – their ailments and family relations – and news of British friends retired back home and recent deaths. The men talked of cricket and horse racing.

Everyone was too full of lunch to want to play tennis. They dozed under newspapers or flicked through magazines in the shade.

Libby went for a walk, keen to escape. She strolled through a beautiful oasis of lawns and trees like an English garden on a hot summer's day. She found it hard to believe that three or four miles to the north lay a teeming Indian city or that there had ever been violence and unrest in Calcutta. Nobody seemed to want to talk about it.

Libby wondered if there was any chance of her father coming to fetch her sooner than in March or whether she could make her way up to Assam alone. If there was no George in Calcutta, the thought of another three weeks of bumping into the Percy-Barratts and their kind made her heart sink.

Yet Libby felt a flicker of triumph at her attempt to contact Dr Fatima Khan. She wanted to get an Indian view on the upheavals of the past year since the post-war elections and the deepening splits between Hindus and Muslims over the future of India. She had found out more in Britain about the worsening political crisis in India than she had since arriving in the country.

She knew all about the Muslim League's demand for a homeland called Pakistan and their fear that a united India under the Congress Party would result in perpetual Hindu domination. But Jinnah, the League's leader, had been largely blamed for inflaming anti-Hindu feeling which had led to the killings in Calcutta the previous summer. The violence had spread into rural east Bengal and had only died down after the charismatic Congress leader, Ghandi, had gone to live among the terrified villagers and calmed the situation.

What did Muslims like the Khans think? The Watsons and their friends seldom mentioned the communal troubles. They only talked about the dwindling numbers of British filling the civil service posts and who among their acquaintances were applying for jobs in other parts of the Empire. Libby determined that she would break out of the British enclave and find out for herself what was going on.

CHAPTER 6

Libby was exultant when, two days later, an invitation to afternoon tea arrived by post from Fatima Khan. It helped lessen her disappointment that she still hadn't heard from George.

'Who is it from?' Helena asked, intrigued. 'Is it your young man?'

'No, it's from a friend of Adela's – a lady doctor,' said Libby. 'She's inviting me for tea tomorrow.'

'Kiran can drop you off and pick you up.'

'That's kind,' said Libby, 'but I've decided to go into town earlier and have another look at the art gallery – take my sketch pad. I'll get the tram to the Maidan.'

'Not on your own, surely?' Helena looked worried. 'Your uncle can go with you.'

'I'll be fine,' said Libby firmly. 'And I'll get a rickshaw to Hamilton Road.'

When her aunt protested, Johnny intervened. 'Libby can look after herself, darling. She's used to being independent and at her age she doesn't need our permission to leave the house, does she?'

'I suppose not,' said Helena doubtfully. 'You will wear one of your nice new dresses, won't you, dear?'

Libby's heart quickened with excitement as she mounted the staircase inside Amelia Buildings. The *chowkidar* had told her that Dr Khan lived at the top, on the fourth floor. The mansion block must once have been a desirable place to live; it had marble pillars in the entrance and large arched windows, but the tiled floors were cracked and some of the ornate shutters hung loose on rusted hinges. There was a strong smell of spicy cooking as she took the stairs two at a time.

A small, dark-skinned woman opened the door to her knocking. Beyond the door was a faded green curtain which the servant pulled aside, with a slim hand beckoning Libby into a large, airy, high-ceilinged room. Seeing a rack of shoes near the door, Libby pulled off her new court shoes.

'Miss Robson.' A handsome bespectacled woman who looked to be in her late thirties came forward with an outstretched hand. She was wearing a calf-length buff-coloured dress and a gauzy cream shawl. 'Welcome. I'm Fatima. No need to take off your shoes.'

Libby shook hands and smiled. 'They're killing my feet anyway. Aunt Helena insisted on buying them. And please call me Libby.' Libby reached into her new handbag and drew out a tin. 'These are for you – Scottish toffees. Adela said you'd like them.'

Fatima exclaimed, 'How kind! I love toffee – ever since my brother Rafi brought them back from Scotland when I was a girl. I'll have to hide them from Ghulam or he'll eat them all. He has a terribly sweet tooth.'

'Is your brother here too?' Libby asked.

'He's still at work,' said Fatima. 'He's a journalist with *The Statesman* newspaper. Perhaps you will meet him another time.'

'Yes, I'd like that,' said Libby, feeling a flicker of disappointment. He sounded like the sort of man who would have interesting views on the current situation.

'Please, come and sit down. Are you ready for tea?'

'Thank you, yes.'

'Sitara will bring it in then.'

Fatima turned to the servant, handed over the tin of toffees and spoke in a language Libby didn't understand. Perhaps it was Punjabi, as the Khan family hailed from Lahore. Adela had told Libby about Fatima's devoted servant, a Hindu widow that the doctor had rescued from the streets years ago.

Libby glanced around the room. It was whitewashed and simply furnished with table and chairs, two cane seats with blue cushions, a desk scattered with papers next to a long bookcase and another pile of books propping up a radiogram. The room smelt of sandalwood and the polished floor was partly covered with a blue-and-gold Persian carpet.

Libby sat in one of the cane chairs, tucking a stockinged leg under her. It was a habit she had picked up at boarding school and which irritated her mother, but Tilly wasn't there to chastise her. Libby wondered what her mother would think of her visiting an Indian home and decided she wouldn't mind. She was less sure what her father might think; she didn't really know his views on a range of matters.

As they waited for tea, Fatima spoke in a calm soft voice, probing Libby with questions. How had her journey been? What had she done so far in Calcutta? What news of Adela and Sam? How were her mother and brothers, her father? Libby was surprised at how much the doctor seemed to know about her family. Adela must have spoken of them all.

Sitara brought in a tray loaded with food: open sandwiches – cucumber and tomato – a Madeira cake, a selection of Indian sweetmeats, and the toffees displayed in a pretty blue-glazed bowl. The servant returned with another tray with a tea set and a large china teapot, beautifully decorated with green and yellow birds.

Libby tucked into the tea. The sweetmeats tasted of rich, creamy fudge. After sugar rationing in Britain, Libby was not used to such sweetness and found them almost too sickly. But Fatima pressed her to eat more.

Halfway through tea, Libby heard a pounding of feet on the stairs to the flat and then the door was swinging open and a stocky dark-haired man in a crumpled linen suit was barging through the curtain.

'They're leaving!' he cried. 'It's just been announced! The Brit—'

Abruptly he caught sight of Libby and stopped, his face registering surprise.

'This is Miss Libby Robson,' Fatima said. 'A relation of Adela Robson's. Libby, this is my brother Ghulam.'

Libby stood. 'How do you do?' She smiled and put out her hand, wishing she had kept her shoes on to look more sophisticated.

Ghulam hesitated, his look suddenly guarded and the excitement gone.

'Miss Robson,' he said with a nod, taking her hand in a brief handshake.

Libby feared he must be thinking her a typical memsahib in her crisp frock and cardigan. She wanted him to like her.

'Through my mother I'm a distant cousin of your sister-in-law, Sophie.'

He gave her a droll look. 'Ah, the glamorous Sophie.'

'Sophie and Rafi were very kind to me when I was a child,' said Libby, 'and they were great fun.'

'Yes,' he said, 'my brother has always enjoyed the company of sahibs more than his own kind.'

Libby coloured at his sarcastic tone.

'Ghulam, you know that's unfair,' Fatima chided. 'Rafi has been a loyal brother to us both – and he works for a rajah, not the British.'

Ghulam gave an amused snort. 'Indian princes are even worse. When Independence comes, the rajahs will be dragged into the modern world or forfeit their wealth.' He glanced at Libby. 'Please, sit down. I didn't mean to interrupt your tea party.'

'Join us,' said Fatima, 'and then you can tell us what it is that brings you rushing home early.'

Ghulam threw off his jacket and straddled one of the hard wooden chairs. His white shirt sleeves were rolled up, exposing hairy muscled arms. His broad face became animated again.

'The news is just coming through from London – the Britishers will hand over by next year.' He gave a triumphant smile. 'It's really happening.'

Fatima gasped in excitement. 'Are you sure? When next year?'

'By next June at the latest,' said Ghulam. 'Even after the elections I never really believed they would give us proper independence. But now they have to – the pressure for them to go is too strong.'

'Congratulations,' said Libby. 'I'm glad. I didn't doubt that the Atlee Government would stick to their promise.'

Ghulam scrutinised her. 'So you are a supporter of the socialist Labour Government, Miss Robson?'

'Very much,' said Libby. 'I would have voted for them but I wasn't quite twenty-one at the election.'

She felt her cheeks grow hotter at his assessing look and wished she hadn't mentioned her age. It made her sound immature when she felt much older. Ghulam looked to be in his late thirties or early forties. She couldn't decide if he was handsome or not. He was heavy-jawed and at some time his nose had been broken but he had the most startlingly green eyes under thick dark eyebrows and his mouth was sensuous. He was well spoken, with a deep voice, and she remembered Adela telling her how she had once seen him hold a crowd enthralled with his oratory at a political demonstration in Simla before the War.

'We hope for a progressive government in India too,' he said. 'Once you Britishers have gone.'

He held her gaze as he stretched over and picked up one of the Indian cakes, popping it into his mouth whole.

'Not all of us intend going,' said Libby. 'I've only just returned. My father thinks the tea planters will still be needed.'

'Does he think we Indians are incapable of running our own tea gardens? We do all the hard work as it is.'

'I'm sure he doesn't think that,' said Libby. 'He is training up a very capable deputy manager, Manzur, to take his place.'

'But not his place on the company board, I imagine?' Ghulam said with a look of derision. 'The Britishers will try and cling on to their wealth as long as possible. But the day will come when the headquarters of the big commercial houses – the tea and jute and oil – must be in India, not London or Dundee. India must have control of its own resources and trade. There will be no long-term future for men like your father.'

'Well, I think you are wrong.' Libby felt her face grow hotter with annoyance. 'And I too plan to stay.'

He looked sceptical. 'And do what, Miss Robson?'

Libby couldn't think of a reply. She hadn't really thought beyond getting back out to India and being reunited with her father.

When she said nothing, Ghulam gave a twitch of a smile. 'Don't you think you'll find the Britisher clubs rather dull and empty once most of your fellow memsahibs have retired back to England?'

Libby flashed back. 'They're not the most interesting of places whether full of memsahibs or not. I shan't miss them.'

'Good reply,' said Fatima with a wry smile. 'Don't let my brother tease you. He's terrible for getting on his high horse.' She shot her brother a warning look, adding, 'I'm sure Libby will find something useful to do. There will be a great need for forward-thinking women in the new India.'

Ghulam reached for a sweet from the bowl.

'Ah, real Scottish toffees!' he said, with a child-like glee that surprised Libby. 'The best thing to come out of Britain apart from cricket.' He unwrapped it and put it in his mouth.

Libby sipped her tea and watched him warily as he chewed, his jaws working hard to soften the toffee. She sensed a deep anger in him; no doubt he disapproved of his sister inviting one of the despised Britishers into his home. And yet Sam and Adela had spoken of him with liking and admiration, so he must have been friendly towards them. She persevered.

'So are you supporters of Congress or the Muslim League?' asked Libby.

Ghulam raised an eyebrow. 'Someone has been doing her homework.'

Fatima said, 'Congress. I want a united India.'

'Neither,' said Ghulam. 'As a radical socialist I'm suspicious of the way Congress is pandering to militant Hindus in order to win support. It's a dangerous game. The new India must be secular; I voted with the communists.'

'So neither of you agrees with the Muslim League?' asked Libby.

'No,' said Ghulam. 'I understand their fears but disagree with their demands. To divide the Punjab and Bengal from India as they suggest would be disastrous; India must stay as one country.'

'But you are both Muslim,' said Libby, 'and would be in a minority. Doesn't that worry you?'

His eyes glittered. 'We are Indians first. We have as much right to live here as anyone. Religion shouldn't come into it.'

'Not all of our family agrees,' said Fatima, her look suddenly sombre. 'Our father is a member of the League in the Punjab.'

Ghulam was scathing. 'He is just keeping in with what is popular in Lahore to ensure his business is safe. He's just like Jinnah – enjoys the good things in life too much to be devout.'

'You shouldn't speak about our father like that,' Fatima reproved him.

Ghulam said dryly, 'I'm sure it's nothing to the things he's said about me over the years.'

'Don't you see your family in Lahore any more?' asked Libby.

Fatima shook her head. 'I went home briefly when our mother died just before the War but not since. They've never understood why I wanted to be a doctor more than get married. Rafi was the only one who always stuck up for me – and he's the only one Ghulam and I are still in contact with.'

'Family are not as important as comrades,' said Ghulam. 'When the Britishers throw you in prison, that's when you know who your true friends are.'

Libby gave him an assessing look. 'But Adela said it was Rafi and the Rajah of Gulgat who helped get you released from prison,' said Libby. She was gratified when she saw him blush slightly.

'I was due to be released anyway,' he answered, glancing away. 'But I count Rafi among my friends.'

'Even though he fraternises with the *sahib-log*?' Libby couldn't resist provoking him.

'Those days will soon be over,' Ghulam said, his eyes flashing, 'and Rafi will have to do his bit for the new India – unless his wife takes him back to Scotland.'

'I can't see Sophie doing that,' said Libby. 'She has no family left there. And is Sophie not just as entitled to stay in India as you or Rafi? She was born here and has spent all her adult life here.'

'Of course she is,' said Fatima. 'She is Rafi's wife.'

Ghulam gave an impatient sigh. 'It doesn't matter what a handful of Britishers and privileged Indians think or do,' he said. 'It's the millions of ordinary Indians whose voices must be heard.' He swung off his seat and stood up. 'Do you know the conditions that most workers in Calcutta endure, day in and day out? The men in the jute mills, for instance? They come from the countryside to find work – but even if they slave all day they never earn enough to pay the high rents or feed their families. That is the legacy that you Britishers are leaving us. That is what Congress and the League should be discussing – how we make

India a more equal society – not turning against each other and dividing up the spoils!'

He plunged his hands into his pockets and strode to the window.

'I agree with you,' said Libby.

'Do you?' He seemed disconcerted by her reply and stared out between the half-ajar shutters as if there was something of importance below.

'Yes,' she said eagerly, 'I too believe strongly in fighting injustice.'

He turned to look at her, his strong-featured face half in shadow.

'And does that include your father's tea pickers?' he challenged.

'What do you mean?'

'I've been to the tea plantations and seen their working conditions,' said Ghulam. 'They're treated like serfs – living in hovels that you Britishers wouldn't keep your dogs in – and working till they drop.' He marched back across the room and stared down at her. 'We went there to try and unionise them but men like your father chased us away.'

Libby was aghast. She had no idea how the tea workers lived; she had been a child at Cheviot View. Were her precious memories of Assam built on an illusion? Had it only been idyllic for the British?

'I was only eight when I left,' she admitted. 'Too young to know about such things.'

'Quite so,' said Ghulam with a look of derision. 'You were being given a privileged schooling at the expense of all those women slaving on your father's plantation. Do their children not deserve a good schooling too?'

'Of course—'

'Well, they don't get one,' he snapped. 'The British Empire is built on the backs of the people they have subjugated and exploited but who reap none of the rewards.'

'I don't agree with British colonialism,' Libby insisted, her heart pounding.

'But you profit from it, nonetheless,' he accused. 'Your education and your fine principles all come at a cost and it's your father's workers who pay the price.'

'That's enough, Ghulam,' said Fatima, intervening. 'Libby is our guest.'

Libby stood up, suddenly furious. 'And what about your privileged education?' Libby accused. 'Did your family's building company not prosper from all the contracts that the British have given it over the years?'

'I have had nothing to do with my father's business,' said Ghulam hotly. 'I turned my back on that at the age of eighteen. I've dedicated my life to getting rid of colonial rule – gone to prison for it– and been cast out from my family. That's what fighting injustice is like for an Indian – it's not about fine words and school debates.'

'You think I'm just another spoilt little memsahib, don't you?' She glared at him. 'It suits you to think we are all the same – all your enemies – but we're not. What are you going to do once you don't have the British to blame for all your woes, Mr Khan? It's not the British who are setting fire to Hindu homes or butchering Muslims, is it? You Indians have to take some responsibility for the violence and for not agreeing to a political settlement – the Labour politicians in London at least have tried to do that.'

She turned to Fatima. 'Thank you for inviting me. I've really enjoyed meeting you but I think I'd better go. I'm very sorry to have caused such upset.'

Fatima rose too, looking distressed. 'Please don't blame yourself. It is Ghulam who should apologise.'

Libby flicked him a look but he remained silent, his expression stormy. Libby picked up her handbag. 'No, he's entitled to his opinions – as I am to mine.'

Libby walked towards the door. Fatima said, 'Ghulam will see you safely into a taxi.'

'There's no need,' said Libby stiffly.

Ghulam followed her. 'Please let me, Miss Robson.'

'You will call again, won't you?' Fatima said, as Ghulam opened the door for her.

Libby nodded as she jammed on her shoes. 'Thank you, Dr Khan.'

She descended the stairs with Ghulam a surly presence at her elbow. Her heart hammered. She could barely contain her anger. What right did he have to preach at her when he knew nothing about her? He was just as prejudiced and narrow-minded as the people he railed against. She had no idea why Sam and Adela liked him; to her, Ghulam Khan was rude and arrogant.

As soon as they reached the street, Adela was hailing a rickshaw.

'Let me summon a motor taxi,' said Ghulam.

'There's no need,' she said with a frosty glance. She could hardly bear to look at him. 'I can look after myself. And don't worry – I shan't embarrass you by coming here again. Your sister was only being polite.'

'Miss Robson,' he began. 'I shouldn't—'

But she was already clambering into the rickshaw. Libby couldn't wait to get away and put distance between them. As the rickshaw-wallah jostled his way down the lane, avoiding two boys in *dhotis* who were heaving an overloaded cart in the opposite direction, she clung on to the sides of the vehicle. Her eyes stung with angry tears. Libby didn't look back.

Ghulam stayed in the street, watching Libby's rickshaw merge into the traffic and the throng of passers-by. He pulled out a squashed packet of cigarettes from his top pocket and searched for matches. Realising they were in the jacket that he had left upstairs, he sighed in frustration. He put the packet back in his pocket and ran his hands through his thick hair with a groan of annoyance.

What an infuriating woman! Her remarks about his past life in Lahore had particularly riled him. It was true he had benefited from an elite education at Aitcheson College but he had rejected such a privileged life. Instead of training as a lawyer as his father had wanted him to do, he had joined the Free Hindustan Movement and been thrown out of his father's house.

Libby Robson had no idea of the sacrifice he had made to follow the path that he had; five years in prison then living hand-to-mouth as he tramped the country encouraging resistance to colonial rule, always keeping one step ahead of the authorities. Only with the outbreak of war did he agree a temporary truce in his revolt against the British. Communists and socialists like him had agreed that the greater evil facing them all was fascism, so they had co-operated with the war effort. Ghulam thought bitterly how he had been vilified by friends in the Congress Party for doing so, and how he had lost the trust of some comrades dear to him – one in particular.

For a time, he had turned his back on politics. When the appalling famine had hit Bengal four years ago, Ghulam had thrown all his energies into helping the starving. It had been a hopeless job. Fatima had arrived in Calcutta and found him worn out and dispirited. If it hadn't been for his caring sister, he might have driven himself into an early grave. It was through friends of hers that he had secured his part-time job at the newspaper.

Ghulam looked up at the top-floor flat. He felt a wave of remorse for spoiling Fatima's tea party. She allowed herself so few moments of relaxation from her demanding hospital job. What had got into him?

The Robson woman had not deserved his anger either. She had struck him as one of those do-gooder missionary types – well-meaning but patronising – in her prim dress and straw hat. Was it her insistence on agreeing with him about ending colonial rule that he had found so irritating? Or was it the way she had regarded him with those dark-blue eyes as if she somehow found him wanting that had goaded him into rudeness?

He turned and retreated into Amelia Buildings. He would not be judged by some Britisher half his age who thought she knew India better than he did.

'Damn you!' he cursed under his breath as he mounted the stairs. Ghulam wasn't sure if the oath was for the girl or for himself. Now he would have to explain his baffling behaviour to his disappointed sister.

CHAPTER 7

Newcastle, early March

A dela took Sam's hand and squeezed it. They were standing outside the haberdashery shop in Cullercoats owned by Sam's adoptive mother, Mrs Jackman. The sign said closed. It was a raw, sunless Sunday afternoon; the on-shore wind was bitter and the sea a churning steel-grey.

With a flood of emotion, Adela remembered how she had stood here over eight years ago, heavily pregnant and torn with indecision: should she go into the shop and make herself known to Sam's estranged mother or not? Her courage had failed her. She had feared interfering in Sam's life. Sam had been so bitter about his mother's desertion in Assam when he was such a young boy.

But later, as a mother herself and knowing the agony of separation, Adela had gone to see Mrs Jackman. She still recalled how Sam's mother had almost collapsed with shock and relief to hear word of her son. If it hadn't been for Mrs Jackman, Sam would never have known the true identity of his real parents, the Logans, or been reunited with his long-lost sister, Sophie.

Even though Sam had begun a correspondence with his mother, Adela knew today's meeting was going to be a trial for him. They had been in Newcastle for well over a month yet Sam had put off coming to Cullercoats until now.

'The longer you put it off, the worse it will be,' Adela had said, finally losing patience. 'Let me make the arrangements if you won't.'

So here they were: for the first time in over thirty years, Sam and his mother would come face-to-face.

Adela felt his large hand trembling in hers. Even though outwardly her tall, athletic husband looked strong and in control, she knew that inside he was feeling like that bewildered young boy whose mother had run away and left him. His handsome face was tense and his brow furrowed.

'She loves you,' Adela said in encouragement, stepping forward and ringing the bell to the upstairs flat. 'And this will be just as hard for her.'

Mrs Jackman must have been keeping a lookout, for she answered the door almost immediately. She was less plump than Adela remembered and her hair – bound into a neat bun – was now completely silver. She wore a well-cut purple dress that would have been the height of fashion twenty years ago.

'Adela! Sam!' Mrs Jackman exclaimed, her arms outstretched and eyes burning with tears. 'Sam, you've grown so tall!'

It was a ridiculous remark to make to a man who was almost forty but Adela felt a stab of pity. All these years, the woman must have tried to imagine what Sam looked like growing up, yet in her mind's eye he would forever be the skinny, grinning seven-year-old that Mrs Jackman had last set eyes on.

It was like that for Adela. Her son was now eight but to her he was still that bright-eyed baby with soft dark hair sucking contentedly at her breast.

Sam, too overwhelmed to speak, ignored the woman's attempt to hug him and stuck out a hand. His mother's face fell but she shook his hand, holding on to it for longer than a casual handshake.

Adela gave her a kiss on the cheek. 'It's lovely to see you again.'

Mrs Jackman's chin wobbled. 'I've been so looking forward to this, dear.'

'So have we,' said Adela, her heart going out to the woman. 'Haven't we, Sam?'

Sam nodded, swallowing hard. He was staring at his mother as if trying to find something familiar about her.

'Please,' said Mrs Jackman, recovering some poise, 'come away out of the cold. What terrible weather we're having. You must find it freezing after India. I've got the kettle on.'

She bustled ahead up the steep staircase. 'Pull the front door behind you, Sam, dear.'

Adela gave Sam an encouraging smile and, for the first time since arriving in Cullercoats, he smiled back.

Mrs Jackman must have been saving up her ration coupons because the tea trolley that she wheeled into the neat, brightly lit upstairs sitting room was groaning with sandwiches, pies and cake. Sam followed her back into the kitchen offering to help brew the tea. Ignoring her half-hearted refusal, he set about pouring boiling water from the steaming kettle into the waiting teapot. Watching from the doorway, Adela knew Sam needed to expend his nervous energy; he was like a caged animal in the small flat. She wondered if Mrs Jackman would let him smoke.

The tea made, Adela and Sam were invited to sit down on the chintz-covered sofa. Pale-green plastic trays were clamped to the arms on which, Adela presumed, they were to balance their tea cups and plates. Mrs Jackman made Sam pile his plate high with food.

'I made your favourite bacon-and-egg pie,' she said, with an anxious smile. 'And take another slice of ginger cake. You always liked ginger cake.'

Sam complied. They talked of trivial matters – or rather Mrs Jackman did – while Sam and Adela ate. She began a rambling commentary on the long snow-bound winter they had endured and about the possibility of renting out her shop to someone younger.

'And have you managed to pick up work, Sam?' she asked.

He swallowed and nodded. 'I'm doing a bit of photography work for a local newspaper. Not much – just a handful of weddings – but it's a start.'

'Photography,' gasped his mother. 'That's grand.'

'Sam's been helping me in the café too,' said Adela.

'Fixing things up,' said Sam, 'and re-decorating.'

'It's going to be quite a struggle to keep it going,' said Adela. 'It's pretty run down – Lexy did an amazing job keeping it open during the War but such a lot needs doing.'

'With a bit of hard work, we'll manage,' Sam said, smiling at his wife. 'This spring, I'm going to get the café allotment going again.'

'It's Sam's idea.' Adela smiled back. 'It's so overgrown and neglected since the end of the War but my green-fingered husband will bring it back to life. My mother grew a lot for the tearoom in the early days.'

'You'll be good at that, Sam,' said Mrs Jackman. 'I was proud to hear of you planting orchards for the natives before the War.'

She plied him with more cake and watched intently for signs of enjoyment.

Adela said, 'The food's delicious, Mrs Jackman. I think I should get your recipes for the café. Now our manager Lexy's retired, I'm in charge of the menu.'

'I could make some pies and cakes for you,' she offered at once.

'Goodness, I didn't mean that,' said Adela. 'You have your own business to run.'

'I'm winding down the shop – my eyesight's not good enough for such close work these days – and I've always enjoyed cooking.'

'That's very kind of you but it would be quite a commitment,' Adela cautioned.

'I'm fit and healthy,' said Mrs Jackman stoutly, 'and I'd love to help you out.'

Adela looked at Sam. 'Perhaps we could have a think about your kind offer and let you know?'

'Of course, dear.'

Sam said, 'It's up to Adela – she's in charge. But I can vouch for her being a good boss.' He grinned and brushed his wife's cheek with affection.

Adela saw Mrs Jackman holding back sudden tears.

'I'm so happy that you've come back to live here,' she said. 'I know it must be very strange for you, Sam, when you've always lived in India. But I'm so grateful. I never thought I'd ever get the chance to see you again. I know I don't deserve it.'

She fumbled for her handkerchief and dabbed at her brimming eyes. Adela went at once to put her arm about her.

'Please don't upset yourself. Sam now understands that you wanted to take him with you but that his father wouldn't let you.'

'I know,' said Mrs Jackman, 'but I will never get over the guilt.' She looked at Sam in distress. 'You were the most precious thing to me, yet I couldn't stand being in India a minute longer – or with your father. We were never suited but it wasn't really his fault either – it was like a fever that I couldn't control. I had to get out. But I should have stayed for your sake. You poor boy! It breaks my heart to think of what you must have gone through. What you must have thought of your mother.'

She broke down sobbing. Adela held her. She looked at Sam and saw the struggle of emotions in his tortured expression. She knew he still bore anger towards his adoptive mother for what she did – for not telling him that she was going – but she also knew what a compassionate and loving man he was. Sam was incapable of holding a grudge forever. Adela felt emotional to think of all those years of misunderstanding between mother and son. It made her all the more determined not to waste time in getting down to searching for her own son.

Sam stood up and came to his mother's side. Crouching in front of her, he gently took the handkerchief from her and wiped her face of tears.

'I did miss you,' he said, his voice hoarse, 'but I had a happy life in India on the boat with Dad. Don't think of me as a miserable boy who didn't enjoy life – 'cause that wasn't me.'

He took her hands in his. 'But the bravest thing you ever did was to send Adela the shawl and bracelet that allowed me to find out about my blood parents and my sister. My wonderful big sister, Sophie, who I love very much. If you knew her, you would love her too. I will always be grateful that you did that.' He hesitated, then said, 'Thank you, Mam.'

Mrs Jackman gave a tearful cry. 'You haven't called me Mam since you were a lad!' She threw her arms around him and kissed the top of his head.

Adela blinked away her own tears. Then Sam buried his head in his mother's lap and let out a sob.

'Oh, my bonny lad,' Mrs Jackman said tenderly, stroking his head. The three of them held on to each other as Sam wept.

CHAPTER 8

Calcutta, March

It was George Brewis turning up on the Watsons' doorstep – bearing a huge bouquet of flowers for Helena and a dinner invitation for Libby – that made Libby swiftly abandon her plan to leave Calcutta early. She was thrilled at his sudden appearance. George had been to Dacca with work and had only just picked up her message.

'Of course, I'd love to go out to dinner!' she agreed eagerly.

'Good,' he said with a wink. 'I'll pick you up at seven and we'll go to the club for cocktails first.'

How glad she was to see him. Her heart soared at the sight of his handsome ruddy face grinning at her from under his topee. She spent more time than usual getting ready to go out. She chose a red-and-black dress with a heart-shaped neckline that Josey had helped her adapt before leaving Newcastle. Piling up her dark-auburn hair in a loose bun and putting on make-up, Libby stared at her reflection in the mirror and hoped she looked sophisticated enough for the worldly George.

The hairstyle showed off her oval face and the red lipstick emphasised her full mouth. But there were dark shadows beneath her eyes that betrayed the string of sleepless nights she had had since her disastrous visit to the Khans. She had been shaken by the encounter with the activist Ghulam; furious at his dismissal of her opinions and his hostility towards her and her father. How dare he be the judge of them?

She had taken her revenge by drawing a cartoon of Ghulam; his thick shoulders and torso turned into those of a tiger, his face snarling and contorted through the bars of a cage. The cage is open but he won't come out. A young woman in trousers is throwing away her topee and saying, 'Well, stay and sulk about Britishers if you like. I'm off to an Independence Day freedom party.'

Tossing in bed, too hot for sleep, Libby had wondered why she minded Ghulam's disapproval so much. Perhaps it was because, ever since she had been the eager pupil of her radical history teacher, Miss MacGregor, she had seen herself as enlightened and on the side of the oppressed. In Britain, Libby was seen as a progressive young woman with a mind of her own. She had thought it would be the same in India. But at the first chance of making Indian friends, she had failed. Fatima had not been in touch all week. To Ghulam Khan she would always be a privileged white woman: one of the *sahib-log* who had kept his people downtrodden and disenfranchised for two hundred years.

Perhaps he was right and she should be packing her bags and booking a passage to Britain. Maybe this wasn't her country after all. Since the news broke that the British were to hand over power within the next year, the chatter in the Calcutta drawing rooms had abruptly switched from sport and films to how long they should stay in Bengal. There was a flurry of calls to shipping lines and air companies to book summer passages home just in case trouble was brewing again.

'Well, I'm not going to run away,' Libby said, with a mulish pout at her reflection. 'I'm staying in India – and no man is going to tell me that I can't.'

George took her to the Saturday Club near to his digs and they drank pink gins with some of his bachelor friends before joining a party of diners at Firpo's on Chowringhee Street. Libby knew it was one of the most popular restaurants in Calcutta. By day it served up robust lunches of Scotch broth and steak and kidney pie, as well as lavish afternoon teas; by night it laid on five-course dinners. Libby had heard that it boasted a lively orchestra and a full-sized sprung dance floor, which she hoped George would guide her around. Chandeliers sparkled and fans whirred in the large dining room, which buzzed with conversation and laughter. Mellow with gin, Libby was seduced by its glitzy opulence.

She was disappointed to discover that she was not dining alone with George as expected, but the group of friends were a lively mixed crowd of young people. Several of the women were obviously Anglo-Indian and two of the men wore Sikh turbans. Libby relished a renewed feeling of adventure.

'This is Flowers Dunlop, a friend of Adela's,' George said, introducing her to a petite woman in a slinky silver dress with gleaming dark hair fashioned into a short perm. She had huge dark eyes and a quick smile. Libby felt ungainly as she shook Flowers's slim hand.

'Oh, Adela spoke fondly of you. You're a nurse, aren't you?'

'Yes,' said Flowers, 'at the Presidency General Hospital. Are you enjoying Calcutta?'

'Yes,' said Libby, 'well, some of the time. I've been meaning to contact you – Adela said I should – I'm sorry I haven't up till now.'

'Don't be,' said Flowers, 'I'm sure you've had plenty to do. But you're very welcome to visit. My father would love to meet you. He's from a tea planter family too.'

'Oh, which one?' Libby asked with interest.

Flowers gave a vague wave of the hand. 'Oh, I'm not sure. You'd have to ask him. Assam not Darjeeling.' She slipped an arm through Libby's as if they were old friends. 'Come on; let's sit together so you can tell me all about yourself.'

It was the first of several dinner-dances that Libby was taken to by George and his friends. Sometimes they danced in the open-air winter garden at the Grand Hotel as well as returning to Firpo's to quickstep and tango across the crowded ballroom. Libby loved it when George chose her for the last waltz; she felt intoxicated being held close in his arms and feeling the brush of his chin against her cheek.

'I'm glad you came out to Calcutta, bonny Libby,' he murmured in her ear.

'I'm glad too,' she said with a dreamy smile.

Although she had been disappointed that George hadn't attempted to kiss her on any of their evenings out, she was sure it was only a matter of time before he did.

Libby attended tennis parties with George and went swimming at the Saturday Club after he had finished work. He invited her to a long, alcohol-fuelled dinner party at his chummery which spilled out on to the flat roof and ended with them all dancing in bare feet to an old wind-up gramophone.

Flowers and her nursing friends were nearly always there too. Flowers was a wonderful dancer but she never allowed any of the men to monopolise her on the dance floor. Libby couldn't work out if Adela's former school friend was keen on any man in particular and hoped it wasn't George.

Extravert George was friendly to everyone and usually the instigator of these parties but Libby liked to think he was especially attentive and affectionate towards her. A couple of times she met him for lunch too and she revelled in having him to herself. They chatted about family and news from Newcastle.

'Adela and Sam seem to be settling okay,' said Libby one lunchtime. It was a hot day – a taste of the higher temperatures to come now that it was the middle of March – and she was grateful to be in the airy dining room at Firpo's under the electric fans. 'Sam's met his mother at last – well, the woman who adopted him as a baby. Adela says they're getting on well and might be moving in with Mrs Jackman. Adela thinks she's quite a lonely woman and she's over the moon to see Sam again.'

'And Herbert's tearoom?' asked George. 'Has Adela saved it from collapse?'

'She's trying her best, by the sounds of it,' said Libby. 'She's even got Mrs Jackman helping with the cooking.' She eyed him before continuing.

'What does that look mean?' asked George.

'Adela says she's twisted Joan's arm to come in and help with waitressing,' Libby answered. 'Don't you hear from her at all?'

'From Joan?' George asked in surprise. 'No, why should I?'

'Doesn't she tell you how Bonnie's getting on?'

George hesitated, a forkful of sausage and mashed potato halfway to his mouth. 'Bonnie's not my bairn,' he said, 'so I don't need to know, do I?'

Libby felt uncomfortable. She would have understood if George had been bitter about Joan's infidelity but his indifference struck her as odd – perhaps not towards Joan but towards three-year-old Bonnie. After all, George himself had said how much his mother Olive adored the child and Adela was fond of her too, saying she was a sunny-natured little girl. Libby wondered if Adela found comfort in having Joan's daughter around to spoil or if it just made her hanker after her lost child? But did George really feel no affection towards Bonnie at all? Or was he pretending not to care so that he could start a new life out in India without any emotional ties?

She watched him carry on eating with his usual relish. George did everything with enthusiasm; it was one of the things she liked about him. Libby decided not to mention Bonnie again. Strange how different people could be: Adela had travelled halfway round the world to try and find her illegitimate baby, whereas George appeared to feel nothing for the child he had taken on during the War.

His plate cleared, George leant closer and took her hand across the table.

'Enough talk about Newcastle,' he said, giving her one of his disarming blue-eyed looks. 'I promised to give you a good time in Calcutta, didn't I?'

'You did' – Libby smiled – 'and you are.'

'That's grand.' He grinned. 'So when would you next like to go dancing, bonny lass?'

The moment George finally kissed her took Libby quite by surprise. After every dinner-dance, Libby had been hopeful that George would take her in his arms and kiss her goodnight but there had always been others around sharing the taxi, dropping her off in Alipore first.

One Sunday afternoon, on a picnic in the Botanical Gardens, while their friends dozed and chatted, George and Libby wandered off to look at the lake. She began talking about what concerned her; the ominous rumours that violence was erupting in the Punjab.

'Do you think it's possible that hundreds of Hindus have been massacred near Rawalpindi?' Libby asked. 'Or is it scaremongering? I know it's over a thousand miles away but the killing could spread to Bengal as well, couldn't it? It sounds too awful. Was it very terrible here last summer?'

'Luckily I was in England for most of August,' said George.

'Oh, of course,' Libby said, remembering. 'That's when we met up again.'

Perhaps it was the sudden memory of their night out in Newcastle that prompted George or perhaps he just wanted her to stop dwelling on the grim news. But the next moment he was taking her by the hand and pulling her behind the dense foliage of a tree. Tilting her chin, he leant towards her and covered her mouth with his in an eager embrace.

Libby's heart jolted in astonishment, then she was kissing him back with enthusiasm. His moustache smelt of curry and cologne and he tasted of beer as his tongue explored her mouth.

'Oh, lass,' he murmured, taking a breath, 'you're just as tasty as I remember.'

Libby stifled her amusement. He made her sound like a steak and kidney pie. He pressed her up against the trunk of the tree and kissed her again. Libby's heart hammered. Was he a little drunk?

'Brewis!' a voice called from a few yards away. 'Brewis, where've you gone?' It was Eddy Carter, one of his fellow lodgers from Harrington Street. 'We're going to play croquet – need you to make up the numbers.'

George and Libby broke apart. He gave her a wry look.

'To be continued,' he said with a conspiratorial grin.

Libby couldn't speak; her feelings were a mix of arousal and frustration – and something else she couldn't quite name. How far would they have gone if Eddy hadn't interrupted them?

Libby, her heart still hammering, had no idea how George managed to play croquet with his usual casual banter as if nothing had happened under the willow tree. She caught his look a couple of times and he gave her the slightest of winks but apart from that, he didn't single her out for attention.

She was aware of Flowers eyeing her during the game and knew that she must have seen them wander off together. Libby tried not to blush under her scrutiny. Had Flowers sent Eddy to look for George, jealous of them being alone?

At the end of the afternoon, when Libby was being dropped off in Alipore, Flowers said to her, 'I'm off work on Tuesday – come round for tiffin. You still haven't met my dad.'

Libby felt a pang of guilt that she hadn't done so; she had been too obsessed with George and trying to see him as much as possible.

'Thanks, I'd like that,' she agreed.

George saw her to the gate of New House. 'I have to go away this coming week,' he told her.

Libby was dismayed. 'For how long?'

'Ten days, but I'll be back in time for your birthday, I promise.'

Why hadn't he told her before? Ten days seemed like an eternity.

He grinned. 'And perhaps we can arrange a night out alone sometime soon?'

Libby smiled and nodded. He leant forward and pecked her on the cheek. 'Don't do anything I wouldn't do while I'm away,' he said.

She watched him hurry back to the waiting car and climb in beside Flowers. Libby felt a tug of jealousy. They waved. She raised her hand in farewell and watched until the car was out of sight. She was encouraged by George's increased ardour towards her at the picnic but was left wondering what it meant. Did George want her for his girl or not?

Flowers lived in busy Sudder Street behind Hogg's Market. Libby arrived by taxi. Since George had taken to organising her social life, her Aunt Helena had stopped fussing about Libby venturing out on her own. The taxi driver sounded his horn as he inched around bullock carts, porters, street sellers, cows, mangy dogs, shoe-shine boys and rickshaws. Stepping out of the car, Libby was almost deafened by the cries of vendors, the blare of horns and the shriek of scavenging birds.

The block of flats where Flowers lived with her parents was set back from the pavement behind tall iron gates and fronted by a small dusty courtyard with a banyan tree full of noisy sparrows. Flowers was looking out for her.

'We're on the second floor. I hope you're hungry.' Flowers grinned. 'Mum has laid in provisions for a small army.'

Whereas the Khans' living quarters had been sparsely furnished, the Dunlops' sitting room was crammed with dark, heavy mahogany furniture. Ornate side tables jostled for space with high-backed uphol-stered chairs, a chaise longue, a sideboard, a dining table and chairs and a harmonium. The walls were covered in old prints of Calcutta, gilt-framed mirrors and sconces that must once have held oil lamps. The walls were papered in faded green stripes and any parquet floor that wasn't hidden by furniture was covered in red durries.

A small, friendly-looking woman greeted her. 'I'm Flowers's mother – welcome to our home! We are so pleased to meet you. Call me Winnie.' She was dressed in a flowery frock and had dark hair kept in order by tortoiseshell combs.

Flowers's father was propped up in a long cane chair. Despite his baldness, he looked much younger than Libby had imagined, with a trim moustache and light-coloured eyes under bushy eyebrows. But then most of her contemporaries had fathers far younger than her own. Mr Dunlop didn't look Anglo-Indian either. Flowers evidently got her darker looks from her mother.

'How do you do, Miss Robson?' He reached for his sticks and Libby saw at once that he had only one leg.

'Please don't get up, Mr Dunlop,' she said, quickly crossing the room to shake his hand. 'It's very nice to meet you.'

He beamed. 'The pleasure is mine.'

Flowers tried to help her father to the table but he shrugged off her attempt with an impatient 'I can manage'. He beckoned Libby to sit beside him. It struck Libby how a man of his age – he didn't look more than fifty – must find enforced retirement a trial.

Tiffin was a four-course lunch of mulligatawny soup, chicken liver on toast, fried fish with tartare sauce, mashed potatoes and cabbage, finished off with a pudding of pink blancmange and stewed apple. It was washed down with iced jugs of homemade lemonade.

All the while, Mr Dunlop asked Libby questions about life in Assam and he reminisced about his time in the railway colony at Srimangal in East Bengal where he was once stationmaster.

'We were happiest there, weren't we, Winnie? Things went downhill when I was moved to Calcutta during the War. Realised too late I had diabetes – lost my leg.'

'It's not so bad here, Danny, dearest,' said Winnie. 'There's more to do than up-country – and we have family here.'

'Your family,' he muttered.

Libby saw Flowers roll her eyes. Libby tried to distract Mr Dunlop from thoughts of his reduced life in Calcutta.

'Flowers tells me that you are from a tea planter family from Assam too,' said Libby. 'I don't know any Dunlops. Whereabouts in Assam?'

Danny Dunlop gave a regretful shrug. 'That I don't know. You see, my parents died young and I was raised in an orphanage – so many planters succumbed to disease in those days; it's a tough climate. But I don't need to tell you that. I was always told they were British and that my father was Scottish. It's obvious from my name, isn't it? Dunlop is Scottish.'

Flowers said, 'Dad's always wanted to go back and trace our family one day, haven't you, Dad?'

'The journey would be too much for you,' fussed Winnie.

'You're probably right,' he said with a sigh. 'Still, I would have liked to go back to Shillong and seen where I grew up.'

'Shillong?' Libby looked at Flowers. 'Isn't that where you and Adela went to school too?'

'Yes, we overlapped for a short time,' said Flowers. 'Adela left and went to Simla but she was the best friend I had in that place. The other girls didn't treat Anglo-Indians like us very well.'

'You were just as British as they were!' Mr Dunlop protested. 'They had no right to be so unkind.'

'Mum turning up on speech day in a sari didn't help,' said Flowers.

'I only did that once,' said Winnie, 'and I looked twice as elegant as those horsey army women.'

'I'm sure you did,' Libby agreed.

Winnie gave a proud jut of her chin. 'My family can trace their roots back to some of the first Europeans in India – St Thomas Christians – but many of the newly arrived British look down their long noses as if we're no better than Untouchables.'

'Libby's family are not like that,' said Flowers.

'Sorry, I didn't mean you, Libby,' said Winnie quickly.

'Mum's right about the snobbery towards us though. It's something we've always had to live with but now it's really worrying. What will happen to us now that the British will be handing over to the Indians? We've worked for the British Raj for generations yet there's no guarantee that the jobs we have will be secure in the future.'

'We'll go back to Britain,' Danny Dunlop insisted. 'It's our home too.'

Winnie was outspoken. 'We could never afford it – and it's not our home.'

'Well, it's mine!' he protested. 'If my father hadn't died young I'd have been brought up on a tea plantation like Libby.'

'Don't get upset, Dad,' said Flowers. 'I shouldn't have mentioned it.'

'I'm sorry too,' Winnie apologised again. 'You just make me anxious with your talk of going to England. I think we Anglo-Indians should stick together and make the best of it here. Be a special kind of Indian in the new India.'

Danny exclaimed, 'The Indians have an even lower opinion of Anglo-Indians than the British – they hate us for doing our patriotic duty during the War – so don't expect any special treatment from the likes of Nehru and his Congress-wallahs.'

'What do you want to do, Flowers?' Libby asked.

The young woman shrugged.

'Flowers could get a good job back home nursing,' her father answered for her.

'But where would we go?' Flowers asked.

'Adela would help find us somewhere to live in Newcastle,' he suggested. 'And the climate would suit me better. I could enjoy a happy retirement there. Watch cricket and live by the sea. Find other railway-men to share a *chota peg* with at the club. Look up Dunlop relations.'

Winnie shook her head in disbelief. 'What other Dunlops? They won't all live together in a colony like a railway family here.'

'I'll find them,' he said with conviction.

Libby wondered how often they argued about their future. She hadn't realised how especially difficult and uncertain it must be for those families caught in the middle – the half-halfs, as Helena unkindly called them, accepted as neither truly British nor properly Indian.

Flowers looked embarrassed. 'I didn't invite Libby here to witness a family squabble. Let's talk of something else. When are you going up to Assam, Libby?'

'In a week or so – after my birthday – when my father comes to Calcutta.' Libby smiled.

'Lucky you. I haven't been out of the city for over two years,' said Flowers. 'I nursed in Assam during the War.'

'My daughter was on the Front Line in Burma,' said Mr Dunlop proudly, 'caring for our boys.'

'Yes, Adela told me,' said Libby. 'You were much braver than I was. Being a Land Girl was hard work but I was never in any danger.'

'We were too busy to think of the danger,' said Flowers with a rue-ful smile, 'but the conditions were hardly the Ritz.'

Eventually, Libby stood up to go and turned to Winnie. 'Thank you for such a lovely lunch. I've really enjoyed meeting you and Mr Dunlop.'

'You must call again before you leave Calcutta,' said Winnie, 'now you know where we are. Please call in anytime.'

'Yes,' agreed Danny, 'you must. I'd love another chat about Assam.'

'Thank you, I'd like that very much,' Libby said, touched by their warmth. 'I hope you'll all come to my party. My aunt and uncle are insisting on hosting one.'

The Dunlops seemed overwhelmed. Flowers answered for them. 'We'd love to!'

'It'll be a chance to pay back some hospitality before I leave Calcutta,' said Libby. 'Everyone's been so kind and generous. And you will get to meet my father.'

'Our fathers could talk about Shillong together, couldn't they?' Flowers smiled. 'That would be the next best thing to visiting, wouldn't it, Dad?'

But this seemed to upset Danny. 'How I wish I could travel back with you as far as Shillong – go and see my old school – just one last time.'

In alarm, Libby saw the man's eyes welling with tears. Perhaps her coming here and stirring up old memories had not been a good idea after all.

Suddenly Flowers put a hand on Libby's arm and said, 'Perhaps I could travel with you as far as Shillong? Then I could visit Dad's old school for him – see if there's any information on our family.'

'What a splendid idea!' Mr Dunlop said.

Libby was taken aback. She was looking forward to travelling with her father and having him to herself. She'd even daydreamed that George might travel up and join them to see Assam for himself; Flowers didn't fit into that plan. 'But your work – wouldn't it be difficult taking holiday at such short notice?'

'I'm due some leave – I never take time off. But if you'd rather I didn't come with you . . .'

'No, I didn't mean that,' said Libby hastily, feeling guilty at her selfish thoughts. 'It would be fun to have you with us.'

'And you could visit Adela's mother at Belgooree,' Flower's father suggested. 'That's not far from Shillong. Adela was always inviting you.'

'I wasn't thinking of going further than Shillong,' said Flowers.

'I'm sure Clarrie Robson would like that,' said Libby. 'If you can get more than a few days off, then you must spend some time with us in Assam.'

'What about your father?' Flowers asked.

'He's probably wondering how on earth he's going to keep me occupied while he's at work.'

Flowers's pretty face lit up. 'Then I'd love to.'

'Good,' Libby said. 'I'll write to him and tell him.'

Leaving the flat, Libby wondered why she had encouraged the impromptu idea. She didn't know Flowers well and had no idea how her father would really react to having her to stay.

Flowers accompanied her out of the building. At the entrance she stopped Libby with a hand on her arm again. 'Sorry about inviting myself along with you. We don't have to do it. I just thought it might keep Dad happy to say I'd look into his family background. This whole Independence thing – he and Mum never used to argue about anything but they can't agree on the future. None of us really knows what to do or think – least of all me.'

Libby felt a stab of sympathy and was ashamed at her reluctance to have Flowers go along with her to Shillong.

'Of course we must do it. I'll arrange it with Dad.'

'Are you sure?'

'Yes, I am.'

'Thanks.' Flowers gave her a cautious smile. She kept her hand on Libby's arm. 'There's one other thing I wanted to say while we're alone. It's about George.'

Libby's insides tensed. 'Oh?'

'I think you have feelings for him. Am I right?'

Libby reddened. 'Why are you asking? Do you feel the same?'

Flowers's dark eyes widened. 'Me?' She gave an embarrassed laugh. 'George is very attractive and good fun, but I don't think of him as a suitor.'

Libby felt a wave of relief. 'Oh, I thought perhaps you did.'

Flowers shook her head. 'But neither should you, Libby.'

'Why not? His divorce will be coming through any day and it doesn't bother me that he's been married before.'

Flowers gave her a pitying look. 'Don't let him lead you on. He likes the married ones – women who don't want commitment, just an affair.'

Libby was incredulous. 'I don't believe you! George is a gentleman. He'd never—'

'George is charming but a philanderer. He's carrying on with a woman in Dacca. He won't be serious about her because he's just after fun, not another marriage. I just thought you should know.'

'Stop it!' Libby said, pulling away. 'He's there on business.'

'Yes he is,' agreed Flowers, 'but he stays on longer to see her too.'

'How could you possibly know that?'

'Eddy told me. I asked him to keep an eye on you. I don't want to see you getting hurt.'

Libby was stunned. She couldn't speak. She hurried out of the building. Flowers followed. 'I'm sorry.'

Libby waved goodbye and fled towards a waiting rickshaw, her cheeks burning.

CHAPTER 9

L ibby didn't go straight back to Alipore; she went for a walk across the Maidan in the late afternoon sunshine. Indian families were picnicking, and boys were playing cricket. She passed a holy man lying on a piece of homespun cloth, asleep in the shade of a cassia tree.

She was shocked by what Flowers had told her. Could she be believed? Perhaps Flowers was warning her off so that she could have George to herself. Then Libby felt ashamed of such a thought. Flowers had shown her nothing but friendship. Besides, Flowers appeared to have no particular interest in George; in fact she kept all the young men from the chummery at arm's length. Was this because Flowers was unsure about her position in the social group? Even though people were mixing far more freely since the War, did Flowers feel her Anglo-Indian-ness more keenly now than ever in the shadow of Independence?

Libby thought again of George kissing her under the willow tree. Why had he done so if he was involved with another woman? She had to admit that he had drunk a lot of beer that lunchtime and it was the first time he had attempted to kiss her since their brief embrace in Newcastle the previous year. But then, she was the one who had instigated that kiss. Libby felt a wave of embarrassment.

Perhaps their recent embrace had meant nothing to George. Apart from that impromptu moment, had he given her any encouragement beyond inviting her along to social events? Not really, Libby had to admit. She was just one of several young women that were always included in his dinner-dance parties. Yet she had felt special to him. Libby felt a kick of anger. If he was carrying on an affair with a married woman, he had no right to be encouraging her at the same time.

Libby caught the tram back to Alipore. By the time she got home, she had decided not to judge George until she had seen him again and confronted him with what she'd been told.

'Had a nice tiffin with the Dunlops?' Uncle Johnny greeted her, breaking off from his conversation with the *mali* as she crossed the garden.

'Very,' said Libby. 'I've invited them to my birthday celebrations. Hope that's okay?'

'Course it is – you invite anyone you want. Got any room left for a spot of tea?' he asked. 'I'm going to join the Colonel on the veranda.'

'No more food, thanks,' said Libby, smiling, 'but I'll happily sit with you both.'

'A letter came for you, by the way. It's on the hall table.'

Libby's heart lurched. Perhaps it was from George. She longed for it to be reassurance that he was in Dacca merely for business and that he was looking forward to seeing her on his return – making some arrangement just for the two of them. Flowers might have been misled by Eddy; perhaps Eddy wanted Flowers to himself?

She hurried into the house and picked up the letter. The handwriting was unfamiliar.

Dear Miss Robson
My sister Fatima has been castigating me since last week for my rudeness to you. You were her guest and I was the interloper. I must apologise for ruining your tea party

and causing you both upset. There was no excuse for my behaviour except perhaps a rush of blood to the head at the news of Attlee's announcement.

Please forgive the hasty things I said to you – especially my unkind remarks about your father in particular and memsahibs in general. You are obviously not in the usual category of lady Britisher and, having had time for my hot head to cool down a little, I have to admit to being more than a little impressed with your knowledge of Indian politics and your socialist sympathies.

So there, apology made and I hope accepted – in the spirit of comradeship if nothing else. If you were interested in seeing the other side of Calcutta – away from the dull clubs and drawing rooms of the wealthy – then I would be happy to volunteer as your guide. You could contact me at the newspaper office in Chowringhee Square. I quite understand if you would rather not. But please visit Fatima before you leave for Assam – otherwise I will be confined to the 'dog-house' for the rest of the year.

Yours in comradeship
Ghulam Khan

Libby was astonished. She re-read the letter, trying to stifle her amusement at his droll humour, not quite sure if his apology was genuine or ironic. She had felt cross with him every time she'd thought of the fractious tea party and the way he had spoilt her visit to Amelia Buildings. But now she felt guilty for not having made any attempt to see Fatima again; she should not have left it up to the doctor to issue another invitation. Perhaps she would send a note. Libby tucked the letter into her skirt pocket.

Later that evening, lying in bed under the mosquito netting, she read the letter twice more. What should she make of it? The thought of being shown the Indian side of Calcutta filled her with an excited curiosity. But she should probably ignore the letter. She suspected her father would be horrified at her going to meet this radical Indian journalist unaccompanied. Miss MacGregor, on the other hand, would no doubt applaud it.

Two days later, Libby stood outside the offices of *The Statesman* newspaper in slacks, a plain cotton shirt and with her hair tied back, waiting nervously. Trams and traffic thundered by. Ghulam had acknowledged her note and replied saying he would take her for lunch.

He appeared, ten minutes late, his jacket slung over his shoulder and his sleeves rolled up. He was better-looking than she had remembered, a lick of dark hair falling over his vivid green eyes.

'You should have come into the building, Miss Robson,' he said, 'I was delayed by a phone call.'

'I'm not clairvoyant, Mr Khan,' Libby answered.

'Sorry,' he said hastily, with a lop-sided smile. 'Are you hungry?'

'Nearly always.' She ignored the fluttering in her stomach.

'Have you been into Hogg's Market?'

'No, my aunt had to reach for the vapours when I suggested it. But I have a vague memory of going there with my dad years ago.'

Ghulam gave a grunt of amusement. 'Then we shall risk your aunt fainting at the news and go to Nizam's.'

He hailed a rickshaw. Libby was acutely aware that they were sitting with their arms touching – the dark hairs of his forearms tickling her pale skin – as they were jostled south down Chowringhee Street. They passed the Grand Hotel and turned into Lindsay Street. She felt suddenly tongue-tied but he appeared preoccupied and didn't seem to notice. Perhaps meeting up with him was a mistake; they might find nothing to say to each other or end up arguing again. At the clock tower, Ghulam helped her down and paid the driver.

He led her into the covered market past pyramids of fruit and vegetables: bananas, apricots, okra and aubergines. Porters stepped around them with wide flat baskets on their heads, carrying packages of foodstuffs and cloth, while traders called out for business. Corridors spread out in different directions. She was struck anew by the plentiful supplies in India compared to the ration-weary Britain she had left behind. Any returning British would be in for a shock.

'This way,' said Ghulam, nodding. Libby was amazed at the variety on offer: stalls packed with china and hardware, drapery and shoes, flowers and hot peanuts. They pushed on through a butcher's hall, the floor sticky with fresh blood. Overhead, fans whirred in the gloomy gaslit alleyways and pigeons flapped and darted. Passing a cheese stall, Libby could see daylight again. Ghulam stopped and waved her forward into a restaurant. She wondered if he had brought her the long way round so that she could experience the market in all its chaotic glory.

Ghulam was welcomed as if he often came there. A series of booths, some of them curtained, lined the room. From the chatter, Libby could hear that they were providing privacy for women and children. The people she could see were all Indian. Ghulam sat opposite her in one of the booths, leaving the curtain drawn back. She wondered who else he had dined here with in these intimate cubicles. Libby felt her insides flutter again.

'What would you like to eat?' he asked. 'I come here when I'm in need of some Punjabi food. The Bengalis live on fish – sometimes I crave a well-cooked mutton curry.'

'I like the sound of that too.'

He raised an eyebrow quizzically.

'Auntie's cook is probably the worst in Calcutta,' she explained. 'I've had my fill of soggy veg and rubbery chicken.' She pushed escaping tendrils of hair behind her ears in a nervous gesture. 'Oh dear, that makes me sound like a typical memsahib complaining about the servants. I didn't mean it like that. I just meant I'd love a decent curry.'

Ghulam's mouth twitched in amusement. He ordered swiftly. The waiter brought them glasses of *nimbu pani*. As they waited for the food, Ghulam took a swig of his lime drink and then leant on his elbows and fixed her with a direct look. Libby smirked.

'What's funny?' asked Ghulam.

'I was just remembering how Mother always nagged me about keeping my elbows off the table,' said Libby, planting her own firmly on the tabletop too.

Ghulam gave his charming uneven smile again, the one that made his face suddenly very handsome and Libby's stomach curdle. 'We got off on the wrong foot, didn't we?' he said. 'Let's start again getting to know each other. Tell me about your mother with the exacting table manners.'

Libby found herself telling him not only about Tilly, her brothers and Josey, but about Newcastle, the café and Lexy, and her unhappiness at school and how she would have run away if it hadn't been for her mentor Miss MacGregor. She spoke enthusiastically of her time as a Land Girl, of the anti-climax of living back at home again, of teaching Doreen to type and her frustration with the typing pool at the bank.

'They didn't expect a woman behind a typewriter to have any brain cells,' said Libby. 'I was forever getting into trouble for making alterations to the manager's letters.'

This made Ghulam laugh, a deep, amused chuckle that made her laugh too.

A series of dishes came: mutton curry in rich gravy, black bean dal, fried aubergine, spicy potatoes and rice. Ghulam scooped up his food with chapattis so Libby ignored the cutlery brought for her and did the same. They both ate with relish.

'This is all delicious,' said Libby, licking her tingling lips. 'Now it's your turn – you've led a far more exciting life if everything Adela says is true. I want to hear about it all.'

After a bit of prompting, Ghulam began to tell her about growing up in Lahore in a tall mansion house in the heart of the old city, with three brothers and two sisters.

'Rafi was always my favourite big brother,' he said. 'He was the dashing one who could ride and play sport and make friends easily. I idolised him. Being bright, he was sent away to school in Simla and I couldn't wait for him to come home in the holidays – I was always pestering him to play cricket with me. Then he enlisted in the Lahore Horse and was sent to France. After that he went to Scotland to do a forestry degree. By the time he came home he was a stranger – aping the manners of the sahibs he worked with – and I was an angry young man.'

Ghulam drained off his drink. Libby poured him some more from the cool metal jug.

'So you grew apart?' guessed Libby. 'A different war, but the outcome's the same – a family split by long years of separation – I know how that feels.' She saw the struggle in his face and knew that, deep down, he must still love his brother Rafi as much as he did as a boy. 'You shouldn't blame Rafi too much for that.'

Ghulam shrugged.

'And you still had Fatima as an ally,' said Libby with an encouraging look. 'What was she like as a girl?'

Ghulam smiled with affection. 'My little sister was the quiet rebel. I was the one who had the blazing rows with my father and older brothers but Fatima just got on with what she wanted to do – she studied hard at school and went on to university. She had an inspirational teacher like you did – her headmistress – but she also credits our mother. On the surface Mother was a very traditional woman who kept strict purdah and didn't have an education – but Fatima told me our mother had lost three babies because there were no purdah doctors and she wanted Fatima to be a doctor to women like her.'

'She must have been a remarkable woman to have raised such independent-minded children,' said Libby.

'That is my only real regret,' Ghulam admitted, 'that I never saw my mother again before she died.'

'When did you last see her?' asked Libby.

'When I was released from prison in '28. I went to see her when my father was out at work. She scolded me and made me eat a huge meal and wept over me when I left. I think we both knew we'd never see each other again.'

Libby saw his eyes gleam with tears. She waited while he sipped more of the lime-flavoured water and then said, 'Tell me about your time with the communists – when you went to Simla campaigning for the rights of the hill people.'

He looked at her in surprise. 'So Adela told you about that too? And did she tell you how her husband Sam saved me from arrest at the Sipi Fair?'

'Not in any detail,' said Libby. 'I want to hear it from you.'

'I was intent on making a scene at the Fair – in front of all those champagne-swigging Britishers and their rajah friends – but Sam saw me and barged me out of the way. Later, he helped hide me in the hills and got me safely away. If either of us had been caught he would have been in very grave trouble.' Ghulam looked reflective. 'He also intervened to save a Gaddi girl – one of the nomadic shepherds – from an abusive uncle. Sam is the bravest and most principled man I know.'

'High praise for one of the despised sahibs,' Libby said dryly.

'There are exceptions to every rule,' he said with the flash of a smile.

'So, thanks to Sam's intervention, you were able to carry on your campaigning?'

Ghulam nodded. With Libby's encouragement he spoke about his hand-to-mouth existence all over northern India, speaking at rallies, evading the police and eventually coming to an uneasy truce with his persecutors during the War.

'Unlike many of my comrades,' said Ghulam, 'I thought the greater evil was Hitler and his fascists, not the Britishers. Neither did I relish the prospect of a Japanese dictatorship taking over India.'

'So you supported the Allies against Japan?' asked Libby.

Ghulam nodded, a wry smile playing on his lips. 'I believed that the quickest way to get rid of the Britishers for good would be to support the war effort – I wasn't going to see the Japanese march in and impose a new Raj.'

'So what do you think of the Indians who supported the Japanese in Burma?' Libby pressed. 'The ones who joined the Indian National Army – they're treated as heroes now, aren't they?'

She saw the sudden tension in his jaw and a flash of anger in his eyes.

'I lost friends for good over my stance,' he admitted, 'but I don't regret choosing to speak out against fascism.'

'What did you do?'

'Became a volunteer fireman here in Calcutta.' He told her of how he had grown disenchanted with politics for a while, of his futile attempts to help the dying on the streets of Calcutta and of Fatima saving him. 'She nursed me back to health – not just my body but my spirit – and helped me find my passion again for the things that matter.'

Libby was moved by his words and in awe of how much he had been prepared to give up for his beliefs. It was easy to spout forth political opinions but quite another to act on them. 'Deeds not words' had been Miss MacGregor's mantra and the slogan of the women suffrage campaigners Libby had so admired. Ghulam had lived his whole life putting his ideals into practice too. She wondered if he had lost anyone special to him along the way.

'So you've never got married or had a family?' she asked.

His eyes widened, startled by her blunt question. 'No,' he spluttered. She saw his jaw darken with embarrassment. 'Besides,' he said, recovering, 'marriage is a bourgeois institution, don't you think?'

'Well,' said Libby, 'it's nice to be dining with a man who isn't married. I'm not very good at choosing men.' She stopped, realising she'd been thinking out loud. He was giving her a curious look. 'Not that there's anything implied in our meeting for lunch. I don't want you to think that's why I came – that I expect anything more than – er – lunch . . .'

Libby felt her cheeks burning. She put her hands to her face. 'Oh dear, sorry. I don't know why I said that.'

Ghulam started to chuckle. 'Well, now we've both been embarrassed, so we're even on that score.'

Libby laughed out loud.

'Do I take it,' he said, 'that you've had a bad experience with a married man?'

'Well, it wasn't bad at the time,' said Libby candidly, 'just disappointing to discover he was married. He was an Italian POW.'

'You are a startling young woman,' Ghulam said, his face creasing in amusement. 'I can't say I've ever had such a frank conversation with someone I've only known for a couple of hours – especially a woman.'

'Not what you expected of a memsahib?' Libby teased.

He laughed. 'Not in the least. But I can't deny I find it most refreshing.'

She eyed him. 'You only invited me out to lunch to keep your sister happy, didn't you?'

He hesitated and then nodded. Libby felt a flicker of disappointment but tried not to let it show.

'Well, I only accepted because I was curious about seeing bits of Calcutta I've never been taken to before.'

'Good,' he said. 'Then neither of us have any expectations apart from a good lunch.'

He ordered tea and drew out his cigarettes, offering one to Libby. She took one and he lit hers and then his. Their conversation turned to his work at the newspaper.

Libby asked, 'So what is the latest news? I've been hearing terrible rumours about unrest in the Punjab. I hope it's all been exaggerated.'

Ghulam's expression turned grim. 'It's not, I'm afraid. Amritsar and Lahore are going up in flames. Sikhs against Muslims. The Punjabi prime minister, who was trying to hold together a coalition, has resigned.'

Libby saw the tension in his face. 'What about your own people?'

He frowned. 'Meaning?'

'Your family,' said Libby. 'Even if you don't speak to them any more, you must be worried.'

He sat back and blew out smoke. 'Yes, I worry. I have nephews and nieces . . .' He ran his fingers through his hair in agitation.

'Have you had news of them?' asked Libby.

He shook his head. 'I've been trying to ring Rafi in Gulgat to see if he has heard anything.'

'Is that the telephone call you were on when I was waiting for you?'

He shot her a look. 'Yes. You're perceptive.'

'And?'

'He knows less than I do,' said Ghulam impatiently, 'stuck away in the jungle.'

'At least he will be safe there – and Sophie too.'

'Perhaps,' said Ghulam.

'What does that mean?'

'Even in Gulgat things are changing, it seems. The old Rajah died last year and the new prince doesn't seem as well disposed towards Rafi as his uncle was.' Ghulam's lip curled. 'He's one of those princely leeches who bleed the people dry in order to finance a life of excess. Always getting his photo in the papers for attending society parties – usually with some film star on his arm.'

'Prince Sanjay?' asked Libby.

'Yes.' Ghulam looked surprised. 'Do you know him?'

'I know of him,' said Libby, thinking of Adela's confession. It made her angry to think that her cousin had been a victim of Sanjay's selfish behaviour. 'I don't like the sound of him at all. Is Rafi's job in danger?'

Ghulam shrugged. 'Possibly. He was very guarded on the phone but recently I got a letter from him, posted in Shillong, that said for the first time he's thinking seriously of returning to the Punjab – that's if Pakistan becomes a reality.'

'Really?' Libby was shocked. 'But Rafi's not religious and he's lived in Gulgat for over twenty years!'

'That's his choice,' said Ghulam.

'But you don't agree with him,' Libby guessed.

'I think it's a disastrous idea. We need Muslims like Rafi to stay and help build the new India.'

Libby stubbed out her half-smoked cigarette and sipped at the hot sweet tea. She thought again how war and division had ruptured families all over the world, including her own. Was India heading for civil war now? The thought filled her with anxiety.

'Will the violence spread to Calcutta again?' she asked. 'What are you hearing?'

He lit a second cigarette from the stub of his first, inhaled deeply and gave her a direct look. 'We've had one thing in our favour these past months – Gandhi has been living in Bengal. Just having that man here seems to calm people's nerves, it's quite extraordinary. Last summer, we communists went out on the streets to show our solidarity – Muslims and Hindus together – but we couldn't stop the butchery. But Gandhi with his spinning wheel and hunger strikes somehow takes the poison out of our veins.'

'So that should give us optimism?' Libby pressed.

'Except Gandhi is leaving and going west to try and bring calm. We need a thousand Gandhis. I fear the violence is going to escalate again.'

'I don't understand why it should suddenly get worse now that the British government has announced they are definitely leaving.'

'Power and fear,' said Ghulam starkly. 'Everyone is afraid and all sides are stoking up that fear to gain the upper hand in the negotiations. Just like last year, people are already leaving their homes and moving into villages or parts of the city to be with their own kind.'

'Perhaps it will make a difference having a change of viceroy,' Libby suggested. 'Mountbatten knows India well from the War and he might be able to bring the differing sides together. He's due here any day now, isn't he?'

Ghulam gave her an impatient look. 'A change of Britisher at the top is not the solution. It's far too late for that.'

Libby went quiet; she didn't want to antagonise him again. She already regretted her high-handed remarks at Amelia Buildings about Indians being to blame for the escalating violence. Up till now, she had enjoyed every minute of his company. She hadn't had such interesting conversation in a long time, and never with such a fascinating man – this former revolutionary with the mesmerising green eyes.

Ghulam scrutinised her. She felt her heart pound faster under his gaze. He stubbed out his cigarette and began fishing out money for the bill. Libby felt a wave of disappointment that the lunch was coming to an abrupt end.

'Let me contribute something,' she said.

'Certainly not.'

'I've really enjoyed this,' said Libby. 'The meal – and talking to you.'

Abruptly he asked, 'Have you ever had cake from Nahoum's Confectionery?'

'No.'

'Then you must. You cannot leave Hogg's Market without a visit to the Jewish bakery. That's if you have room for something sweet?'

Libby smiled. 'I always have room for cake.'

'Then we share something else in common apart from socialism and Indian Independence,' he said with a grin.

Nahoum's had the biggest selection of cakes and pastries that Libby had ever set eyes on: cheesecakes, lemon sponges, Madeira slices, seed cakes and plum puddings. She took ages to decide what to choose and in the end Ghulam picked a selection and had them boxed up. When Libby gasped over the range of boiled sweets, he insisted on buying lemon drops and mint humbugs too.

'No toffees as good as your Scottish ones,' he said with a quick smile.

'They didn't last long then?' Libby guessed. He shook his head. 'Then I'll get Mother to send some more out.'

To her delight, Ghulam didn't seem in any hurry to get back to work. He suggested they walk through to the Maidan but she feared bumping into some of her aunt's friends watching cricket at Eden Gardens. She didn't want him subjected to any snide remarks or hostile looks.

'I'd rather you showed me more of the streets around here,' Libby replied.

They walked north, through a maze of lanes and side streets bustling with life and noise. Some of the buildings must once have been palatial with their intricately carved doorways and balconies but their façades were now crumbling and dirty. This was old Calcutta. They passed a steaming laundry, the rooftop with drying linen flapping like a ship in sail. Chinese merchants were selling paper lanterns and food-stuffs next to a dairy and piggery. Banging and hammering came from a row of leather workshops and cobblers. They got some curious looks as they walked by.

'Don't worry, they'll just think I'm your bearer carrying your packages,' Ghulam murmured.

Libby had a strong desire to slip her arm through his to show that they were equals but was worried he might rebuff such a gesture.

Eventually emerging on to a broader street, Libby recognised the road that led down to the Duff Church.

'Let's go this way,' said Libby. 'I know somewhere quiet to sit down.'

A few minutes later, they were turning left and passing through an iron gate into the church garden. The whitewashed building was shuttered and locked but the steps were in the shade of tall palm trees. Libby climbed on to the top one.

She smiled. 'Time for eating cake, don't you think?'

Ghulam followed, pulling off his jacket. 'Sit on this if you like.'

'I'll share it with you,' she said, spreading it out and settling on to one half. She kicked off her sandals and wriggled her toes, enjoying the feel of the warm stone on the soles of her feet.

Ghulam untied the string and opened the box. 'You go first.'

She picked out a slice of walnut cake and bit into it. The icing was made with dark cane sugar, a taste that made her think of holidays in St Abbs and afternoon tea with her Watson relations. She closed her eyes. 'Mmm, I haven't tasted cake this good in years.'

She let it melt on her tongue and then took another bite, larger this time. Opening her eyes, she saw that Ghulam was watching her. Libby felt suddenly aware of how close they were sitting and how alone they were. Birds chirruped drowsily in the surrounding trees. Her heart began a slow thud; she could feel perspiration break out on her forehead and between her breasts.

She pushed untidy hair behind her ear. 'What cake are you eating?' she asked, her voice sounding breathless.

'Lemon,' he said. 'Want to try it?'

Libby nodded. He offered his half-eaten cake. She leant forward and bit into it. The pulse in her throat made it suddenly difficult to swallow. The tart lemon juice flooded her mouth and mingled with the sweetness already there.

'Good,' she whispered and held her slice out to him. 'Try this at the same time.'

Ghulam hesitated. She thought she had never seen eyes quite so compelling, the green almost translucent and framed by such dark lashes. Then he steadied her hand in his and took a bite from the walnut cake. Libby could hardly breathe. Her hand trembled in his. Was he feeling the same intensity as she was? He pulled his hand away and munched the cake with a frown of concentration. She wanted to push the wayward strand of hair out of his eyes and run her fingers over his uneven features – the broken nose and the dimpled chin that was already showing dark bristles.

'What are you thinking?' he asked.

She went a guilty puce. 'About nice things like cake.'

He swallowed down his mouthful and smiled. 'Time for another then.'

They sat in the shade munching cake until the box was empty, while Libby told him about long-ago tea parties on the cliffs at St Abbs, of swimming in the sea and playing cricket with her brothers.

'I have to admit,' said Ghulam, 'there's one thing I will thank the Britishers for when they leave and that's cricket.'

'Not cake?' Libby teased.

'The Indians have been making sweetmeats for far longer,' he teased back. 'So no; you memsahibs can't claim to have invented cake.'

Libby gave a raucous laugh, wondering if it was possible to be intoxicated by sugar. She felt lightheaded.

He stood up. 'I really should be getting back to the office.'

'Pity,' said Libby.

He offered his hand and pulled her to her feet. For a brief moment, they didn't let go. He leant towards her and Libby held her breath. But he bent to retrieve his jacket. She hid her disappointment by scrambling for her shoes.

As they gained the street again, Ghulam hailed a rickshaw. 'I'll come with you,' said Libby, 'and get the tram back from town.'

They sat close together but the intense intimacy of the quiet garden had evaporated. Libby sensed that his mind was already preoccupied with work. He must be so worried about the reports of communal violence coming out of the Punjab.

Disembarking at Chowringhee Square, Libby said, 'Thank you for lunch – and cake – I've really enjoyed it all.'

Ghulam nodded and gave a distracted smile. 'Remember to call on my sister before you go to Assam.'

Libby felt dashed; he was not going to make another assignation. As far as Ghulam was concerned, he had made amends for his rudeness and done his duty to his sister.

'Would you and Fatima come to my birthday party?' Libby blurted out. 'It's next Tuesday. At my uncle's house. Nothing grand. But it's a way of seeing my friends before I leave.'

He looked astonished. 'I can't imagine your uncle and aunt will want the likes of me at your party, Miss Robson.'

'Uncle Johnny won't mind in the least – and anyway the guest list is up to me, not my aunt. And Fatima deserves a night out – you told me she works too hard.'

He looked undecided.

She pressed him. 'Please come. You won't be the only Indians there, I can promise you that.'

'Well, if you really want—'

'Yes I do.' Libby cut in. 'I'll send an invitation with the details. I don't want any presents – just a bit of fun.'

His mouth twitched in amusement. 'Well, if my sister wants to go, then I shall bring her.'

'Good.' Libby smiled. 'And thank you again for today.'

He raised a hand in farewell and strode off into the building. Libby could imagine her mother's disapproval at Ghulam leaving her unchaperoned in the street and expected to find her own way home. But Libby was pleased. It showed Ghulam thought of them as equal – and Libby as mature and independent.

With a tremor of excitement, she set off down the street to catch a tram. Something unexpected had happened today. She had gone half reluctantly to meet Ghulam Khan, convinced he would be as dismissive of her as he had been on their first meeting. But she had had the most stimulating lunchtime and afternoon since coming to Calcutta. Libby had revelled in his company and was fairly sure he had enjoyed hers. Why else would he have suggested extending their time together by going to the cake shop and then showing her more of central Calcutta?

Yet, sitting in the Duff Church garden, she had felt something deeper: a powerful physical attraction. Had Ghulam felt anything similar? As the tram swayed, she went over in her mind every scrap of conversation, gesture and look she could recall. She felt exhilarated. Soon she would have the party to look forward to – not only the excitement of being reunited with her adored father, but also the anticipation of seeing Ghulam again.

It was only when she alighted in leafy Alipore that it occurred to Libby: for the whole afternoon she hadn't thought of George once.

CHAPTER 10

Assam

James jerked awake. In panic he sat up, his heart pounding. He listened. Someone screamed beyond the darkened bedroom. He scrambled under the mosquito net and fumbled for his revolver. Breckon, his black retriever, leapt up, barking. Dashing for the door James rushed out on to the veranda, Breckon at his heels. The scream came again. He strained to see but the night was so dark that he could make out nothing of the garden or the forest beyond.

'Sahib?' A voice spoke from close by. 'It is a jackal, sahib.'

'Sunil, is that you?' James panted.

'No, sahib, it is Aslam. There is no Sunil here.'

James stared in confusion at the grey-haired servant who emerged out of the dark carrying a kerosene lamp. His bearer, Aslam. The screech of a jackal came again from further off. Not a human scream at all. He felt foolish.

'I thought I heard an intruder . . .' said James, bending to calm his dog.

'Sahib is not sleeping well again?' asked Aslam. 'Can I get you a milky drink?'

James huffed. 'I'm not a boy.'

'Robson memsahib would always order hot milk for bad sleep,' said Aslam.

'Yes, she would, wouldn't she?' James sighed. 'Well, she's not here now so you can pour me a large whisky instead. I'll sit for a while out here.'

He couldn't bear the thought of returning to the dark bedroom and tossing sleeplessly, plagued by his thoughts. Were they bad dreams or memories? Sunil Ram had been there, the *punkah-wallah* from the old days at Dunsapie Cottage. Why on earth had he been thinking of the long-dead servant? Was it Sunil who had screamed in his head?

With Breckon stretched out beside him, James sat in the long cane chair covered in a rug, and slugged at the whisky Aslam brought him. The night seemed as restless as he was; the air pulsed with crickets and rustlings came from the undergrowth.

It was Libby's recent letter that had stirred up old memories. He picked it up from the side table and re-read it.

> *Dearest Dad*
>
> *I can't wait to see you! Just another week and you'll be here in Calcutta. I'm having an interesting time. Uncle Johnny and Aunt Helena have been so kind, but I'm impatient now to see you and get back to Assam.*
>
> *I hope you don't mind but I've asked an old school friend of Adela's to come on holiday with me. She's a nurse and she hasn't taken any leave for ages. Her name's Flowers Dunlop. Her father was a railwayman but thinks he's related to Scottish tea planters in Assam. She's promised him that she'll try and find out about the family connection while she's with us. He's an invalid and not very well so it's really just to keep him happy that Flowers said she'd look into it all. Do you know any Dunlops? He's called Danny (I presume short for Daniel). He was*

*orphaned and went to school in Shillong by the way. I
said we could go and visit on our way home. I hope that's
okay? You'll like Flowers, she's good fun.*

*Let me know what train you will be arriving on next
Monday and I'll meet you. Aunt Helena is insisting on
having a party for me on Tuesday so I'm inviting a few of
my new Calcutta friends along. You'll be my VIP guest!
I simply can't wait!*

A big hug soon,

Your loving daughter Libby xxx

*PS I've invited the Percy-Barratts too so that you'll
know someone from Assam. Muriel's a bit of a headache
but Reggie's quite sweet.*

James felt a hot flush of panic. He hated parties or being the centre
of attention. He didn't want to meet crowds of sophisticated Calcuttans
or talk gossip with garrulous women like Helena Watson or Muriel
Percy-Barratt. As his nearest neighbour on the plantation, Muriel had
mothered him for years but she'd never really approved of Tilly as a
pukka planter's wife. He had grown tired of her endless criticism at
Tilly's desertion of him during the War and had been silently relieved
when Reggie had decided to retire from the Oxford Tea Estates and
move to Calcutta.

'Oh, Libby,' he sighed.

When he thought of his daughter she was still an eleven-year-old
with a plump, grinning face and long auburn pigtails, a robust girl who
was more athletic than her brothers and twice as talkative. He knew that
he had spoilt her as a small child because she had reminded him of a
young, warm-hearted Tilly but with his stronger sense of adventure. It
was Libby and not Jamie who had always insisted on going riding with
him in the early mornings and who had loved to accompany him on

fishing trips. She had been a delightful companion, full of exuberance and affection.

Even as a schoolgirl back in England, Libby had soon overcome the bashfulness between them when he had taken a brief leave to see his children in 1936. He would have cherished that holiday to St Abbs even more if he had known it was to be the last time they would all be together for the next decade – perhaps ever.

He was eager to see his daughter again and yet frightened of meeting her. Tilly complained that Libby could be rude and headstrong, constantly challenging her mother's authority and arguing back. Tilly said Libby ranted about politics at inappropriate times such as when the vicar came round to take tea. Tilly also suspected that Libby had lost her virginity and was over-sexed. All these criticisms had been listed in reproachful letters from his wife, blaming Libby's wild behaviour and views on his failure to be a firm father.

'And how was I supposed to do that when you refused to come back to India with the children at the start of the War?' James exclaimed aloud. 'You're the one who should have been firmer with her. You're a failure as a mother! You've deprived me of my children. You've turned the boys against me – they don't even want to come back to India. I bet you've just encouraged Libby to come so you can get her out of your hair!'

James reached for the decanter and poured another large whisky. He must stop talking to himself out loud; Aslam would be summoning the doctor again. The new young tea garden doctor, Dr Attar, thought James was suffering from exhaustion and wanted to give him something to calm his nerves.

'Nothing wrong with my nerves,' said James, gulping another mouthful.

He sat on, feeling the welcoming numbness from the whisky seeping through him. With any luck he'd fall asleep in the chair and not have a repeat of the nightmare that had woken him. He couldn't remember any of it now.

'Oh, Libby,' he murmured, 'I do want to see you, I really do.'

She had written such a loving letter, it melted his heart. Tilly must be quite wrong about the poor girl. So what was it that had made him so agitated?

'He's related to Scottish tea planters . . . orphaned and went to school in Shillong . . .'

James felt his chest go tight. He found it hard to breathe. He was back in the convent in Shillong, pushing the infant boy at the nun. The Brat. James couldn't now remember if Logan's son had ever had a proper name. *He's called Aidan.* James had invented a name for the boy. He hadn't thought of Logan and his illegitimate son for years. Why should he feel a renewed surge of guilt now? It had happened so long ago and he'd done nothing wrong. It was his loathsome boss who had fathered Aidan and cast him aside, not he. How could he, as a young planter, have stood up to Logan and refused to do his bidding?

James took the letter in a shaking hand and searched again for the name. Daniel Dunlop. It couldn't be the same boy; was hardly likely to be. Half a century ago, orphanages were full of illegitimate Eurasian children whose tea planter and army fathers had refused to acknowledge them. Still, it left James feeling anxious that he might have to return to Shillong and help this nurse probe into her father's background. It would only stir up more unwanted memories and bad dreams.

'Why would you want to know?' cried James. 'It's obvious this Dunlop, whoever he was, didn't want to keep Daniel. You'll just uncover some shameful tale that will upset your father more than the not knowing. Let sleeping dogs lie, I say.'

James drained off his second whisky and closed his eyes. Sleeping dogs. He fondled Breckon's ears. The dog snuffled.

'If only I could sleep without dreaming,' James sighed.

What was it that had so disturbed him? It lurked just beyond his consciousness like a wild animal ready to attack the moment he drifted off. Something terrible, something his mind had closed off for years.

Exhaustion, the doctor said. Take some leave. But he was fearful of going to England and facing Tilly, frightened that his marriage was over. Last month he had turned seventy; perhaps he had already left it too late to patch things up between them? For the first time in his life he was feeling his age and questioning his own mortality. He didn't want to leave Assam. Increasingly he was finding it hard to leave his sanctuary of Cheviot View. Other than his own bungalow, only Clarrie at Belgooree provided anything like a safe haven. The thought of Clarrie lifted his spirits. His cousin's widow was kind and sensible; she understood him. Perhaps he should talk to her about these strange dreams – and his anxiety at meeting Libby again after all these years. He would go and see Clarrie.

With that comforting thought, James fell into an uneasy sleep.

CHAPTER 11

Calcutta

'He's not coming,' said Aunt Helena briskly.

'He's been delayed, that's all,' Uncle Johnny said, trying to break the news more kindly.

'Dad's not coming to Calcutta?' Libby asked in dismay.

'I'm sure he'll come as soon as he can,' said Johnny.

'But not in time for the party,' said Helena. 'You would have thought he might have made the effort for your birthday.'

Libby felt winded.

'Darling,' Johnny chided, 'he's not well or he would be coming.'

'Not well? What did Clarrie say?' Libby asked, suddenly anxious.

'Well, the line from Belgooree wasn't very good,' said Johnny, 'but she said your father had taken ill a few days ago and was resting at Belgooree.'

'What sort of ill?' Libby asked, her insides knotting.

'Nerves,' said Helena bluntly.

'Exhaustion,' Johnny said. 'So he needs complete bed rest.'

'He could do that here,' protested Libby. 'I could look after him. It shouldn't be left up to Clarrie.'

'The journey would be too much at the moment,' said Johnny gently. 'But he's welcome here to recuperate whenever he wants.'

Libby's eyes stung with tears. How much she had been looking forward to his arrival! 'I wish I'd been here when she'd called.'

'She rang from the factory telephone,' said her uncle, 'so your father wasn't there. Perhaps you could ring in a day or two and see how he is. You really mustn't worry; it's nothing life-threatening – Clarrie insisted on you knowing that.'

'Do you still want the party to go ahead?' asked Helena. Her aunt seemed more concerned at James spoiling the party by not turning up than about his health.

'Of course it must go ahead,' insisted Johnny. 'We can still make a fuss of our lovely niece on her birthday, can't we?'

Libby did her best to hide her hurt at her father's failure to turn up in Calcutta. She couldn't believe he was suffering from nerves – that was the excuse of the work-shy to men like her dad; surely he was merely over-tired. It was probably Clarrie being ultra-cautious and making a fuss at the thought of James undertaking a long journey. It wasn't his fault. He would have come if he could.

Swallowing her bitter disappointment, Libby determined to put on a brave face and make the most of her birthday party.

'It's not as if I'm used to having Dad there on my birthday,' she said breezily at breakfast, 'and there'll be plenty of others to spend together.'

'That's the spirit,' encouraged the Colonel. 'Carry on!'

The day was spent pleasantly, starting with a ride across the Maidan, tiffin with the Colonel, a swim at the club and a rest before the party.

She decided to wear the green satin evening dress that Josey had retrieved from the theatre wardrobe and helped her have altered. It was pre-war fashionable, strapless and figure-hugging with a slit showing leg up to the knee. At twenty-two, she was not going to let Helena bully her into wearing something more demure. Libby wore her wavy hair long and unbound, applied mascara to embolden her blue eyes and red lipstick to accentuate her full mouth. She sprayed herself liberally with French perfume that Colonel Swinson had instructed Helena to buy as a gift from him. She wanted to look her most sophisticated for George – and for Ghulam.

By seven the guests had started to arrive. Libby was a bundle of nerves inside but she greeted them with as much composure as she could muster. There were friends and neighbours of the Watsons, including the Percy-Barratts, and a dozen new friends from the Tollygunge and Saturday Clubs. George came with his chummery friends, Flowers with her parents and a couple of fellow nurses, and a handful of young people arrived from the Duff Church. Nearly thirty people were expected. Danny Dunlop was positioned in a bath chair on the veranda next to the Colonel and they fell into deep discussion about the railways.

George kissed her on the cheek. 'You are looking like a film star, Miss Robson. I hope you've missed me half as much as I've missed you.'

Libby gave him a cool smile. 'That depends.'

'On what?' His grin was quizzical.

'On what you've been up to in Dacca,' she answered, turning away to meet the next guest and leaving him gaping.

She milled around, cocktail glass in hand, chatting to the new arrivals. She was touched that her aunt and uncle had gone to such trouble for her: the hallway was cleared for arrival drinks, the dining room laid out for a buffet and the garden and veranda decorated with balloons and strings of coloured lights that kept flickering faultily. Three jazz musicians from the Saturday Club had been hired to play music and were positioned under an awning on the lawn.

Libby deliberately kept her distance from a bewildered George while keeping an eye out for the last of her guests. As it drew near to seven-thirty, she doubted that the Khans were going to come. Libby didn't like to admit that the knot of disappointment in her stomach was as much for Ghulam's absence as for her father's. Of course he wouldn't come. Fatima probably hated parties and Ghulam would be thankful not to have to accompany her to a Britisher celebration in the heart of wealthy Alipore.

Johnny clapped for people's attention and beckoned her into the centre of the hall. The hubbub died down.

'This last month has been one of the happiest we've spent in Calcutta since retirement,' said her uncle. 'And it's all because we've had our niece Libby staying with us. You've all got to know her too so you will agree with me that she is a wonderful girl – fun to have around, interesting to talk to and our croquet has improved no end thanks to her competitiveness in all things sporty.'

Shouts of 'Hear, hear!' punctuated his speech.

'It's a disappointment that her father, my brother-in-law James Robson, can't be with us for the occasion. But let's raise our glasses to the birthday girl – as well as to absent family and friends.'

'To Libby!' they chorused. 'Absent friends!'

Libby took a sip of her drink. 'And can I just say,' she added, raising her voice, 'a big thank you to my very generous aunt and uncle – and to Colonel Swinson – for hosting the party and being so very kind to me in Calcutta. Please enjoy the evening.'

'We will! Well said!' people cheered and conversation broke out again.

Libby, turning to smile at her uncle, caught sight of Fatima standing in the doorway dressed in a beautiful peacock-blue sari. Her heart knocked to see Ghulam beside her, immaculately turned out in a knee-length black silk kurta and white trousers. She rushed over to greet them, taking Fatima's hand.

Libby beamed. 'I'm so glad you could come.'

'I was delayed at the hospital,' said Fatima, 'or we would have been here sooner. Sorry.'

'Don't be; you haven't missed anything. I love your sari.'

'And your dress is fabulous,' said Fatima. 'Did you have it specially made?'

'Sort of.' Libby smirked. 'It's from a theatre props cupboard – but don't tell anyone.' She glanced up at Ghulam. 'A socialist theatre group,' she said with a smile, 'so it's not a degenerate bourgeois dress.'

He smiled and shook her hand. Libby felt a tingle go up her arm at the contact. 'We can forget the revolution for one evening,' he said with an admiring look, 'especially for such a dress.'

He looked more handsome than ever with his hair groomed and his chin freshly shaven. He smelt of sandalwood or something musky. She let go of his hand with reluctance.

'What would you like to drink?' Libby asked. 'The gin cocktails are good but there's fruit juice if you prefer.'

A waiter with a tray of drinks appeared beside them.

'Fruit juice for both of us, thank you,' said Ghulam, lifting two tumblers. 'You go and mingle with your friends, Miss Robson. There's someone over there wanting your attention.'

Libby turned to see George waving her over. She tensed. Her feelings about him were still very mixed and she was yet to have the conversation about Dacca.

'He can wait,' she said. 'Let me introduce you to Flowers Dunlop – she's a nurse and a friend of Adela's but I don't think you know her.'

Libby steered the Khans on to the veranda where Flowers was keeping her mother company and introduced them. Soon Libby was being led away by Helena to go and speak to one of her acquaintances from the club.

'She remembers your mother from Assam – name's Bradley.'

Libby hid her reluctance. Mrs Bradley was sitting with the Percy-Barratts in the sitting room and she knew it would be hard to get away.

'What an interesting mix of people you know, dear,' said Muriel, her tone disapproving. 'Would never have happened when we were young.'

'It's the face of the new India to come,' said Mrs Bradley, 'and I think it's rather fun.'

It turned out that Mrs Bradley had been a good friend of Tilly's when she'd first arrived in Assam. The reminiscing made Libby ache for her absent father. She had tried to speak to Clarrie on the telephone that morning but had only got Daleep the factory manager, who promised to pass on a message that she had called.

The evening passed quickly. A large buffet was served mid-evening and then her aunt and uncle organised a game of charades on the veranda. George kept seeking her out and paying her special attention. He made sure that they were chosen in the same group and they acted out *A Midsummer Night's Dream*, with Libby playing a sleepy Titania and George doing a slapstick Bottom. Although she was flattered by the fuss he made of her, it also left her feeling uncomfortable. She didn't want Ghulam to assume she was George's girlfriend.

Afterwards there was dancing in the garden to the jazz band and people drifted between the house and the veranda, drinking and laughing, sitting and chatting. Libby saw Fatima talking to Danny Dunlop and wondered if he was asking her for medical advice. At least the Khans were still here; she had lost sight of them since the charades. While George went off for more drinks, Libby went in search of Ghulam.

She found him smoking under the trees with a young hillsman from the Duff Church whose father had been in Johnny's regiment.

'Putting the world to rights?' Libby asked.

'Talking cricket,' Ghulam answered, offering her a cigarette.

'No thanks,' said Libby. 'To be honest, I don't really like smoking.'

They stood chatting for a few minutes about the party and then the young Gurkha excused himself.

'I was hoping for a dance,' Libby said after he'd gone.

'I'm a hopeless dancer,' said Ghulam.

'Well, I'm quite good,' she said, 'so we stand a chance of getting it right.'

He eyed her. 'There are men queuing up to dance with you tonight who are younger and far more suitable than me.'

'Perhaps,' she said, holding his look, 'but I want to dance with you. It would be bad manners to refuse me on my birthday.'

Ghulam ground out his cigarette. 'Very well, Miss Robson.' He held out his arm.

'Please call me Libby.' She curled her fingers around his arm, enjoying the feel of muscled strength beneath the thin shirt.

'Comrade Libby,' he said with a twitch of a smile.

On the shadowed lawn, they attempted a waltz to the strains of 'Smoke Gets in Your Eyes'. Libby could hardly believe she was being held close by this man who had dominated her thoughts for the past week. She leant into his shoulder, thrilling at the feel of his warm hand on her back and the soapy smell of his chin as it brushed against her cheek. She felt desire surge inside her. If only the dance could go on forever.

'I'm sorry your father couldn't be here,' Ghulam said. 'Will you still go to Assam this week?'

'I don't know. I'm not sure what's wrong with him. He needs to rest. Perhaps it's just an excuse not to come to Calcutta.' She looked into his eyes. 'Have you heard any more about your family in Lahore?'

'No,' said Ghulam.

'But you haven't had bad news?'

'No, nothing.'

'Well, then that's something. I hope you get good news soon.'

His grip on her tightened a fraction as they continued to waltz. She thought her heart would burst out of her chest it was thudding so hard.

The tune came to an end. Ghulam dropped his hold. Libby didn't step away. 'Dance to the next one?' she suggested.

'I think Fatima wishes to go,' he said, glancing over her head. 'And that red-faced sahib is making a bee-line for you again.'

Libby's heart sank as, looking over her shoulder, she saw George approaching.

'Can I see you again?' Libby said quickly.

His look was guarded. 'I'm not sure that's a good idea, Libby.'

'You offered to be my guide around Calcutta, remember?'

'This is your Calcutta here,' he said, an edge to his voice. 'Safer if you stick to it.'

'I don't care about safety,' she replied. 'I want to see what's going on beyond this world. I had a glimpse of it with you the other day – please show me more. How can I adapt to the new India if I stay confined to the old?'

She saw his indecision. He was on the point of saying something when George arrived at her side.

'There you are, bonny lass.' He grinned. 'My turn for a dance, eh?'

Libby was choked with disappointment as Ghulam nodded and withdrew without another word. In frustration, she watched him walk off across the lawn, his shoulders broad under the black kurta. He didn't look back.

George led her swiftly into a fox-trot. 'He's a strange one to invite,' said George. 'Caused a bit of a stir among the burra memsahibs in the drawing room. Did you know that Khan went to prison for terrorism?'

'Yes,' said Libby, 'a long time ago when he was a youth.'

'They say he's a communist too,' said George. 'God help us if his kind take over Calcutta after Independence. They'll ruin the economy. Still, his sister, the lady doctor, is a good sort. Old friend of Adela's apparently. I suppose you had to invite him along to chaperone her.'

'I invited them both because I like them both,' said Libby in irritation.

George gave her an astonished look. 'You've met him before?'

'Yes, twice. I've been to their flat and he's taken me out to lunch.'

George was shocked. 'I really don't think that's a good idea. Your uncle and aunt won't want you getting mixed up with his sort at all. Promise me you won't see him again, lass?'

Libby stopped dancing. 'Don't tell me who I can and can't see!'

'I care about you and I don't want to see you being led astray by the wrong kind.'

'At least he's not married,' Libby said bluntly.

'I'm nearly divorced,' George said defensively. 'And I would never take advantage of you.'

'So what were you doing kissing me at the picnic?'

'I may have had a bit too much to drink,' he admitted. 'But you were looking so kissable. I thought you wanted to.'

'I did,' said Libby. 'I've wanted you to kiss me since I was fifteen.'

'Really?'

'But I no longer feel the same about you, George. Not since I was told you're carrying on with a married woman in Dacca.'

He caught her hand to stop her walking off. 'Who told you that?'

'It doesn't matter who.' She gave him a fierce look. 'I know I don't mean anything to you so let go of me, George.'

'Lass, I do care about you,' he insisted. 'There's no woman in Dacca – no one special at least.'

'It doesn't matter,' said Libby. 'What I felt for you was just a girlish crush. I didn't realise it until tonight.'

George looked bemused. 'I had no idea you ever felt like that.'

'No, George, because you don't really think about how other people feel, do you? Just as long as you're having fun.'

She pulled away from him.

'Don't say you're in love with that communist?' George said in disbelief. When Libby didn't answer, George warned, 'Don't be a fool, Libby. He's too old for you – and he'll only use you for what he can get out of the British.'

Libby rounded on him. 'He doesn't want a single thing out of us British,' she said angrily, 'except for us to get out of India. And as for his age – I like older men – or hadn't you noticed?'

She turned from him but he kept pace with her back across the lawn.

'Sorry, Libby,' George said contritely, 'I won't interfere. It's up to you how you live your life. Say you'll forgive me for upsetting you.'

Libby slowed, glancing to see if he meant it. George took her hand and pulled her round.

'I'm truly sorry for messing things up between us,' he said. 'You're right; I am a bit selfish. But after getting my fingers burnt with Joan I'm wary of getting involved again. I feel bad if you think I led you on – you know how fond I am of all you Robsons – I just thought you might be up for a bit of fun too. I never meant to hurt you. Please forgive me. Are we still friends?'

His fair face looked so pained that Libby relented. She couldn't help liking George. She knew he was a hopeless womaniser but he was also fun and generous and she didn't want them to part on bad terms.

'I suppose we're still friends,' she relented.

He beamed and kissed her on the cheek. 'Grand! Let's get another gimlet and dance till dawn.'

Libby suppressed a laugh as they retreated to the veranda. Flowers met them on the steps with an enquiring look.

'It's okay,' Libby mouthed.

'The Khans have just left,' said Flowers. 'Fatima said to say goodbye – she didn't want to stop you dancing.'

Libby flushed to think that Ghulam's last sight of her was dancing with George. She would have no chance to find out if he wanted to see her again. But why should he? To him she was still one of the despised *sahib-log* – a privileged white woman – despite her Indian sympathies. Would they ever be able to get beyond that unseen but powerful barrier that divided them?

For a brief moment as they had danced, Libby thought she had seen desire in his eyes. But perhaps she had been wrong. Ghulam had not encouraged her suggestion that they meet up again and he had been swift to leave without a word of goodbye. The truth made her heart heavy; Ghulam Khan would never allow himself to fall for a Britisher. He had come out of duty to his sister and not from any desire to see Libby again.

George's friend Eddy Carter appeared beside her. 'Can I finally get a dance with the birthday girl?' he asked.

Libby, suppressing her longing for Ghulam, smiled at Eddy. 'You certainly can,' she said. Linking her arm through his, they set off down the steps.

CHAPTER 12

April

Libby hung on to the telephone, anxiously twisting the cord around her fingers. It had taken all morning to get through to Belgooree but Clarrie Robson had sounded pleased that Libby had called.

'It will cheer your father to know you've called.'

'So can I speak to Dad?' Libby had asked.

'I think he's sleeping.'

'*Please*, Clarrie.'

'Of course. Let me go and fetch him.'

It seemed an age before Clarrie returned. Libby heard a crackle at the other end and then Clarrie's warm reassuring voice was speaking again.

'Libby, sweetheart, your father's only just woken up. He's been sleeping so badly. He's rather groggy. Can I get him to ring you tomorrow or the day after?'

Libby felt a spasm of anger: despite several attempts to get through on the telephone she still hadn't managed to speak to her dad. 'Is he really so weak that he can't come to the phone to speak to me?'

'It's a long walk from the house to the factory,' Clarrie reminded her.

Libby felt a guilty pang; was she being unreasonable? 'What's wrong with him? You told me it was nothing serious.'

There was a hesitation then Clarrie said, 'The doctor thinks he's worn out – complete exhaustion. Something seems to be troubling him but he won't talk about it. Perhaps he will to you.'

'Not if he won't even drag himself to the phone for two minutes,' Libby said in frustration.

'It's not that he doesn't want to,' said Clarrie, 'it's just that he's finding it hard to say anything at the moment.'

Libby was suspicious. 'So he is capable of coming to the phone, he just doesn't want to. He's avoiding me.'

'It's not like that . . .'

'Well, that's what it feels like,' Libby said, her eyes smarting with tears. 'I've been longing to see him.'

'I know you have,' Clarrie sympathised. 'And you know you are welcome here any time. Perhaps your uncle could travel with you as far as Shillong.'

'I don't need my uncle as a chaperone,' Libby said.

'Your father doesn't want you and Flowers travelling alone,' said Clarrie. 'I think he's being overcautious but things are growing unsettled in the countryside. People are on the move.'

Libby felt a moment of anxiety. Was the violence in the Punjab finally beginning to seep across the northern plain?

'I don't like to ask Uncle Johnny any more favours,' said Libby. 'He's been so kind to me as it is.'

'Let's see how James is in a few days' time,' said Clarrie. 'He might get his energy back and decide to travel to Calcutta after all. Why don't we speak at the weekend?'

Libby swallowed her disappointment. 'Give him my love, won't you?'

'Of course I will. Goodbye, Libby, sweetheart.'

Libby hung up. She sat on the chair by the telephone in the hallway feeling numb and knowing that her aunt had heard every word through the open drawing-room door. Helena appeared.

'It's too bad,' said her aunt. 'Do you think he's having some sort of mental breakdown, poor man? Muriel thinks so. The planters worked so damn hard during the War to keep out the Japs and help the troops. Men your father's age deserve to retire.'

Libby knew her aunt, in her own brusque way, was trying to be kind. But her words distressed Libby. When she finally got to see her father, would she find a broken husk of a man? Was it too late for them to recapture their special bond? She realised how much she was relying on her father to be the same strong, protective figure that she remembered from childhood. It frightened her to think of him as weak and debilitated, worn out by years of war and a lifetime of working in the unforgiving tropics. She was clinging on to the belief that her father would be the one to reunite the family; that once they were all together again her mother would rediscover her love for James and for India – and for Libby.

The thought startled Libby. Perhaps she did care what Tilly thought of her after all.

'Would you like to come with me to bridge at the Percy-Barratts' later, dear?' Helena asked. 'You look like you need cheering up.'

This galvanised Libby, who stood up. 'Thanks Auntie, but I've got plans.'

'Seeing any more of George Brewis?'

'Maybe later,' Libby said vaguely.

'They're such fun, the Strachan's men, aren't they?' Helena said. 'In my day, one rather looked down on box-wallahs as marriage material, but perhaps we were the fools. They're the ones with the money and a future here. It's we army types who will have to go.'

Libby scrutinised her aunt. Something in her tone belied the flippant words.

'Auntie, are you worried about what will happen?' Libby asked.

Helena glanced out at the veranda where her father sat snoozing. 'Yes, I worry. I can't imagine ever leaving – I think it would kill Papa

– but it will never be the same again. So many of our friends are talking seriously now of going home – people who have been here a lifetime. It's so unsettling.'

Libby reached out and put a hand on Helena's shoulder. 'I know, it doesn't seem fair, does it, when you've lived here all your life.'

'That's it,' Helena said, her voice wavering. 'It's all so unfair.'

'But then that's how the Indians have felt about us being here,' Libby said as gently as she could. 'British rule has been unfair to them for too long.'

Helena gave her a sharp look. 'I suppose that's what your friend Mr Khan says, is it? That the Indians have been put upon? But does he ever stop to think what we British – generations of British – have given to India?'

'He would argue that we have taken a lot more than we've given,' said Libby. 'And I think he would be right.'

Helena stiffened. Libby dropped her hand.

'Well, I must get ready for bridge.' Helena stalked off.

Libby felt bad about upsetting her aunt but she had only spoken the truth.

After an afternoon of aimless wandering around the Maidan, making half-hearted sketches, Libby found herself outside Amelia Buildings as the sun was going down. Perhaps deep-down she had always intended coming here, hoping to bump into Ghulam. Her stomach knotted with nerves. What would she say to him? What if he should rebuff her and send her away? She screwed up her courage; if she didn't act now, she would never know what Ghulam really thought of her. She entered the building. If the Khans were out, she would leave a note inviting them to have tea in town – perhaps at the Kwality Café or Firpo's.

Sitara answered the door with a welcoming smile. Fatima was making ready to go out. There was no sign of Ghulam.

'You've just caught me,' said the doctor. 'I'm sorry – I wish I'd known you were coming . . .'

'No, it's me who's sorry,' said Libby. 'I know I should have sent a note but I was just passing. I've been sketching on the Maidan.'

'Alone?' Fatima gave her a look of concern.

'Yes.'

'You must take care,' Fatima warned. 'Do your aunt and uncle know where you are?'

'Not exactly. They'll assume I'm with George or Flowers.' Libby smothered an impatient sigh. 'But I can look after myself.'

Fatima gave her a long look and then nodded. 'Of course you can. So you've delayed going to Assam? How is your father?'

'Needing more rest,' said Libby. 'I'm at a bit of a loose end until I know what he wants me to do.'

'I'm sorry to hear that,' said Fatima. 'Would you like to talk about it?'

'Thanks, but I mustn't make you late. Perhaps I could call another evening?'

'Well, if you're sure?'

'Where are you going?' Libby asked.

'To a meeting in Bowbazar – Ghulam is hoping to speak.'

Libby's heart lurched. 'What kind of meeting?'

'A discussion about what should happen to Bengal – and Calcutta – once the British go.'

'Can I come?'

Fatima looked worried. 'It might get rowdy.'

'But you're going to risk it,' Libby pointed out. 'Please let me go with you, Fatima? I'll just keep quiet at the back; people won't know I'm there.'

Fatima gave her a dry smile that reminded Libby of Ghulam. 'From what my brother's told me about you, I find it hard to believe you'll sit like a mouse through a political meeting.'

Libby blushed. 'Ghulam's spoken about me then?'

Fatima nodded. 'I think – against all his expectations – you've impressed him. And it takes a lot to impress Ghulam.'

Libby grinned. 'Good. He impressed me too. I've never known a man quite like him with so much passion and single-mindedness to a cause.'

Fatima pushed her spectacles up the bridge of her nose and studied her.

'My brother is very single-minded. I love him dearly but I accept that he puts his campaigns and beliefs before anything or anyone else. He's always been like that and he won't ever change.'

'I admire that in him,' said Libby.

'But it has turned him into a man who doesn't allow others to get close to him.'

Libby felt herself go hot. 'Why are you telling me this?'

'May I be frank, Libby?'

'Of course.'

'I have seen you with my brother and I think perhaps you have grown a little fond of him?'

Libby swallowed. 'Is it so obvious?'

'To me, yes. And I also know that he likes you – perhaps in other circumstances would allow a friendship to develop – but these are difficult and uncertain times. If you come with me to the meeting it must be as my friend and not because you want to see Ghulam. Don't fall in love with him, Libby; you will only get your heart broken.'

Libby put her hands to her burning cheeks. She was mortified that Fatima had guessed her feelings for Ghulam so easily. Had the brother and sister also discussed Libby's growing infatuation? She had to know.

'Have you talked about me in this way with Ghulam?'

'No,' said Fatima, 'I am just advising you in confidence – as one woman to another.'

Libby felt wretched. But Fatima only confirmed her own fears: that the time and place would never be right for her and Ghulam. He was not the kind of man to put his own feelings or desires before his politics, and that was part of why she was attracted to him. He had spent his whole life fighting for a free and socialist India. Affairs of the heart would always be secondary. Fatima was being frank to save Libby a lot of heartache, although she couldn't help but wish she might be the one to change Ghulam.

'Has Ghulam ever been close to another woman?' Libby asked.

Fatima hesitated. 'Once, yes. He has had many casual friendships with women over the years – mostly comrades in the party – but this woman was different.'

Libby swallowed. 'In what way? Did he love her?'

'Yes, very much. But they argued badly – she became a fighter with the Indian National Army and accused Ghulam of betraying India. You can imagine how much that hurt him.'

'How cruel of her,' Libby said indignantly.

Fatima gave her a pitying look. 'Yes, but he still keeps her photograph.'

Libby felt a stab of jealousy. 'Where is she now?'

Fatima shrugged. 'Probably back in Delhi where she came from. That's if she survived the War. Ghulam never talks about her.'

Libby's heart clenched for Ghulam and also for herself – for her hopeless love.

Fatima touched her arm gently. 'I'm sorry but it's best you know. I will understand if you don't now wish to come to the meeting.'

Libby dug her nails into her palms; she would show no emotion. 'Of course I still want to come. My interest in what happens to this country isn't any less because of what you've just told me. I hope you don't think I'm that shallow.'

Fatima smiled. 'I don't think you are at all shallow, Libby. You are a remarkable young woman. If only there had been more British like you, we would have got independence a generation ago.'

Libby felt a wave of gratitude for the generous words. 'Thank you.'

'Do you speak Bengali?' Fatima asked.

'Very little,' Libby admitted.

'You may not understand everything that is said,' said Fatima, 'but I'll try and explain what's going on. Ghulam will probably speak in English so everyone will understand him. Come on, let's not be late.'

Despite the whirring of ceiling fans, the hall was hot and stuffy and packed with people, mostly men. The meeting was already underway and a man dressed in the white clothing and cap of a Congress party member was speaking in English to the crowd, exhorting them to remain united.

'I think he's one of the leaders from Delhi,' whispered Fatima.

With nowhere to sit, Fatima and Libby stood at the back next to a handful of other young women. Libby, ignoring the curious looks of those around her, craned for a view of Ghulam. Her heart lurched as she spotted him behind the speaker. As the man finished, a handful of men rose to clap him but others began to shout their opposition. The clamour grew and the exchanges sounded ill-tempered, though Libby couldn't understand much of it.

Ghulam stepped forward and held up his hands for calm.

'Comrades!' he bellowed. 'There is a saying in our country that if you have one Calcuttan you have a poet; if you have two, you have a political party; and if you have three – you have two political parties.'

There was a ripple of laughter and the noise began to subside.

'These are exciting times for our nation and some of us have different visions of what that nation should be. But what binds us all is our desire for freedom and the right to decide our own destiny. Don't let brother fall out with brother – this is not the time for disunity.'

'It's too late,' a man shouted, jumping to his feet. 'The Muslims are butchering our brothers in the Punjab. It's a matter of time before it happens in Calcutta again – just like last year.'

'The violence was on both sides,' said Ghulam. 'As a journalist I witnessed atrocities against Muslims in our city too.'

'Hindus only acted in self-defence!' the man protested.

'No,' Ghulam contradicted him, 'the violence was organised – the Hindu militants had been preparing for weeks, collecting weapons and teaching impressionable youths that Muslims were their enemy. But it's the rich Hindu landowners who are to blame – inflaming the lowest castes to fight, all so that they can have the rich spoils of West Bengal to themselves. The ordinary people don't benefit from partition – far from it: they are the ones who will be uprooted and lose their homes and livelihoods. The winners will be the rich Marwari merchants who want to push out their rivals – they are the ones who finance the violence in our city.'

'That's a lie!' someone else shouted.

'Not your city, Khan!' the first protester said, jabbing an accusing finger. 'You're a Punjabi.'

'And a Muslim,' another called out.

Libby's chest tightened in fear for Ghulam; she felt the sudden tension in the room.

'I'm an Indian,' Ghulam cried, his expression passionate. 'We all are! That is why we must hold fast together,' he urged. 'Don't let the British tactics of divide and rule live on in our new India. There is no place for a separate Bengal – or for a divided one.'

'We don't agree,' said a Congress worker standing near to Ghulam. 'The Bengal Congress Party has come to the conclusion that dividing the state is the only way of guaranteeing the safety of all.'

'Whose safety?' Ghulam challenged. 'The up-country migrants from East Bengal who struggle to make a living in Calcutta?'

'The Muslim Bengalis will be better off going back to East Bengal – that's what they want too.'

'And what about the Hindu minority in East Bengal?' Ghulam said heatedly. 'Are you saying that they must leave the only home they've ever known? Did Gandhi waste his time there this last winter and starve himself half to death for nothing?'

'Gandhi is out of touch! Non-violence means nothing to Jinnah's League or his half-caste lackey Suhrawardy who runs our city for the benefit of his own kind and not ours.'

'It shouldn't matter whether we're Muslim or Hindu,' Ghulam said in exasperation. 'We all want the best for Bengal and India.'

'We're not all the same,' his original opponent shouted. 'We have an enemy within – and that's the Muslim living among us pretending to be our friend while plotting to kill us.'

'That's ridiculous!' Ghulam retorted.

Libby's heart began to pound. The atmosphere simmered with hostility. She admired Ghulam for standing his ground yet was anxious on his behalf.

The Congress supporter standing beside him put a hand on his arm. 'We don't all believe that, Comrade, but sadly too many do. The only way to stem the bloodshed is to agree to some measure of partition. Give the League their Pakistan and let us get on with forging a new India. Don't waste your energy fighting your fellow Indians when there are other battles to be won – such as taking power and wealth from the maharajahs.'

'Yes,' agreed the man in the crowd. 'We want our own state for West Bengalis.'

'*Jai Hind!* Victory to India!'

Then someone countered with a defiant chant: '*Pakistan Zindabad!* Long live Pakistan!'

The room erupted in shouts and argument. Libby saw the frustration on Ghulam's face. He searched the room for support – perhaps looking for Fatima – and for an instant their eyes locked. His mouth fell open in astonishment. The exhortation that he was about to make died on his lips. People began to look round and stare at the women. Some started to mutter and ask questions but Libby didn't understand. Moments later Ghulam was being manhandled from the platform as the meeting broke up in chaos.

Fatima gipped Libby's arm. 'We need to get out of here,' she gasped. 'It's not safe.'

Her face was so worried that Libby did not argue. But as they tried to move towards the door, they were blocked by the press of people around them as others attempted to leave. The mood was volatile; some arguing, some anxious to be gone. Libby heard the word Britisher being hissed. Fatima squeezed her way through, hanging on to Libby's arm. Then someone pushed between them in their eagerness to get out and the two women became separated.

Fatima looked on helplessly as she was carried on a sea of people towards the entrance while Libby was jostled and shoved in the opposite direction.

'Go!' Libby called. 'I'll see you outside!'

As Fatima disappeared from sight, the belligerent man in the black hat appeared beside her and pressed himself against her. He snarled at her with teeth stained red with paan.

'Get out, Britisher spy!'

'I'm no one's spy!' Libby glared back, trying to push him away. 'I'm India born and bred – I've every right to be here.'

He spat in her face. 'Quit India, Britisher whore.'

Libby recoiled, closing her eyes and wiping at her cheek. Her assailant cried out in fury. She opened her eyes to see him being grabbed from behind by a taller man, who shoved him out of the way. Libby gasped to see it was Ghulam. Without a word, Ghulam seized her hand

and barged his way through the throng of agitated people. He cut a way to the door, pulling her behind him. Men shouted threateningly. Heart slamming against her chest in fright, Libby clung on, fearful of being separated.

Minutes later they were out on the street. They looked around in vain for Fatima. The sun had now set. Oil lamps flickered in stalls and shadows loomed. He hurried her behind an old colonnade and its sheltering darkness.

Suddenly he rounded on her. 'What on earth are you doing here with Fatima?' he demanded.

'I wanted to hear the debate,' Libby panted. 'I called round to your flat and Fatima was just on her way out.'

'She had no right to bring you,' he answered angrily.

'Don't blame your sister,' said Libby, 'I made her take me. And why shouldn't I be here?'

'Do you have any idea how dangerous you made it for her – and for you?' he blazed. 'This is no polite debating society – we're fighting for India and passions are running high.'

'I realise that—'

'Yet you expect to swan in and spectate as if it was one of your pig-sticking shows.'

Libby was suddenly aware that he was still gripping her hand. She pulled free.

'You think I came to lord it over you?' she asked, impassioned and shaking with adrenaline. 'Nothing could be further from the truth. At least your sister knows I'm genuinely interested in India's future – otherwise she wouldn't have brought me.'

'I thought you made her take you?' he retorted.

'But she agreed with me,' said Libby. 'Because we both believe that we women have just as much right to be there as you men – it's our future too.'

Ghulam leant very close, so that Libby could see the fury flashing in his green eyes.

'No, Libby,' he growled, 'it's not your future. You British no longer have a say in what happens to India – except the date of when you give us freedom from your Raj. That is the last decision over us Indians you will ever make. It's time you accepted that.'

His words hurt Libby more deeply than the hostility and spitting she had just endured in the hall.

'I thought we were on the same side,' she said, glaring back at him. 'I agreed with all you said in the meeting. I think partition would be a tragedy too. I'm not asking for a say in India's future but I'll fight for my right to live here.'

'You are a British citizen,' he pointed out, 'not an Indian one. You have a choice about where you live – we real Indians don't.'

She held his look. 'What's a real Indian, Ghulam?' she demanded hotly. 'Shouldn't that include all the minorities here? Or don't you want to think about the inconvenient ones – the Anglo-Indians like Flowers or my cousin Adela – or even the Indian-born Europeans like myself? Are we not pure enough for the new India?'

'That's not what I meant—'

''Cause if that's your attitude then you are no better than the Hindu extremists who want to rid India of the Muslims and Sikhs. Because once you start excluding one group then where do you stop?'

They glared at each other. Libby could see the muscles in his jaw clenching in anger. Abruptly he turned from her with a curt reply. 'I need to find my sister. I'll fetch you a rickshaw to take you home.'

'I want to know that Fatima is safe too,' Libby said. 'I'm coming with you.'

Ghulam gave a sigh of impatience. 'Very well.'

They emerged from the shadows and watched the people milling around the entrance. The numbers had already dwindled as people hurried for home, perhaps unnerved by the ill-tempered meeting.

'There she is!' Libby cried, catching sight of Fatima on the opposite pavement, standing anxiously at a rickshaw stand.

They hurried across. The women clutched hands in relief.

'Are you all right?' Fatima asked. 'I'm sorry for leaving you.'

'I'm fine,' Libby assured her. 'I'm sorry for putting you at risk.'

'You didn't.'

'Your brother thinks I did,' said Libby, flicking Ghulam a look.

'You were both needlessly reckless,' he said angrily. 'We must get away from here in case those men have *goondas* waiting to cause trouble.'

Libby felt queasy with fear again. Ghulam summoned two rickshaws. He helped his sister into one.

'Go straight home, Fatima,' he ordered. 'I'll see Miss Robson to Alipore.'

The women said a hasty goodbye as Libby scrambled into the second rickshaw, followed by Ghulam.

Libby and Ghulam sat in silence as they were jostled down the road. Libby's heart hammered with annoyance and upset. Why was he so infuriating and stubborn in his prejudice against her? And yet he had saved her from an ugly situation in the hall – a chivalrous gesture that would probably harden the Hindu militants' dislike of him. By being there, she had made a bad situation worse. She had been deeply shaken by the anger and hostility in the hall; until then she hadn't fully grasped how uncertain and dangerous the future was for India – and for men like Ghulam.

On Chowringhee Street, they transferred to a taxi to take them out to Alipore. By the time they neared New House, Libby was feeling wretched.

'I'm sorry for causing you and Fatima trouble,' she blurted out. 'You're right; I should never have gone to the meeting. I didn't think. I was just curious. It's a big fault of mine – nosiness. But if I'd known there was such animosity . . .' She turned to look at him in the seat beside her. 'Have I made it very much worse for you?'

He studied her with his intense gaze. 'No, I don't suppose consorting with memsahibs will make any difference. The Hindu Mahasabha already hate my guts.'

'Because you're a communist or a Muslim?'

He gave a mirthless laugh. 'Both. And for the articles I've written against them and their warped version of nationalism.'

Impulsively, Libby reached out and covered his hand with hers. 'Tell me what I should do. I want to be useful here but I feel so helpless. It's as if the world is spinning out of control and everyone's angry or afraid of something. It should be a new dawn – but it doesn't feel like it.'

The taxi slowed as it turned into the quiet leafy street in Alipore where the Watsons lived and came to a halt. Libby thought Ghulam wasn't going to say anything, yet he hadn't pulled his hand away.

'Do what is in your power to do, Libby,' he said. 'It doesn't have to be anything big or newsworthy.'

'Such as?' she asked, searching his face.

'Go and see your father,' he answered. 'He's ill and he needs you.'

She was taken aback by his suggestion. She wanted to do something grand and noble that would make a difference to people. She hadn't meant something small-scale and personal.

'He hasn't asked for me to go,' she countered.

'He might never ask. Are you going to kick your heels around Calcutta because you're afraid to face him? Because if so, you're not the brave woman I think you are.'

His challenge jolted Libby. She thought how Ghulam had been cast out from his own family and it surprised her that he should think it important for her to see her father. Perhaps he had guessed that, despite her insistence on wanting to see her father again, she was also nervous at meeting him. Or maybe Ghulam just wanted her gone from the city. As if reading her thoughts, he added, 'It is perhaps my only regret that I did not see my mother again before she died.'

Libby's eyes prickled with sudden emotion. He seemed such a strong man – one who would never show any weakness – and yet his words were edged with a bittersweet tenderness. For all that they had argued and the evening had been fraught, Ghulam still had the humanity to think of her relationship with her father – a man whose position of power in the tea gardens he despised. She was only just beginning to grasp the depth of Ghulam's wisdom and compassion for people – even for his adversaries.

'Thank you,' Libby said.

Instinctively, she leant towards him and pressed her mouth against his in a robust kiss. Then she was pushing open the door and clambering out before he had time to react.

They watched each other as the taxi moved off. Ghulam's handsome face was impassive. Libby felt a fresh wave of remorse – not only for angering Ghulam with her earlier impulsive behaviour and for causing upset between Fatima and her brother – but now for her foolish kiss. It would make things ten times more awkward between her and Ghulam should they meet again. What on earth had taken possession of her?

Libby retreated up the garden path, her cheeks burning with more than just the evening heat. By the time she had reached the house, she had made up her mind. She would contact Flowers in the morning and if her friend still wanted to come with her to Assam, Libby would make arrangements for their travel as soon as possible. If not, she would go anyway.

Only later, lying in bed, going over the events of the evening, did she remember. She had left her jute bag with the sketching pad and pencils at the Khans' flat in Amelia Buildings. Libby stifled a gasp of embarrassment. What if Ghulam should flick through it and find the cartoon of him portrayed as a caged sulking tiger? Libby lay back with a sigh. She and Ghulam Khan would probably never set eyes on each other again – no doubt that would be what he wished – so what was the use in worrying?

With a deep sigh of regret, Libby forced herself to think of something else. She would go to her father. Soon she would be back in Assam. After all, that's why she had come all this way, wasn't it?

Unable to sleep, Ghulam went up to the flat roof of Amelia Buildings to smoke. Something that Libby had said kept nagging at his thoughts: *It's as if the world is spinning out of control and everyone's angry or afraid of something . . .'*

That was how he felt – as if things were slipping out of his control. The meeting had been bad-tempered and seething with hostility. People had already made up their minds that the partition of Bengal was coming whether they wanted it or not, and they talked of the Punjab in the same way. There was a fatalistic belief overtaking the Congress Party that the only way to salvage India was to sever its two arms: Punjab in the west and Bengal in the east.

During the meeting, Ghulam had begun to feel dispirited. He had searched around the room for Fatima; his younger sister's presence always calmed and reassured him. He had come to rely on her more and more. Whatever happened, Fatima always maintained her quiet optimism that things would work out for the best. Then he had spotted Libby standing with Fatima at the back wall. For a moment he had been speechless with surprise, thinking he must have made a mistake. But the large blue eyes with their challenging look and the expressive mouth that curved in a smile of encouragement as their eyes met could belong to no other.

Ghulam felt his heart begin to thud again at the memory. His instant feeling was one of elation that she had come to hear him, followed immediately by anger that she would put herself and also Fatima in danger by coming openly to the rowdy meeting. Of course as a memsahib she would attract suspicion and resentment.

Ghulam took a deep drag on his cigarette. He should never have told his sister about the meeting in the first place. The atmosphere had been openly hostile towards Muslims. Yet Fatima continued to reassure him that once a political settlement was reached then the anger and fear between the communities would dissipate. He had to believe that.

He leant on the parapet, welcoming the evening breeze that licked his hair and face, and looked south towards Alipore. An indistinct mass of dark trees obscured the housing.

'Oh, Libby,' he sighed.

He felt such a clash of emotions towards the young woman: annoyance and resentment, admiration and liking. Seeing her being accosted at the meeting by the odious heckler, Ghulam had been astonished by the surge of protectiveness he had felt towards her as he'd rushed to her aid.

He lit another cigarette. He had to admit that it wasn't just the world slipping out of control that preoccupied him but his feelings for the Robson girl. How many times had the image of Libby in the green satin evening dress come to mind in recent days? Seeing her on the Watsons' veranda had taken his breath away: her voluptuous figure and lustrous hair, her hypnotic blue eyes and translucent skin that betrayed her emotions as the blood rushed up from her chest to her cheeks at the slightest compliment. She was beautiful.

Ghulam had gone with reluctance to the birthday party just to please Fatima and had intended staying for as short a time as possible. But he had been unable to stop gazing at Libby or to quell the kick of jealousy he felt at seeing her dancing with her other male friends. He had feigned indifference to her plea to dance with him and yet when he took her in his arms he was flooded with a desire that he had not felt in years.

It was ridiculous to feel this way about a Britisher – and one nearly half his age – and yet he could not help it. He found himself thinking about her when trying to write articles, when he heard a snatch of band music on the radio or when over-tired and sleepless in his bed. Restless, Ghulam could not help wondering about other lovers she might have had.

He knew such surges of desire were fruitless; nothing could come of a relationship with Libby and it would be wrong to give her hope. Besides, Fatima had just told him how she had cautioned Libby against developing feelings for her brother and that he was wedded to his causes. He was grateful for his sister's frankness towards the British girl.

But what about that moment of intimacy in the taxi earlier that evening? His pulse had throbbed at the touch of her hand on his and then that brief electrifying kiss on the lips. If she had stayed any longer, would he have pulled her into his arms and kissed her properly? Ghulam let out a long sigh. He had been genuine in wanting her to be reunited with her father and realised what an ordeal it would probably be for both of them after such a long separation. He had not suggested it as a means of putting her out of temptation's way but there was a certain relief in thinking Libby would be leaving for Assam. He could get on with his work without worrying about bumping into her – and perhaps he could rid his thoughts of her more easily.

Ghulam stubbed out his cigarette and went below.

CHAPTER 13

Herbert's Café, Newcastle, England, April

Adela glanced out of the hot kitchen to see Joan loitering with Sam in the back yard and sharing his cigarettes. She'd wondered where the lazy woman had got to. Sam, on his way in from the allotment, had obviously been distracted. He had a box of spring greens at his feet. With a stab of irritation, Adela made for the door.

'As soon as the divorce comes through, me and Tommy are ganin' to get wed,' Joan was saying, with a toss of blonde hair. 'He doesn't care about me being married before – not like all the gossips round here – and he's twice as respectable as them, him being in charge of Major Gibson's stables.'

'It's good that Tommy wants to take on your daughter Bonnie,' said Sam, tipping up his battered hat and scratching his head. His face was glistening and his hands were ingrained with soil. Adela felt a familiar pang of affection for her husband but it was quickly replaced by annoyance at Joan.

'Joan, you're needed in the café, please,' Adela said. 'Doreen can't manage the waitressing *and* the washing up.'

Joan blew out a smoke ring. 'Well, she'll have to manage without me soon. I'm not stoppin' to help out much longer. Tommy's got a house on Major Gibson's estate and I'll be moving up to Willowburn once we're wed.'

'So you keep telling us,' Adela said.

'The only job I'll have will be taking care of Tommy,' Joan said, staring into the distance with a dreamy smile.

'And Bonnie,' Sam reminded her.

'I hope Tommy's good at cooking his own meals and cleaning up after himself,' Adela muttered.

'Adela!' Sam said with a look that was half amused, half reproving.

She ignored his appeal. 'Well, in the meantime, Joan, you can practise in our kitchen, if that isn't too much of an inconvenience. You are getting paid, remember?'

'Talking of which,' said Joan, 'Tommy thinks I should be getting paid a lot more than I am. He thinks you're taking advantage of my good nature.'

'Good nature?' Adela snapped. 'I'd call it lazy nature. You swan in here when it suits you and leave early.'

'Only 'cause I have to pick up Bonnie from Mrs Brewis,' Joan said.

'Or sneak off to the pictures,' Adela accused.

Joan flushed pink. 'Well, we all need a bit of time off now and again – it's hard work being a mam.'

Adela was stung by the comment. Joan was one of the few who knew she had given up her baby; was she trying deliberately to hurt her?

'Hard work for Aunt Olive you mean,' retorted Adela. 'I can't imagine how you're going to manage when you haven't got my aunt to look after Bonnie all day.'

'I won't need George's mam once I'm up at Willowburn,' Joan said with a dismissive wave. 'It'll be just me and Bonnie and Tommy – a perfect life.'

Adela bit back a waspish reply about Joan being completely unsuited for a life in the country.

'Smells like something's burning,' Sam said.

'Oh hell!' Adela turned on her heels and dashed back into the kitchen. She had forgotten all about the rhubarb pies. Wrenching them out of the old oven, she saw that the pastry crusts were burnt black. Acrid smoke billowed around.

'Eeh, you've ruined Mrs Jackman's pies,' said Joan who had followed her inside. 'What a shame. That'll be her ration of butter gone. And Sam was so proud of that rhubarb; weren't you Sam?'

Sam stood scratching his head. He caught Adela's thunderous look and quickly said, 'There's more – I'll go and pick some.'

'No!' Adela turned back to the pies. 'They're not ruined. We'll cut the tops off and serve them with whipped cream. They'll still be delicious. Mohammed Din did a recipe like this. We'll put ginger in the cream.'

'They'll not eat that round here,' said Joan.

'Of course they will,' Adela said, her temper rising, 'and you are going to serve it to them. Put that cigarette out and get your apron back on again.'

With a pout, Joan did as she was told.

Sam said, 'I'll stay and wash the vegetables, shall I?'

'No,' Adela said quickly, not wanting Joan to have any more distractions. 'You can go back to the allotment.'

Joan rolled her eyes at him as she sauntered back into the café. Adela felt her teeth clench. Sam put a hand on her arm.

'Let's go for a walk up the Tyne this evening after work,' he suggested. 'I'll take the camera. Just you and me.'

Adela felt exhausted just thinking of it. 'There's so much to do here. By the time I get cleared up I'll just want to soak my feet in a basin of hot water and drink gin.'

'After the gin then,' Sam said with a smile.

'Anyway you can't. Your mother's expecting you for supper. Last thing she said before she got the bus home. Though why you should have to trek miles across the city to see her when she's at the café every other day, I don't know.'

Sam frowned. 'Because I'm down on the allotment or out taking photos. I don't see her that often – and I only go over to the coast when you're staying here late.'

'I wouldn't have to stay late if you helped out more,' she snapped.

'I thought we agreed that I was of most use in the allotment?' Sam said.

'Well, if Joan goes then you'll have to help round here more,' Adela said with an impatient sigh.

'Perhaps if you were a little kinder to her,' said Sam, his voice suddenly steely, 'then she might stay longer.'

With that he dumped down the box of vegetables and strode out of the kitchen. Adela felt immediately contrite and hurried after him.

'Sam, I'm sorry,' she called.

He turned, halfway across the yard. Her stomach somersaulted at his handsome face, but his look was wary.

'Go and see Mrs Jackman this evening,' said Adela. 'I didn't mean to criticise her; your mother's been a godsend. We'll have a walk on Sunday – just the two of us.'

She couldn't read his expression; was he relieved or disappointed? She was too weary to work it out. She blew him a quick kiss and then doubled back inside.

It was after seven o'clock before Adela was finished in the café and locking up. She knew Sam wouldn't be at home and she didn't have the energy to put on a cheerful face for Tilly and Josey. She climbed the stairs and knocked on Lexy's door.

'Come in!' Lexy's deep smoker's voice beckoned.

As Adela entered the cosy flat, Lexy was already heaving herself out of her armchair and making for the kitchen. 'I've got a pot brewing. Thought you might be up shortly. Heard the fun and games earlier. Madam Joan playing up, is she? Little minx.'

'I'll get the tea,' Adela said at once.

'You'll sit down and put your feet up, hinny,' ordered Lexy. 'I might puff like an old steam train but I can still pour a cuppa.'

Adela sank gratefully on to the sofa and closed her eyes. She must have dozed off for a few minutes because when she opened her eyes, Lexy was back in her favourite chair coughing over a cigarette and there was a cup of black tea and a paste sandwich on the side-table by Adela's elbow.

With a deep sigh, Adela drank the tea. She was past being hungry and the grey sandwich didn't look in the least appetising.

'Tell all,' Lexy encouraged.

'Where to begin? It's so much harder running the café than I thought. Even though we aren't on the ration, it's almost impossible to get hold of some ingredients. How can you make a decent shepherd's pie when half the potatoes have been blighted by frost? Thank goodness I've got your contacts at the Grainger Market or we wouldn't have anything on the menu.'

With a sympathetic nod from Lexy, Adela continued to pour out her troubles. 'Joan is driving me mad and Sam just panders to her instead of backing me up, and his mother is really kind but once she gets in the café kitchen she's a real bossy-boots. I know I can't manage without her – I have pretty few cooking skills – but she's taking over our lives. If she's not at the café then she's wanting Sam to go all the way out to Cullercoats to spend the evening with her.'

'She's had a long time without him,' Lexy pointed out, 'so she's only trying to make up for that. She'll calm down.'

Adela felt a twinge of guilt. 'I sound so ungrateful, don't I?'

'It's only natural that you feel a bit jealous over Sam with his mam,' said Lexy.

'I'm not jealous,' Adela protested. 'It was me who encouraged Sam to get in touch with his mother.'

'Aye, it was; but that doesn't mean you don't see each other as rivals for his love,' said Lexy. 'What you should remember is that your lad, Sam, has a big heart and enough love for you both. And he's daft about you. Anyone can see that.'

Adela felt her eyes sting with tears. She thought wistfully of how happy and in love they had been in India, when the prospect of returning to England together had felt like an adventure. 'I don't know. I haven't been nice to him recently. I've turned into this nagging, short-tempered hag and I know I'm being unkind but I can't help saying things. He doesn't deserve it . . .'

'You're both a bit at sea,' said Lexy, 'but things will settle down once you've found your feet here. You're doing your best with the café and Sam's getting more photography work now, isn't he?'

'A bit but not much,' said Adela. 'I feel like I've dragged him half-way round the world for nothing.'

'So you've found out nowt about the bairn?' Lexy asked.

Adela shook her head. 'I've written to the missionary society who arranged the adoption but heard nothing. I'm just going off the address on that piece of paper I signed, so I don't even know if they've got my letter. Maybe they won't tell me anything even if they do know where John Wesley was placed.' Adela felt her throat constrict as tears flooded her eyes. 'I just keep imagining him in some awful orphanage or institution where no one really cares for him and they're strict and leave him to cry himself to sleep—'

'Stop torturing yersel', hinny,' Lexy remonstrated. 'It's just as likely that he's with a canny family who love him and are giving him the best start in life he could have. That's all you can ask for, isn't it?'

Adela gave her friend an anguished look. 'But I want more than that, Lexy. I want to hold him in my arms and ask him to forgive me for abandoning him. I can't be like Sam's mother and live with years of guilt. I want to be a mother to him.'

Lexy's look was pitying. 'You know that's never likely to happen, lass. Even if they know where he is, you have to be prepared that they might never let you see him. Are you prepared to lose him all over again?'

Adela's heart ached. 'But at least I would *know*. It's the not knowing what's happened to him that is breaking my heart.'

'What does Sam say?' Lexy asked.

Adela gave an unhappy shrug. 'He knows I'm trying to find out about my boy but we don't really speak about it – there's precious little time to talk about anything these days. All I know is that he wants us to have our own child.'

'That's to be expected,' said Lexy. 'Surely that's what you want an' all?'

'Of course it is,' said Adela. 'But nothing's happening on that front. Not that we get much time for baby-making these days. We're up at the crack of dawn to get to the market while there's still something to buy – and at night we just fall into bed, dog-tired.'

'Well, make time,' said Lexy.

'I know we should,' sighed Adela. 'But it's not just that. I can't think about another baby when all my thoughts are with John Wesley. I thought time would make my longing for him lessen but it's quite the opposite. And I know Sam would love him too. Once we find him, all our quarrelling will stop. Sam would make such a wonderful dad to John Wesley.' She gave Lexy a pleading look. 'Can't you help me, Lexy? You used to know some of the people from that missionary church, didn't you?'

'No, not really,' said Lexy. 'It was the minister at the seamen's mission who knew them. I never met any of 'em – except the two wives who came to take the bairn away and I can't remember what they were called.'

'I could ask the minister then?' Adela's hope flared.

Lexy shook her head. 'Poor man went down on a ship during the War.'

Adela felt leaden. 'Is there no one you can think of who would know about the adoption? There must be someone I can ask!'

Lexy said, 'Don't fret, hinny. You might hear back from the folk at the adoption society before long. These things tak' time. And I'll gan and have a word with Maggie – see if she remembers what them lasses from the church were called. Mind you, her memory's not what it was.'

Adela thought with affection of Lexy's friend Maggie who had taken her in when she was pregnant and homeless. Maggie, with a passion for purple and an earthy sense of humour, had given Adela sanctuary and helped bring John Wesley into the world. The Cullercoats cottage where Maggie had cared for the elderly Ina had also been John Wesley's first brief home and a safe haven for Adela at a traumatic time.

'How is Maggie?' asked Adela. 'I've called round a couple of times to the cottage but she's never in.'

'She's hard o' hearin',' said Lexy. 'Bang louder next time. She doesn't gan far these days.'

'I will,' said Adela. 'The next time I get a spare minute.'

Lexy gave her a direct look. 'The next time you get a spare minute, you spend it with that man of yours and have a bit o' fun. Promise me you will?'

Adela gave a tired smile. 'Okay, I promise.'

On Sunday, heeding Lexy's advice and encouraged by Tilly, Adela and Sam borrowed Tilly's car and drove out west beyond the city outskirts and into the countryside. It was a blustery April day of scudding clouds and sudden bursts of tepid sunshine. The winter seemed to have lasted forever. For one day, Adela determined she wasn't going to worry about blighted potatoes or the lack of supplies of bread or cheese for the café. She didn't want to think of the café at all.

They had a picnic packed and a tartan rug. Sam whistled as he drove, his battered pork-pie hat – the fourth one he had owned since Adela had first known him – perched at a rakish angle on the back of his head.

Adela took sly glances at his face in profile; his long features were weathered from working outdoors and his hair was still a youthful honey brown. He caught her staring and gave her a quizzical smile.

'A penny for your thoughts?' he asked.

'I was just remembering the very first time I ever sat in a car beside you,' said Adela. 'When I'd escaped from school and made you drive me back to Belgooree.'

Sam laughed. 'I should have known then that the rebellious tea planter's daughter would turn my world upside down.'

Adela smiled and traced a finger down his lean face. 'I fell in love with you that day, Sam Jackman.'

'Lucky me,' Sam said with a grin. She could tell he was pleased with her sudden show of affection. She felt bad that she hadn't made an effort to be more loving in recent weeks.

Sam said, 'I first fell in love with you when I saw you at the top of the veranda steps in Simla looking divine in a red dress at your birthday party.'

Adela gave a wry laugh. 'It was a pink dress.'

'Was it? Well, it looked red in the setting sun.'

'You arrived after dark,' Adela said in amusement.

'Did I?' Sam gave a rueful smile. 'Well, you looked delectable and I had a hard time trying not to kiss you that night.'

Adela laughed. 'I spent the evening wishing you would.'

He put out a hand and squeezed her knee. 'I'm not always very quick to understand what you want, am I?'

'I wish we had kissed back then,' sighed Adela. 'It would have saved a lot of trouble—'

She bit off her words, suddenly remembering how misunderstandings between her and Sam had led to her allowing Prince Sanjay to seduce her and leave her pregnant.

Sam withdrew his hand. 'It worked out well for us in the end, didn't it? I hope you don't have any regrets – I certainly don't.'

'Of course I don't,' Adela said quickly.

After that, they drove in silence. Adela stared out of the window at the passing scenery. Trees were finally in bud after the severe winter frosts and the fields were sprouting the first tiny green shoots of wheat and barley. Sam didn't whistle any more; he seemed lost in his own thoughts. She had an unexpected pang of longing for Belgooree and her mother. At this time of year Clarrie would be busy overseeing the first flush of tea. Adela was gripped with sudden worry that she had made a terrible mistake in leaving India. Perhaps she and Sam could only ever be really happy in their old surroundings?

But things were changing in India. Within the next year many of the British would have to retire from service and return to Britain. Even some of the tea planters might not want to stay on, knowing that their way of life might have to change too. The last letter she had had from her mother had been full of concern for Libby's father James. He appeared to be recuperating at Belgooree from some nervous condition and was yet to be reunited with Libby.

Sam broke into her thoughts. 'Shall we picnic near the river? I don't want to use up too much of Tilly's petrol ration.'

'Yes, that would be nice.'

A few miles on they drove through an attractive village of stone houses called Wylam and parked up. Sam hauled the picnic basket out of the boot and Adela carried the rug. They walked through a wood, upriver, passing an occasional courting couple and boys skimming stones at the river's edge. After a while, they came to a deserted patch of grass by a sandy bank, sheltered by trees and undergrowth.

Spreading out the rug on the damp grass, Sam opened up the basket. They shared a bottle of beer and munched on egg-and-cress sandwiches and slices of corned beef. Adela had got hold of some oranges through a contact at the Grainger Market. They sat sucking segments of the sweet fruit.

Then Sam produced something wrapped in greaseproof paper.

'I got Mum to make this,' he said, glancing at her cautiously as he unwrapped it.

'Ginger cake?' Adela exclaimed. 'My favourite!'

'And there's butter to go with it,' Sam said, smiling, as he cut off a slice and spread butter on it.

'Is that your mother's own ration?' Adela asked guiltily.

'She's happy for us to have it.' He held out the slice. 'Eat it.'

'Delicious,' said Adela, biting into the cake. Silently she thought it lacked the richness and spicy tang of Mohammed Din's ginger cake but she was touched by Mrs Jackman's offering and Sam's boyish eagerness to please her. 'Takes me right back to Belgooree.'

'You haven't told me what was in your mother's most recent letter,' said Sam through a mouthful of cake. 'Is she well? Is Harry still enjoying school in Shillong?'

'Mother's fine as always,' said Adela, 'and Harry too. He couldn't wait to get back to school for the cricket. He's staying over some weekends now that he's in the school's second eleven.'

'Good for him. He's got the height and strength of a sixteen-year-old rather than a boy of thirteen. He'll do well.'

'Yes,' agreed Adela, 'he's so like Dad.'

Adela felt a sudden lump in her throat. Her father had been dead for nearly nine years but she still felt his loss keenly.

Sam leant towards her and put an arm around her shoulders. 'I know you miss him.'

Briefly she laid her head on his shoulder. But she didn't want the day to be overshadowed by sad thoughts; she had promised herself that she would make an effort to get close to Sam again.

'I'm fine,' she said, 'and I'm not worried about Mother. It's James though . . .' She told Sam about Clarrie's concern over Libby's father, how he was resting at Belgooree and hadn't been to Calcutta to meet Libby as promised.

'Does Tilly know he's ill?' asked Sam.

'I don't think she's taking it seriously,' said Adela. 'I tried to mention it the other day but it was a rushed conversation on my way out to work. Tilly just thinks that James likes being at Belgooree and being fussed over by my mother.'

'What do you think?'

Adela shrugged. 'He's not acting normally. James has always lived for his work at the Oxford but he's showing no interest in it at the moment. And Mother says he has terrible nightmares and shouts in his sleep. Privately she thinks he should retire and leave the Oxford.'

'Come back to Britain, you mean?'

'Or take an extended leave,' said Adela. 'She doesn't believe Tilly will ever go back to India, so she's trying to persuade James to come home and patch things up with Tilly before it's too late.'

Sam let out a sigh. 'Where does that leave poor Libby?'

'Goodness knows,' said Adela. 'She's a resourceful girl and will make the best of wherever she is, but she was so looking forward to seeing her father. It worries me how much she was pinning her hopes on resuming a life in India as if nothing had changed since her childhood there.'

Sam nodded in agreement. 'Have you heard from Libby recently?' he asked.

'No, but I've had a letter from Fatima saying that Libby had invited her and Ghulam to her birthday party.'

'Ghulam too?' Sam said with surprise. 'I can't imagine he went.'

Adela smiled. 'He did, and Fatima said they both enjoyed it.'

Sam grinned. 'Well, well, the anti-British radical accepting hospitality in the heart of colonial Calcutta! Whatever next?'

Adela laughed. 'That's how persuasive Libby can be.'

Sam helped them to more cake.

'Talking of the Khans,' said Adela, 'what news of your sister and Rafi?'

Sam stiffened and Adela immediately regretted asking.

'She never complains,' he answered, 'but I think Sanj— I think the new rajah is making life difficult for Rafi. Did I tell you that he's sacked him as his ADC?'

Adela winced at Sam's avoidance of saying Sanjay's name. 'No you didn't. How unfair! Is Rafi still the forest officer?'

'Yes,' said Sam. 'Sophie is putting a brave face on things – says that Rafi is happier being out of the limelight at court and so is she.'

'Well, Rafi has always been a forester at heart, hasn't he?' said Adela. 'And Sophie hates all that stuffy court life. Maybe they really are happier.'

'But for how long?' Sam said. 'It's all so uncertain in India now – even the British in the princely states might be out of their jobs soon.'

Adela slipped her arm through his. 'Wouldn't that be wonderful if Sophie and Rafi decided to retire back to Britain too? I know you miss her and it would make me feel a whole lot better for having dragged you back to Newcastle.'

Sam gave her an intent look. 'You didn't drag me anywhere. I don't mind where I live as long as you are there, Adela.'

Her heart drummed at his loving words. 'Darling Sam, I don't deserve you.'

'Nonsense. I'm the luckiest man in the world, having you as my wife,' he said and leant in to kiss her on the lips.

Adela kissed him back, flooded with love for him. Gently, Sam pushed her back on the rug and began to kiss her more deeply as his hands searched to loosen her jacket and blouse. Adela's arousal turned abruptly to panic. She pushed him away.

'Not here, Sam,' she said. 'It's too public.'

He gave a puzzled smile. 'There's no one around. I want you so much, my darling.' He tried to kiss her again but Adela sat up.

'I can't – someone's bound to come. We're just off the footpath.'

Sam sighed and pulled away. Adela felt confused by her reluctance to make love – she desired him just as much as ever – but she couldn't. The place was wrong, that was all. Guilt swept her at the look of hurt on her husband's face. It was all this talk of India; it was making her homesick and unsettled. It reminded her of how happy they had been in the early days of their marriage, when they had been so easy in each other's company – so spontaneous.

'Let's put our feet in the river,' she suggested, standing up.

'It'll be freezing,' he protested.

'I know.' She smiled and, kicking off her shoes, scrambled down the sandy bank.

The river was fast flowing but they were perched above a shallow pool gouged out of the bank where the current slowed. Adela rolled down her stockings and shoved them in a jacket pocket. Holding up her skirt, she waded into the icy water with a shriek.

Sam was soon rolling up his trouser legs and joining her with a loud bellow at the freezing water. He flicked water at her, making her scream and splash him back. A few minutes later, a worried-looking man appeared on a bicycle.

'Are you okay?' he shouted down.

Spluttering, Adela called out, 'We're fine – just paddling!'

'You're daft in the head,' said the man before cycling on.

After that they climbed out with bashful laughter and pulled on their shoes with numb fingers. Packing up swiftly, they made their way back to the car. It clouded over and the sun went. By the time they got back to Tilly's house, they were chilled through. Tilly scolded Sam for allowing Adela in the river and ordered her into a hot bath. Adela nearly fell asleep in the steamy bathroom and, excusing herself from the evening meal, retreated to bed.

'It's been a lovely day,' she said, 'but I can hardly stay awake.'

Even though it was still light outside, Adela fell asleep in minutes and wasn't even aware of Sam creeping under the covers later that night.

Adela, refreshed after a long sleep, determined that she would make a real effort to be nicer to Sam and her staff in the coming week. She didn't like the fretful, short-tempered woman she had become. Despite the daily grind, she must try and be more like the gregarious Adela of old who would lift people's spirits and encourage harmony. That day at the café she refrained from criticising Joan, complimenting her on being chatty with the customers and thanking her for helping out.

She allowed Mrs Jackman to order her about in the kitchen and retreated to a corner of the café to do her paperwork. She liked to sit half hidden behind a screen and listen to the customers and the waitresses, being on hand to smooth things over if a complaint or problem arose. She was always touched when some of the older customers remembered her mother fondly and told Adela that she reminded them of Clarrie. To her, that was the greatest compliment anyone could give her.

Sam turned down his mother's invitation to go to her house for a meal that evening.

'Maybe Adela and I could come over on Sunday?' he suggested.

Mrs Jackman looked dismayed. 'That's a whole week away.'

'It'll soon be here,' said Sam with a smile of reassurance. 'We've too much to do at the café at the moment – redecorating and odd jobs that can't be done during the day.'

'Very well,' Mrs Jackman agreed with reluctance, 'I'll expect you for Sunday dinner.'

Adela was grateful to Sam for standing up to his mother and told him so. That evening, as they walked from the bus stop to Tilly's, arm in arm, they discussed what they would plant next in the allotment and whether they should alter the style of the café décor.

'The palms and brass urns are all a bit dated, aren't they?' said Adela.

'I like the eastern look,' said Sam.

Adela smirked. 'P&O third-class dining room, you mean.'

'Snob,' said Sam with a nudge.

'We should go for something less imperial,' she said, 'and more modern. Maybe French chic – Mediterranean colours and bright table-cloths instead of those old white ones that are almost yellow with age.'

'Have you suddenly come into money?' Sam teased.

'We can dye the old ones,' suggested Adela. 'Josey will help me – she's full of artistic ideas. And we need to change the waitresses' uni-forms – they're positively Victorian.'

As they reached the house, Adela was filled with a new optimism. Lexy was right: it was just a matter of finding their feet. Her sense of emotional distance towards Sam was nothing to worry about and their lack of intimacy would be temporary. They had just had too many other things to cope with since arriving in Newcastle.

'There's an official-looking letter for you,' said Tilly as they passed on the doorstep. 'I've left it on the hall table. I'm off to a Mothers' Meeting at church. There's tongue and pickle in the pantry – help your-selves. Josey's upstairs making trousers out of black-out curtains for that next play. Toodle pip!' Tilly kissed Adela on the cheek as she went.

Adela grinned. 'Thanks and see you later.'

Adela ignored the envelope on the table and went straight into the dining room to pour herself a gin and lime. A creditors' letter could wait. She was already taking a large gulp by the time Sam followed her into the room. He held out the letter, a strange look on his face.

'It's addressed to you,' he said.

'Well, it would be, wouldn't it? I'm dealing with all of Herbert's admin.'

'It's to Adela Robson, not Jackman,' he said.

Adela's heart missed a beat. 'Is it . . . ? Do you think it's from . . . ?'

'Open it and see,' said Sam. He looked as tense as she felt.

She put down her glass and held out her hand. With shaking fingers, she tore open the envelope. The typed address at the top was different from the one she had written to. The missionary society had moved to London.

> *Dear Miss Robson*
> *I apologise for not replying sooner but your letter has only just been forwarded from Newcastle by the General Post Office.*
>
> *I regret that we are unable to help you. We are a small adoption society and all our records from before 1942 were destroyed in an air raid on the city of Newcastle. Even if they had survived, we would not be at liberty to share our documents with you (as you no doubt realised when you signed over your child into our care).*
>
> *I can, however, assure you that your son will have gone to a loving Christian home, with all the benefits of a stable, moral upbringing, and will be learning to walk in the way of Jesus Christ.*
>
> *May the Lord bless you.*
> *Yours sincerely*
> *Rev A. J. Stevens*

Adela felt numb as she re-read the letter, searching for any tiny clue that would give her hope that she could find her son. But there was none. Bile rose in her throat.

'Adela,' Sam said with an anxious expression, 'what does it say?'

She held it out to him, tears making her vision blur. She couldn't speak. She stood shaking while Sam scrutinised the letter with a frown of concentration. He looked up. His hazel-brown eyes were filled with pity. He opened his arms. 'Come here,' he said.

Adela stumbled into his hold and felt his strong arms bind tightly around her. She buried her face in his shoulder and wept. Sam stroked her hair and murmured, 'I'm sorry, my darling.'

They stood clinging to each other for long minutes. Adela didn't want to break away or think about what came next. She was submerged in a wave of loss and longing for John Wesley. How *could* she have ever given him up? The letter had made her see the brutal truth: she had no right to her own child. Worse still, now that the records of his adoption had been destroyed in the War, she would never be able to find out what had happened to him. The thought was unbearable. If Sam had not been holding her, she would have collapsed to the floor.

He let her sob in his arms until she was exhausted.

'Whatever's the matter?'

They were startled by Josey, dressed in an old red kimono, appearing in the doorway. Sam, keeping an arm about Adela, handed her the letter. Josey read it and came quickly to Adela's side.

'My poor sweetie,' she crooned, putting her arms about her.

Adela moved out of Sam's hold and clung to her old friend and confidante.

'I can't bear it!' Adela cried.

'You have to, dear girl,' said Josey fatalistically. 'There was only a very slim chance you were ever going to find him.'

Adela pulled away. 'I don't accept that. I know I'll find him one day – all my instincts tell me I will. Lexy's going to help me.'

Sam stared at her, baffled. 'My darling, haven't you put yourself through enough already?'

She felt sudden anger towards him. 'The feelings I have for John Wesley will never go away,' Adela said in distress. 'Can't you understand that?'

His face went rigid. 'Isn't it enough that we have each other?'

'No!' Adela cried. 'It's like half of me is missing.'

Sam gave her a harrowed look. 'Then I don't know how to help you.'

Adela watched helplessly as he turned and strode from the room.

'Oh, Adela,' Josey said with a reproachful look, 'don't take it out on poor Sam.'

Adela felt turned to stone. She couldn't move or speak. She heard Sam retreat down the hallway and the front door bang shut behind him. She wished she had the strength and compassion to go after him but even if she did, she could not think of any words that would comfort him.

At that moment, the only person she wanted was the one she couldn't have: the beautiful baby boy with the palest brown skin and the shock of black hair who she had cast away to strangers when she had been young and foolish.

CHAPTER 14

Assam, India, late April

'Is that your father?' Flowers asked, pointing at a white-haired, barrel-chested man of medium height, standing on the *ghat* clutching his hat.

Libby's heart was racing. Even with the morning river breeze on the sluggish Brahmaputra she had been in a permanent sweat since transferring from train to riverboat. She had been ecstatic that her telephone call to Clarrie, insisting that she and Flowers were coming to Assam, had galvanised her father out of his black mood. But for the entire journey she had been dreading the state in which she might find him. Distracted by the dazzling sight of dawn coming up over the wide river, her nerves had steadied. Now her anxiety returned. As a porter grabbed her case and heaved it on to his head, she took a second look.

'No, I don't think . . .'

Then Libby saw the man catch sight of her, wave and chuck his hat in the air. Just like her father used to do. She swallowed her surprise.

'Yes – yes, that's him!'

Libby set off down the gangplank, side-stepping porters and luggage, and breaking into a run. Waving with both hands, she shrieked, 'Daddy!'

Pushing past the other disembarking passengers and riverside ped-lars, Libby reached her father and flung herself at him. He laughed and hugged her self-consciously, patting her back.

'Well, well, little Libby! Can it really be you?'

Libby, her arms around his neck, squeezed him to her and breathed in the dusty smell of his jacket: sweat masked by camphor and soap. His familiar smell brought tears to her eyes. His breath smelt mildly of whisky and peppermint.

They broke away, gazing at each other and grinning. Libby was shocked at how old he looked; his hair and moustache were snowy-white against his lined leathery face, his cheeks sunken and his eyes bloodshot. Her father appeared to have shrunk – she was nearly as tall as him now – and his legs were spindly and hairless in his khaki shorts. But his voice and his bashful smile were the same.

'How are you, Dad?' Libby asked in concern.

'Never better,' he said.

'Cousin Clarrie sounded so worried about you on the phone.'

'A fuss about nothing. Touch liverish that's all. A few days' rest. Right as rain now.' He pulled out a handkerchief and mopped his brow. 'How was your journey?' he asked. 'I really think you should have let Dr Watson accompany you.'

'It was fine, Dad,' said Libby. 'No one troubled us – except to sell us peanuts and chai, which we were happy to buy. There was a very interesting teacher making her way to Kalimpong who shared our com-partment as far as Siliguri. Uncle Johnny sends his very best greetings – and Aunt Helena too of course.'

James raised an eyebrow. 'I bet she didn't – Helena has never been a fan of mine.'

'Okay,' Libby admitted, 'it was largely Uncle Johnny. They've been so kind to me in Calcutta, and old Colonel Swinson's a dear – I wish you'd come for my birthday, you'd have seen your old friends the Percy-Barratts and—'

'Where is your friend?' James interrupted.

'Oh goodness!' Libby exclaimed and swung round; she had momentarily forgotten all about Flowers. She saw her companion walking towards them, neat and cool in her fashionable frock and hat, with the porters following in her wake. Libby waved her over.

'Meet my father,' said Libby eagerly.

Flowers smiled and held out a white-gloved hand for James to shake.

James gave her a bashful welcome. 'Come along then, car's waiting. Manzur's driving. Thought we'd go straight to Cheviot View.'

'Manzur? How lovely! But aren't we going to Shillong first?' Libby asked. 'Flowers wants to see where her father grew up.'

'Plenty of time for that. Imagine you're keen to see home after all this time, Libby?'

'Of course, but Flowers—'

'Don't worry about me,' Flowers said quickly. 'I'm not that interested in Daddy's school life. I'm just happy to be on holiday.'

James looked relieved. 'Good. Come on then, girls.'

At the car, a slim handsome Indian stepped forward, pushing a pair of sunglasses on to his forehead.

'Manzur?' Libby cried in disbelief. He was a taller version of the boy she had liked in childhood, with the same large brown eyes and cheeks that dimpled when he smiled.

'Missy sahib,' he said with a grin.

'Call me Libby, for heaven's sake.' Laughing, she introduced him to Flowers. 'Manzur grew up at Cheviot View – my brother James and he were thick as thieves. I was always trying to join in their games but they used to make me hide and then they'd run away.'

'I'm much more well behaved now,' Manzur said.

Flowers smiled. 'Glad to hear it.'

'Manzur is my very able assistant manager at the Oxford,' said James. 'Now, all aboard.'

Manzur held open a rear passenger door for the women. Libby noticed the look of interest in Flowers's eyes as she slipped into the seat and nodded her thanks to the young assistant. As they set off, Libby leant forward eagerly to speak to her father, trying not to stare at his changed appearance. When had his hair turned so white? But the conversation soon petered out.

'Makes me carsick to keep turning round,' James complained.

Libby sat back, her stomach knotting. She gazed at the back of his head and thick neck – so familiar and yet not. He was still the same man she remembered, just older. It was bound to be a little awkward at first. Once they were back at Cheviot View, they'd rekindle their old closeness.

Libby spent the morning hanging out of the window and gazing at the passing countryside: rice paddies criss-crossed by dusty tracks that wound their way into low forested hills, the occasional corrugated-iron-roofed bungalow and villages of bamboo huts shaded by palms. The sun pulsed in a hazy sky and dust blew up from the road but she refused to wind up the window.

She grinned. 'I want to smell Assam.'

They stopped for tiffin at a dak bungalow. Libby insisted that Manzur join them, sensing too that her father felt more at ease with the young man in attendance. Libby encouraged Flowers to chatter with her father about the War and her time at the Burma Front as a nurse. To her relief, her father made an effort to be sociable to her friend. Libby began to hope that Clarrie had been over-anxious for no reason, though she did notice how her father kept swigging from a hip flask. Manzur was quiet, observing them. Libby engaged him in conversation.

'How are your parents?'

'They are well, thank you.'

'Still both working at Cheviot View?'

Manzur nodded.

'They must be very proud of you becoming a manager on the Oxford.'

'Your father has been very good to me.'

An awkward silence ensued. She noticed him sliding glances at Flowers as he ate. Libby tried again.

'And you've been tutor to my cousin Harry at Belgooree? Adela told me Harry much preferred you teaching him than going to school.'

Manzur smiled. 'Robson chota-sahib is a quick learner, but he prefers to be outdoors riding or playing cricket.'

Libby laughed. 'I think that's the same for all of us tea planter children.'

Back on the road, James fell asleep in the front and Flowers dozed in the back. But Libby was far too excited for sleep as they approached the first of the tea plantations. Acres of green bushes stretched as far as the eye could see like an undulating emerald carpet, shaded by feathery trees and bounded by thickening jungle. They rattled over a narrow bridge. Below, elephants rolled in the mud of the almost dried-up riverbed. The smell of heat, vegetation and dung transported Libby back to her childhood.

As the familiar outlines of the hills around her old home came into view, her eyes prickled with emotion. Plantation gates appeared ahead, proclaiming the Oxford Tea Estates. James abruptly woke up.

'Take us straight to the house,' he ordered.

'But, sahib, there is tea laid on at the clubhouse,' Manzur said. 'A welcome for—'

'No,' James snapped, 'we can do that another time. My daughter wants to get home.'

'I don't mind,' said Libby. 'It would be nice to show Flowers the clubhouse.'

'Not today.'

Libby gave Flowers an apologetic look. Her father was obviously tired by the journey. He must have left Belgooree in the early hours to meet the steamer.

'We'll take you round the estate later in the week,' Libby promised.

Manzur swung the car past the gates and headed for the un-metalled road that wound up to Cheviot View.

Half an hour later, Libby was queasy with anticipation as they rounded the bend and her old home appeared through the trees, perched on the hillside among flowering bushes. Its weathered upstairs veranda was choked in creepers.

'When did you have the roof replaced?' Libby asked, with a twinge of disappointment at seeing the green corrugated roof in place of the old thatch.

'Goodness, it's been like that for years,' said James.

Almost before the car had stopped, Libby was flinging open the door and scrambling out. She rushed round to the front of the house – the lawns were still well cut and the borders were a riot of pansies, violets and wall-flowers. A black flat-coated retriever came bounding across the lawn, barking loudly.

'Breckon!' James shouted, hurrying across on stiff legs. The dog leapt towards his master, dancing around him in excitement. 'How I've missed you, you rogue!' James bent down and patted him vigorously. The dog licked his hand and thumped his tail.

'Mother's canna lilies are still here,' Libby said in delight as her father fussed over his beloved dog.

'I've kept everything as your mother likes it,' he said.

Libby's eyes watered at the tender remark. Just then she saw a movement on the bungalow steps: the servants had lined up to greet her. Manzur's parents, Aslam the bearer and Meera, her old ayah, were among them. Aslam's beard was silver-grey but Meera still looked remarkably young for a woman in middle age. Libby ran up the steps and threw her arms around Meera. Her former nurse rubbed her back and then gently pushed her to arm's length.

'It's so good to see you all again,' Libby said, tears spilling down her cheeks.

'Come, come,' said James, 'no need to get upset.'

'Not upset' – Libby smiled tearfully – 'just very happy.'

She turned back to Flowers who was saying something to Manzur; the young manager was giving an embarrassed smile. Libby waved her over.

'Come on, Flowers! Let me show you around.'

Libby rushed between the rooms, relishing their familiarity; the highly patterned floor rugs and veranda cushions had faded to muted browns but the sitting room was still cluttered with brass ornaments, bookcases and tables crammed with family photographs. Even her mother's stamp collection was still gathering dust on a shelf under an oil painting of a Scottish Highland scene. It was all sweetly familiar and yet there was a neglected air about the place – a smell of mildewed books and decaying flowers – that highlighted the absence of her mother and brothers. How the house needed a family to breathe life back into it! Why had her mother kept them away for so long?

'Your bedroom should be shipshape,' said James, perhaps catching the regretful look on her face. 'I sent a message to Aslam to unpack all your things from the trunk in the godown – as long as the ants haven't made a meal of them.'

'Thanks, Dad,' Libby answered, though she couldn't remember what possessions of hers could have been stored all this time.

Her bed under the mosquito net was covered in her old pale-green counterpane and two dolls with china faces and Edwardian clothing were propped on the pillows.

'Milly and Dilly!' she cried in astonishment. 'I'd forgotten all about them.' On closer inspection, it appeared that moths had eaten away at their outfits.

Libby saw that old toys were displayed on top of a rusted black tin trunk: a collection of metal cars that she had once won off Jamie in a dare, a spinning top, a cracked solitaire board with metal balls and a tennis racket. Libby picked up the racket and curled her fingers around the peeling leather handle.

For a moment she was transported back to a hot afternoon playing tennis with Jamie on the makeshift court at the side of the house. Manzur was acting as their ball boy. Her mother was sitting reading in the shade while Ayah Meera pushed Mungo in his pram up and down the terrace. Libby and her brother must have been arguing over the rules because she remembered Tilly shouting, *'Oh, do be quiet! You're giving me a headache.'* Shortly afterwards, Libby, infuriated at her brother for cheating, had thrown down her racket in protest and stomped off.

Libby gave a sigh of amusement as she put the battered racket back down on the trunk; she'd forgotten how much indignant stomping off she had done as a child.

Turning to the window, she gasped. Sitting on top of the table was her mother's gaudy musical box. She opened it up and wound the key. The tinny strains of Swan Lake played for a few seconds.

'I was always getting into trouble for playing with this,' Libby told Flowers. 'Mother kept it on her dressing table but I used to sneak in and take it to bed. It helped me get to sleep. Meera must have remembered.'

Flowers was given Jamie's old room. 'It's got the best view,' Libby told her. 'Gets the morning sunshine too before the heat – so you can open your shutters and listen to the birdsong.'

After washing and changing, they met on the veranda for drinks. Manzur was staying the night to visit his parents in the compound and James invited him to take supper with them in the bungalow. Libby thought how such a thing would have been unheard of before the War – having an Indian employee dine with them – but she was glad at the change. Her father seemed far less hidebound by social etiquette than she had remembered. Perhaps it was because people like the

Percy-Barratts were no longer keeping a watchful eye on his household. Libby could almost hear Muriel admonishing them: *'Mustn't let the side down by mixing with the natives.'* But such notions would soon be obsolete once Independence came, surely? At least Libby hoped they would.

Flowers and Libby drank gimlets, while Manzur had a lemonade. Libby sensed the young Indian was ill at ease having his father, Aslam, bustle about overseeing the *khitmutgar* in the pouring of drinks. James downed a large whisky and immediately ordered another.

Libby sat contentedly, gazing out over the garden and jungle to the tea plantations in the distance, as the sky turned from gold to orange to red to purple. James and Manzur talked about work. The sky went green then darkness fell abruptly. The air pulsed with the sound of insects and the stars came out in abundance. Before they went into the dining room, Libby saw her father pour himself another large whisky. With dismay she realised he must have drunk half a decanter already. She never remembered him drinking this much.

James ordered a bottle of champagne to be served with the main course.

'I kept it for your mother all through the War,' he said, 'but no point in letting it gather dust any longer. Not when there's a special occasion like this.' When the drink was poured, James got to his feet and raised his glass.

'I last saw my daughter when she was twelve years old—'

'Eleven,' Libby corrected.

'Eleven then,' he conceded. 'A long time ago. So this is a very special day for me.' He turned to look directly at her, his blue eyes softening. 'Libby, you have grown into a beautiful young woman and I'm proud to be your father.' He paused and Libby saw his chin tremble. He bit his lip and swallowed hard. 'To Libby!' he croaked and gulped at his champagne.

'To Libby!' Flowers and Manzur chorused.

Libby felt suddenly overwhelmed, her eyes flooding with tears. She had never before seen her father grow emotional or show his feelings. This man was more vulnerable – and perhaps kinder – than the bullish man of action she remembered. She ought to be pleased but somehow seeing him close to tears made panic rise in her chest.

Flowers came to the rescue with light-hearted conversation about Calcutta parties and outings.

'It sounds like you've been helping my daughter have a good time in the city,' James said. 'I'm afraid we can't offer much to keep you young ladies entertained here.'

'It's just nice to get away and have a break,' said Flowers. 'It's very kind of you to have me to stay.'

'Not at all,' said James. 'You'll be company for Libby.' He turned to Libby. 'So you've seen quite a bit of Clarrie's nephew, George Brewis, eh?'

'For a while,' said Libby, 'but not recently.'

'Any other young men that I should worry about?' he asked.

Libby laughed. 'None to worry about, no.'

'Libby is very popular among the Strachan's men,' teased Flowers. 'She can take her pick on the dance floor.'

'No more than you.' Libby smiled. 'But I'm not interested in anything more than dancing. They're fun but a bit dull at conversation.'

'You sound so like your mother,' James chuckled. 'So who do you like conversing with?'

'The Khans are a very interesting couple.'

'The Khans?' James queried.

'Rafi's sister and brother – Fatima and Ghulam,' said Libby. Even as she mentioned Ghulam's name she could feel the heat rushing to her face. 'Adela encouraged me to meet them and I'm glad I have.'

'Not that terrorist who went to prison for arson?' James cried, horrified.

'He's not a terrorist, Dad,' said Libby. 'He's passionate about freeing India from colonial rule but he turned his back on violence years ago. He's spent the past year trying to stop the bloodshed in Calcutta – so has Fatima.'

'I'm surprised at Adela putting you in touch with such a man,' her father said with a frown, 'or that the Watsons allowed it.'

'Of course they did. Uncle Johnny welcomed them to his home,' said Libby. 'The Khans came to my birthday party.' She gave him a pointed look.

James glanced away and drained his glass. 'Well, I wouldn't have let a communist agitator like Khan over my doorstep.'

'Even though Ghulam is Rafi's brother?' Libby challenged. 'And Rafi is your friend?'

'Rafi is different – he's a civilised Indian. Under Sophie's influence he's practically one of us.'

Libby was jolted by his words; they echoed Ghulam's own earlier disdain for his older brother becoming like one of the *sahib-log*.

'Ghulam is a highly educated and principled man,' said Libby.

'Well, he's put that education to bad use,' snapped James. 'I remember him coming and causing trouble around the tea gardens in the thirties.'

'Trouble for the planters, you mean,' said Libby, 'not their tea pickers.'

'He did them no favours! Stirred them up in the lines with a few speeches and then was gone. So I don't want you defending his revolutionary talk. These agitators have no idea how hard we all work to keep the plantations running and satisfy the demand for tea.'

'What do you think, Manzur?' Libby turned to the young assistant.

He squirmed in his seat and Libby immediately regretted asking him. He had hardly touched his food. She was embarrassed at her father's patronising words about civilised Indians. Manzur cleared his throat.

'The gardens provide work for many people,' he answered. 'Low castes and migrants who can't get work anywhere else. We house them and give them medical care.'

'Well said, Manzur,' James cried. He took out his handkerchief and mopped his brow. 'My daughter is an idealist and easily persuaded by radical talk – her mother said she was like this all through school.'

'Give me some credit for having my own beliefs,' protested Libby, hurt at her father siding with Tilly's critical view of her. 'Anyway, what's wrong with idealism? India will need people with vision and optimism in the coming years.'

'What India needs is pragmatists,' James replied, 'who will see that they still need our expertise in industry and our capital. Men like Khan want to sweep it all away. But India will still need wealth and trade.'

'Yes,' said Libby, 'but after Independence it will be Indians who make the decisions about their own economy. The future should be in the hands of men like Manzur, not you, Father.'

'And it will be. But that's enough politics,' James said in agitation. 'Miss Dunlop hasn't come all this way to listen to you lecture us all about socialism.'

'I'm not lecturing—'

'That's enough, Libby,' James ordered. 'I want no further talk about the Khans or their radical ideas.'

Libby bit back an indignant retort, stung by her father's disapproval. She felt like a child again, being publicly admonished. Her father had no right to silence her; she was just as entitled to voice her opinions as he was. It dismayed her that his way of thinking was so at odds with hers and that they had been so quick to argue. It wasn't what she'd expected. When she was a child, her father had always taken her side.

Flowers quickly filled the awkward silence.

'My father once came on a camping trip to the hills around here,' she said. 'The year he left school. He's always had a fondness for Assam

– that's why he jumped at the chance of promotion to stationmaster in the Sylhet district. That's where I grew up.'

'Good tea-growing area too,' said James. He began a rambling monologue about rainfall and south-facing slopes.

Libby was embarrassed to realise that her father was quite drunk. She admired Flowers for the tactful way she showed an interest and gave encouraging answers. It was just what Adela would have done. Libby felt a stab of guilt for answering her father back. It was the very first night of their reunion and she had allowed herself to lose patience with him. She was upset by their differences – especially over Ghulam – but her father was still recovering from his bout of fatigue. She must try and be more considerate. Besides, he was from such a different generation to hers that he was bound to think differently. The last thing she wanted was to argue with her dad. She would make more effort not to rile him.

When the meal was over Libby suggested, 'Shall we take tea and a nightcap on the veranda?'

'Sounds a jolly good idea,' James slurred. He pushed back his chair and stood swaying.

Manzur took this moment to escape. He stood and gave a courteous bow. 'Thank you for a very enjoyable meal.'

'Stay a bit longer,' James insisted.

'Thank you, but my mother . . .'

'Of course you must go and see your mother,' Libby said, not wanting to prolong his discomfort. 'It's good to see you again.'

'I hope you have an enjoyable stay,' said Manzur, nodding at Flowers.

She gave him one of her dazzling smiles. 'Thank you. And I hope we'll meet again while I'm here.'

Libby saw Manzur blush, his attractive brown eyes widening. 'P-perhaps . . .' he stammered and swiftly took his leave.

Flowers took his departure as an excuse to retire to bed, leaving Libby alone with her father. Libby steered him on to the veranda and into a cane chair.

'Can manage,' he mumbled. But within a minute he was asleep and snoring.

Libby gazed at him. He was almost a stranger to her, his mouth gaping and his face flushed under tousled white hair. Hair grew from his nostrils and ears too. The hands that hung loose over the chair arms were knotted with veins and marked with age spots. He looked so vulnerable: a man well past his prime. She felt engulfed with regret that they would never be able to recapture the eleven years during which they had been separated. They no longer knew each other.

Why had her parents allowed such a long time apart? She and her brothers had been robbed of a father and a proper family life. How she wished her parents had been more like Clarrie and Wesley and sent their children to school in India! Libby thought bitterly of her long cold exile at boarding school in Britain. Why hadn't they returned to India at the beginning of the War as so many other children of tea planters and civil servants had?

Libby felt familiar resentment at her mother twist inside; Tilly had always seen Newcastle as home rather than Assam. But had her father been equally to blame? Why hadn't he insisted that they return? She let out a long sigh. There was no point in hankering after what might have been. At least she was back home now. Libby breathed in the warm scented air. She got up and, leaning over her father, gave him a tender kiss on the forehead. Tomorrow she would try harder to get to know him again. She tiptoed away to the bedroom that she had last slept in when she was eight years old.

James woke briefly as his daughter departed, then fell back into a fitful sleep.

He was standing in Bill Logan's study at Dunsapie Cottage. The start of the cold season was bringing relief after the sweltering monsoon but James still found the room stifling and airless. The rest of the house was crammed with new furniture, china and glassware for Logan's future wife.

'I'll be gone for a month,' said Logan, 'so you will be in charge of the running of my bungalow. Make sure the servants don't cheat me or steal.'

James felt relief that his boss would be gone until Christmas. Perhaps he and Reggie might take a few days off to go on shikar *now that the tea growing season was over. The experienced tea planter Fairfax, who was an expert in tracking tigers, had promised to take the young bachelors game hunting. James could hardly hide his impatience at seeing the back of Logan for a while. And perhaps the man would become more bearable once he was married and responsible for a wife. The new century would bring fresh beginnings, James thought with optimism.*

'And one more thing,' Logan said, pouring them both a whisky. 'You will make sure that native woman is gone by the time I bring Jessie Anderson back. I can't risk my young wife being subjected to one of her crying fits. It might lead to awkward questions.'

James's insides turned leaden. 'Aruna is still coming to the bungalow?' he asked in dismay. On the few occasions he had spotted her among the pickers, she had looked sallow and forlorn, but he'd been at a loss as to how to comfort her.

For a moment Logan looked uncomfortable. 'I have been too weak with her,' he said, 'allowing her to come to – er – visit on the odd occasion.'

James looked at him, appalled. Surely his boss had not resumed taking the tea picker into his bed. Had he not caused the hapless woman enough grief by fathering the Brat and then having him disposed of like an unwanted dog?

'Don't give me that insubordinate look, Robson,' Logan snapped. 'A man has physical needs.'

James couldn't trust himself to speak.

'But she's becoming tiresome,' said Logan. 'Making a scene every time she has to leave. I think it's something to do with the Brat. You can deal with it — you're better with the natives than I am. Make her understand that the boy is in good hands now.'

Logan handed him a tumbler of whisky. James felt nauseous at the smell.

'Come on, drink your dram,' said Logan. 'You look like a condemned man. I'm the one who is giving up my freedom, not you.' He laughed and knocked back his drink.

James hesitated and then put his tumbler down on the desk. 'Stomach's not up to drinking at midday, sir. But I wish you well for your forthcoming marriage to Miss Anderson.'

Logan gave him a look of disdain. 'You'll soon discover, Robson, that whisky cures most ailments out here in Assam. Only men with strong constitutions, who don't allow their feelings to rule them, survive life in the colonies.'

James made for the door.

'Just remember,' Logan called after him. 'I want that native girl kept away from here. Do what you have to do.'

James nearly choked on the bile in his throat. He couldn't get away from the bungalow quickly enough. Poor Jessie Anderson coming to live here with that man!

As he ran down the veranda steps, he caught sight of Sunil Ram sitting cross-legged, staring up at him with accusing eyes. Somewhere in the shadows beyond he thought he heard whimpering. A puppy, no doubt. James hurried away . . .

James woke with a start. Someone was shaking him. He raised a hand to ward them off, ready to punch with his other.

'Aruna?' he gasped. The young woman was standing there, her dark hair curling around her face.

'Mr Robson, it's me, Flowers Dunlop. You've been having a night-mare.' She spoke in a soft reassuring voice. 'I didn't want you to wake Libby.'

He gaped at her. Where was he? His heart beat erratically and his palms were sweating. His head felt as if it were clamped in a vice.

'Shall I help you to bed?' asked Flowers.

James realised with a flood of relief that he was on the veranda at Cheviot View. The dream of Logan and Dunsapie Cottage had been so vivid that for a moment, on waking, he had mistaken Libby's friend for someone else.

'I'm sorry if I woke you,' he said. 'Was – was I shouting? Aslam complains that I shout in my sleep.'

'I think you were crying,' said Flowers.

He felt embarrassed under her dark assessing look. 'Crying? What nonsense.'

Flowers took a step away. 'Perhaps I was mistaken. But you must be uncomfortable in the chair. Wouldn't you sleep better in bed?'

James sighed. 'I can't sleep in there. Too stuffy. Fan's been broken since the War.'

He wasn't going to tell her that he'd promised himself he would fix it once Tilly came back to him. Neither was it any of this woman's business that he found the dark shuttered bedroom too oppressive. He feared most the dreams he had in there. He thought the time at Belgooree had cured him of his nightmares. It was just that he had drunk too much alcohol, nervous at having people under his roof again after all this time. He would curb his drinking, at least while Libby was here.

He had a hot wave of panic. How long was his daughter going to stay here with her Anglo-Indian friend? He had been eager to see Libby but now he wasn't so sure. Perhaps Tilly had been right when she had warned that their daughter was difficult to live with, rebellious and opinionated. Would he be able to love her again? James felt ill. He shivered, even though it wasn't cold.

'I'm fine,' he said. 'Please go back to bed, Miss Dunlop. I'm sorry I disturbed you.'

She left and he closed his eyes. A minute later, she was back, tucking a thin blanket around him.

'My father's the same.' Flowers smiled. 'Sits up too late and falls asleep. I'll see you in the morning, Mr Robson.'

James murmured his thanks but she was already padding away on bare feet. His eyes itched with tiredness. He rubbed them with the heels of his hands. He pulled his hands away, surprised to find them wet with tears. Dread clawed inside. He didn't want to fall asleep again. He didn't want to dream. James sat up in the chair and threw off the blanket. He would force himself to stay awake until dawn.

CHAPTER 15

Assam, May

For the first few days Libby relished being back at Cheviot View. She went out riding before breakfast with her father, who was always up and awake before her, leaving Flowers to lie in.

'I'm not keen on horses,' Flowers had said, 'but drinking tea in bed and reading your mother's old books is a real treat. So don't worry about me.'

Libby suspected her friend was allowing her time alone with her father and was grateful. It was the best time of day, when the sky was a pearly grey and before the heat grew fierce. They rode through the jungle and crossed the tea gardens at the outer edge of the Oxford Estates as the air filled with raucous birdsong. In the distance they could see the tea pickers wending their way to work through the bushes in their brightly coloured headscarves, baskets strapped to their backs. Libby forced from her mind Ghulam's sour words about their exploitation; Manzur had assured her that they were adequately housed and given medical treatment.

Libby cherished this moment alone with her father; it conjured up the happiest part of her childhood when they had gone riding and he had pointed out birds and wildlife and taught her the names of trees. She was certain he was enjoying it too – he seemed more relaxed than in the house – yet he said little. She had steered clear of talking politics since their first evening but, frustratingly, Libby couldn't get him to talk about himself.

'Nothing much to tell – same old routine, year in, year out. I'm much more interested in hearing about you, dear girl. Tell me about that farm you worked on during the War.'

Libby chattered happily and was delighted when her father laughed at her anecdotes about her fellow Land Girls. She decided it was best not to mention Lorenzo.

By the time Libby and her father got home, the dew-sparkling lawns were steaming in the morning sun. While Flowers had breakfast in bed, Libby sat with her father on the veranda eating scrambled egg on toast and drinking tea poured from a huge china teapot that had been a wedding gift to her parents from a retired tea planter called Fairfax.

'Nice to get the old teapot out,' said James. 'Never bother when I'm on my own.'

'It's one of the things I remember,' said Libby, 'Mother insisting on pouring the tea from this and not letting the servants do it. "I'm quite capable of presiding over my own teapot," she used to say.'

Libby hoped that talking about her mother would coax her father into fond reminiscing or at least curiosity about what Tilly's life was like in Newcastle. But all week her father avoided talk of her mother. Every time Libby mentioned Tilly he went quiet or changed the subject. Not that he was particularly chatty about anything. Mostly Libby talked and he half listened, his gaze wandering off beyond the veranda as if his mind was far away. Perhaps he had always been like that and she just hadn't realised it as a child. Was that one of her mother's frustrations with James – that he just didn't listen?

Libby noticed that her father seemed uneasy around Flowers, watching nervously for her to appear and making excuses to go shortly after she joined them.

'Work to do,' he would mutter and hurry away.

Libby felt embarrassed and hoped it wasn't because Flowers was Anglo-Indian. Flowers made no comment and seemed content just to sit around on the veranda between meals, reading and dozing. Libby chivvied her into playing games, hunting out the croquet set and, with the *mali*'s help, having the old tennis court mowed and a net erected. In the godown she found a spare racket for Flowers but the ground was too uneven and the balls had lost their bounce.

'It's really far too hot for tennis anyway,' sighed Flowers, retreating back to her favourite veranda long chair to sip *nimbu pani* and read.

'Perhaps we could go down to the clubhouse and play there when it's cooler in the late afternoon,' Libby suggested one day. 'We could get Manzur and Dr Attar to make up a foursome – Dad says the new doctor is mad about tennis.'

Flowers showed immediate interest. 'That would be fun.'

The next day, James promised to mention it when he left for the office but returned that evening with nothing arranged. By the end of the week, Libby was growing bored and restless.

'Dad, please let us come with you today,' she said on their morning ride. 'You can drop us off at the club. Flowers is going to go home having seen nothing but Cheviot View.'

'She seems happy enough,' he answered.

'She's very easy going,' said Libby, 'and too polite to complain but I don't feel we're being very good hosts. And we still haven't done the trip to Shillong.'

That seemed to galvanise James. 'Very well, I'll drive you down to the club later.'

The afternoon trip to the clubhouse was not a success. By the time James had driven them down the hill and dropped them off, the temperature had soared and there was not a lick of a breeze. Libby's dress was sticking to her as if she'd been caught in the rain. Despite Libby's protests, the young women were not allowed into the main club room and had to sit and take tea in the ladies' room, which was deserted.

They whiled away the afternoon playing half-heartedly at cards and backgammon.

'Mother used to call it the hen-house,' Libby recalled. 'She couldn't bear it. Said the so-called library had nothing to read except out-of-date magazines.'

'It still hasn't,' said Flowers with a dry smile.

'We kids loved coming here for socials though,' said Libby. While the grown-ups danced and had too much to drink, we'd watch cine films and eat so much ice cream and cake that one of us was always sick on the way home.'

'Sounds delightful.' Flowers laughed. 'We did much the same thing in the railway colony – there were always parties and dressing-up, especially at Christmas and Easter.'

'It's so hot,' Libby sighed, fanning herself with a magazine. 'I can't imagine how I thought we could play tennis in this. I've hardly got the strength for cards. Do you want me to order more tea?'

'No,' said Flowers, 'but I wouldn't mind a *chota peg*. Is it too early?'

'Not when you're on holiday,' said Libby. 'But shall we go somewhere more exciting?'

'Such as?'

'Dad says Manzur lives at The Lodge with the old *mohurer*, Anant Ram. He's a sweetie. The bungalow is just further up this road and has one of the biggest verandas on the plantation. We could call in there if you like?'

'Won't Manzur still be at work?'

'Probably,' said Libby, 'but we could visit Anant Ram in the meantime and wait for Manzur to come home.'

Flowers's mouth twitched in a coy smile. 'Won't your father disapprove?'

'Why should he? Anant Ram is an old friend from my childhood and I haven't had a chance to see him yet. Come on. I'll send a *chaprassy* to let Dad know where we've gone.'

The women borrowed bicycles from the clubhouse and cycled along to The Lodge as the sun began to lose its strength. Even though it only took minutes, Libby was beetroot red and panting as they wheeled their bicycles up the garden path towards the secluded red-roofed bungalow.

Flowers stopped suddenly, her look alarmed. 'Do you think this is a good idea?'

'Dad really won't mind,' Libby reassured her. 'And I'm not cycling any further.'

Anant Ram, bald, skinny and in wire spectacles – looking ridiculously like pictures of Gandhi – welcomed Libby enthusiastically and summoned his youngest daughter, Charu. Libby had a vague memory of Charu from years ago and it now appeared that she was looking after her aged father. They ushered their guests on to the deep-set veranda and produced a refreshing jug of lime and soda, along with spicy snacks.

Libby did all the talking, answering the old bookkeeper's questions about the family and life in Britain. Only after a while did she realise that Flowers was sitting tensely on the edge of her chair, her drink almost untouched. She was still perspiring.

'Are you feeling unwell, Dunlop-Mem'?' asked Charu. 'Perhaps you would prefer tea?'

'No, no . . . thank you,' Flowers said, her voice breathless. 'I just feel a little faint.'

'Would you like to go and bathe your face?' Libby suggested.

Flowers didn't answer.

'Come, please,' said Anant's daughter. 'I will show you. And then you will have sweet tea.'

Flowers followed her into the house, glancing back at Libby with an anxious expression. Libby was baffled as to why her friend should feel so uncomfortable among the affable Rams. She wondered if she should go with her but just then she heard the toot of a car horn. Minutes later, James and Manzur were joining them.

'So this is where you've got to,' James said, his voice affable but his look annoyed.

Anant offered him a drink but James declined, turning to Libby. 'Where is Miss Dunlop?'

'She's gone inside – she's not feeling well – I think the bike ride was too much for her.'

'You shouldn't have made her cycle in the heat,' her father chided. 'Manzur or I could have driven you here.'

Manzur stood glancing awkwardly between them but said nothing.

'Anyway, it's time to go home,' said James, 'I want to be back up the hill before sunset.'

Libby got up. 'I'll go and find Flowers then.'

It took a moment for her eyes to adjust to the gloom of the shuttered interior. The layout was simple: a large central sitting room with doors at either side leading off to what Libby assumed were the bedrooms. As with all the old tea bungalows, the kitchens would be in a separate building around the back.

The walls creaked. She heard a sigh.

'Flowers?' Libby called out. There was silence. Perhaps their hostess had taken Flowers to lie down. Libby crossed the room and opened the door on the right. A ghostly light filtered through the shutters. Her eye half caught sight of a figure in the corner.

'Flowers, Dad's here and wants to go.'

But when she turned fully towards the person, she saw that it was merely a shadow. Heart thumping, Libby retreated swiftly from the room to find Flowers hurrying out of the opposite door. All colour had drained from her face; her dark eyes were wide and her hair was stuck to her skin with sweat. She stood rigid.

'Whatever's the matter?' Libby went quickly to her.

'Can we go?' Flowers said.

'Yes, Dad's come to fetch us. You look like you've seen a ghost.'

Flowers flinched and looked behind her. 'Don't say that.'

Libby laughed. 'Sorry, I was only joking.' She took her friend by the elbow – Flowers was shaking – and steered her out of the room.

Charu appeared with tea just as the party were leaving. Libby was apologetic. Flowers said nothing; not even the presence of Manzur was enough to shake her out of her strange mood. James was silent on the drive home too.

Flowers declined supper and went straight to bed. Libby ate with her father but he seemed infected by the bad atmosphere since the visit to The Lodge. Libby tried to remember what it was about the bungalow that she had heard before – some unhappy history – but she couldn't remember.

After the meal, James took a large whisky on to the darkened veranda. Libby picked up the days-old newspaper she had brought from the clubhouse.

'Would you like me to read it to you?' she asked. 'Like I used to when I was learning to read.'

'Not really,' James sighed. 'The news is too grim these days. Violence breaking out again.'

'What will happen here in Assam, Dad?' Libby asked.

'What do you mean?'

'After Independence?'

He took a sip of his drink. 'We'll be all right here.'

'I'd read that Prime Minister Bordoloi wants to get rid of Sylhet to East Bengal,' said Libby, 'because of its Muslim majority. Consolidate the Hindu majority in the rest of Assam.'

James studied his daughter. 'You really do take an interest in politics, don't you? I don't know where you get that from – certainly not your mother or me. I suppose it's that teacher of yours that's to blame – what was her name?'

'Miss MacGregor,' said Libby. 'And yes, I've her to thank for opening my eyes to the world. She made me see that everything in life is political.'

'Everything?' James scoffed.

'Yes. Take this afternoon at the clubhouse,' said Libby. 'They're still not letting women into the main building.'

'They do for dances at Christmas race week,' said James.

'Not much use in May when we wanted a drink in a comfortable, air-conditioned sitting room.'

'Well, you should have stayed here if that's what you wanted,' he replied. 'I don't see why you had to go traipsing off down the hill. Your friend looked quite ill – I hope she's not sickening for something.'

'She was fine until we got to The Lodge,' said Libby. 'Something unnerved her there. What is it about that place? Wasn't there a death there years ago or some tragedy?'

James took another swig. 'Just some foolish gossip.'

'About what?'

Her father looked away. 'I don't remember the details.'

'But you remember something?'

James stared into his glass. 'It used to be the burra bungalow when I was a young planter. But it fell out of favour – too small and not luxurious enough – that's why Anant Ram was happy to rent it.'

'Oh, yes,' Libby said, a memory stirring, 'it was supposed to be haunted. The kids at the club used to talk about it. Didn't they change its name?'

Her father shifted in his seat.

'I'm sure they did,' Libby persisted. 'I remember Anant Ram saying something about it when I was little. To take away the bad luck.'

Suddenly Flowers appeared out of the dark. James gave a startled cry.

'Goodness you gave us a fright,' said Libby. 'Are you feeling any better?'

'A little now I've slept,' said Flowers, though she still looked drained. She sat down next to Libby.

'Would you like a nightcap?' asked James.

'Yes, please.'

James got up and poured her a whisky, generously replenishing his own glass. She thanked him and took a gulp.

'I heard you talking about The Lodge,' said Flowers.

James said, 'Libby shouldn't have taken you. The cycle obviously exhausted y—'

'I think it's haunted,' Flowers interrupted. 'Going into the house made the hairs stand up on the back of my neck. I've never believed in ghosts but I'm sure I saw something.'

'So did I,' said Libby, 'but it was only a shadow. The place is a bit creepy though.'

'That's old bungalows for you,' said James. 'All creaks and dark corners.'

'It was more than that,' said Flowers. 'There was a definite presence and a terrible atmosphere.'

'I think you are being fanciful,' said James.

'It was like a great cloud of sadness,' said Flowers with a shudder. 'Didn't you feel it, Libby?'

Libby was unnerved by her words. She had experienced a strange feeling in the room beyond the sitting room but that was just because it was dark. But her father seemed agitated by the conversation and she didn't like to see him upset.

'No, not really,' she answered. 'As Dad says, it's just an old house.'

Flowers asked, 'So what was it called before it became The Lodge?'

'What does it matter?' James said short-temperedly.

'Dad! She's only asking,' said Libby.

James knocked back his whisky. Libby thought he wasn't going to answer. Abruptly he said, 'Dunsapie Cottage.'

'That rings a bell,' said Libby.

'Isn't it time you young ladies retired to bed?' James asked.

Flowers shivered though it wasn't chilly. 'I know it sounds pathetic, but can I sleep in your room tonight, Libby? I don't feel like being on my own.'

'Of course you can,' Libby said. 'You can take my bed and I'll go on the truckle bed. Ayah Meera sometimes slept on it next to me before Mungo was born.'

'Thank you,' Flowers said with a look of relief.

❧◦☙

Libby took a long time to fall asleep and when she did it was only fitful. All week she had slept deeply, drugged by the scented heat of the warm nights and the long alcohol-fuelled dinners. But she had been disturbed by the events of the day; the trip to The Lodge, Flowers's strange reaction and her father's reluctance to talk about the old bungalow. What was it that eluded her about the place? Where had she heard the name Dunsapie Cottage before?

She knew there was a Dunsapie Loch in Edinburgh – her Uncle Johnny had mentioned it when reminiscing about being a student at Edinburgh University. So the bungalow had probably been named by a homesick Scotsman working at the Oxford plantation . . .

Libby came awake with a start. Something had woken her. The sound of an animal howling? She sat up and listened. It was more of a whimpering and was coming from somewhere very close by. She scrambled off the truckle bed and peered through the mosquito net that draped over both beds.

'Where are you going?' Flowers's voice made her jump. Her friend was swinging her legs over her bed to follow.

'That noise,' said Libby. 'Did it wake you too?'

'I haven't been asleep,' whispered Flowers. 'But he wakes me every night with his crying.'

'Who does?'

'Your father.'

'What?' Libby exclaimed.

'He sits on the veranda and doesn't go to bed.' Flowers reached for her dressing gown. 'Haven't you heard him before? He shouts and cries in his sleep. I've tried to get him to go to bed but he won't. I think it's the whisky giving him nightmares – or maybe it's memories of the War.'

Libby was aghast. 'Why didn't you tell me?'

'I've wanted to but he asked me not to.'

Libby hurried outside to the veranda, Flowers at her heels. Her father was standing gripping the veranda railing and talking to someone, his voice pleading but his words incoherent. For an instant, Libby thought he was remonstrating with one of the servants, but the veranda was deserted.

She went to him. 'Dad . . .'

He swung round at her touch, confusion on his perspiring face.

'No, no,' he gasped. 'Don't let her!'

'Dad, it's me, Libby. You're all right.'

But he was staring beyond her, raw fear on his face. 'Get her away! Tell her to go!'

Libby glanced round to see that it was Flowers he was looking at. Libby felt a wave of shame at her father's rudeness.

'It's Flowers – my friend,' said Libby.

James started babbling again.

'He doesn't see us,' said Flowers. 'He's sleepwalking. We must be careful with him.' She came forward and took him gently by the arm. 'Come on, Mr Robson. Come and sit down and rest.'

He seemed to respond to her soothing voice. Flowers and Libby coaxed him back into his chair.

'Shouldn't we try and get him to bed?' whispered Libby.

'He won't go,' said Flowers. 'He's frightened of falling asleep indoors.'

As they settled him, Aslam appeared, looking sleepy but anxious.

'The *chowkidar* woke me, Missy-Mem',' he said. 'Is sahib having nightmares again?'

'So you know about them?' asked Libby.

Aslam nodded. 'For a long time he is having bad dreams.'

Libby put a protective hand on her father's head. He was murmuring but calm. 'He's fine now,' she said.

'He's not fine,' said Flowers. 'Your father's mind is disturbed.'

Libby's insides tensed; she didn't want to believe he could be mentally ill. 'It was all that silly talk about The Lodge being haunted that upset him,' Libby said firmly. 'I should never have brought up the subject.'

'The Lodge, memsahib? What has sahib been saying?'

Libby's heart lurched at the bearer's anxious expression.

'Nothing much,' she said. 'Do you know what could be worrying him in particular, Aslam?'

The servant glanced away. 'I cannot say. But it is a bad place. I do not like Manzur living there.'

'I wouldn't live there if you paid me,' said Flowers.

'For goodness' sake,' Libby hissed, 'you're all over-reacting. It's just an old bungalow.'

'I don't think I'm over-reacting,' Flowers said. 'But whether I am or not, your father needs medical help.'

'Shall I call for Dr Attar?' Aslam asked.

Libby shook her head. 'No point dragging him out at this time of night just 'cause Dad's had a bad dream. I'll sit with him till the morning. When he's awake we can decide what to do.'

'I'll sit up with you,' said Flowers.

'There's no need – you go back to bed.'

'No,' said Flowers, 'I'm a nurse: let me help.'

James was in a buoyant mood; two days ago he had shot his first tiger. A clean shot through the neck and a follow-up bullet between the eyes. An old

tiger, admittedly, but it had still taken skill to track and kill it. Fairfax told him that the taxidermist would be able to repair the damage to the head and it would make a prized trophy on the sitting room wall at Cheviot View.

He was sauntering out of the office for tiffin when he saw a commotion at the gates. Someone was remonstrating with the guard. Hurrying over, James was surprised to see the punkah-wallah from Dunsapie Cottage.

'What's all this fuss about?' he demanded.

'Please, sahib, come!' Sunil Ram pleaded. 'Oh, master . . . !'

James's stomach clenched at the look of distress on the man's face. 'What's wrong, man?'

The servant gabbled so rapidly in Hindustani that James couldn't comprehend him. But the beseeching tone he did understand.

'Very well,' said James, 'wait here.'

He doubled back and ordered a syce to fetch his pony. In a few days Logan would be back with his new bride and James could hand over responsibility for the burra bungalow once and for all. There would be a mistress in charge and no need for him to be summoned like a lackey by the bullying Logan to do his distasteful bidding. As James made his way to Dunsapie Cottage he thought with satisfaction how he had impressed on Aruna that her son was being well cared for but in future she must stay away from Logan sahib. A brisk talking-to was all that was needed. He was discovering from old hands like Fairfax how best to deal with their workers. 'Firm but fair. Just like with children. That's how to get the best out of them. No need for cruelty.'

The bungalow was strangely quiet. Even though the master was away, James still expected to see and hear servants about the place – a mali or a sweeper. Not even a dog barked. The burra bungalow seemed deserted.

Sunil Ram came dashing past him, panting from running all the way from the office compound. He got to the bungalow steps and stopped. James dismounted and came up behind.

'Well, what is the matter?'

To James's irritation, the man would go no further. He pointed into the house and moaned. Perhaps some wild animal had found its way into the house and the servants had fled in fear. He drew out his pistol and climbed the steps.

There was nothing on the veranda to cause alarm. He ventured inside. The cool tiled floor and darkened interior made him give an involuntary shiver. But there was nothing untoward. James crossed the sitting room and opened the door to Logan's study. He waited while his eyes grew accustomed to the gloom. All was silent. He walked behind the desk and, throwing open the shutters, looked round warily. There was nothing.

He let out a sigh of relief. Sunil Ram would feel his wrath if this was a fuss about nothing. James strode back across the central room and flung open the opposite door. Realising it was Logan's bedroom, he hesitated. He could see the outline of the large bed draped in nets. He walked in. It was the smell that hit him first. James stopped in his tracks. Confusion gave way to disbelief and then horror. His chest went tight. He couldn't breathe . . .

James cried out.

'It's me – Libby. You're okay. Dad, you're okay.'

James was still in the grip of his nightmare. He could still see . . . He shuddered in fear. But the spectre was receding. He wasn't inside that terrible room after all. He was on his own veranda in the early dawn. With Libby. James gulped for breath. His heart palpitated. He was close to tears. The relief.

'Libby?' he gasped.

'Yes, it's me,' she reassured him, squeezing his hand.

'Oh, Libby . . .'

To his utter disbelief he felt a sob rise up inside that he couldn't control. It burst out of him. Once he started weeping, he couldn't stop. Great wracking sobs shook and convulsed his body. His daughter – this half-stranger – held him and stroked his hair as if he were the child. He felt grateful and humiliated in equal measure.

It was then that he noticed the Eurasian girl. She looked familiar. Should he know her? She regarded him with pity and handed him a glass of soda. He couldn't take it. Libby took it for him and tried to get him to sip. It slopped down his chin.

'I'll ring for Dr Attar,' said the woman whose name he couldn't remember.

Who was Dr Attar? The garden doctor was called Thomas. Did she mean him? And who needed him?

'Dad, tell me what's wrong.'

He stared at the young woman holding his hand. She looked like Tilly. Was it Tilly? James opened his mouth to speak but no words came out.

He felt utterly weary. He was glad he didn't have to speak. A comforting numbness settled inside. Perhaps that's why people cried, because it washed away pain like a river in spate washes away stones.

He clasped the hand of the young woman and closed his eyes. He welcomed the fog that enveloped his thoughts. He didn't have to think about anything.

CHAPTER 16

I've given him a sedative,' said Dr Attar, joining Libby and Flowers on the veranda. 'At least it will help him sleep.'

The sun was up and the air already hot and humid.

'Thank you,' said Libby. 'That's what he needs – he must be exhausted from not having slept properly for months.' She invited the doctor to sit down and take tea and toast.

'It's more than lack of sleep though,' said Flowers, 'isn't it, Doctor? You said he's been near to a mental breakdown before.'

'He's not mad,' Libby protested.

'Nobody's saying he is,' said Flowers, 'but he is ill. All that drinking till he passes out – it's the sign of a troubled mind.'

'You're exaggerating. All tea planters like their *chota peg* after a hard day's work,' Libby said.

'Not as much as that,' said Flowers. She turned to the young doctor. 'What is your opinion?'

Dr Attar put down his cup and gave Libby a compassionate look.

'I believe Robson sahib is suffering from nervous exhaustion,' he said. 'It's not something that's happened overnight – he was under considerable strain during the War helping the relief efforts on the Burma Front. That is when I first came to the plantation here. Your father worked like a Trojan, organising canteens and transporting supplies. He drove himself so hard.'

'I had no idea he was so involved in the war effort,' said Libby, feeling guilty. 'We thought that in Britain we were doing far more.'

'But many people worked hard during the War,' Flowers pointed out, 'my own father included. It doesn't explain why Mr Robson should be suddenly worse now.'

Dr Attar looked pensive. 'It may be a delayed response to the stress of that time – but he is also a man who has just turned seventy. That is old to still be working on a tea plantation. I have suggested retirement – or at least a period of home leave – but the most he would do was go to Belgooree for a bit of rest and recuperation. In my view he did not stay long enough.'

Libby flushed. 'That was probably my fault, insisting on coming to Assam and the Oxford Estates. I was so impatient to see him and my old home. He cut short his stay at Belgooree for me.'

'You're not to blame,' said the doctor. 'Robson sahib is not a man who takes easily to sitting around – he sees it as idleness, not a well-earned rest.'

'Doctor,' said Flowers with a puzzled frown, 'I have seen soldiers that have been affected by war – not just physically but from battle shock – and Libby's father reminds me of them. It's as if they are reliving the moments under gunfire – like it's very real to them – and it makes them suffer all over again. Is there something traumatic that could have triggered this for Mr Robson?'

Dr Attar nodded. 'I have wondered this too. His health does seem to have deteriorated in recent weeks – though why, I can't say.'

Libby's heart began to thud. 'Could it be because of my coming back to India?' she asked.

'Surely not?' said Flowers. 'He must have been longing for that.'

'Or nervous about it,' said Libby. 'Perhaps it stirred up all his unhappiness that my mother wasn't coming too. He hasn't been himself since

I've been here – not the happy, larger-than-life father that I remember. There's a distance between us that I hadn't expected.'

'I don't think that is to do with you,' said Dr Attar. 'He has been withdrawn for a while – keeping himself to himself at Cheviot View rather than socialising at the club.'

Libby said, 'Clarrie Robson thought there was something troubling Dad but that he wouldn't talk about it. She thought I might be able to find out what it was, but I can't get him to talk about anything personal.'

'Why don't we take him back to Belgooree?' suggested Flowers. 'Get him away from what's worrying him here. Perhaps then he will open up to you about what is troubling him. I could help you do that before I return to Calcutta next week.'

Libby considered this. Clarrie might be just the calm, practical person to help, whereas staying here, isolated at Cheviot View once Flowers had gone, was a daunting thought. What if her father's mental state got worse? How would she cope if he refused to confide in her about what troubled him? The place no longer seemed the idyllic childhood home after which she had hankered for so long. Its heat and remoteness were growing oppressive. A green prison, her mother had called it, and for the first time Libby had a sense of what it must have been like for Tilly – a young woman used to city life – having to make her home here.

'I think that would be a good idea,' encouraged Dr Attar.

Libby gave Flowers a grateful look. 'Okay, I'll ring Clarrie and see if that's possible.'

❧ ☙

To Libby's surprise, her father made little protest at the suggestion of going to Belgooree. He was groggy and confused when he awoke, saying little and allowing Libby to make the decisions.

'Belgooree . . . yes . . . if you like . . .' he said.

Libby had been encouraged by Clarrie's instant acceptance of the arrangement.

'Of course you must come,' she urged on the crackly telephone line. 'It will be wonderful to see you – and Flowers too.'

It was arranged that Manzur would share the driving with Libby. Two days later, they loaded up the car and waved farewell to Aslam and Meera, leaving them in charge of the bungalow.

'We'll be back soon,' Libby promised, though more to pacify her father who, at the last minute, grew agitated that neither Aslam nor his faithful hound Breckon were going with him. 'Manzur can always bring Aslam over to Belgooree if you find that he's needed. And the servants will spoil Breckon here.' Libby knew that Flowers was wary of dogs and would hate a long car journey confined with the boisterous Breckon.

They drove all day, the steering wheel too hot to touch without driving gloves, and stopped only to picnic at dak bungalows along the way and to get temporary relief in the shade.

It was dark by the time they began the ascent up to Belgooree, the car headlights catching fireflies in their beam and a welcoming breeze cooling the travellers. Manzur was driving so Libby was able to hang out of the window and see the familiar outline of the Belgooree factory come into view, as they bumped up the pot-holed track through the tea garden. Her father had been asleep since their tea stop an hour ago.

The nostalgic heady scent of flowers and pines made Libby's eyes prickle with emotion. It brought back memories of family trips to see her father's Belgooree cousins and how ridiculously excited she would become. *'Sit still!'* her mother would cry. But her father would let them out at the bottom of the track and allow Libby and Jamie to run all the way from the factory up to the house. Libby resisted the urge to jump out and do so now in the dark. But as they pulled up outside the old bungalow, gleaming silver in the moonlight, Libby was leaping out of the car and up the veranda steps.

Clarrie was waiting on the veranda to welcome them. Her black hair now held a few silver threads, but at sixty-one, Libby thought the woman still beautiful. Her fine-featured face glowed in the lamplight and her dark eyes were lively. Despite her old-fashioned frock, Clarrie still had the figure of a young woman.

Libby hugged her warmly. 'This is very good of you, Cousin Clarrie. Dad's not well.'

'You know I would do anything for Tilly's family.' Clarrie smiled. 'I'm so happy to see you.' She turned. 'Harry, darling, go and help Uncle James out of the car.'

It was then that Libby saw a tall youth standing in the shadows. 'Cousin Harry?' she gasped. 'We've never met – but you look so like your dad, it couldn't be anyone else.'

The boy gave a bashful smile and an awkward handshake before jumping down the steps to help his elderly cousin. 'Manzur!' he cried in delight, on catching sight of his former tutor.

'That was kind,' murmured Clarrie. 'Harry loves to be compared to his father, though I'm afraid he has little memory of Wesley . . .'

'I meant it,' said Libby. 'He's got his father's dark good looks. In a few years the tea planters' daughters will be fighting over him at the club dances.'

Clarrie laughed softly and put a hand on her arm. 'And you have grown so pretty, Libby – you have the lovely Robson eyes.'

Libby blushed with pleasure; none of her family had ever said that.

As Harry led a disorientated James up the steps, Libby noticed Flowers sharing a cigarette with Manzur. They made an attractive couple. On the journey while James had slept, the nurse had been quizzing Manzur about The Lodge but he seemed vague about its previous occupants. She wondered what Flowers was talking to him about now.

'Clarrie!' James exclaimed.

'James.' Clarrie smiled and kissed him on the cheek. 'Come and make yourself comfortable. How was your journey?'

Libby watched in amazement as her father followed her meekly to a cane sofa and sat down beside her. But it was the look on her father's face that surprised her the most: a tenderness that she had not seen before. It was the sort of expression that Libby had longed to see pass between her parents. The concern that she had felt in England, that her father and Wesley's widow might have grown close during Tilly's long absence, resurfaced. How intimate had they grown during the War?

Libby banished such thoughts; Clarrie was merely being kind. That's the sort of generous person she was. Libby was over-tired from the driving and the past few days of little sleep and was reading too much into a couple of glances and a kiss on the cheek.

Declining supper, Libby went thankfully to bed in the small back bedroom which she used to share with Adela on long-ago holidays. She dozed off to the sound of crickets and muted conversation and slept soundly.

Two days later, as Libby walked with Flowers in the garden, Flowers told Libby of her decision to get a lift to Gowhatty with Manzur and take the train back to Calcutta.

'Your father is in good hands here,' she said to Libby. 'I think you should have time together as a family and not worry about having to entertain me.'

'I'm sorry,' said Libby, 'it's been no holiday for you at all.'

'I've enjoyed a lot of it,' said Flowers, 'so you mustn't feel guilty. I just hope your father's health improves quickly.'

'He already seems calmer here,' said Libby. 'Perhaps all he needs is a change of air.'

Flowers looked sceptical. 'Try and get him to talk about what's concerning him.'

Libby, silently hoping that recuperation was all her father needed, changed the subject. 'What about our trip to Shillong? We still haven't been to the orphanage. Are you sure you don't want to stay a little longer?'

'I'm not sure I want to find out about Daddy's past any more,' said Flowers. 'I think it's more important to decide what our future is going to be.'

Libby gave her a teasing smile. 'And you'd rather spend a car journey with a certain assistant manager than visit orphanages?'

Flowers grinned. 'Perhaps. He is very charming. Not that he's interested in a half-half like me.'

'Don't say that,' Libby said. 'Manzur's not prejudiced.'

'Maybe not,' said Flowers, 'but our communities are. Daddy would hate the idea of me fraternising with an Indian – and Manzur's parents will no doubt have a good Muslim wife picked out for him.'

Libby slipped her arm through her friend's and continued their stroll across the lawn. 'Things are changing fast. It might not always be like that. Our generation will be different.'

Flowers asked, 'Are you still holding out hope for the handsome Ghulam?'

Libby's heart jumped at his mention. She had confided her feelings to Flowers on one of the hot afternoons they had spent aimlessly flicking through books and lounging on the veranda at Cheviot View. He was rarely out of her thoughts but she knew it was fruitless to hanker after him; her love was unrequited.

'Not really,' Libby said. 'He doesn't feel the same way about me.'

'I think you're wrong,' said Flowers. 'The night of your party he couldn't keep his eyes off you.'

Libby reddened. 'You're just saying that to be kind.'

'Not at all – I'm good at observing people and I think Ghulam finds you very attractive. Not just that, but he's the sort of man who wouldn't bother being friends with a woman unless he found them interesting too.'

'Thank you for saying that.' Libby gave a wistful smile. 'But even if he does, he won't act on it – I'm still one of the despised British. He will never let such a relationship develop. His sister warned me off too – didn't want me to get hurt.'

Flowers gave her arm an encouraging squeeze. 'What was that you were just saying about things changing? Be optimistic. And carry on being who you are, Libby, whatever men like Ghulam think. Don't let others define you. Your cousin Adela taught me that. She stood up to the bullies at our school and didn't change who she was to fit in with them. She showed me how to be brave and I'll always be grateful to her for that.'

Before Flowers's early morning departure, she gave Libby an envelope.

'If you get the chance to go into Shillong, then these are the details that I know of Dad's schooling. But don't feel you have to.'

'If I can, I will,' promised Libby.

'And if you ever need somewhere to stay in Calcutta,' said Flowers, 'then you are always welcome in our home.'

'Thanks.' Libby hugged her. 'You've been so helpful and under-standing. And I hope I'll get back to Calcutta soon – when Dad's feeling better.'

'Write to him,' Flowers said in a soft voice that the others couldn't hear.

'To who?'

'Ghulam, of course. It's sometimes easier to say things in writing. The worst that can happen is that he doesn't reply.'

Libby was startled by the idea. She still treasured the amusing, friendly letter that Ghulam had written to her in Calcutta offering to show her the city. She had read it so many times it was in danger of falling to bits. How she would love to hear from him again! Yet she doubted he would want to write to her so she shrugged off the suggestion.

'Don't worry about me. I'm not the kind to pine away over a man.'

Flowers laughed. 'No, I've noticed. Shall I give your regards to George if I see him?'

'Regards, yes, but nothing more.' Libby grinned. 'I'm still fond of him even though he doesn't deserve it. But don't tell him that.'

It was true that she still felt something for the pleasure-seeking George Brewis, but it wasn't as strong as her feelings for Ghulam. Best to put them both out of her mind. It looked like she would be at Belgooree for some time and it was her father who needed her attention. That was her priority.

Libby felt sorry waving Flowers away – she had enjoyed her company – but felt a tinge of relief too. Her father seemed to have been on edge having Flowers around. Libby hoped fervently that his health would repair more quickly in the tranquil surroundings of Belgooree – and that she would get her old dad back.

Libby breathed in the cool scented air of the dawn. Her spirits lifted. Her mother had loved coming here; there was something very special about this place. She turned and walked back to the bungalow, glad that she wasn't leaving just yet.

CHAPTER 17

Newcastle, late May

Since Sam's fortieth birthday at the end of April, Adela had been attending church on a Sunday morning. The congregation of the Gospel Missionary Church met in a small redbrick building in Sandyford, a modest suburb of railway workers' terraces. Their grander church had been destroyed during the War.

'Don't know why you want to go there instead of St Oswald's with me,' Tilly had said in bafflement. 'I bet the sermon's twice as long and you don't get all the local gossip afterwards.'

'Lexy likes to go,' Adela had said, 'so I said I'd take her.'

Sam had given her sceptical looks but didn't question her sudden interest in religion. They didn't talk about much any more. Her attempt to give him a special birthday by inviting his mother to a picnic tea in the local park had been a disaster. The cake Adela had made collapsed in the tin and Mrs Jackman had spent the afternoon chiding Adela for not asking her to make it. A dog had run off with the cold sausages and rain finally chased them indoors. Sam had taken his mother home and didn't return in time for Adela to take him to the cinema. By then she had polished off a bottle of sherry with Josey in the kitchen while Tilly worked in the sitting room on the stamp collection she was building up since leaving her old one in India.

Adela had not been able to hide her annoyance. 'Your mother knew we were going to the pictures. I really wanted to see *Black Narcissus*.'

'We can go another night,' Sam had said, eyeing the empty bottle. 'Anyway, you seem to have made the best of your evening without me.'

'At least Josey knows how to have fun,' Adela had retorted.

'Leave me out of this,' Josey had said, getting up from the table. 'You lovebirds need time alone.'

Adela had tried to curb her resentment at Sam's mother spoiling the birthday but in bed that night, she pretended a headache so they didn't make love.

'Drinking too much gives you that,' Sam had muttered and rolled away from her.

Adela had lain awake feeling wretched and wracked with guilt. Why had her interest in sex shrivelled so quickly? It wasn't that she didn't love Sam, so what was the problem? But after that, Sam only spoke to her about the mundane day-to-day running of the café and kept out of her way. His commissions for wedding photography were increasing and took him all over Newcastle. On Sundays he went off with his camera on long walks and sometimes didn't return until suppertime. Adela knew that she should be putting more effort into her marriage but all she could think about was tracking down her lost son.

She felt achingly alone. Why did Sam not understand her yearning to find her boy? Surely, he of all people should realise how she felt? He had been wrenched from his mother at an early age and knew how damaging it was to have the mother-son bond severed. If only he would let her talk about it, she could make him understand, but he never brought up the subject. Adela consoled herself with the hope that finding her son would bring her and Sam together again in a common purpose – loving John Wesley and giving him a home. That was her unspoken dream; it's what kept her going through the relentless drudgery and worry of running the café. She would patch things up with Sam soon.

At least Lexy still understood her need to find John Wesley. When Adela had shown her the letter from the Reverend Stevens of the mission society, her friend had been indignant at its patronising tone. 'Thinks he's better than the likes of us lasses – the cheek of it!' It had spurred her on to help in the search.

It was Maggie, Lexy's old friend, who had remembered the name of the women who had come from the mission church to take away Adela's baby in 1939. Mrs Singer and Miss Trimble.

'Reminded me of sewing machines and thimble,' Maggie had said in a rare moment of lucidity. 'Singer and Trimble.'

Adela had tracked down the congregation – now reduced to a couple of dozen mostly female attendees – to the small hall in Sandyford. Lexy had agreed to go with her if Adela would drive her in the café van. This had been another cause of friction with Sam, when he'd wanted the van to get to an outlying village to take photos at a christening. Tilly had quelled the argument by offering Sam her car instead.

It was three Sundays before Adela plucked up the courage to ask about Singer and Trimble. She stayed behind to talk to the elderly preacher.

'Miss Trimble died last year,' the pastor said. 'But Mrs Singer is still very much with us, I believe. How do you know her?'

Adela hesitated. Lexy said, 'She used to come in the tearoom where I worked. Lost touch during the War. It would be canny to see her again.'

'I'm afraid she doesn't live in Newcastle any more,' the preacher said.

'Where is she?' asked Adela.

He frowned. 'I think it was Durham. She went to live with her daughter.'

Adela's insides twisted in disappointment. 'Do you know where?'

He gave her an enquiring look. 'I'm not sure I do.'

'But you know she's still alive?' Adela persisted.

'She keeps in touch with Mrs Kelly, the organist.' He looked around. 'It would appear she's already gone home.'

Adela could hardly curb her impatience for the following Sunday morning to come. She made sure that she spoke to Mrs Kelly before she left church. The woman was large and wheezed as loudly as the bellows on the ancient organ that she wrestled with each week.

She beamed at the mention of her friend. 'I was that sad when Lily moved away. But her daughter married and settled down Durham way and Lily was already widowed so she followed her. Friends of hers you said? Not regular church people though? Lovely voice you have, pet. Noticed it straight away. Makes a difference to the hymns.'

'Thanks.' Adela smiled. 'We were wondering if you could put us in touch with Mrs Singer – with Lily. The minister said you'd know her address.'

'Well, I'm sure she'd like a letter from an old friend,' Mrs Kelly agreed. 'My memory's like a sieve but I've got it written down. I'll bring it for you next Sunday.'

With a warning look from Lexy, Adela hid her frustration. 'That's canny of you, Mrs Kelly,' said Lexy. 'We'll see you next week.'

It was early June before Adela got the address for Lily Singer. Afterwards Lexy said, 'Does that mean I divn't have to gan to church again? That preacher could put me to sleep standing up.'

'I really appreciated you coming – but you can have a lie-in from now on,' Adela said.

'So are you going to write to her?' Lexy asked.

'No, I'm going to go over and visit her.'

Lexy shook her head. 'I don't think that's a good idea. You can't just turn up on her doorstep.'

'If I write she will just palm me off with the usual reply that she can't tell me where John Wesley is.'

'And what if she never knew where he was sent?' Lexy asked.

'Then I won't be any worse off than I am now,' said Adela. 'At least if I can look her in the eye, I'll be able to tell if she knows something.'

Lexy scrutinised her. 'And are you going to tell Sam why you're waltzing off to Durham?'

Adela felt a familiar pang of guilt over Sam. 'I don't think so. Not until I have something worth telling him. He'll only get annoyed at me. I don't think he really wants me to find my son at all.'

'Well, maybe's he's right,' Lexy said bluntly. 'You should be looking to start your own family together. That's the best way to get over losing the bairn.'

Adela gave her a bleak look. 'That's the problem – I can't.' She tried to put her deepest feelings into words. 'It's like I would be betraying John Wesley by having another baby.'

'Don't be daft!'

'I know it sounds selfish of me – Sam longs for a child – but once we have one then I'm admitting that I've given up on my boy. And I just can't bring myself to do that.'

'Stop being so hard on yersel', hinny,' Lexy said with a pitying look. 'You did what any young lass would have done in your position.'

Adela's look was full of sorrow. 'I can't help it. And I won't ever forgive myself if I don't find out what's happened to my boy.'

'Then you must let Sam know how you feel,' said Lexy. ''Cause he's going around with the look of a dog that's been kicked.'

Adela winced. 'I just need to meet this Mrs Singer and find out what happened – then I'll be able to put it behind me.'

Lexy gave her a look of disbelief which left Adela feeling hollow inside. She didn't want to hurt the people she loved the most but she had to find out about John Wesley or she would go out of her mind.

After Adela had time to think it through, she realised it would be better to write to Mrs Singer first rather than risk travelling to Durham to find she wasn't at home. She wrote a vague letter saying that she had recently joined the church and wished to meet so she could talk to Lily about her work with the adoption society. Lily Singer wrote back inviting her to visit on her next day off.

On the following Saturday afternoon, Adela arranged for Josey to cover for her at the café. She chose that day knowing that Sam was being hired by a local newspaper to take pictures of people at the annual races and would be out all day. Only Lexy and Josey knew where she was going.

That morning, Sam was in a good mood with his day of photography ahead.

'What do you want to do for your birthday next week?' he asked. 'Would you like to go to the pictures? There's a Ronald Colman film on at the Gaumont.'

She was touched that he had given it some thought and felt a guilty pang that she was going behind his back to see Mrs Singer.

'That would be lovely,' she agreed.

'Good,' he said with a smile – that familiar dimpled smile that used to make her stomach do flips.

She almost confessed there and then about tracking down the woman from the adoption society but didn't want to wipe the cherished smile from his handsome face. She would explain everything to him when they had time alone on her birthday.

'Off you go,' said Adela, brushing his lips with a quick kiss. 'You don't want to be late for Plate Day.'

He strode from the house, whistling. It was the first time she'd heard that for weeks. Adela's insides tightened with sudden anxiety; she hoped what she learnt from Mrs Singer wouldn't drive a wedge further between her and Sam.

As Adela walked down the steep hill from Durham railway station in warm sunshine, the Cathedral bells were striking three o'clock. She had only ever seen the city from the train – the fortress cathedral set on its wooded peninsula – and if she hadn't been so intent on seeing Mrs Singer she would have been curious to see more.

Following instructions that took her under a viaduct, Adela descended into tightly packed terraces of blackened brick houses and on down a wider street of shops that led to an ancient stone bridge spanning the River Wear. Crumbling housing clung to the riverbank on one side, while the other was crammed with twisting lanes flanked by tall elegant buildings. The narrow streets were busy with shoppers and traffic. It struck her how Sam would enjoy photographing all this.

Quelling thoughts of her husband, Adela walked briskly on through the market place, where a policeman was directing traffic from a central box, and made for the far side. Here the street banked steeply once again. She was perspiring and breathless by the time she climbed to the top of Claypath and turned into a cluster of terraced housing.

Adela's heart was drumming with nerves as she knocked on Lily Singer's door. She was surprised to see a dark-haired woman not much older than herself answer it.

'You've come to see Mam?' she asked.

Adela swallowed and nodded, realising this was Lily's daughter.

'Come in. I'm Dorothy.' She opened the door wide so Adela could step into the tiny hallway. 'Mam's just in there.' She pointed to an open door. 'Mam! Your visitor is here.' She turned and beckoned Adela into the room. 'Go on in, I'll bring tea in a minute.'

From somewhere deeper in the house, Adela could hear the chatter of children's voices.

She stepped into a small, neat sitting room which felt chilly after the heat of outside. The furniture was plain and functional: an oval table with wooden chairs, and an upright green sofa with wooden arms. Sitting in a high-backed chair next to it was a stout woman with badly

236

swollen legs. Lily Singer had wavy greying hair and a double chin which increased when she smiled, which, judging by the wrinkles around her mouth and eyes, was often.

'Forgive me if I don't stand up, Mrs Jackman,' she said. 'My legs aren't what they used to be.'

'Don't apologise, Mrs Singer,' Adela said quickly, crossing the room to shake her hand. It still surprised her when people called her by her married name: she still thought of herself as a Robson.

'Please sit down,' said Lily, waving her to the sofa. 'It's so nice to get a visit – I don't see many folk these days.'

Adela perched on the edge of the sofa and smoothed her skirt over her knees. It was a plain utility one to go with the modest blouse and cardigan she was wearing; she wanted to impress on Mrs Singer that she was a respectable married woman. At Lily's feet was a basket of wool and some abandoned knitting.

'What are you knitting?' Adela asked, for something to say.

'Jumper for my grandson.' Lily smiled. 'I've unravelled two old jerkins that my husband used to wear. Our Michael says he doesn't like brown but I've told him waste-not-want-not. Fancy being eight years old and fussy about clothes!'

Adela's stomach fluttered. Lily's grandson was the same age as John Wesley. For a wild moment, she wondered if it was possible that this woman might have kept the baby herself. Perhaps daughter Dorothy couldn't have children.

'Is he your only grandchild?' Adela asked.

'No, I've got five in all,' said Lily. 'Dorothy's three and my other daughter has twins. I don't see them as much as they live in Cumberland but I knit for them too. Like to keep busy – 'specially as I don't get out the house much.'

Adela felt a kick of disappointment, yet she would still like to see this Michael just to be sure. Then doubt gripped her. Would she know if it was John Wesley or not? How would she recognise a boy she hadn't seen since he was a few days old? Adela nearly lost her nerve. She shouldn't have come. She was here under false pretences and poor unsuspecting Mrs Singer didn't deserve to be put in this situation.

'But I've got nothing to complain about,' Lily continued. 'I'm blessed to have my grandchildren – they've kept me going since my dear husband was taken from me five years ago.'

Adela licked her dry lips and nodded, trying to calm her erratic heartbeat. 'Mrs Kelly sends her warmest regards.'

'Dear Doris!' Lily exclaimed. 'How I miss her and the folk from church. Tell me all about them.'

Adela tried to answer Lily's many questions about the congregation and the move to the Sandyford hall but it was obvious the woman was disappointed with her lack of detailed knowledge.

'I haven't been going there very long,' Adela admitted. 'But they've been very welcoming.'

'They are, aren't they?' agreed Lily. 'So tell me about yourself, Mrs Jackman.'

Adela hadn't really wanted to say much about herself but Lily had a warmth of personality that invited confidences. She found herself telling the widow about being brought up in India, marrying Sam and coming back to Newcastle to help run the family tearoom founded by her mother.

'You see my family were from the North East originally. My Belhaven grandfather was from North Northumberland and I have an aunt and cousins in Newcastle.'

Mrs Singer's eyes were wide with interest. 'Which tearoom is it?'

'Herbert's,' said Adela, 'in the West End.'

Lily nodded enthusiastically. 'I remember going there when Dorothy was little. There was that nice park nearby. We'd go there for a cup of tea and the lady in charge would always give Dorothy a toffee. Would that be your mother?'

'Probably the manageress Lexy.' Adela smiled. 'Mother went back to India with my father after the Great War.'

They were interrupted by Dorothy bringing in a tray of tea things, a girl of about three following and clinging on to her skirt while peering at the visitor. She reminded Adela of fair-haired little Bonnie.

'Hello.' Adela smiled at her. 'What's your name?'

The girl darted behind her mother.

'This is Maureen,' said Dorothy. 'Say hello to the lady, Maureen.'

Adela went down on her knees as the girl peeped out again. 'I see you!' Adela grinned. 'Hello, Maureen.'

The girl gave a shy smile.

'Where's your big brother Michael?' asked Adela.

'Playing football,' Maureen whispered. Then she turned and ran out of the room.

Dorothy said to Adela, 'I hope you don't mind if I leave you to pour the tea while I keep an eye on the children?'

'Of course not,' said Adela, relieved that she would not have to ask awkward questions in front of the younger woman.

As Adela put a cup down on the side table next to Lily, the older woman asked, 'Do you have children, dear?'

Adela's stomach lurched. 'My husband and I haven't managed to have a baby yet.'

'All in good time.' Lily gave her a sympathetic look. 'I know you haven't come here just to chat to me – pleasant as that is. What is it you would like to know, Mrs Jackman?'

Adela sat down again and tried to calm the thumping in her chest.

'I – I wanted to ask you about your work with the adoption society – the one the mission church used to run in Newcastle.'

'I'm not sure I can help you. I haven't been involved with the society since early in the War,' said Lily. 'You'd be better off speaking to the minister if you're thinking of adopting. He can put you in touch with the society.'

'But you used to help with the children – the babies – that were given up for adoption?' Adela asked.

'I wasn't one of the inner circle who made decisions,' said Lily, looking puzzled. 'But I did help with fostering now and again before the babies were found parents.'

Adela's heart drummed to think this woman might have cared for John Wesley and cradled him in her ample arms. She took a deep breath.

'Did you foster a baby boy just before the War? A baby with black hair and skin a bit darker than mine?' She ploughed on. 'You went to Cullercoats with Miss Trimble to fetch him . . .'

Lily's expression changed. She stared at Adela.

'You remember him, don't you?' Adela pressed her.

It seemed an age before Lily spoke. The clock on the mantelpiece chimed four o'clock.

'Are you the mother?' Lily finally asked.

Adela's eyes smarted. 'Yes,' she whispered. 'Please tell me what happened to him.'

Lily gave her a pitying look. 'He went to a good home – to parents who wanted him.'

Adela was cut by the remark. 'I wasn't able to keep him – not then – but I've regretted it ever since.'

'Many girls have made the same mistake,' said Lily. 'But at least you've got a husband now, so be thankful for small mercies. Does he know about the baby?'

Adela nodded.

'And does he know you're here?'

Adela shook her head. Her throat was so constricted she couldn't speak.

'Go home to him, Mrs Jackman,' said Lily, her tone sharper, 'and just be grateful for what you have.'

Adela gave her a pleading look. 'Just tell me something about my boy.'

Lily sighed. 'I don't have anything to tell – I hardly saw him.'

'Did you look after him?'

'Just for a couple of nights at the most. There was a childless couple ready to take him.'

'What were they like?'

Lily looked agitated. 'I shouldn't be talking about them and you shouldn't be asking. I'm sorry for you, dear, but if I'd known this was why you'd come I wouldn't have agreed to see you.'

Adela felt tears spilling down her cheeks. 'I'm so sorry, Mrs Singer. I know it's wrong of me. But I can't go on not knowing what became of John Wesley. It's eating away inside me. I've tried to forget and get on with my life but I can't. Coming back to Newcastle has made it worse. Please, I beg of you – tell me something about his adoptive parents – so I can picture him happy. Your grandson Michael is the same age. Imagine if you never knew what had happened to him!'

'My daughter is a good Christian girl,' Lily protested. 'She would never have got herself into such a mess.'

Adela fumbled for a handkerchief and wiped her face. 'I'm sorry, Mrs Singer, I shouldn't have said that.' She stood up to go. 'Please forgive me for coming here like this. You're a good person and don't deserve to be tricked.' Adela picked up her handbag. 'Thank you for looking after my son – even for a short time. I'm glad it was someone caring like you. That gives me comfort.'

She walked to the door. As she reached for the handle, Lily spoke.

'She used to come to the church – the lady that adopted your boy. She was a kind soul but a bit lonely. They weren't from round there, didn't know many people. Husband had come to Newcastle for work.'

Adela turned towards Lily and held her breath, willing her to say more. When she didn't, Adela dared to ask, 'Where were they from?'

'I don't rightly know,' said Lily, 'but they were foreign.'

'Foreign?' Adela gasped in surprise.

'Yes, French, I think. That's why we thought the baby would suit them, with him not being quite white-skinned. They looked the same, you see – especially the father.'

Adela felt light-headed. She wasn't aware of a Frenchwoman among the congregation but surely it would be possible to trace a French couple in Newcastle?

'Don't ask me anything more about them,' Lily cautioned. 'I don't know what happened to them. Probably went back to France. But you mustn't tell anyone that I told you. It's in strictest confidence. You won't go bothering them if they're still in Newcastle, will you?'

'No, Mrs Singer,' said Adela, blinking away fresh tears. 'I promise you I won't bother them. I'm so very grateful for what you've told me. My worst fear was that my son was in an institution with no one really caring for him.' Adela managed a tearful smile. 'But I like the sound of this French couple – so thank you.'

She went swiftly so that she wouldn't have to explain her distressed state to Dorothy or the curious Maureen. Adela closed the front door behind her and hurried blindly down the hill.

❧～❧

Adela saw Sam pacing outside Tilly's house, smoking, as she rounded the corner. She tensed, ready for his anger. Her head was fuzzy from the couple of sherries she had stopped to drink in the station buffet. She had wanted to clear her head and think about everything Lily had told her. The third sherry had been a mistake.

'Where have you been all this time?' Sam demanded, stamping out his cigarette. 'It's practically dark. Mother said you left Josey in charge. What's been going on? Josey went off to the theatre without saying a word.'

'I'm sorry,' said Adela, 'I didn't realise it was so late.'

'Who've you been with?'

Seeing his troubled look, Adela couldn't lie. 'I've been to Durham – it took longer than I thought.'

'Durham? Why?'

'To see a widow from the church.'

'What widow?'

'You don't know her – it was a pastoral visit.'

He searched her face. 'If you'd told me about it sooner we could have gone together – had a day out.'

'You had your work for the paper,' said Adela. 'Did it go well?'

'It did,' he answered, his tone sharp, 'but I want to know more about this mysterious visit to Durham that has taken till nine at night.'

'Let's go inside, Sam, and talk about it there. I'm tired.'

Sam grabbed her arm as she tried to step past. 'Do you expect me to believe that you spent all this time with a devout widow when you come home reeking of booze? Don't treat me like a fool!'

Adela gaped at him. Did Sam suspect her of infidelity? She felt terrible for making him worry about such a thing, yet she was aghast he could even think it.

'Please, Sam, don't make a scene in the street,' she hissed. 'Come inside and I'll tell you.'

He let go his grip and followed her in. The house was quiet.

'Where's Tilly?' Adela asked.

'Out to dinner with Jamie and Mungo,' said Sam, 'celebrating Mungo's end of term.'

'Oh, I'd forgotten she was doing that. Nice to think of Mungo being around for the summer.' She headed for the kitchen. She needed black tea to clear her head. 'I'll put the kettle on.'

Flicking on the kitchen light, Adela winced at the glare of electric light. Sam could not contain his impatience. He took her by the shoulders and forced her to look into his face.

'Don't treat me like a stranger, Adela,' he said, his jaw clenching. 'Tell me what's been going on.'

She flinched at the stormy look in his hazel eyes – eyes that were usually filled with compassion and love – and looked away.

'It's not what you think,' she said. 'I really have been to Durham to see a woman from the church.'

'Then why all the secrecy?' Sam asked, the traces of suspicion still evident in his voice. 'I don't see why you want to keep me away from your church friends. I'm the one who used to be a missionary, remember? I'm not allergic to religion.'

Adela gave a ghost of a smile. Sam always tried to defuse arguments with humour – until recently when they had begun to grow apart. She realised that it was largely her fault for pushing him away but she knew he wouldn't like what she had to tell him.

'It wasn't really a pastoral visit,' Adela admitted. 'I went to see Mrs Singer for my own benefit – for what I hoped she could tell me.'

'So who is Mrs Singer?'

Adela braced herself to tell him. 'She was one of the women from the church adoption society who took John Wesley away.'

Sam dropped his hold and stepped back as if he had been physically struck. 'How did you find her?'

'Through the church.'

'So that's why you've suddenly found religion,' he said with a bitter laugh. 'Why didn't you say so?'

'Why else do you think I go there?' said Adela, willing him to understand.

'But you didn't want me to go with you – not to church – and not to see this Mrs Singer.'

'I didn't want to put you through all this,' said Adela, 'in case nothing came of it.'

'But I am part of this,' Sam protested. 'How can I not be? I'm your husband!'

''Cause I know you don't really want me to find my baby,' Adela cried.

'I've never said that!'

'But it's true – deep down it's true – and I don't blame you, Sam. Finding him can never mean the same to you – and I don't expect it to – though I want you to love him too. But I can't go on any longer pretending that it isn't the most important thing in my life.' She saw him flinch, yet she had to explain or the unhappiness that was gnawing inside her would destroy them both.

'Today I discovered that my son was adopted by a childless French couple – here in Newcastle. I'm so happy to hear that he's not in an institution. Mrs Singer said they were kind people.'

Sam's eyes glistened. 'I'm happy to hear that too.'

'But I don't know anything else – whether he's still in the city – or whether they've taken him back to France.'

'What are you saying?'

'It can't be so hard now to find him,' said Adela. 'At least if they've stayed in Newcastle.'

Sam looked horrified. 'So you're going to pursue him even now? Even though you know he has parents who are looking after him well. Are you going to barge into his life and tell him that these people aren't really his mother and father?'

'No, of course not,' said Adela, 'but I just want to see him . . .'

'Good God, woman! Just listen to yourself. You won't stop at that, will you? You'll carry on with this obsession till you've got him back, no matter who gets hurt in the process. Why can't you just let it rest, now you know that he's with a kind family?'

'You of all people should understand why!' Adela cried. 'Would you rather not have known about your real parents – that you were a Logan? To have gone through your life not knowing you had a loving older sister? Imagine a life without Sophie.'

'That's not fair,' Sam said angrily. 'You know it's not the same. Nobody got hurt by my finding out about Sophie and my parents. But you risk tearing this boy's life apart.'

'I would never do that!' Adela said, wounded by his words. 'How could you think it?'

'I don't know what to think any more,' he growled. 'Except that our marriage appears to mean a lot less to you than it does to me.'

'You know that's not true,' Adela said, tears choking her throat. 'I love you, Sam.'

'Do you?' he demanded. 'Or are you still in love with Sanjay?'

Adela reeled from the accusation. 'Sanjay?' she gasped.

'Yes, the man you had a child with, remember?' He looked at her in fury. 'You've never really got over him, have you? That's why you can't give up on finding his son.'

Adela gaped at him in disbelief. She was so shocked at his suggestion that she could not speak.

Sam clenched his fists. They stood glaring at each other.

'If that's what you think, then just go, Sam,' Adela hissed.

Abruptly his angry expression turned to one of desolation. He spun round on his heels and strode out of the kitchen. Adela wanted to call him back but in seconds the front door was slamming shut behind him. She sank to her knees, buried her face in her skirt and wept.

CHAPTER 18

Belgooree, Assam, June

They huddled around the wireless in the sitting room to hear the announcement. Libby, her stomach in knots, sat close to her father on the sofa, while Harry perched on the arm of his mother's chair. Clarrie had encouraged the servants to come in and listen too. Their *khansama*, Mohammed Din, stood tall and erect behind the sofa, keeping an eye on the others.

Libby watched James warily to see how he would take the news. Her father was still listless and withdrawn at times but he seemed more content since coming to Belgooree and had regained some of his old vitality under Clarrie's attention. It was Clarrie too who had suggested that Breckon be brought over to help revive James's spirits; the dog now lay at his master's feet. But this broadcast from the outside world might set her father back. Lord Louis Mountbatten, the new Viceroy of India, was to make a pronouncement on India's Independence.

Before Libby had left Calcutta she had seen newsreels of the dashing naval officer and his glamorous wife meeting with the top Indian political leaders, Nehru and Jinnah. There had been brief clips of the viceregal couple touring the country with their daughter to witness the devastation that communal violence was bringing to parts of the Subcontinent. There was no sign of the aloofness of viceroys of the past:

the Mountbattens appeared refreshingly unstuffy. Even Gandhi had warmly welcomed them.

Yet here in the hills, Libby felt guilty that she and the family at Belgooree seemed cocooned from the unrest and far removed from the tensions of Calcutta and Bengal. How were Ghulam and Fatima? Libby had eagerly read any copies of *The Statesman* that Harry had brought up from Shillong at the end of the school week to see if there were any articles by Ghulam. There had been one about the council in Calcutta attempting to house Hindu refugees arriving from East Bengal and another covering a heated debate at the council about the future of Calcutta that had led to punches being thrown. But she could glean nothing from the newspapers that told her about how life really was for him and Fatima.

Despite Flowers's encouragement, Libby had not written to Ghulam. Many times she had got out her typewriter with the intention of typing a letter. But she had not even been able to decide on the endearment, let alone pour out her feelings to him. She felt sure he would scoff at any soppiness or be embarrassed by a declaration of love. So no letter had ever gone further than the passionate thoughts in her head.

Libby tried to put Ghulam from her mind and concentrate on the broadcast. The Viceroy was speaking. He was talking about his last two months in India spending every day consulting with as many communities and people as possible.

'Why doesn't he just get on with telling us what's happening?' James fretted.

'Shush, Dad,' Libby said, 'he will do.'

'. . . *a unified India would be by far the best solution of the problem.*'

'Unified India?' James seized on the words. 'Did he say unified? Does that mean—?'

'Dad!' Libby exclaimed. 'Please, just listen.'

Clarrie put a hand on James's arm which calmed him. Libby didn't miss the fond look they exchanged. Mountbatten spoke about India being a single entity with unified communications, currency and services and his hope that communal differences would not destroy this. Libby held her breath. Perhaps there was still a chance that India could remain one country and that the Viceroy had a plan. The room went very still as Mountbatten said he had urged the political leaders to accept the Cabinet mission plan of 1946 which had met the needs of all the communities.

'. . . *To my great regret it has been impossible to obtain agreement either on the Cabinet mission plan or on any other plan that would preserve the unity of India.*'

Libby's brief hope was immediately dashed. The Viceroy continued. There was no question of coercing large communities into living under a government where another community had the majority.

'. . . *and the only alternative to coercion is partition.*'

'Oh, God!' James cried. 'Surely not?'

Libby felt leaden inside as Mountbatten went on to say that because the Muslim League had demanded the partition of India, Congress was demanding the partition of Punjab and Bengal. He, himself, was opposed to both.

'*For just as I feel there is an Indian consciousness which should transcend communal differences, so I feel there is a Punjabi and Bengali consciousness which has evoked a loyalty to their province. And so I feel it was essential that the people of India themselves should decide this question of partition.*'

'What does that mean?' asked Harry. 'Can people vote against it?'

Clarrie held up her hand. 'Listen, he's saying something about Bengal and Assam.'

'. . . *but I want to make it clear that the ultimate boundaries will be settled by a boundary commission and will almost certainly not be identical with those which have been provisionally adopted.*'

'Provisional?' James echoed in bewilderment. 'What provisional boundaries?'

'They must have made an attempt at drawing state borders,' said Libby unhappily. 'So that people have an idea of what partition might look like. How else can they vote on it?'

'Will Assam be split in half too?' Harry asked anxiously.

As they questioned his words, Mountbatten was speaking about the Sikhs and his sorrow to think that the partition of the Punjab would definitely split them but saying that they would be represented on the boundary commission.

'The whole plan may not be perfect, but like all plans its success will depend on the spirit of good will with which it is carried out. I have always felt that once it was decided in what way to transfer power, the transfer should take place at the earliest possible moment . . .'

They listened to him explaining that the British Government would transfer power to either one or two new governments with Dominion status rather than wait a long time for a whole new constitutional set-up for India to be agreed.

'This I hope will be within the next few months. I'm glad to announce that his Majesty's Government have accepted this proposal and are already having legislation prepared . . . Thus the way is now open to an arrangement by which power can be transferred many months earlier than the most optimistic of us thought possible, and at the same time leave it to the people of British India to decide for themselves on their future . . . This is no time for bickering, much less for the continuation in any shape or form of the disorders and lawlessness of the past few months. We cannot afford any toleration of violence. All of us are agreed on that . . . I have faith in the future of India and I am proud to be with you all at this momentous time. May your decisions be wisely guided and may they be carried out in the peaceful and friendly spirit of the Gandhi-Jinnah appeal.'

As soon as Mountbatten finished and handed over to Nehru to speak next, the room erupted with more questions.

'So will there be one India or two countries?' Harry asked.

'Sounds like partition is coming,' said Clarrie.

'He kept saying *if* partition is chosen,' Libby pointed out. 'It's still not a foregone conclusion.'

'I don't see how it can be otherwise,' Clarrie said, her face etched with sadness.

'Mountbatten is washing his hands of it all,' said James in agitation, 'like Pontius Pilate.'

'What else can he do?' Clarrie said. 'He can't get any of the warring sides to agree.'

'He could knock some heads together,' insisted James.

'He could give it more time,' said Libby, annoyed by Clarrie's fatalism. 'He's only been here two months. Gandhi took weeks of talking and listening to get enemies to stop killing each other. Mountbatten hasn't tried hard enough.'

'It's easy to criticise,' said Clarrie, 'when we aren't the ones making the difficult decisions.'

Libby was stung by the remark. 'But he's taking the easy way out by blaming the mess on the other parties and saying Indians will have to decide over partition when he has no other plan.'

Clarrie sighed and sat back, her hand slipping from James's arm. Libby could see she didn't want to argue. How she wished Ghulam was with her as the news was breaking; she longed to know what he was thinking of it all. Would he be hunched around a wireless set with Fatima or listening at work?

'So when *is* Britain going to hand over to the Indians?' Harry asked.

'He talked about months rather than next year,' said Libby. 'Perhaps by the cold season. At least Mountbatten's not reneging on that.'

'Far from it,' said Clarrie. 'And he offered that British officials and officers would stay and help if they were asked.'

'Does that mean we'll be allowed to stay at Belgooree?' Harry's serious expression lightened.

'Of course it does,' said Clarrie. 'It's our home.'

Libby bit back the retort that they didn't even know what country this part of Assam might end up in, let alone if they would be welcome to stay on. But she didn't want to frighten Harry, even if Clarrie's avoidance of the issue irritated her.

'And what about you, Uncle James?' asked Harry. 'Will you carry on at the Oxford like you always have?'

Libby saw doubt flicker across her father's face.

'I don't know,' James said. 'It's all so uncertain . . .'

It shocked Libby to see her father's reluctance; she never thought the day would come when he would contemplate leaving Cheviot View for good. But since coming to Belgooree, he had shown no interest in going back to their home. In fact, he hardly talked about the Oxford at all.

Clarrie was soothing. 'You don't have to make any final decisions yet.' She patted his hand. 'Would you like us to turn off the wireless?'

Libby glanced at the servants behind who were murmuring anxiously amongst themselves.

'Let's hear what Nehru and Jinnah have to say,' Libby suggested. 'We might get more clarity and the servants have a right to hear it.'

She saw Clarrie flush. 'Of course they do; that was selfish of me.'

Nehru was speaking in Hindi. As the others listened intently, Libby didn't like to admit she understood almost nothing of what was said. Then Jinnah spoke in English on behalf of the Muslim League.

'That's because his Urdu's not good enough to address his own people in it,' muttered James.

By the end of the broadcast, Libby was left in no doubt that Jinnah was demanding a separate Muslim state called Pakistan. Ghulam would be desolate at the news; all his worst fears appeared to be coming to fruition.

'But where will this Pakistan be?' asked Harry.

No one seemed able to answer his question. Libby felt a jolt of alarm at the look of consternation on the face of Mohammed Din. The *khansama* was usually so genial, as if nothing could upset his mild nature. Libby wondered if he had family back in the Punjab. She remembered hearing that Mohammed Din – or M.D. as the family affectionately called him – had been Wesley Robson's servant in his bachelor days and had come to work at Belgooree after Wesley and Clarrie's marriage.

At that moment, it hit Libby how huge were the ramifications of the announcement of possible partition. It was too late for political debates in the council chambers or demonstrations in the streets. Partition – that amputation of India that Ghulam and others had spent the last year trying to prevent – was looming. This room was full of people from different communities who didn't know how independence would change their lives. Across the Subcontinent, this same uncertainty must be striking doubt and fear into millions of others.

Later that evening, they sat subdued on the veranda, saying little yet not wanting to retire to the solitariness of their own rooms.

Clarrie tried to rally their spirits with a potful of the new second-flush tea and by playing Wesley's old Gilbert and Sullivan records on the gramophone. James hummed along and shared some in-joke with Clarrie about major-generals. But Harry kept asking questions and probing them for answers.

'What about the princely states? Will they just carry on as before?'

'I suppose so,' said Clarrie. 'The British government can only decide what happens to the bits of India under British rule, not the parts belonging to the maharajahs.'

'So even if Pakistan doesn't happen,' said Harry, 'there won't be just one big India, will there? There'll be India plus lots of separate states.'

'Unless the new India persuades the princes to join the new country,' suggested Libby.

'Why would they do that?' said Harry. 'If I was a maharajah I wouldn't want to give up my land.'

'Their people might want the benefits of being part of a new country with a constitution and citizens' rights,' said Libby, 'so they might be forced to.'

'Or bought off with large pensions,' grunted James.

'What do you think will happen in Gulgat?' asked Harry. 'Will Sanjay want to carry on being rajah and do you think the Khans will stay?'

Libby saw Clarrie stiffen. She felt a pang of pity for the widow: every time Gulgat was mentioned, Clarrie must think of her husband's gruesome death there.

'Why shouldn't the Khans stay?' said James.

'Rafi and Sophie are Muslims,' said Harry. 'Won't they have to go to Pakistan?'

'Of course not,' said Clarrie. 'No one is going to be forced to go if they don't want to.'

Libby's stomach somersaulted at the mention of Ghulam's brother and sister-in-law. In confidence, Ghulam had told her how Rafi had been considering migrating to Pakistan if it became a reality. She wondered how vulnerable Ghulam and Fatima might be in a Calcutta fought over by Hindus and Muslims.

'Ghulam Khan says the new India will be secular,' Libby said stoutly, 'and all faiths and none will be welcome to stay.'

Her father shot her a look. 'A bad dose of wishful thinking,' he muttered.

'So all the violence should stop now,' said Harry, looking happier. 'If all sides are agreeing about the future.'

'Let's hope so, darling,' said Clarrie. 'That's what the leaders are urging.'

Harry nodded. 'Then even if people vote for partition there should be no need for fighting because they'll have got what they want.'

'But I don't believe it is what most Indians want,' said Libby. 'It's a rushed plan. The British should be handing over to a united India and then they can make their own decisions.'

Harry frowned. 'But they're rushing it because of the violence, aren't they? They want to stop the killings.'

Libby looked at Clarrie's young son; he was mature beyond his years. She remembered Harry's father Wesley as being forthright and decisive, organising the children into games and taking a great interest in people. Harry was like his father in more than just looks.

'Let's hope that this announcement will calm things,' said Clarrie, placing a hand gently on her son's head. 'We must pray for a peaceful handover.'

'I wonder when it will be,' said Harry.

Libby smiled at him. 'Perhaps by the time of your fourteenth birthday in October,' she suggested.

'Who knows?' James sighed.

They fell silent, each lost in their own thoughts as the jungle beyond stirred restlessly in the hot night.

❧❧

Startling news reached them a few days later. At the weekend, Manzur arrived unexpectedly from the Oxford bearing *The Statesman* newspaper.

Harry, with Breckon at his heels, went dashing out to meet him. Manzur's handsome face lit up with pleasure as he caught sight of Libby on the veranda steps.

As he approached, he said, 'I didn't think you'd still be here.'

'Why wouldn't I be?'

'The pull of the city . . . ?' He gave her an amused, quizzical look.

Libby smiled. 'I'm a country girl at heart, remember.'

'How is Robson sahib?'

'Snoozing inside. Come up and have a drink. I'll play hostess as Cousin Clarrie is at the factory.'

Libby led him out of the sultry heat into the deep shade of the veranda. Harry followed like his shadow. As Manzur sat down, he handed Libby the newspaper. Her heart lurched.

'Is this a recent edition? Does it tell about Mountbatten's announcement?'

Manzur nodded. 'And the press conference. I thought I'd come over and tell your father in case he hadn't heard.'

'Heard what?'

'The date for the hand-over.' His brown eyes shone with suppressed excitement.

'The day for Independence?' Harry queried.

Manzur nodded.

'When?' Libby's heart began to pound.

'August the fifteenth.'

She stared at him. 'August *this* year?'

He nodded. 'It seems to have caught everyone by surprise.'

'So soon?' Libby gasped. 'But I thought there were to be votes on partition and all sorts of arrangements to be made . . . ?'

Manzur said, 'It will all have to be done in the next few weeks – many Hindu astrologers are saying the date is inauspicious and terrible things will happen if it falls on the fifteenth. It's thrown a cat at the pigeons.'

Despite the gravity of his news, Libby couldn't suppress a smile.

'What is funny?' he asked.

'The expression is to "put a cat among the pigeons",' she said. 'Not throw one at them.'

Manzur gave her a bashful smile. 'Well, it has the same effect.'

'So is this good or bad news?' Harry asked, unsure.

Libby and Manzur exchanged glances. He shrugged.

'It's hard to say,' said Libby.

'Time will tell,' said Manzur, with an expressive gesture of the hands.

Manzur could not linger as the Oxford plantation factory was at full production for the 'second flush' of tea. It surprised Libby that her father showed scant interest in Manzur's updates on the plantation. It was as if he had shut his mind off to the Oxford Estates and didn't want to think about them. When she tried to talk to him about it he grew agitated.

'Manzur and the others can cope without me.'

On the other hand, James seemed more interested in what was going on at Belgooree and in recent days had begun accompanying Clarrie on her early morning rides to inspect the tea garden. Libby was glad that her father was showing a renewed interest in life and regaining some of his former energy. But she couldn't help a twinge of jealousy at these dawn rides and it alarmed her to see him becoming more and more settled at Belgooree and content in Clarrie's company to the exclusion of others.

In dismay, Libby witnessed a deepening fondness between Clarrie and James. What if this grew out of control and her father abandoned any thought of being reconciled with her mother? She had such mixed feelings about her cousin's widow. In childhood she had loved her visits to Belgooree; Clarrie had been so warm-hearted and always made a fuss of Tilly's children. But in those days she had been Wesley's wife and no rival to Tilly in any way; in fact, her father had made critical remarks about Clarrie in front of the children for which Tilly would admonish him.

'*You can't bear the thought of Clarrie being a successful tea planter because she's a woman!*' Tilly accused him.

'*That has nothing to do with it,*' James blustered.

'*Well then, you're a snob, James. You don't like Clarrie because she's not quite pukka.*'

Now that she was grown-up, Libby knew that what her mother had meant was that Clarrie was Anglo-Indian. Her father had carried the usual prejudices of his generation towards those of mixed blood in India, whereas her mother had not. It hadn't struck Libby before that her sense of fairness and justice might have been instilled by Tilly long before the influence of Libby's teacher, Miss MacGregor.

At a distance, Libby was beginning to view her mother differently. She could imagine how overwhelming it must have been for Tilly – at the age that Libby was now and having grown up in a northern city – to come out to this remote part of India. Everything would have been bewilderingly alien: the landscape, the climate, the people, the seasons, the heat and the strict hierarchical rules of a colonial society that lingered in India even though they were changing in the home country.

It was only with the onset of the stifling, pre-monsoon heat that Libby had recalled her mother's plaintive comments: '*It's like sitting in soup*' and '*Oh, for a downpour of cold British rain!*'

Libby remembered her mother's inability to cope with the summer heat, driven to distraction by prickly heat and swollen ankles. None of the family had been sympathetic and Libby had never understood why Tilly had never followed James's advice. '*A morning ride before chota hazri would set you up for the day, my girl. You'll go as mouldy as one of your books if you stew indoors.*'

Her poor mother! Libby felt a twinge of remorse at the way she had berated Tilly for not returning to India with her. Her mother was happy in Newcastle with her many interests and friends. What would she do out here in Assam? Who would be her kindred spirits? There was her mother's old friend Sophie Khan. But Sophie lived a day's drive away from Cheviot View in Gulgat and who knew for how much longer she would remain there? And there was Clarrie. Libby's insides twisted with anxiety. Clarrie was making James's life too easy here. She was not helping James's marriage.

Libby couldn't help feeling sorry for Clarrie: she had lost her husband so cruelly and abruptly, and everyone talked of what a devoted couple Clarrie and Wesley had been. But Clarrie was bound to be lonely and she was still an attractive woman. Libby didn't think Clarrie would be deliberately trying to steal James away from Tilly, but circumstances had thrown them together during the War. Libby was well aware that affairs had been commonplace when couples had been forced apart for years on end. Libby couldn't allow this to happen to her parents.

For the first time since returning to the country of her birth, Libby began to wonder if perhaps it really would be better for James to leave India and return to Britain. Not only his marriage but his health was suffering out here. Unpalatable as it was, she had to admit that her father's mental state was fragile and could probably not be fixed by rest and fresh air alone. Maybe she had been wrong to try and force the family together in Assam. Their childhood idyll could not be recreated – and Libby had to face the uncomfortable truth that Cheviot View might never have been as idyllic as she had remembered.

With her mind in turmoil about how best to deal with her father and their uncertain future, Libby felt in limbo at Belgooree. Being idle did not suit her; she was used to working and being useful and independent. She was torn between staying to keep an eye on her father and returning to her friends in Calcutta to where she might be of some use.

The dilemma prompted her, late one steamy night, to write to Ghulam. Not wanting to disturb the household by tapping on her typewriter, Libby fetched a writing pad, pen and ink and went out on to the veranda. By the light of a hissing kerosene lamp, she drew ink into the fountain pen and began to write. After several attempts to strike the right tone, Libby kept it short and friendly.

Dear Ghulam

How are you and Fatima? I hope both of you are well. I've been thinking about you and wondering what you are making of the announcements from the Viceroy and the other leaders. Are you very disappointed (as I am) at the plans for partition? Or are you pleased that it will all be decided sooner than expected and the tiresome British will be out of your hair in a matter of weeks? It all seems a bit unreal up here in the hills.

My father's health took a turn for the worse about a month ago, so we are staying with Adela's mother at Belgooree while he rests again. He seems to have lost his zest for tea planting and our old home. Perhaps it really is time for him to retire back to England. No doubt you will approve of that!

If you felt like writing back, I'm eager to know what is happening in Calcutta and Bengal. Manzur, my father's assistant manager, brought us a copy of The Statesman recently but otherwise we don't get much news as our wireless is very temperamental. To be honest, I'm going a little mad with boredom here!

I hope the news of your family in the Punjab is good and that they are safe. Please give my fond regards to your sister – and please take good care of yourself.

Libby

She hesitated over that final signing off, wanting to express some endearment but not wanting to embarrass him. She longed to tell him more about her anxieties over her father – her failure to get to the bottom of what troubled him – but decided that was unfair on Ghulam. What could he possibly do or advise? He didn't know her father and none of it was his responsibility. Besides, he must have so many worries of his own.

Later, lying on top of her bed under the mosquito net, Libby wondered whether she should send the letter at all. She got up at sunrise and walked down to the factory office, adding the letter to the office dak before she could change her mind.

In the days that followed, Libby looked out for a return letter from Calcutta but none came. At Clarrie's suggestion, she took to joining her father and Clarrie on their morning rides and accepted Clarrie's offer to join her in the tea-tasting room at the factory. Libby was grateful for the distraction.

'What do you think of our second flush?' Clarrie asked.

Libby sucked the liquid through her teeth like Clarrie did and spat into the spittoon.

'It tastes good,' said Libby, 'though I don't really know what I'm looking for.'

Clarrie smiled. 'Strong body, deep golden colour. More fruity than floral. Bit more earthy than first flush.'

'Dad said you were good at this.' Libby grinned. 'I think my taste buds were ruined by army tea in the War. The judge of a good cuppa was whether the spoon would stand up in it.'

Clarrie laughed. 'Wesley used to talk like that about the tea the troops drank in the Great War.'

Libby felt a sudden pang for the dark-eyed woman. 'What was Cousin Wesley's favourite tea?'

Clarrie gave a wistful smile. 'The autumn plucking when the leaves are more mature and the tea full-bodied. Wesley said it tasted of the monsoon. And he loved that time of year when things grew less hectic in the gardens and there was more time for riding and hunting. We'd take Adela off camping.'

'Both of you did?' Libby asked.

'Yes,' said Clarrie. 'Wesley always insisted on that. We first met when he was out in camp – up the hill from here. That was always our favourite spot—' She broke off, her eyes filling with tears.

Libby said, 'Adela was a lucky girl. Mother wouldn't have gone camping with me and Dad even if you'd promised her tea with the Viceroy.'

'No, she never did like the outdoor life,' agreed Clarrie. 'Dear Tilly.'

Libby eyed her. 'What should I do about Dad?'

'What do you mean?'

'He can't stay here forever,' said Libby, 'but he's showing no signs of wanting to go home – either to Cheviot View or Newcastle.'

Clarrie gave her a considering look. 'Let's talk about this away from the factory,' she said.

Libby's insides tensed as Clarrie led the way out of the building and into the heat. The sky was low and oppressive. The restless sound of insects crackled around them as they walked back towards the bungalow. Clarrie spoke as she walked.

'You think I'm keeping your father here out of selfish reasons?'

Libby flushed. 'I didn't say that.'

'You don't have to,' said Clarrie. 'I know you find it difficult that your father and I . . . that we've grown close as friends. But I can assure you that is all we are – just friends. He helped me when Wesley was killed – in practical ways with the business. Sometimes I sent him away because he fussed too much but I could see it was only because he missed your mother and was lonely. We both gave each other companionship. And I was grateful that he was kind to Harry and arranged for

Manzur to tutor him. It made such a difference to my boy – brought him out of his misery over losing his father. Manzur was so kind and good fun.'

'I'm glad about that,' said Libby. She felt embarrassed at Clarrie's sudden confiding in her and didn't know what to say.

Clarrie led Libby towards the garden at the back of the bungalow, an area beyond the tennis court shaded by large oaks.

'But if you think I'm standing in the way of your father going back to your mother,' said Clarrie, 'then you are wrong. I have been encouraging James to go and see Tilly since the War ended.'

'Then why hasn't he?' Libby asked, baffled.

'I think it frightens him,' said Clarrie. 'Not that he'd ever admit it.'

'Frightened of what?'

'That Tilly might reject him. I suspect it's a matter of pride for James. She chose to stay with her children in England rather than come back out to be with him. He thinks she should make the first conciliatory move.'

'But that's ridiculous,' cried Libby. 'He's punishing Mother for staying with us during the War?'

'I suppose he is in a way,' Clarrie said. 'But don't be hard on him for that. He pleaded with Tilly to come back out to India with you all in the early years of the War. We didn't know then that it would become so dangerous here in Assam. He wanted to keep you all safe and it drove him to distraction that he was powerless to look after you.'

Libby looked at her in astonishment. 'He wanted us all to come back out?'

'Of course,' Clarrie said. 'He was angry with Tilly for staying in Britain where there was imminent danger of invasion. Other tea planters arranged for their wives and families to join them but Tilly wouldn't. I suppose she didn't want to risk the dangerous sea voyage with you all.'

'I didn't know that,' said Libby. It distressed her to think that they could have all returned as a family to Assam years ago. Silently she wondered if it was just the excuse her mother needed to not have to re-join James in India.

'The point is,' said Clarrie, 'that James missed your mother terribly – and coming to Belgooree was a distraction. For a short while he could take his mind off the worry about you all and fuss over me and Harry.'

Libby couldn't help a twist of jealousy that it was Clarrie and Harry who had had her father's attention all those years. She looked at Clarrie.

'You underestimate your importance to Dad. It may have started as a distraction but I can see the way he looks at you. He cares for you and he's come to rely on you too much.' Libby forced herself to go on before she lost her nerve. 'I don't blame you that my father has grown fond of you, Cousin Clarrie, but if he's ever to see my mother again then you have to persuade him to leave here.'

Clarrie's dark eyes filled with sadness. She stood very still, considering Libby's words. 'Yes, you're right,' she said softly. 'Your father is worn out by India. Perhaps the time is right for him to leave. I'll do what I can to make him see he must go back to Tilly. Perhaps she can revive his spirits.'

Clarrie turned. 'Let me show you something.'

She walked a little way off to an area of the garden deep in the trees where roses and jasmine were growing over a trellis. Libby followed. With a start, Libby realised Clarrie was standing by a gravestone. Wesley's name and dates were engraved on it. It was almost the ninth anniversary of his death.

Clarrie looked at Libby. 'This is the only man I have ever loved with all my heart. Even in death. My love for Wesley goes beyond the grave.' She gave a sorrowful smile. 'So you have no need to worry about me falling for your father.'

Libby's throat tightened. She was ashamed of the resentment she had felt towards this brave, big-hearted woman, and hoped she hadn't offended her by speaking her mind. But as they stood gazing at Wesley's final resting place, Libby couldn't help wondering if her father would find it so easy to give up Clarrie and go back to Tilly.

CHAPTER 19

Newcastle, late June

Every conversation that Adela started with Sam seemed to end in an argument. She couldn't forgive him for accusing her of still being in love with Sanjay – that man who had used her for his own gratification and had been the cause of her father's traumatic death! She hated Sanjay and wished she'd never met him. Yet the accusation seeped into her mind like a poison and she found herself thinking about the handsome, selfish prince more and more.

Was there some truth in what Sam suspected? Was her single-minded pursuit of John Wesley partly to do with reclaiming a piece of her former lover? Perhaps, deep down, she still hankered after those heady days in Simla when she had been desired and courted by such a charismatic and wealthy Indian. Adela was aghast at the thought. She refused to believe it. Sam was cruel to even suggest it.

Yet a part of her yearned to be that carefree, fun-loving young woman she had been in India, when nothing had daunted her and everything seemed possible. Life in post-war Britain was so relentlessly drab and anti-climactic after the tumultuous times when she had toured with ENSA during the War. She and her fellow entertainers had encountered danger and hardship, but her time with the Toodle Pips had been one of the happiest in her life, a time when she had looked forward to married life with Sam with such anticipation and joy.

But the reality of married life was proving to be an anti-climax too. Her life was reduced to a daily grind of dragging herself out of bed at dawn to go to the market, long hours supervising in the café, cooking, washing up and then wrestling with the accounts until late into the evening. She was surrounded by people but had never felt so lonely – and with each day, she and Sam seemed to be drifting further apart.

'I think we should move out of Tilly's house,' Sam announced abruptly. It was the end of another tiring day at the café and Adela was looking forward to getting home, kicking off her shoes and helping herself to a drink.

Adela stretched her aching back. Sam had a smut of dry soil on his cheek and smelt of sweat and earth from the allotment. She resisted the urge to lick her finger and wipe his face clean.

'And go where?' she asked.

'To Cullercoats – to my mother's.'

Adela gave a cry of disbelief. 'I'm not moving in with your mother.'

'Well, I am,' Sam said.

She stared at him, wondering if he was joking, but his expression was serious.

'Come with me,' Sam said, though there was no enthusiasm in his voice. 'It's time Tilly had her home back and Mungo shouldn't have to be sleeping in the attic all summer – it's like a furnace up there.'

'Cullercoats is too far from the café,' Adela said, alarmed by the idea. 'I'm not going to spend my petrol ration and what little free time I have driving back and forth. We could move into the attic if you like.'

'You know Mungo won't let us do that,' Sam said. 'He's far too polite. It's time we gave up our room. Besides, Jamie has no bed of his own when he comes home for visits – just a camp bed in the box room.' Sam gave her a look of appeal. 'We never meant to stay this long.'

'I know,' said Adela, 'but Tilly doesn't mind.'

'Well, I do,' Sam said impatiently. 'We shouldn't be taking advantage of her good nature – we should be standing on our own two feet.'

'We'll hardly be doing that by living with your mother!'

'It'll just be temporary until we find a place of our own,' Sam insisted.

'We're as far away from that as the day we set foot back in Britain,' Adela exclaimed.

'But at least we won't be beholden to friends,' he said.

'They're family,' Adela pointed out. 'More than Mrs Jackman is.' She saw him wince at her words and immediately regretted them. 'Sorry, what I mean is—'

'Adela, I'm trying hard to make a go of our marriage,' he said in exasperation, 'and I don't think it's helping living there. We're never alone together – you spend any free time with Tilly or drinking with Josey and avoiding me.'

'And being at your mother's is going to solve that?' Adela cried. 'She monopolises you as it is. I'll be like a spare part.'

'Mother has always been kind to you,' Sam said, sounding hurt.

'Only to humour you,' she retorted. 'What she really wants is you all to herself.'

Sam glowered. 'Well, at least she wants me around – which is more than my wife does.'

'Oh, for goodness' sake, I'm too tired to argue about it!' She pulled off her apron and flung it over a chair. 'You go running to mummy if you want.'

She watched him stalk out of the back door. She felt angry at his stubbornness and yet wretched that his feelings for her seemed to be shrivelling before her very eyes. Adela didn't think he would really go to Cullercoats without her but, two days before Adela's twenty-seventh birthday, Sam went to live with his mother.

When Tilly asked if they were having difficulties, Adela brushed off her concern.

'Sam's just worried about his mother living on her own. It's a temporary move. You don't mind if I stay on here a bit longer do you? We do intend to get our own place – it's just so difficult to find anywhere decent to rent or that we can afford.'

'Of course you can,' said Tilly with a reassuring smile. 'You know I love having you to stay. As long as it's not causing friction between you and Sam.'

'It's nothing we can't work out,' Adela said, turning away quickly so Tilly wouldn't question her further.

In Sam's absence, Adela redoubled her efforts to find out about the French couple who had adopted John Wesley. There was no point questioning the minister as he had only come to the church towards the end of the War. Frustratingly, Mrs Kelly was on holiday visiting her son in Yorkshire for two weeks but when the organist returned, Adela lost no time in asking if she could call on her one evening.

Doris Kelly lived in a ground-floor flat in a terraced row in Sandyford with three cats and a budgerigar. Adela was astonished to see the bird flitting above the furniture while the cats washed their paws and made no attempt to catch it.

'They're all the best of friends,' Doris laughed, leading her into the kitchen. 'Just as the Good Lord intended.'

It was a warm evening and Doris left the back door wide open for the cats to roam in and out; a welcome breeze wafted in. Doris poured two glasses of homemade elderflower cordial.

'My son makes it,' she said with a proud smile. 'He's handy at all sorts, is my Wilfred.'

For a few minutes Adela asked her about her trip to see Wilfred in Yorkshire but soon Doris was quizzing her.

'You never told me about your visit to Lily Singer,' she prompted. 'Did you have a good catch up?'

Adela nodded and took a gulp of her drink. At least it didn't appear that Lily had written to Doris warning her not to speak to Adela. Perhaps Lily feared it would prove she had said too much.

'She was very interesting about her work for the adoption society,' Adela replied. 'We had quite a discussion about that.'

'Lily was always daft about the babies,' said Doris. 'She'd have taken them all in if she could. Some women are natural mothers. I'm more a cat person myself – though I love my Wilfred, of course.'

Adela's heart began to thud, making her breathless. Was *she* a natural mother? How could she be when her first instinct had been to get rid of her child and pretend she had never been pregnant? Yet she felt deep in her being that she *was* a mother – that there would always be an invisible cord tying her to her baby wherever he was in the world. That feeling was so strong that she knew she had to keep asking awkward questions until she found out all there was to know.

Adela took another sip of cordial and said, 'There was another woman like that at the church during the War, wasn't there? A woman who helped with the adopted babies? Mrs Singer said she was French.'

'French?' Doris frowned, trying to remember. She shook her head. 'No, I don't think so.'

Adela's heart plunged. 'Oh, maybe I'm mistaken but I'm sure Mrs Singer said there was a French couple who adopted a baby boy just before the War. The woman was a regular at church – I'm not sure if the husband came that often.'

Mrs Kelly gave her a bemused look. 'What were they called?'

'It's silly of me,' said Adela, 'but I can't remember now what Mrs Singer said.'

One of the cats – a thin tabby – padded in and distracted her mistress.

'Come here, Polly!' Doris picked up the cat and began to stroke her. Polly purred and kneaded Doris's lap with her paws.

Adela feared the woman would change the subject back to cats. 'Mrs Singer said that the Frenchman was swarthy so they found a baby that was suitable.'

Suddenly, Mrs Kelly's eyes widened. 'The ones who took the coloured baby?'

Adela felt herself flushing but nodded agreement.

'Oh, I remember them!' said Doris. 'Yes, they were foreign. Such a nice woman. But they weren't French – though they spoke it.'

'Oh, so what were they?'

'Belgian. He worked on the railways – or built engines – something mechanical – over Birtley way. Now what were they called?' She frowned in concentration and stroked Polly. 'Segal. That's it. Elene Segal was the wife. Can't remember if I ever knew her husband's Christian name.'

'Ah, yes, Segal,' Adela murmured, as if recalling the name too. 'But they don't come to church any more?'

Doris shook her head. 'No, dear, they haven't been for years. Unfortunately, once the original church was bombed we didn't have anywhere to meet so the membership dropped off. And then some got drafted and others moved away. We lost touch with a lot of folk. And the dear chaplain from the Seamen's Mission who used to come and preach – he was killed at sea.'

The woman's eyes welled with tears.

Adela touched her arm in sympathy. 'Yes, I heard he was a kind man,' she said. 'I am sorry.'

A tear dropped on to Polly. The cat leapt down and hurried back outside.

'Did the Segals move too?'

Doris sighed. 'I can't recall. Yes, I think so. I think Elene might have been evacuated with the baby – well he was a little boy by then.'

Adela's heart thumped. 'Do you remember him?'

Doris smiled. 'He was a cheery thing – always smiling and babbling away trying to talk. And his mam was devoted. You would think she was his real flesh-and-blood mother the fuss she made over him.'

Adela's heart ached with a mixture of pride and jealousy.

'But it's possible they might still live in Birtley?' Adela pressed.

'Oh, they didn't live in Birtley,' said Doris. 'That was just where Mr Segal worked. No, they lived in Newcastle.'

'Whereabouts?' asked Adela, trying not to sound too eager.

Doris gave her a look of surprise. 'Why are you so interested in the Segals? Did you know them?'

'No,' Adela admitted, 'but I'm interested in the adoption society. I'd like to do something worthwhile like that.'

'You should ask the pastor about it, dear.'

'Yes, but it would also be useful to talk to mothers who know about these things.'

Adela held her breath, hoping Mrs Kelly would believe her. Or was the organist growing suspicious of her string of questions? Adela felt bad about lying to the woman but it wasn't far from the truth. She did want to talk to this Elene Segal – or at least find out where she lived.

Doris pursed her lips in thought. 'Heaton,' she said. 'They lived in Heaton. Now where was it? Railway Terrace, I think. Yes, Railway Terrace near the goods yard. But there's no knowing whether they're still there. In fact, I'd be very surprised if they were.'

'Why's that?' Adela asked.

'Because she would still have been coming to church, wouldn't she?' Doris shook her head. 'No, I think it more likely they were evacuated – or moved with his job. I was away in Yorkshire a lot of the War looking after Wilfred's young ones but the Segals had gone by the time I came back. I've never seen or heard of them since.'

'You're probably right,' Adela agreed, trying not to show disappointment.

'Or there's the other possibility,' Doris mused. 'They might have gone back to Belgium when the War ended.'

Adela's chest tightened at the painful thought. If that was the case, it would be almost impossible to find her son.

Doris pressed her to stay for a cup of tea and a biscuit. Adela realised that there was no Sam at home to nag her about staying out late, so she accepted. They talked about other things; Doris was interested to hear about her growing up in India.

As she got ready to go, Adela turned the conversation to the Segals one last time. She was plagued by one question in particular.

'What did the Segals call their baby?' she asked.

Doris frowned in thought. 'Let me think.'

Adela went very still, even though her heart was hammering. She thought it unlikely they would have kept his real name, yet she hoped unrealistically that they had.

'Jacques, I think it was,' said Doris. 'Maybe it was Mr Segal's name.'

Adela nodded, her throat suddenly too tight to speak. It may have been the adoptive father's name but it was also the French name for John. Adela's eyes prickled with emotion and she made a hurried departure, afraid that she would break down crying in front of Mrs Kelly.

꧁ ꧂

It was after nine o'clock but still light when Adela left Mrs Kelly's flat. Full of a restless energy, she began walking in the direction of Heaton and the railway line. She couldn't wait another day to discover if the Segals still lived in Railway Terrace. She wouldn't knock on anyone's door; she would just walk the street and casually look around. What if she were to spot John Wesley playing in the street?

Adela's heart pumped and her stomach churned with nervous excitement. She had gone to Mrs Kelly's expecting to find out little about a nameless French couple, not wanting to raise her hopes too much. But the friendly organist had given her a precious gift. Not only did Doris remember John Wesley as a cheerful, engaging baby called Jacques, but she had told her where he lived.

As Adela walked briskly in the soft twilight, she felt a clash of emotions about the Segals. She was grateful that such a caring couple were bringing up her son. Both Lily and Doris had had nothing but warm words for the Belgian couple. She tried to imagine what they looked like. Perhaps Elene was dark-haired like she was. Would Mr Segal be as handsome as Sanjay? Adela thought that was unlikely.

It was unsettling thinking of her former lover. The only good thing that had come out of their brief, intense affair had been their beautiful baby. But now another couple would spend a lifetime bringing him up. A sharp stab of envy made Adela stop and clutch her stomach as if she'd been winded.

Two women standing gossiping on a nearby doorstep stopped and stared.

'You all right, hinny?' one called out.

Adela gulped for breath. 'I'm fine,' she gasped, trying to control the palpitations in her chest. 'Just walking too quickly.'

'I'll fetch you a cup o' water,' the woman said and dived into the house before Adela could refuse.

A minute later, Adela was gulping at the tepid water the kind woman had brought her. 'Thank you.' She gave her a grateful smile.

'You're not from round here, are you?' the older neighbour asked.

'No,' said Adela. 'I'm looking for Railway Terrace.'

'You're the wrong end of Heaton, hinny,' said the bearer of the water. She gave Adela directions.

Adela set off, annoyed at herself for not asking the way sooner. She had been in such a state after her visit to Doris Kelly that she hadn't been thinking straight and had headed in the vague direction of the railway line.

Perhaps she should give up and come back in full daylight when there would be people about and children playing in the street. Yet she was so close now that she couldn't give up the hunt.

Twenty minutes later, Adela was standing at the end of a street proclaiming itself as Railway Terrace. It was identical to the streets on either side: soot-blackened red-brick rows with neat lace-curtained windows and uniform doors. Pulse quickening, she set off down it, looking eagerly from side to side, though she wasn't sure what clues would tell her where the Belgians might be living.

Halfway down the street, the houses came to an abrupt stop and open waste ground took over. In the half-light, she could see the earth was pock-marked with craters and strewn with piles of brick and rubble like crude temples. A large part of the street had been bombed and not rebuilt. At the far end, factory sheds clustered around a railway siding.

Doris's words came to her clearly: *'Railway Terrace near the goods yard.'*

Adela realised in horror that this was the end of Railway Terrace where the Segals had lived with John Wesley. She gasped aloud. 'Please don't say he's dead!'

She picked her way across the bomb site, scouring the ground, as if she would suddenly come across some evidence that they had been here. Perhaps she would find the precious pink swami's stone that she had bundled into the baby's blanket as a good luck charm when they'd come to take her son away. Her mother had given it to her as a talisman: *'I want you to wear it and always be under the swami's protection and my love.'* Adela had treasured the stone and it had been all she could think of to give John Wesley as a token of her love.

As Adela searched fruitlessly, she knew how ridiculous she was being. She made herself stop and take deep breaths. She didn't know for sure if the Segals' house had been bombed and even if it had, that didn't mean anyone had died in the raid. They might have been rehoused nearby. Or they might have moved away from Railway Terrace before the bombing. An hour ago, she had felt jealous of the Belgians who were raising her child. Now she prayed fervently that they were alive and well and looking after her son somewhere safe.

Her emotions in shreds, Adela turned for home. She would return another day and make enquiries about them. She had to believe John Wesley was alive – the alternative was too unbearable to contemplate.

It was the following week before Adela was able to get away from the café and return to search Railway Terrace. She told no one what she was planning to do – least of all Sam. They only spoke to each other about the running of the café and allotment: mundane arrangements as if they were merely business partners and not husband and wife. He brought in the baking that his mother did, muttering that his mother was tiring of the travelling and preferred to stay at home.

On the day she was planning to slip off early to go to Heaton, Sam caught her attention.

'You might have to find someone else to make the pies,' he said, glancing warily at Adela. 'Mother is finding it's getting too much for her.'

'That's all we need!' Adela said in exasperation.

'You'd be better off finding someone younger and more local anyway,' Sam suggested, before leaving swiftly for the allotment.

Adela felt overwhelmed by responsibility for the café; when would it ever stop?

'It's always me who has to sort out the problems,' Adela complained to Doreen. 'Mother must have had the patience of a saint to run this place.'

'He's right, you know,' said Doreen forthrightly. 'Mrs Jackman's not reliable – she comes in when it suits her and you've never got on with her in the kitchen. We need a proper cook who can do the whole menu.'

Adela sighed, knowing Lexy's grand-niece was speaking sense.

'You're the only one I can rely on around here,' said Adela, swinging an arm around Doreen's shoulder. 'Don't you go leaving me for some office job too soon, will you?'

'Shan't promise,' Doreen said with a teasing smile. 'Would you like me to have a word with Lexy and Mam? I bet they can find a suitable lass.'

'Would you?' Adela asked in relief.

'Aye, of course,' the waitress agreed. 'Then maybe's you and Sam will have one less thing to argue over.'

Adela blushed with guilt. Was it so obvious to everyone that she and Sam were not getting on? She dismissed the thought. She had too much else to think about. Sam would soon tire of living at Cullercoats and once she had tracked down the Segals, she would have more time to repair her unravelling marriage.

Adela approached a group of boys playing football with a tin can on the bomb site in Railway Terrace. Pulse racing, she searched their faces for any similarity to her or Sanjay but found none. They paused in their game, eying her in curiosity.

'What d'yer want, Missus?' demanded a red-haired youth who looked older than the others.

'Do any of you know a boy called Jacques?' she asked. She hadn't meant to come straight out with such a direct question but the boy had asked and he looked old enough to have remembered people who had lived round there before the War.

'Jack who?'

'Jacques Segal.'

The boy laughed. 'Jack Seagull? Na, there's neebody here called that!'

Another boy made a squawking bird noise and the others started laughing too.

Adela smiled. 'It's a Belgian name. He'd be eight years old. I know they lived in this street in the early part of the War.'

'Sorry, Missus, never heard o' him.' The red-headed boy turned away.

Adela's heart sank. Perhaps Doris Kelly had remembered the street incorrectly.

'There were them people who talked foreign, remember, Micky?' said the squawking boy. 'Lived at number twenty-eight. Me mam used to speak to the wife.'

'Oh, aye,' said his friend, 'they were Frenchies or some'at.'

'That could be them,' Adela said, hope flaring. 'Which is twenty-eight?'

The older youth, Micky, pointed at one of the piles of rubble. 'Right there, Missus.'

Adela's worst fears were confirmed. 'Do you know if they survived the bombing?'

'Divn't kna,' said Micky with a shrug. 'But Billy's mam might remember.'

'Aye,' his friend agreed. 'Me mam knew everyone in the street before the War.'

'Would she speak to me?' Adela asked.

'If you give me a tanner,' intervened Micky, 'I'll tak' you to Billy's mam's.'

'She's my mam not yours,' Billy protested. 'I should get the tanner.'

'It's my can,' said Micky, picking up the battered tin they were using as a football. 'And I say who gets to play wi' it.'

Swiftly, Adela fished out a coin each for Billy and Micky. 'You can both take me, please.'

The other boys whooped and hollered behind the two leaders as they led Adela back up the street to Billy's house. Adela was ushered into a dark passageway as Billy called out, 'Mam! Someone to see yer!'

'Well, bring them in,' a voice replied. 'Unless it's the Grim Reaper.'

Adela found herself in a narrow galley kitchen that smelt of boiling vegetables, facing a wiry woman in a faded apron. She gaped at Adela.

'You didn't tell me it was Vivien Leigh!'

Adela laughed, despite her nervousness. 'I did used to work for ENSA,' she joked. 'But my name's Adela.'

'Eeh, hinny, has our Billy gone and smashed yer car window or owt? He's that clumsy. He'll have to pay for it with odd jobs, 'cause I haven't got the money—'

'Mam!' Billy protested. 'I've done nowt wrong.'

'No, it's nothing like that,' Adela reassured her. 'Billy's just trying to help me track down some people who used to live in the street. He thought you might know them.'

'Try me,' said the woman, wiping her hands on her apron.

Adela explained who she was looking for.

'Oh, aye, the Belgians,' she said with a nod. 'Canny couple. He worked over the river. Terrible thing, the bombing. I was on nightshift and Billy was evacuated up Alnwick way, thank heaven.'

Adela forced herself to ask. 'So were the Segals caught in the bombing or did they escape it too?' She could hardly breathe as she waited for the answer.

The woman gave her a pitying look and shook her head. 'House took a direct hit. Caught in the shelter so I heard. Didn't stand a chance of getting out.'

Adela felt nauseated. She put her hand to her mouth to smother a sob.

'Eeh, hinny, you've lost all your colour,' said Billy's mother. 'Sit yersel' doon.'

She pulled out a stool. Adela sank on to it, trembling.

'I'm sorry if it's a shock. Were they friends of yours, hinny?'

Adela felt completely numb. All she could think about was the randomness of a bomb falling on the very place where her son was living. Her mind filled with horrific images: the Segals grabbing John Wesley and hurrying to the shelter – fearful, praying, clutching each other tight – while the small boy wailed in fright. Would they have felt anything as the blast ripped them to pieces? Did they all die at the same time or did her son linger on, terrified and consumed with pain and completely alone?

'They would have died instantly,' said Billy's mother, as if reading her dark thoughts. 'No time to suffer.' She patted Adela's hand. 'A crying shame. And such a bonny bairn they had an' all.'

Adela let out a howl and doubled over, clutching her sides. Nothing the woman said could comfort her. As quickly as she could, Adela left, mumbling her thanks, and fled from the house, the gang of boys staring at her in astonished alarm as she ran up the street.

⁂

'Wherever have you been?' Tilly asked when Adela finally returned home late that night. It was dark but Tilly and Josey were in the sitting room waiting up for her.

'I'm not sure,' Adela said, numb and weary. 'Just wandering . . .'

Josey steered her into an armchair. 'You look terrible. What's happened? Have you had another row with Sam?'

'Sam?' Adela said in confusion. It occurred to her that she hadn't thought about her husband for hours – not since she'd learnt the shocking news of John Wesley's death. She closed her eyes. She couldn't think about Sam – couldn't contemplate the idea that he might be relieved her relentless search was over.

'So you haven't been to Cullercoats?' prompted Tilly.

Adela shook her head.

'Then where?' demanded Josey.

'Do you want to talk about it?' Tilly said more gently.

Adela felt her chest tighten in grief. 'No . . . yes.' She leant forward, face in hands, and burst into fresh tears.

'Darling girl!' Tilly rushed to comfort her.

Adela groped for her and buried her face in Tilly's plump shoulder. 'How can I bear it?' she wept.

'Bear what?' Josey asked.

'My baby!' Adela wailed. 'My darling boy!'

'What baby?' Tilly asked, baffled. 'Are you pregnant?'

Adela let out an anguished sob and pulled away. 'No . . .' She looked at Josey in distress and saw realisation dawn on her friend's face.

Josey went straight over to the drinks cabinet and poured out a large whisky.

'You've had a shock, haven't you?' she said, thrusting the glass at Adela. 'Drink this down and then you can tell us.'

'Tell us what?' Tilly frowned in concern. 'Josey, what do you know that I don't?'

'Adela can tell you,' said Josey.

Adela shook her head.

'Best to get it all off your chest,' Josey said. 'Tilly's been such a support to you; she deserves to be put in the picture.'

Adela gulped at the whisky and spluttered at its fiery taste. She took another mouthful and almost instantly began to feel calmer. The women waited for her to speak, Tilly's expression fearful.

Hesitantly at first, Adela began to unburden herself of the shameful secret she had kept from Tilly for so long. When Tilly exclaimed in shock, Josey silenced her and encouraged Adela to continue. Soon, Adela was pouring out her feelings about her lost baby and her increasing desperation to try and find him.

'So is that what has been the cause of the rift between you and Sam?' asked Tilly.

Adela nodded. 'He can't bear that I wanted my son back more than anything else in the world – even him.'

'Poor Sam,' said Tilly, 'and poor you.'

'So what has happened today,' pressed Josey, 'that has made you so upset?'

Adela told them about going to Railway Terrace and her terrible discovery about the death of the Segals. She dissolved into tears again.

'I don't think I can b-bear the pain,' Adela sobbed. 'I always believed . . . deep down . . . I'd get John Wesley b-back.'

Josey sighed. 'That's the real reason Adela came back to England – and dragged Sam with her.' She gave Tilly a rueful look. 'Sorry – I don't like having secrets, but Adela asked me not to tell you.'

Adela met Tilly's look, and was pained at the shocked expression she saw on her friend's face. She made an effort to calm down and explain.

'Mother and Lexy know too,' Adela said, 'and Joan found out. But I couldn't bring myself to tell you, Tilly. I knew you'd think less of me.'

Tilly was staring at her as if she were trying to work out who she really was.

'I'm so sorry,' whispered Adela. 'I shouldn't have made Josey keep secrets from you.'

'It's terrible what you've discovered,' said Josey, 'but at least now you know – and it was the not-knowing that was eating away at you, wasn't it? The whole thing is an awful tragedy. But you still have Sam. Perhaps now you can begin to patch things up with him before it's too late.'

'What do you mean, too late?' Adela asked, with a prick of alarm. 'Things aren't that bad between us—'

'Where did you say the Segals lived?' Tilly suddenly interrupted. 'Railway Terrace?'

'Yes,' said Adela, feeling her queasy grief return at their mention.

'And they were from Belgium?'

'Yes. Why . . . ?'

'I was on ARP duty the night of the bombing,' Tilly said, a strange look on her face. 'I was one of the first on the scene at that street near the railway yard.'

Something about Tilly's words made the back of Adela's neck prickle.

'And?' said Josey.

'There was a Belgian couple dead in a shelter in a back yard – the warden wouldn't let me go and look – but he came out carrying an infant – covered in dust but alive . . .'

'Alive?' Adela gasped.

'Yes, and unharmed.'

'Was it a boy?' Adela asked, her ears drumming.

'He was,' Tilly answered. 'I remember taking him back to the relief centre and worrying about what would happen to him without his parents – and thinking that the rest of his family might be in Belgium and wouldn't be able to look after him. It stuck in my mind that he was Belgian.'

Adela grabbed on to Tilly, trembling. 'You held my baby?'

Tilly clutched Adela. 'I must have done.'

'What happened to him?' Adela demanded. 'Can you remember? Please try!'

Tilly's eyes filled with pity. 'I'm sorry, I don't know.'

Adela was seized by fresh hope. 'Can you find out? There must be records. He must have gone somewhere.'

'Adela!' Josey chided. 'We don't even know if it was your boy. They can't have been the only Belgians living in Heaton.'

'I know it's him,' said Adela.

'Don't put yourself through any more upset—'

'Please, Tilly,' Adela urged, ignoring Josey's appeal, 'can you try and find out?'

Tilly gave Josey a helpless look.

'Tilly,' Adela pleaded, 'you've held my baby boy in your arms. You must know how my arms ache for him! I can't live without knowing whether it was him.'

Tilly pulled Adela into a hug. 'I'll try, dear girl. But don't get your hopes up.'

Josey gave a sigh of disapproval and walked out of the room.

CHAPTER 20

Belgooree, late June

*D*ear Libby
I was surprised but pleased to receive your letter out of the blue. I'm sorry for not replying sooner but I've been away in East Bengal covering stories for the paper and didn't get your letter until my return this week.

By now you will probably have heard that both the Legislative Assemblies in Bengal and Punjab have voted for partition. It is a catastrophe. I am not just disappointed but angry. The country that I have campaigned for all my adult life – a free, democratic, secular India for all Indians, unshackled from the yoke of British rule – is never to be.

I have already seen the turmoil this is bringing to Bengal – there is a new wave of refugees on the move from the east to the west of the state. The Hindus don't feel safe staying in the east when they know they will be under Muslim rule in a few weeks' time – though no one knows where the border is actually going to be and this is beginning to cause panic. Also there is to be a referendum in Assam over Sylhet – but you probably already know that. It's a foregone conclusion – the majority Hindus will vote to get rid of Sylhet and its Muslim population. So no doubt you will see Muslim workers on the move from Assam into East Bengal in the weeks to come.

My editor is a decent man but he isn't interested in lots of bad news stories from East Bengal. Perhaps I won't have a job for much longer. Still, I can always find other work with my pen and my loud mouth – as my sister keeps reminding me. No doubt you, as a good socialist, would also add that I have rich relations in Gulgat and Lahore who will bail me out if, like the Prodigal Son, I go cap in hand and beg forgiveness.

It was kind of you to ask after my family. Fatima assures me they are all safe and well. She has heard from our older sister Noor.

I'm sorry to hear that your father's health is still a worry but if the time has come for him to return home then I'm glad to hear he will be handing over to an Indian assistant. That shows foresight. Who is this Manzur you write about? I seem to remember you mentioning him to me once before.

What do you intend to do, Libby? Will you go home with your father? If so, I hope that Fatima and I will have the chance to see you in Calcutta before you leave.

Kind regards
Ghulam

Libby had read the letter a dozen times since it was delivered to the house that afternoon by Nitin, a grinning Khasi youth and a grandson of Banu, the tea garden overseer. She could hear Ghulam's voice in her head as she committed his words to memory, his tone serious one moment and sardonic the next.

He was pleased to hear from her and wanted to see her again – even if it was only briefly on her way back to England. But was he just being polite or was there warmth behind the words? He sent his 'kind regards', not just 'yours sincerely' or some other formal farewell.

Unable to keep still, Libby went for a ride through the gardens despite the sapping heat. There had been a few rumbles of thunder in recent days but no real let-up to the oppressive atmosphere. The monsoon was late this year.

After half an hour, she reached the glade where Clarrie had taken her on a previous ride to show where she had first met Wesley and where the family had liked to camp. The ruins of an ancient temple lay strewn across the clearing, close to a stream and a hut with a fallen-in roof where a holy man had once lived. Later, the swami's dwelling had been occupied by Adela's old ayah whom Libby remembered from childhood visits to Belgooree. Her brothers had been frightened of the wrinkled old woman but Libby had been fascinated by her and often sat with her and listened to her high-pitched singing. Ayah Mimi still lived in the compound at Belgooree, though she was very old and virtually a recluse. Only Clarrie was encouraged to visit her.

Despite being armed with a rifle, Libby found the solitary camping site unnerving; the jungle was alive with squawking birds and animals rustling. The cloud was low and hid any mountain views. It wasn't a burial ground and yet it had the feel of somewhere peopled with ghosts from the distant past. Libby shivered; she preferred the company of the living. She pulled out Ghulam's letter from where she'd tucked it beneath her blouse. She imagined his dextrous hands folding the paper and pushing it into the envelope, and his tongue licking the gum. Her yearning for him was suddenly overpowering. He had asked her questions so she had an excuse to reply to him. Kicking her pony into a trot, Libby hurried away from the swami's dell.

Dear Ghulam

I was so pleased to get your letter yesterday. I wish I could whisk you here on a magic carpet so that you could tell me in person about your travels in East Bengal. It annoys me that your editor is not interested in your reporting but I suppose your newspaper is biased towards what goes on in Calcutta and what they think will interest the English-speakers.

I hope that you keep your job and don't have to go begging to your father like the Prodigal Son. Who would be the jealous older brother? Not Rafi – I know he wouldn't begrudge you anything. But to be a prodigal presupposes that you've had a riotous time in Calcutta, spending a fortune and thinking only of your own pleasure. I don't know you well, but you don't strike me as a man who has lived anything remotely akin to a debauched life. Although you do have a weakness for cigarettes and Scottish toffees.

My father still won't face up to what he should do next. I'm worried about him. Both Clarrie and I are urging him to return to Britain to see my mother and brothers – even if it's just for a spell of leave. I think he is coming round to the idea that he may not be going back to work at the Oxford – he really does seem to agree that his days as a planter are over, even if his ones in India aren't. I feel I must stay here and help him until he decides what to do.

You ask about Manzur. He is my father's assistant manager at the Oxford and a very able man. He wanted to be a teacher but my father offered to train him as a planter and his parents encouraged it. Manzur's father is our bearer at Cheviot View and his mother was my ayah.

No doubt you will roll your eyes at such colonial exploitation but believe me when I say that Ayah Meera was the person I loved most as a child.

My mother was so grateful to Meera for her help with us children that she encouraged my father to put Manzur through school. Manzur and my brother Jamie were like brothers, always playing together and teasing me when I tried to join in. Of course, when Jamie was sent back to England to school they could no longer be best friends.

But Manzur is still just as friendly as I remember. Perhaps he will end up being a teacher one day – he's very enthusiastic but also patient with people. During the War he used to come over to Belgooree and tutor my cousin Harry as Clarrie didn't want to send him away to school so soon after Harry's father had died. I think I told you about Wesley being killed by a tiger on a hunt in Gulgat, didn't I? He saved Adela's life but died of his wounds. I think the family are still struggling to get over his loss.

Anyway, that's probably more information than you ever wanted to know about Manzur and my family. Is it unbearably hot in Calcutta? I wish I could go and drink ice-cold nimbu pani with you at Nizam's. Do you still go there?

I think of you often.

Warm regards

Libby

When Libby walked down to the factory to hand in her letter for posting, she went looking for Clarrie and found her in the withering shed with her factory manager, Daleep. The noise of the vibrating belts and pounding machinery drowned out their conversation but they were looking concerned. Clarrie waved at her and mouthed she would be five minutes.

'Is everything all right?' Libby asked, when Clarrie joined her in the shade of a peepal tree.

'Yes,' said Clarrie. 'Well, mostly. Daleep is worried about the situation deteriorating in Assam – not knowing whether we'll still be part of India come August. It could affect our trade – if the railways or waterways are cut off by a new border, that sort of thing.'

'Are you worried too?' asked Libby.

'My feeling is that whatever country we end up being in, they will still need tea – either for the domestic market or to trade for foreign currency. As long as we still have access to the auction houses we'll survive. And that will be up to agents like Strachan's to act as brokers.'

'But what about politically?' Libby said. 'Are you worried about this vote over Sylhet and workers being displaced?'

Clarrie sighed. 'I don't think it will affect us at Belgooree whatever the outcome – our workers are mainly Khasi and there's little communal tension here in the hills. It might be a different matter at the Oxford Estates and the bigger tea gardens where there are much larger numbers of migrant labourers. But . . .'

'But what?'

'I think this area will stay as part of India – we are too far from Sylhet to be affected. But my worry would be for the Muslim labourers left in Assam.'

Libby felt sudden alarm. 'Do you mean Aslam and his family might be in danger?'

'I'm sure they won't be,' said Clarrie hastily, 'but until everything is clearer, they are bound to be worried.' She put a hand on Libby's arm. 'I think it best not to talk about this to your father – it'll only make him fret more.'

Libby was struck again by how much Clarrie cared for her father, even though she had so many other concerns. It made her more determined to say what she'd come to say.

'I won't mention any of this,' said Libby, 'but I haven't come to talk about Dad.'

She saw a flicker of relief cross Clarrie's face. 'Oh?'

'I want to be more help to you while I'm here,' said Libby, 'around the garden or the office. I don't want to take anyone else's job away from them but just do some helping out. I'm very organised and I'm good at accounts; I can type – I was teaching typing to Lexy's grand-niece before I left Newcastle. Or I could help muck out the horses – anything.'

'Dear Libby! But don't you want to spend your time with your father?'

Libby grimaced. 'I think I'm getting on his nerves, being around all the time.'

'Don't think that,' said Clarrie. 'James is very fond of you.'

Libby shrugged. 'Yes, but I think I also irritate him. The sad thing is we don't seem to have very much in common any more.'

Clarrie squeezed Libby's arm. 'Adela and Wesley used to go hammer and tongs at each other from time to time – he could be overprotective and she was impulsive – but deep down they adored each other.'

Libby felt her insides twist. 'But they saw each other lots while Adela was growing up and that makes all the difference. Dad and I missed out on that and I don't think we'll ever have that closeness.'

'Give it time,' Clarrie said, her look compassionate. 'And I'd be glad of your help. That's very kind of you.'

'No it's not. I'm at a loose end and feeling bad about not doing my share of the work here.'

Clarrie gave her a broad smile. 'You are very like your father in that.' She slipped an arm through Libby's and steered her towards the factory buildings. 'Well, there's something I can think of straight away.'

'What's that?'

'Banu's grandson Nitin is helping in the office now. He's a quick learner and will make a good *mohurer* one day. But it would be very useful if he could type. Would you consider teaching him?'

Libby brightened. 'Of course I would.'

They smiled at each other.

'Good,' said Clarrie. 'Come and have a word with him now. You can start this afternoon.'

Calcutta

'There's another letter for you,' said Fatima, holding up an envelope, 'from Assam.'

Ghulam felt the heat rise into his jaw at his sister's enquiring look. He always felt like the naughty younger sibling when she scrutinised him through her spectacles, even though he was four years her senior. He tried not to show his excitement.

'Oh?'

'So you wrote back to Libby?' she asked.

'I thought it polite . . .' Ghulam threw off his jacket. His shirt stuck to his torso. He had lived in Calcutta for years but he had never quite got used to the draining humidity of the hot season.

'Tea?' said Fatima.

'I'll go and wash first,' Ghulam said, hastily plucking the letter from her hand.

He went to his room and stripped off his sweat-soaked clothes. Padding to the washroom, he scooped tepid water from the bucket and dowsed himself. He let out a sigh of relief as the water trickled over his hair and down his body. All the time, he savoured the thought of the unopened letter propped on the table next to his bed, wondering at its contents. Would it be a few polite lines confirming that Libby was leaving for England? Or would she confide in him further? He had felt that in her first letter, Libby had held herself in check, unsure of the response she would get. Had she expected him to rebuff her? As it turned out, she had waited weeks for a reply. He had felt bad about that and had written at once to explain his silence.

So why had he replied? Since she had left for Assam, he had tried so hard to put the vivacious Libby from his mind by cramming his days with work and political lobbying. But come the long, unbearable nights, Ghulam had been unable to banish thoughts of her sensual beauty. He had not craved a woman like that since his passionate, tempestuous affair with Cordelia. But that had ended in bitter wrangling and her devastating accusation that he was a traitor to the cause of freedom for India. He had thought he would never recover from the hurt and certainly never imagined he would ever feel such attraction again. He had not wanted to; he had sworn to close off his heart to such pain and dedicate his life to his socialist ideals. Then Libby had burst into his life like a monsoon storm and knocked him over.

He gave a dry laugh at the irony of it. For over half his life he had fought the British for independence in any way he could: protests both peaceful and violent, boycotts, seditious speeches, imprisonment and passive resistance. Yet on the eve of grasping *Swaraj* – freedom – he had fallen in love with a Britisher.

If God existed then he had a sense of humour. But try as he did to overcome his desire, Ghulam was left sleepless by the memory of Libby in a green satin evening gown, with her auburn hair rippling over her bare shoulders and her mouth curving in a generous smile. Those kissable lips.

Ghulam dried his hair vigorously on a thin cotton towel. He retreated to his room and pulled on a simple white kurta and drawstring trousers. Then, with fingers trembling in anticipation, he reached for Libby's letter and opened it.

Belgooree

Libby poured over Ghulam's second letter.

My dear Libby
I was delighted to get your letter by return. I too wish I could climb on a magic carpet and be transported to the hills – the relief from the Calcutta heat would be welcome. We alternate between dust storms and a few listless drops of rain that can't really be bothered to fall.

But more than that, it would be very agreeable to land on the lawn at Belgooree and take tea beside you. This would have to be done out of sight of your father who, no doubt, would be disapproving of his precious daughter consorting with such a Prodigal. I wonder, does he even know we are corresponding?

You are quite right in spotting my faults – a misspent adulthood of excessive toffee-eating and a weakness for tobacco have been my undoing. Those two – and perhaps a third: finding myself distracted from work by thoughts of a pretty Britisher with red hair and a taste for nimbu pani.

Manzur sounds a worthy young man. I suppose it was my own fault for asking about him, but little did I expect that he would take up over half your letter. Do you berate him for selling out to the capitalist system by accepting a managerial post in a tea company? I fear you are probably far too kind to him and offer him toffees instead.

Tell me more about Belgooree. I have never been to the Khasia Hills, though my brother Rafi tells me they

*are beautiful and the people are good-humoured cattle
herders.*

> *My fond regards,*
> *Ghulam*
> *PS The India Independence Bill is to be introduced
> into the House of Commons in London next week.
> Assuming that the Indian-hating Churchill doesn't try
> to sink it, then it should be full steam ahead.*

Libby could hardly contain her glee at Ghulam's second letter. It was so much more playful – even flirtatious – than the first and she wondered if he had written it after chewing paan. He didn't drink liquor but she had heard how the betel nut narcotic could also have a stimulating effect on the senses. Whether he had or not, to Libby the words were intoxicating. Could it be that Ghulam was a little bit jealous of her friendship with Manzur? Or was he just teasing her with his jesting comments about capitalist tea planters and toffees? She traced her finger over the closing endearment: fond regards.

Libby sensed that a shift in their relationship was taking place, a deepening of feeling which they could express in writing but had been unable to say face-to-face. She kissed the letter and slipped it into the pocket of her dress.

Calcutta

As the city broiled in oppressive heat and the tension between communities rose daily, Ghulam took to sleeping on the flat roof of Amelia Buildings. Lying on the old lumpy bedroll that he had carried all over northern India in his campaigning days, he smoked and looked up at the sky. Sometimes the clouds cleared to show a scattering of stars. On other nights the sky glowed an ominous red from distant fires – whether started deliberately or from the accidental catching fire of bleached-dry grass and timbers, he couldn't be sure. If only the rains would come and bring relief – and cool off rising tempers too; this heat was enough to send the sanest of men mad.

Ghulam pulled out the latest letter from Libby. He didn't like to keep re-reading it in front of Fatima. His sister didn't approve of his corresponding with the Robson girl. *'She's too young for you – and it's not fair to lead her on. Nothing can come of it. With the worsening situation here, she'll probably decide to go back to England soon, just like Adela did. Don't give her false hope, brother.'*

Was that what he was doing: giving her false hope? Ghulam searched his heart. It was true that he was flattered by Libby's attraction towards him. He had never thought of himself as handsome, unlike his brother Rafi who had been gifted the even features and white-toothed smile of a matinee idol. But Libby was the first woman since Cordelia who had excited his interest, not only physically but also because she shared so many of his ideals and a droll sense of humour.

Wasn't that more important than them coming from the same background? It would be hypocritical, surely, to spout about freedom and democracy for India but refuse Libby's friendship because she was British and he was Indian. She had once taken him to task for his reverse snobbery in dismissing the Anglo-Indian and European minorities as being of less importance than Indians. At the time, he had smarted at the accusation that he was being just as prejudiced as the British or Mahasabha Hindus, but later had seen the truth in it. Ghulam pulled on his cigarette.

Friendship? Was that what they were offering each other: purely friendship? He felt a familiar tug in his guts as he thought of her. He knew he wanted more, but what did Libby want? He remembered the way she had kissed him in the taxi; the supressed desire had been palpable, though he had denied it at the time. Would they ever get the chance to act on it? That was another matter.

Perhaps this letter-writing was all a pleasant distraction from worrying about the uncertain future and the imminent British handover. They were hurtling towards the August deadline and yet there was no clarity on where partition would be and there were still referenda to be held in Assam and the North West Frontier over their futures. In the light of such seismic shifts, what harm was there in a little intimate correspondence?

Ghulam stubbed out his cigarette and reached into his pocket for the last uneaten toffee from a tin that Libby had sent with the letter. He had been saving it for just such a moment. Ghulam sucked on the toffee, his mouth filling with the delicious sweetness, and read Libby's latest letter again.

> *Dearest Prodigal,*
>
> *I hope you don't mind me calling you dearest? Perhaps it is the only way I can convince you that you are very dear to me – far more than a certain assistant tea planter (no matter how kind and passably handsome he may be!). I shan't mention his name again, as you accused me of overuse in my previous letter. As for toffees: rest assured, I haven't shared sweets with M since we were children. I seem to remember he preferred coconut, which is far below toffee in the hierarchy of best sweets.*
>
> *You wanted to know more about Belgooree. It's probably the nicest place I've ever been to. The bungalow is old and almost completely covered in bougainvillea and other flowering creepers I don't know the names of, and it has an upstairs veranda with a beautiful view over the garden and the track down to the tea bushes and the forest beyond. It's almost like living in the jungle. In the*

*evening, you can see the Khasi boys herding the cattle
back into the village and everything smells perfumed from
the wood fires and the night-flowering creepers.*

*I'm getting to know and like my cousin Clarrie
more and more. I have to say I've been a bit jealous of
her because my father is so obviously fond of her when
he should be thinking about my mother and saving his
marriage. Sorry, does that sound very bourgeois of me? I
can't help it – they're my parents and I want them to be
together because I know it's only the years of separation
that have made them grow apart. They deserve to have a
few happy years together to make up for the time they've
missed. At least that's what I think.*

*I know now, first hand, how damaging being apart
can be. I love my dad dearly but he's not how I remember him. As a child I adored everything about him but
meeting him again as an adult, I see that we have very
different opinions about life. Also, I can't help feeling he's
deliberately keeping something back from me – perhaps
because he thinks I'll disapprove – and it's created this
distance between us. I know he's unwell and I shouldn't
judge him too harshly – I feel disloyal even writing this
– but I can't deny our reunion has been a bit of a disappointment. I think it's the same for him too – he's not used
to a young woman answering him back in the way I do!
It's made me more sympathetic to my mother – I think
life with my dad was probably quite difficult out here at
times. She's independently minded too but I keep remembering times when she would have to pacify my father
and try and keep the peace amongst the family. I'd forgotten how much we all argued as kids! But she was never
the least bit snobby or prejudiced. Perhaps my outlook on*

life is more thanks to her than I've ever realised. I hope you don't mind me telling you all this – I've not admitted it to anyone before.

Anyway, I've been helping Clarrie at the factory. She's teaching me tea-tasting. There's a lot more to it than I ever imagined and she's very skilled. I've never done so much sipping and spitting in my life! I'm also teaching a boy called Nitin to type so that he can do the office work for the mohurer *who is getting old and his eyesight's going. I know it's not much in the great scale of things but I was going up the wall with nothing to do and at least I'm feeling more useful while I have to be here.*

Sometimes I wish I could climb on our magic carpet and fly down to Calcutta and sit on the roof with you and discuss the matters of the day. No one here wants to talk about what's happening. Clarrie won't let me mention politics in front of Dad in case he gets anxious. I think it's a mistake as he will have to make a decision soon about what he's going to do. And so, I suppose, will I.

My fondest regards,

Libby

PS I have indeed told Dad that I'm writing to you. When he began huffing and puffing, Clarrie told him to be quiet and said it was nice that I'm keeping up with my friends in Calcutta!

CHAPTER 21

Belgooree, July

I t was the arrival of Rafi and Sophie from Gulgat that proved to be the turning point for Libby's father. They had written ahead asking for Sophie to stay while Rafi went to Delhi to attend the disbanding of his old regiment, the Lahore Horse. The Indian Army was being broken up and divided into two new national armies ahead of Partition.

The nearer the date loomed for Independence, the greater the unrest. The pace of change was dizzying. While the vote in Assam had supported the secession of Muslim Sylhet to Bengal, a Partition Council had been formed to help with the splitting of Bengal. The hastily appointed Bengal Boundary Commission was holding public sittings to hear people's views. A lawyer called Radcliffe had arrived from London to help draw up the borders that would divide India from a newly created East and West Pakistan.

The Boundary Commission will be toothless, Ghulam had written in disgust to Libby, *and they won't want to be held responsible for where the knife falls on Bengal. It will be left up to your British lawyer to do the dirty work. I hear he's never even set foot in India before and would be hard-pressed to find Punjab or Bengal on a map. And with only a month to do it in. The rumour is that the partition won't be announced till after the Independence celebrations, so even on the day of liberation millions of people won't know under which government they will be living.*

Can you imagine the government in London treating the people of Britain like that? No, because it would never happen. So why are Indians being treated in such a cavalier way? The Britishers – arrogant to the very end!

I'm sorry, Libby. I know you do not think like that – you are in the minority of British who think of Indians as your equals and not some sub-species. I am just angry and frustrated at the situation. Things are volatile in Calcutta. Each side is arming their goondas *for a fight over the city. Both want it for themselves but neither side knows whether Calcutta will end up in India or East Pakistan.*

She had written back to him at once to tell him to be careful and avoid any violence, though she knew he was unlikely to take notice. If there was a story to cover or an injustice to expose, Ghulam would be there.

He had written by return, making a joke of danger. *I'm in more danger in the office from back-stabbers than I ever am on the streets. Fatima is taking far greater risks than me. Her women's organisation is now rescuing families from East Bengal escaping by boat and train. They go to the stations east of here, taking medicines and food. Then we try and find them temporary shelter.*

Libby had been quick to notice his slip into 'we'. Ghulam was obviously helping his sister too. All she could do was hope that Fatima would keep an eye on her brother and prevent him from doing anything too impetuous.

At the sound of tooting, Libby rushed out of the factory office to see the Khans' car appearing on the track below the house. She waved enthusiastically for them to stop. Their old black Ford went past, stopped abruptly and reversed. Libby ran up to it. Her heart lurched painfully to see a moustachioed man with a look of Ghulam grinning back at her in surprise.

'Libby?' he exclaimed, jumping out of the car with the engine still running.

'Yes,' she laughed.

He put out his hand to shake hers but she grabbed him in a hug. 'It's so lovely to see you,' she said, her eyes prickling with unexpected tears.

For a moment he squeezed her back and then held her at arms' length. 'Look, Sophie darling,' he called to his wife, who was scrambling out of the passenger seat, 'our sweet Libby is all grown up.'

A moment later Libby was being clasped in Sophie's strong, lithe arms and having her cheeks kissed. Long-ago memories of happy picnics and holidays at Belgooree, with the Khans organising games of tennis and hide-and-seek, came flooding back. Libby clung on to her mother's oldest friend and burst into tears.

'Oh, Libby dearie!' Sophie crooned as she stroked Libby's hair tenderly. 'We've missed you too.'

Libby quickly tried to compose herself. Half laughing, half crying, she said, 'Sorry, I'm not usually such a crybaby. It's just seeing you again – it reminds me of being here with Mother and the boys. We kids used to love it when you and Rafi turned up – you were always much more fun than our parents.'

They all grinned at each other. 'We're a bit creakier around the joints these days,' said Rafi, 'but we can still take you on at tennis.'

'Great,' said Libby. 'I'll get Harry to partner me so I'll have a chance against you old pros.'

'Not so much of the old, lassie,' said Sophie. Her voice still held a trace of Scottish burr even after so long in India. To Libby, she hardly looked any older. Sophie had the same bobbed blonde hair and pretty fair face that Libby remembered.

'Hop in,' ordered Rafi. 'We've been dreaming of M.D.'s ginger cake and Clarrie's tea since we left this morning.'

'You ride up to the house with Rafi,' said Sophie. 'I'm going to stretch my legs and walk.'

As Libby sat next to Rafi, she kept sliding glances at him while he chatted about their journey. He looked older than Ghulam and was grey around the temples but his strongly built physique was similar to his brother's. Rafi was more conventionally good-looking, with an even smile and a trim moustache, and was immaculately turned out in a cream shirt and flannel trousers. Ghulam, by contrast, had uneven features and sometimes looked like he slept in his clothes and forgot to shave. But it was Ghulam's imperfections that Libby found so sexy. Both brothers had the same startlingly attractive green eyes fringed by dark lashes. When Rafi glanced back at Libby, she felt her insides twist with longing for Ghulam.

Round the dinner table that night, Sophie was frank about the situation in Gulgat.

'It's not the same since Sanjay became Rajah,' she said. 'Rafi's no longer ADC. Sanjay consults with his grandmother and her astrologers over affairs of the court. That's when he's there, which isn't often.'

'To be honest,' said Rafi, 'I've been happier just being in charge of forests.'

'But the bullying has been getting worse,' said Sophie indignantly.

'Bullying?' said Clarrie.

'The old witch in the palace is constantly stirring up trouble against Rafi to undermine any influence he might still have over Sanjay. That's why the former rajah's wife left; Rita couldn't bear the palace intrigues any longer. She's gone back to Bombay permanently. I miss her terribly.'

'Is that why you don't want to stay in Gulgat while Rafi's away?' asked Libby.

Sophie and Rafi exchanged knowing looks.

'Not just that,' said Sophie. 'This picking on Rafi has taken a worrying turn. The palace cabal are using the excuse of him being Muslim to attack his character further.'

'That's terrible!' cried Libby. She remembered Ghulam confiding in her that Rafi's job might no longer be safe under Sanjay's careless rule.

'But surely,' said James, 'the Rajah won't hold with that?'

'Sanjay's too weak to stand up to his grandmother,' said Sophie.

'And he's hardly been there this past month,' said Rafi. 'He's in Delhi being sweet-talked by Mountbatten. The Viceroy's putting all his charm into persuading the princely states to give up their autonomy and join either India or Pakistan.'

'The old Rani is putting about the rumour that Rafi is trying to force Sanjay to join Pakistan,' said Sophie.

'It's nonsense of course,' said Rafi. 'When Sanjay asked me, I told him it would make sense to join India as most of the population of Gulgat is Hindu. And Gulgat is too small to stand on its own.'

'But since Sanjay has been away,' said Sophie, 'there have been disturbances in the east of the state.'

'What kind of disturbances?' Clarrie asked in concern.

'Some refugees have arrived from East Bengal,' Sophie explained. 'Horror stories are spreading like wildfire of how Hindus were butchered by Muslim gangs.'

'Some Gulgat Muslim fishermen have had their boats and homes set on fire,' said Rafi. 'Nothing has been done to stop the retaliation.'

'Rafi has telegrammed Sanjay about it,' said Sophie, 'but he says it's a matter for his chief of police and not to worry.'

Clarrie stretched across the table and put a hand over Sophie's. 'I'm so glad you've decided to come here while Rafi's in Delhi, my dear. You can stay as long as you want.'

'Thank you,' Sophie said with a grateful smile.

'Quite right,' said James. 'You can't possibly go back to Gulgat until things have settled down. The Rajah will have to put his house in order first.'

Rafi cleared his throat. 'We won't be going back, ever.'

They all looked at him, startled.

'What do you mean, not ever?' gasped James.

'I have no confidence in Sanjay keeping Sophie and me safe,' said Rafi. 'There is a backlash going on already over Partition and we will be in a vulnerable minority if we stay in Gulgat.'

'But if Gulgat becomes a part of a democratic India,' said Libby, 'you'll be safe from the scheming in the palace, won't you?'

'We will still be at the mercy of this Hindu nationalism that is being stoked up everywhere,' Rafi said. 'It will only get worse. Sanjay's grandmother will see to that.'

'We couldn't risk telling you this in a letter or telegram,' said Sophie, 'in case the palace got wind that we were escaping for good. They might have whipped up a crowd to cause us trouble.'

Libby felt her stomach churn. Were things really so bad in Gulgat? Ghulam had feared they might be. She remembered him telling her of a letter from Rafi that hinted he was contemplating moving back to the Punjab if Pakistan became a reality. How despicable Rajah Sanjay was, not to stand up for Rafi who had served the royal family so loyally. But knowing how Sanjay had manipulated and used Adela for his own gratification, Libby wasn't surprised to learn that he was a weak and selfish man. So if it was unsafe for a couple like the Khans, who were well integrated into the princely state where they had lived happily for years, then how much worse would it be for Muslims like Ghulam and Fatima in the overheated cauldron of Calcutta?

'I think it's awful that you're being harassed out of Gulgat,' said Libby, her eyes stinging with angry tears. 'Is there nothing that can be done?'

'I don't see what,' said Rafi, sadness clouding his eyes.

They sat in silence as the enormity of the Khans' situation sank in. Eventually James asked, 'So what will you do?'

Clarrie hazarded a guess. 'Go back to Scotland?'

Sophie leant close to her husband and said, 'Neither of us wants to leave India.'

Rafi raised his chin in a defiant gesture that reminded Libby of Ghulam. She tensed, fearing what he was about to say.

'I'm going to Lahore after the ceremony in Delhi,' said Rafi, 'to see about a forestry job back in the Punjab.'

'It's where Rafi first started as a forester,' said Sophie.

'Yes, I remember,' said Clarrie. 'And your family are there too.'

Rafi nodded.

'It's time Rafi made peace with his father,' said Sophie. 'For years he hasn't gone because his family wouldn't accept me as his wife.'

'But,' said Rafi, 'now that I'm considering returning to help in the new state of Pakistan, I think my father will relent and want to meet Sophie.'

Libby gaped at them in dismay. Ghulam would be deeply saddened at the news. His words rang in her head: *We need Muslims like Rafi to stay and help build the new India.*

'But Ghulam says Lahore is a tinderbox,' said Libby. 'Surely you won't risk going there at the moment?'

'You're in touch with Ghulam?' Sophie asked in surprise.

Libby flushed. 'Yes, I am.'

'The dak from Calcutta is almost daily,' teased Clarrie.

'Well, well,' said Rafi, 'my little brother showing some sense at last.'

'I think that's wonderful,' encouraged Sophie. 'I can see that you both would have a lot in common.'

'Apart from Khan being rabidly anti-British,' exclaimed James, 'and Libby being half his age.'

'Like Tilly was to you, James,' Sophie said with a wry smile.

Libby felt a surge of gratitude to the Khans for their approval. She saw her father go red; he looked about to protest but Rafi swiftly intervened and said, 'I'm sure the reports about Lahore are exaggerated – I hope so at least.'

'Rafi's family no longer live in the old city,' said Sophie. 'After the death of his mother, they moved to a quiet suburb that hasn't seen any violence.'

'So when do you hope to join Rafi?' Clarrie asked.

'That depends on how quickly Rafi can find a job,' said Sophie. 'But with him being an experienced forester and a Punjabi, it shouldn't take long.'

'I'd rather Sophie waited here till after Independence,' cautioned Rafi, 'just in case . . .'

Libby's heart thudded. 'So you are expecting trouble in Lahore?'

Rafi tried to hide his concern. 'No, I just think it will take longer than Sophie thinks to arrange a forestry job and somewhere to live.'

'It's such a big step to take,' Libby said. 'Do Ghulam and Fatima know you are leaving Gulgat for good?'

Rafi shook his head. 'They know I've been thinking about it but we decided not to tell anyone until we were safely out of Gulgat.'

'Ghulam is so upset about the whole Partition thing,' said Libby. 'He's very against the idea of a separate Muslim state.'

'We didn't want it either,' said Sophie, 'but we're just being realistic about the future.'

'It won't last,' said James.

'What won't?' Libby asked.

'Partitioning Bengal and Punjab. The borders won't work – the people on either side are too alike. Give it five years and it'll all be one country again.'

Rafi smiled. 'I hope you are right.'

After that, Clarrie steered the conversation to lighter topics, planning picnics with Sophie and a shopping trip to Shillong. Rafi spoke about the regimental dinner planned in Delhi and his excitement at seeing his old Sikh comrade, Sundar Singh, again.

'Adela and Sam always said how Sundar had a soft spot for your sister Fatima,' Clarrie said.

'Really?' Libby's eyes widened. 'Did Fatima like him too? I've never heard her talk romantically about anyone.'

'My sister is too dedicated to her work,' laughed Rafi. 'Always has been.'

'I think Adela thought Fatima was fond of Sundar,' answered Clarrie, 'but not enough to marry him.'

'Because he's a Sikh?' asked Libby.

'That's possible,' admitted Rafi. 'My parents would never have approved.'

'I think if Fatima had wanted to marry,' said Sophie, 'she wouldn't have let that put her off. Poor Sundar, he's such a nice man – and widowed so young. He has a son in the Punjab, doesn't he?'

'Rawalpindi, I think,' said Rafi. 'His sister was caring for him while Sundar worked in Simla.'

'What will happen to his son now?' asked Libby. 'Will any of the Sikhs stay in West Punjab?'

Rafi shrugged.

'It's a bloody mess!' cried James suddenly.

'A British mess,' said Libby.

'Not entirely,' said Rafi gallantly, 'despite what Ghulam might say.'

That night, upset by the Khans' flight from Gulgat and an underlying fear over Ghulam and Fatima's safety, Libby gave up on sleep and went on to the veranda. She found her father there, slumped in a long chair and staring into an empty whisky glass.

She pulled a chair next to him, put his glass on the inlaid side table and slipped her hand into his.

'I can't sleep either, Dad. Penny for your thoughts?'

He gave out a long anguished sigh. 'What am I doing here, Libby? I'm behaving like a coward. I'm burying my head in the sand while the world is going mad around me. This business with the Khans has really shaken me up. I had no idea they were in any danger. Now Clarrie's worried about M.D. and his family and I can't stop thinking about Manzur and his parents. Are they in danger too? It's all so ghastly.'

Libby bit back a soothing platitude. There was no use in pretending things would go back to normal; the old way of life was coming to an abrupt end and none of them knew what the future would bring. She held on to his hand and let him continue talking, encouraged that he was beginning to confide in her.

'I really believed that handing over political power wouldn't affect us planters,' said James. 'India has always needed its box-wallahs – and probably appreciates them more than the snooty British "heaven-born" administrators ever have. But I never expected all this religious division – this hatred that is spreading like a fever. Where's it all coming from, Libby?'

Libby grimaced. 'You might say we British have done our best to play one community off against another for the past century. Our colonial service is second to none at cataloguing and labelling people for our own ends.'

James muttered, 'I might have expected you to blame it all on us. No doubt that's what your comrade Khan says?'

'Actually, it's not,' said Libby. 'He's been very critical of the Indian political leaders on all sides for stoking up petty nationalism for political gain. But I don't think he'll ever forgive the British for not handing over independence a generation ago, before separatist ideas had taken hold. Thirty years ago, Indians died in their thousands helping us win the

Great War, but their reward was greater repression. That's what made Ghulam take up the fight for freedom.'

'India wasn't ready then,' said James.

'Only the British thought that,' Libby answered.

James sighed again. 'Perhaps you're right. Who knows? It's all too late now.'

'So what do you want to do about Manzur and his family?' she asked.

Her father stared into the darkness. She thought he wasn't going to answer and then he said, 'I'm not going to do anything until I've spoken to Manzur. I've spent a lifetime telling people what to do. This time the choice has to be his.'

Libby squeezed his hand. 'I think that's a good idea.' She smiled, grateful that he was finally being open with her and treating her like an equal. Maybe Clarrie was right and they just needed a little more time.

James raised her hand to his lips and kissed it. Libby was taken aback by the tender gesture. Her heart swelled with affection. She raised his hand and kissed his back. James gave a soft laugh. It was the first time she had heard him laugh in an age and the sound brought tears to her eyes.

CHAPTER 22

Two days later they said farewell to Rafi. Sophie was going as far as Shillong with him, and then returning in the car with Daleep. Libby gave Rafi a fierce hug, trying not to cry. No one knew when they would see him again but no one wanted to say so.

'Have fun in Delhi,' she said.

Rafi smiled and kissed her forehead. 'Tell Ghulam, I'll look forward to playing cricket with him in Lahore when he comes to visit after Independence.'

Libby gave him a tearful smile. 'I'll write and tell him everything,' she promised.

They waved him away with shouts of encouragement, watching as the car bumped down the drive and went out of sight beyond the factory compound.

Later that day Manzur arrived from the Oxford. Libby saw the strain on his handsome face, despite his smile of greeting.

Over lunch James asked his assistant what his parents wanted to do.

Manzur looked embarrassed. 'Sahib, that depends what you intend to do – whether you will be coming back to Cheviot View. If you return they will stay as long as you want them.'

'And if I don't?' asked James. 'Would they want me to find them another employer?'

Manzur shook his head. 'They only want to work for Robson sahib.'

James put down his knife and fork, his lunch hardly touched.

Libby asked, 'With all the uncertainties going on, are you worried about them staying in such an isolated place?'

Manzur held her look and nodded. 'For them, yes. I am not afraid for myself.'

'So if we don't return to Cheviot View,' she said, 'where would you want them to go?'

'They would want to go back to Bengal – to family.'

'Then that is what I will arrange,' said James. 'I shan't be returning to Cheviot View. But I'll provide them with a pension, so you mustn't worry about them.'

'There is no need,' said Manzur at once. 'I will take care of my parents.'

'I'm sure you will,' said James, 'but I insist on giving them something. Aslam has served me and my family loyally since I arrived in India.'

'And Ayah Meera,' added Libby. 'Mother would want her to be rewarded too.'

Manzur looked overwhelmed. 'They will be very grateful – as am I. Thank you, sahib.'

'That's settled then,' said James, relief on his face. 'You can put the wheels in motion for packing up the house. No point delaying. I imagine your parents will want to travel before . . . before the fifteenth of August.'

Manzur nodded. 'And where shall everything be sent?'

'Sent?' queried James.

'Your household possessions,' he said. 'Or will we store them in the godowns till you decide . . . ?'

James glanced at Libby and then said, 'No, I want everything sent to Bombay to be shipped to England.'

'Dad?' said Libby in surprise.

'I've decided to return home,' he said, his voice strained. 'I'm retiring for good. Leaving India.'

Libby gaped at the sudden announcement. She saw from Clarrie's astonished look that she had not known of his decision either. Libby could see tears welling in her father's eyes and knew he was too overcome to speak.

Manzur stood up. 'May I wish you many happy years of retirement, sahib. It has been a pleasure working for you. You have taught me a lot and been a good friend to me and to my parents.' He looked at Libby. 'All the Robsons have been like friends to me.' He put his hand to his heart. 'Thank you.'

James nodded as he got to his feet and hurried from the room. Libby heard a strange grunt – like a strangled sob – before a far door closed. Her heart lurched. She wanted to rush to comfort her father but knew it would only embarrass him. Yet her mind was in a whirl: what did this mean for her? Would she have to leave India with him? How would her mother take the news of his sudden return? She sat, pinned in her chair, unable to speak.

Despite Clarrie's protestations that Manzur should stay the night and Harry badgering him to give him some bowling practice, Manzur insisted on getting back to the Oxford. The wind was strengthening and the sky looked heavy with rain. It felt like the monsoon was approaching at last and he didn't want to get marooned at Belgooree.

'Dad and I will visit before your parents leave,' Libby promised.

Her initial shock at her father's abrupt announcement had given way to relief that he'd finally broken the impasse and come to a decision. Yet now, as she waved Manzur away, she felt weighed down by the realisation that she too was going to have to give up her childhood home for good.

Only after he had gone, did she realise that no one had actually asked Manzur what he wanted to do. They had all assumed he would stay on at the Oxford to support his parents financially. That's what he'd said – or at least implied. *'I am not afraid for myself.'* His words haunted Libby. Why were so many people being put into the position of having to fear for their own safety or that of their loved ones? Her thoughts went at once to the Khans and Ghulam – they were never far from Ghulam – and she sent up a silent prayer for them all.

As dusk fell, an emotional Sophie returned. Rafi had started his long journey to Delhi. 'We haven't been apart for more than an odd night in the last twenty-four years,' she said tearfully.

Libby hugged her. 'You'll be together again soon. And at least Rafi will be much happier knowing you are safe here at Belgooree.'

Her father didn't appear until breakfast the next day. Libby was encouraged to see him more jovial than she had in weeks.

'Libby tells me you've decided to go back to Newcastle?' Sophie quizzed him. 'Tilly will be so pleased.'

'I hope so,' said James. 'I'll send a telegram once the house is cleared and I've sorted a passage for me and Libby. There's no point hanging around now. If we fly we can be home in a couple of weeks from now.'

Libby's insides jolted. 'For me too? I haven't decided . . .'

'Surely you'll want to come home with me?' said James. 'Heavens, girl! You've spent the last two months badgering me to make the family complete again, so I'm doing what you want. It *is* what you want, isn't it? For your mother and I to be in the same place at last and you to be with us?'

'Yes,' said Libby, unsure how she really felt. 'But two weeks! Your decision is so sudden – you never talked it over with me. I don't want to travel back that quickly. I want to stay for the Independence celebrations.'

'Whatever for?' he demanded. 'They're not our celebrations.'

'They are for Libby,' said Clarrie quietly. She hadn't spoken since they'd sat down for breakfast. 'She was born here after all.'

Libby exchanged a grateful look with the older woman, noticing the smudges of tiredness under her pretty eyes. It struck her that Clarrie had taken the strain of having them to stay for weeks while trying to keep her business going and now had responsibility for looking after Sophie too. She must be just as worried as they all were about the future. Belgooree was her life: her family home and her living. She had a young fatherless son to bring up and a daughter on the other side of the world. Yet never once had she heard Clarrie complain or burden others with her troubles.

Her father seemed annoyed at Clarrie's reproof. 'It's not the same and you know it.'

'Well, I, for one, will be throwing a party on the fifteenth,' said Clarrie defiantly, 'and I hope Libby will be here to join in if she wants to.'

'I second that!' cried Sophie, throwing an arm casually around Libby's shoulders and squeezing her in a hug. 'I'll still be here no doubt. We'll have fancy dress and games and lots of cocktails and dance to all Clarrie's ancient rag-time records.'

Clarrie laughed. 'Not so ancient.'

'That sounds wonderful.' Libby smiled. 'I'll make sure I'm here for that.'

'Good,' said Sophie. She got up from the table. 'Harry and I are playing tennis in half an hour. Want to join us?'

'I'm giving Nitin a lesson this morning,' said Libby. 'Maybe play later?'

'Of course, lassie.' Sophie smiled and sauntered off, whistling.

James sat back with a sigh. 'I can see I've been outmanoeuvred by women again.'

Libby exchanged an amused look with Clarrie.

Things moved quickly after that. By the end of the week, Manzur sent a message to say that the house packing was nearly complete and he was eager to get the trunks and furniture transported downriver before the Brahmaputra swelled to twice the size in the monsoon.

Clarrie loaned Libby and James a car and sent her servant Alok to see to their meals on the way. They set off before dawn and were pulling up at Cheviot View by mid-afternoon. Libby's initial excitement at seeing her childhood home again soon turned to dismay. The downstairs rooms were stacked with furniture, rolled-up carpets and battered trunks bulging with household goods.

Upstairs, the sitting room was denuded of its bookcases, pictures, family photos and dusty curtains. Worse still, her bedroom was bare but for a pile of discarded mosquito nets. The heart of the house had been dismantled and packed away. It no longer felt like home – just a tea planter's bungalow waiting for a new occupant.

Libby ran outside and down the garden steps to the pond below and burst into tears. Manzur found her there. His young face looked stricken.

'Libby-mem',' he said, handing her a pressed cotton handkerchief, 'your father sent me.'

Libby grabbed at the handkerchief, grateful but embarrassed, and blew her nose. 'Th-thank you, Manzur.'

'It's hard for my parents too,' he said. 'This has been their home since they married.'

'Of course,' said Libby, feeling ashamed that she had not thought of that. 'And yours.'

He gave a sad smile. 'Do you remember making a den in the roots of the banyan and you said it was a secret cave.'

Libby gave a tearful grin. 'Yes, and Jamie said it was impossible to have caves in a tree and that I should go away and play with my dolls.'

Manzur's smile broadened. 'And instead you sneaked higher up the tree when we were making mud pies and threw sticks on to our mud castle, saying you were a warrior princess come to attack.'

Libby laughed. 'So I did!'

'And after that Jamie let you play castles with us,' said Manzur. 'I always admired you for standing up to your brother.'

'I must have been a nuisance,' she said, blushing.

'Only sometimes,' he said, his brown eyes shining with amusement.

Libby turned and looked up at the bungalow. Its shuttered windows made it look like a slumbering beast.

'I'm not sure I can bear to spend the night here,' she sighed.

'You can come to The Lodge,' he suggested. 'There is a spare room for your father and I can give up mine . . .' He stopped, his face flushing.

'That's sweet of you,' said Libby, briefly touching his arm. 'I'll see what Dad wants to do.'

But her father dismissed the idea at once. 'No need,' said James hastily, 'we can camp out on the veranda for one night. Say our farewells to the old place.'

Libby felt a flicker of relief. She didn't really want to return to The Lodge after the disturbing episode when Flowers thought she had seen a ghost.

That evening, they invited Manzur to take dinner with them at a camp table on the veranda, with Aslam in charge of the serving. Afterwards, James insisted that Aslam join them for a smoke.

'We'll share a hubble-bubble pipe like we did when I was a young planter and we went out in camp,' said Libby's father. 'Do you remember being so young, Aslam, my friend?'

Aslam touched his heart. 'We are still young in here, even if we are white on top,' he joked.

The men sat on the floor on a rug and shared a water-pipe. Libby curled up in a camp chair and watched them. She had never seen her father so relaxed and casual with his oldest servant. He hadn't drunk as much as usual at dinner either. The trappings of the sahib had been boxed away and it was as if her father had shed the burdens of keeping his distance and playing the master. Here, in the sultry night with only the sounds of the jungle around them, his world was reduced to sitting on a rug smoking and chatting with an old friend.

As the kerosene lamp hissed, Libby sat in the shadows and listened to them reminisce about long-ago hunting trips and treks into Burma, and of people long dead or retired. James's voice was animated as he talked about his younger days; she drank in his stories of adventure. This was the father of her childhood.

'Do you remember when we tracked that tiger for three days?' said James.

Aslam nodded. 'With Fairfax sahib.'

'And we'd decided to give up when – blow me down – the beast comes strolling past our camp at breakfast time! And we all went scrambling for our guns.'

Aslam chuckled and said, 'Except Fairfax sahib, who carried on shaving.'

James guffawed. 'Dear Fairfax. They were made of sterner stuff in his day.'

Libby asked, 'Is he the Mr Fairfax in that nursing home in Tynemouth that Mother still visits?'

'Yes,' her father replied. 'It's good of her to bother.'

'Soon you'll be able to see him again too,' Libby said.

'I suppose I will,' said James. For a moment, his expression in the lamplight was reflective and then he was carrying on with further anecdotes.

Libby's eyes watered to think of how this would be their very last night at Cheviot View – in all likelihood her father's last visit to the Oxford tea gardens – and then that chapter of his life would be over forever.

This was not how she had imagined it being during all those years of exile when she had yearned to return here. She had been so fixated on getting back to Cheviot View that she hadn't really stopped to think what life would really be like as a grown woman here. Her mind had been full of rosy memories of riding, tennis, swimming and exploring, of films at the clubhouse and cook's kedgeree.

Libby chided herself for not thinking beyond her fairy-tale memories. After a short time back at her old home, she had realised it was just a bungalow – albeit with a breathtaking view of shimmering greenery – inhabited by a lonely, careworn father and reduced numbers of loyal, ageing staff.

Libby hadn't expected that. But neither had she expected to find India in such a ferment of change nor guessed at the diverse friendships that she would make. Least of all could she have possibly imagined that she would fall heavily in love with a charismatic, sensuous, amusing, infuriating, passionate Indian revolutionary called Ghulam Khan.

Tonight, as her father shed his responsibilities as a tea planter and master, she felt she was finally shedding her childhood – that distant, idealised world she had clung to and that had helped her get through the grey years in England.

Libby slipped out of her chair and round the side of the veranda. Taking a thin cotton sheet that was shrouding an old wicker chair that was to be left behind, she lay down on the floor wrapped in the sheet and fell asleep to the low hubbub of the men's voices.

The next morning they didn't linger. Libby had wanted a final dawn ride but James seemed eager to be gone. The horses were being sold to Dr Attar and two other young planters who enjoyed *shikar*.

The *syce* and the *mali* were going to work for the doctor. The other servants were being pensioned off and given train fares to return to their relations.

They lined up on the terrace. James went stiffly along the line shaking hands and giving out presents of money and keepsakes from the house. Libby followed, half embarrassed at playing the memsahib and half in fear that she would break down crying. In return, the servants hung garlands of marigolds around their necks and wished them well.

Her father stopped when he got to Aslam. James's chin wobbled. The old servant looked him in the eye and Libby could see the sadness in both their faces.

'Aslam, you have been . . .' James said, his voice breaking, 'a good . . . faithful friend . . . Thank y—' His voice cracked. He swallowed hard and then his strong craggy face crumpled like a small boy's.

Aslam touched him gently on the arm. 'Thank you, Robson sahib. Peace be with you, all the days of your life.'

James stifled a sob and, stretching out his arms, embraced his old bearer. Libby's eyes filled with tears at the sight. She had never seen her father so demonstrative or emotional with Aslam.

She turned to Meera and at once they were hugging like they used to do. The years fell away and Libby was eight years old again being comforted by her ayah because she was having to leave Cheviot View and didn't know when she would be coming back. Only this time it was she, Libby, who was a head taller than Meera as they clung to each other and wept quiet tears.

'We'll meet again, I promise,' Libby said, as Meera dabbed both their eyes with the hem of her shawl.

'You will always be my daughter,' Meera said softly, her brown eyes full of sorrow.

Libby thanked her and stumbled away after her father. At the car, Manzur was waiting. He must have anticipated their being upset for he said, 'Let me drive you down to the offices.'

Libby nodded in thanks. Her father sat in the front. No one spoke as they drove slowly down the drive. James did not turn around but Libby craned for a last view of her old home and the waving servants. She glimpsed the lawns and the pond and her mother's canna lilies. Her nose filled with the scent of her garland. She closed her eyes and tried to commit the final poignant sight to memory.

Libby had no appetite for any further goodbyes, so said she would wait by the car with Alok while her father went to say his farewells to the plantation staff in the large factory compound. He had declined a retirement party or any fuss.

Manzur reappeared having escorted James into the building. Even before their journey started, Libby felt drained by emotion and the heat.

'Libby-mem',' he said, 'I wanted to tell you something in private.'

He looked at her with his dark eyes, so like his mother's. As he led her out of earshot of Alok, Libby felt her insides flutter, nervous at what it might be.

'Go on,' she said.

'Once your father has gone – and my parents are safely in Bengal,' he said, 'I am going to resign from the Oxford.'

'What?' Libby gasped. 'Why would you do that? Are you worried you won't be safe here?'

He gave a dry smile. 'I'm not running away from danger,' he said. 'But since your father decided to retire I have been thinking of my future. I don't want to be a tea planter. That was your father's idea – and I will always be grateful for what he has given me. Your father is a good man – a courageous man. But I want to choose my own life.'

320

Libby stared at him. She had never seen him so determined in speech and manner. 'Dad will be sad to hear that – he thinks you will make an excellent manager.'

Manzur said, 'Please don't tell him yet. I don't want him to worry about it or make his leave-taking any harder. When I have a new job I will write and tell him.'

Libby asked, 'You want to be a teacher, don't you?'

Manzur nodded. 'Yes. I would have left the Oxford five years ago and taken a teaching job if your father hadn't persuaded me to stay.'

'Insisted you stay, more likely?' Libby said with a quizzical smile.

'It was thanks to Robson sahib that I became a tutor at Belgooree,' Manzur reminded her. 'So he found a way for me to do both. Those times at Belgooree were the happiest I have known. That's why I know I want to be a teacher.'

Libby touched his arm. 'You'll make a very good one. Harry is your fan for life. And an inspiring teacher is the best gift a child can have.'

Manzur grinned at her, his cheeks dimpling. 'Thank you.'

'I wish I was as certain about what I wanted to do,' Libby sighed. 'I never really thought beyond getting back out to India – and now I find that dream is suddenly coming to an end and I don't have a home here any more. I want to be useful but I'm not sure how.'

'You could be a teacher too,' Manzur suggested. 'Your father is proud at the way you are teaching typing to the Belgooree clerk.'

'Is he?' Libby glanced at him in surprise. 'He's never said that to me.'

'Robson sahib is not one to waste words or flatter,' said Manzur, 'so when he does speak, it is praise indeed.'

'That's true,' Libby agreed.

She fell silent, thinking about her father. In his fragile mental state he needed someone to care for him and she worried that her mother would not be sympathetic enough. Perhaps she really could be of some use to her father helping him settle back in Newcastle. She didn't want to leave India – her heart felt leaden at the very thought – but in the short term it seemed to be the only course open to her.

'Perhaps when I get back to Britain and my family, I'll discover what it is I'm destined to do in life.' Libby grimaced. 'I hope it's not just a return to the typing pool.'

'You will find your own path.' Manzur smiled. 'Just like you always did when we were children.'

Shortly afterwards, James joined them. Her father was red-faced with emotion.

'I'll drive first,' Libby offered. She turned to Manzur and shook his hand. 'Goodbye, friend,' she said, 'and good luck in all you do.'

He held on for a moment, his hand felt warm and had a wiry strength.

He smiled. 'I hope we meet again, Libby-mem'.'

'Me too,' she said and disengaged her hand.

Soon they were driving off down the plantation road and the buildings of the Oxford Estates – where her father had spent all his working years – receded into a sea of green tea bushes until they disappeared completely in the shimmering heat.

'Good man, Manzur,' said James. 'He's a good man.'

'Yes, he is,' Libby replied.

'He'll make a fine manager one day,' said her father. 'He's the future here. Good reliable intelligent men like him.'

Libby could hear the emotion in his voice. She kept quiet.

'We haven't all been good men out here,' James said, 'some bad apples in the barrel. But I've tried my best.'

Libby reached out and squeezed his hand. 'I know you have. Manzur was just saying what a good and courageous manager you've been.'

'Did he say that?'

Libby smiled. 'Yes.'

James let out a sigh. 'No, not always.'

Libby waited for him to say more. Perhaps now, on the long journey together, her father might confide in her. But after that, he fell into silence as Libby drove. Was there something that still nagged at his conscience – some secret about his time at the Oxford that he couldn't bring himself to tell her? She longed to ask him but didn't want to upset him more than he already was. Perhaps he didn't want to say anything with Alok sitting in the back of the car. Or maybe there was nothing to divulge and his erratic behaviour was due to the stress of getting too old for his job and knowing that he would have to return to England and face his estranged wife. Part of her wanted him to unburden his secret to her as a fellow adult, but part of her feared what he might say. Libby realised she would probably never know.

As they got further away from Cheviot View and nearer to Belgooree, Libby held on to the secret that Manzur had just entrusted her with, and let her mind wander to what she would do next. There was less than a month till Independence. Her desire to get back to Calcutta to see Ghulam, before she had to follow her father to England, was like a feverish itch.

Libby determined she would not leave India without seeing him again.

CHAPTER 23

Newcastle, July

A dela existed in a strange state of numbness, going through the motions of her job and daily routines but feeling detached from it all. In her mind and heart, her life was suspended, waiting for a break-through in news about John Wesley's whereabouts. Daily she expected Tilly to walk through the door waving some document to prove John Wesley – or Jacques Segal – was alive and still living in the area.

But all Tilly's enquiries had come to nothing so far. The resettlement of the homeless after bombing raids had been chaotic and much of the paperwork had been lost in a fire at the end of the War.

At night Adela would toss in bed alone with her imaginings, which would become more fearful as the long dark hours dragged on. Her son had lost his happy home with the kind Segals and was now in an institution – her original nightmare – unloved and unhappy. She grieved for the Belgian couple and felt wretched at her former envy of them. She wished that they were still alive, for at least her son would then have been growing up in a loving home. Now what was happening to him? Had he been evacuated as an orphan to another part of the country? What if he had been adopted once more but his name had been changed so that she would never be able to find him?

Adela had lost interest in eating. Increased smoking blunted her appetite but temporarily calmed her nerves. The face she glanced at in the bathroom mirror each morning was growing hollow-cheeked and wan. She knew she was drinking too much cheap sherry; she kept a bottle in the café pantry for small nips during the day.

The only good development at the tearoom was that Lexy had persuaded Freda, one of her unmarried nieces, to come as cook for a trial period. Freda was slow but methodical and had a knack of being inventive with whatever random ingredients Adela managed to get hold of at the city market.

Once Mrs Jackman stopped working for Herbert's, Adela saw even less of Sam. She felt sore at heart when she thought of him. How was it possible to be so estranged from a man whom she had adored with a passion until a few weeks ago? She was a failure as a wife as well as a mother. Adela cauterised her feelings of uselessness with alcohol and clinging to the hope that she would find her son and at least make up for her past failure towards him.

Occasionally Sam would appear with produce from the allotment and linger to try and speak to her but Adela didn't want them to argue in front of the others.

'I know you're continuing to search for him,' he said, keeping his voice low. 'Josey told me.'

Adela bristled to think her friend was going behind her back to tell Sam her business. 'So?' said Adela, bracing herself for his criticism.

'We need to talk,' said Sam.

'Not now, Sam.'

'Then when?'

'Soon.'

As she turned away, he caught her arm and steered her into the yard. His look was grim.

'We can't go on like this, Adela,' he growled.

She tensed. 'Like what?'

'You know what I mean,' he said in exasperation. 'Living apart. This isn't marriage.'

'You're the one living with your mother,' Adela pointed out.

The look he gave her was so desolate, Adela felt leaden inside. She saw him struggle to say something, and then think better of it. Dropping his hand, he turned from her and strode out of the yard without another word. Adela bit her inner cheek to stop herself crying. She felt confused and angry but more with herself than Sam. They were both hurting but she was too exhausted to work out what she should do about it.

After nearly a month of fruitless searching through archives and making requests in council offices, Tilly had found out nothing about the small boy she had rescued from the bombed street in Heaton.

Adela came back one evening to find Tilly and Josey sitting at the kitchen table waiting for her.

'I thought you had a Mother's Union meeting, Tilly?' said Adela.

'She cancelled,' said Josey, 'so we could speak to you while Mungo is out with friends.'

'Speak to me?' Adela's pulse quickened. 'Have you found out something?'

'No, she hasn't,' Josey answered. 'That's what we want to talk about. You might as well sit down.'

Adela clutched the table. 'If it's bad news please just tell me.'

'Sit down, darling girl,' said Tilly, pouring out a glass of milk and placing it in front of Adela as if she were a child.

'No, thanks,' Adela said, sitting down but not touching the drink.

Josey offered her a cigarette. Adela shook her head, watching nervously as Josey lit up one for herself.

'Adela, sweetheart,' said Tilly, her eyes full of compassion. 'You're making yourself ill with this business about the baby. We can't bear to see you like this.'

'I'm not ill,' Adela said, feeling suddenly agitated. 'I'm fine.'

'No, you're not,' said Josey, blowing out smoke. 'And neither is Sam.'

'That's got nothing to do with you,' Adela snapped.

'It has,' Josey said bluntly. 'He's our friend too.'

Adela gripped her hands in her lap to stop them from shaking. She looked at Tilly for help.

'Adela,' said Tilly, 'you know I love you like a daughter but I can't stand by and see you suffer in this way. I've done what I can to trace the Segal boy – if it was the Segal boy that I rescued – but I've found nothing. It's just the bloody awfulness of war.'

'But you'll keep trying?' Adela asked, panic rising in her chest.

Tilly shook her head. 'If I thought it would do any good I would. But it's not. It's making you ill and it's turning you into . . .'

'What?' Adela whispered.

'Into someone you're not,' said Tilly gently. 'You are the most generous, warm-hearted girl I know – you used to be so fun-loving. But this obsession with finding your baby has changed you. I wouldn't have imagined you could be so callous to poor Sam.'

'Sam?' Adela croaked. A wave of anger and humiliation engulfed her.

'Yes, Sam,' Josey repeated. 'There's precious little hope of you ever finding your son – and even if you did, you'd never be prepared to see him live with anyone else but you, would you? No matter what his circumstances, you'd be prepared to barge into his life as if you were the only one entitled to have him.'

'That's Sam talking,' said Adela, her eyes stinging.

'And he's right,' said Josey, not denying it. 'But you risk losing your husband over this too. Can't you see that?'

Adela was going to protest but bit back the denial. She knew in her heart that Josey might be right.

'I'll work things out with Sam,' Adela insisted, 'just as soon as he comes back from his mother's.'

'This has nothing to do with Mrs Jackman,' Josey said with impatience. 'It's you who is pushing Sam away.' Josey ground out her cigarette and leant across the table. 'He's thinking of going back to India, Adela.'

'India?' Adela gasped. 'He's never said anything—'

'He's tried to but you're not listening,' Josey replied. 'Wake up, Adela. Sam's prepared to go back to India without you because he thinks you don't love him any more.'

'But that's not true,' Adela protested, her heart pounding like it would burst.

'I hope not,' said Josey, 'but that's how it seems to Sam.'

Adela could see that Josey was angry but it was the look of disappointment on Tilly's face that upset her the most.

'You seemed such a happy couple,' said Tilly. 'I thought you had a real love-match. But it's no good just being in love with someone – that doesn't always last. The real test comes when things get tough; that's when you find out if you really care for each other.' A look of regret flitted across her face. 'Not that James and I have been very successful at that.'

Adela thought she might be sick. Had she really been so awful to Sam? Was this single-minded pursuit of finding John Wesley purely selfish indulgence on her part? It couldn't be! She was doing this for her son's sake, trying to make up for abandoning him at birth.

'Do you really love Sam?' Tilly asked gently.

Adela's eyes flooded with tears. She bowed her head, unable to speak.

Josey gave a sigh of impatience. 'Stop chasing an impossible dream of being a mother to John Wesley and go and talk to Sam before it's too late.'

Adela pushed back her chair and rose on shaky legs. 'I'm sorry—' Her throat was too tight to utter another word. Unable to stand another moment in that kitchen, she hurried blindly from the room.

That night Adela didn't sleep, her mind in turmoil. She rose just before dawn, dressed and went out. She would not be needed at the café for several hours. She set off walking with no particular direction in mind, hoping that the mindless repetition of putting one foot in front of the other might relieve her fevered thoughts.

As dawn broke she found herself walking along the banks of the River Ouseburn through leafy Jesmond Dene to a chorus of birdsong. For a fleeting moment she was reminded of Belgooree and her heart ached with sudden longing. She had to stop to catch her breath. Homesickness engulfed her – stronger than any she had felt since returning to Newcastle – and the strength of her sudden yearning for India and her mother left her winded. Was this how Sam was feeling? Was he bitterly regretting leaving the only country he had known as home to come to Britain with her? Was he feeling lost and lonely and wondering if all the upheaval had been worth it? How would she know when she hadn't asked him anything personal in weeks?

Adela put a hand to her thumping chest, as dizziness blurred her vision. Her legs gave way and she crumpled on to a patch of damp grass. Sam! She had tried to keep painful thoughts of her husband at bay but now memories assaulted her. Sam appearing at her seventeenth birthday party in an ill-fitting dinner jacket and grinning as he handed over cherries; Sam rugged in an old work shirt, riding beside her at dawn in the Himalayan foothills; Sam in his pilot's uniform searching for her through a crowded hotel in Calcutta and his face breaking into a huge smile on catching sight of her. Sam's smile that could both melt her heart and weaken her knees at the same time.

Adela thought back to the time, long ago, when she had stowed away in the back of his car to escape from boarding school. She had fallen in love with him the very moment he had discovered her; the young Sam with the battered green pork-pie hat pushed back on his brush-like hair, with the sportsman's hands and lanky gait.

The day they had married – a swift wartime ceremony in Calcutta – and the wedding night they had spent making love in Sophie and Rafi's small flat had been the happiest in her life. That was less than three years ago and yet it seemed so remote, as if it had happened in another lifetime.

Was there any going back to that intense happiness they had shared? She didn't know. Adela put her face in her hands and wept. Cold seeped up from the dew-soaked grass. She got to her feet, feeling utterly drained. She couldn't think straight; lack of sleep and fits of crying had left her mind fuzzy with fatigue. For so long now, she had been so completely focused on finding her baby that she'd had no energy for thinking about any other aspect of her life. Her days were fraught with running the café and her spare time was filled with the quest for John Wesley.

As she dragged her footsteps towards the city and Herbert's Café, Adela was struck by sudden clarity: she was still searching for the tiny baby that she had given up before the War. But her son was no longer that baby; he was a boy of over eight years old. For all of his young life he had been experiencing the world without her; she had been no part of it. He had known the love of the Segals and maybe at this very moment he was being cared for by another family who loved him. Yet, at no point would he be thinking of her – or his blood father, Sanjay. Sam and Josey were right; she had been determined to find him and claim him, no matter what his circumstances, without any thought for who might have adopted him. She didn't just want to know where he was or if he was happy; she'd wanted him for herself.

Adela felt sick with shame. How would that be helping her beloved son? She had assumed that the best thing for her would be the best thing for him too. But that wasn't necessarily the case. Her impulse had been selfish. She was trying to assuage her guilt at having had him adopted in the first place. But she couldn't change the past. All the remorse she felt would not wipe out the painful truth; she had given up her baby willingly and she would have to live with that.

Somehow, Adela got through another day at the café. She went through the motions of supervising Freda and Doreen, and of chivvying Joan to try and concentrate on one more week of work before she left to marry Tommy. Adela kept glancing at the back door, waiting for Sam to appear with some contribution from the allotment. This time she would not brush off his attempts to talk to her; she'd make an arrangement for them to meet after work and have a heart to heart. It was the one thought that kept her going through the day.

Yet, towards closing time, Sam still hadn't come. Adela asked Doreen to finish off and lock up while she went to check on the allotment. But there was no sign of Sam there. His tools were locked in the shed and a man in the neighbouring plot said that he hadn't been there for two days.

Adela felt the first twinges of alarm. Was he ill? Perhaps he was away on a photographic assignment that he hadn't told her about. She hadn't asked him about his photography business for ages. Josey's warning echoed in her mind: *'Wake up Adela. Sam's prepared to go back to India without you because he doesn't think you love him any more.'*

Surely he wouldn't have done anything so drastic without telling her first? It was unthinkable. But then Sam had acted on impulse before when life had got too difficult. Long ago, he had forfeited his steamboat in a card game and disappeared from Assam, only to be rescued from vagrancy and drink in Delhi by the kind missionary, Dr Black. Adela would never forgive herself if her neglect of Sam had pushed him back towards liquor and depression.

Adela had a sudden craving for a drink herself. She stood clenching her fists, fighting the urge to go back to the café and help herself to a tumblerful of sherry. Instead, she hurried into town and caught a bus to the coast.

Alighting in Cullercoats, Adela was assailed by salty sea air and a stab of memory of when she had been pregnant and living with kind Maggie and Ina. She pushed the thought away. She had come to see Sam, to apologise and make up. She would even take a reproof from Mrs Jackman if it helped repair her strained relationship with Sam.

Adela knocked several times before the door was opened. She tried to hide her dismay that it was Mrs Jackman who stood there and not Sam.

'I thought you would have come here before now,' Sam's mother said with a frosty look.

Adela swallowed. 'I'm sorry, Mrs Jackman. I'm not going to make any excuses but I'm here now. Can I come in and see Sam?'

She shook her head. Adela tensed. 'Please, I need to speak to him – to try and explain—'

'He's not here,' she interrupted.

'Oh, when will he be back? Perhaps I could wait upstairs with you?'

A look of pity crossed Mrs Jackman's face. 'No, dear, he's gone away for a few days.'

Adela's heart began to thump. 'Gone where?'

'To Edinburgh to see some tea planters about getting a job. I thought he might have told you.'

Adela felt her panic rise. 'No, he hasn't. Is he really planning to go back to India?'

Mrs Jackman nodded. 'Out East anyway. He's talking about the tea plantations in Ceylon.'

'Ceylon?' Adela cried in disbelief. 'Why would he . . . ?'

'He's not happy here. It'll break my heart if he goes away but I'll bear it if it makes him happy.' Sam's mother shook her head in sorrow. 'I hoped you would have made him happy, Adela, but I was wrong.'

The accusation winded Adela. 'I'm sorry, really I am,' she said, trying not to break down on the doorstep. 'Please tell him I need to see him when he comes back – not to do anything rash till we've spoken. *Please* tell him that, Mrs Jackman, I beg you!'

The older woman relented. 'I'll tell him – but I think you might be wasting your breath. When my Sam gets a notion in his head, it's very hard to stop him.'

'Thank you,' Adela managed to say. In distress, she walked away from the closing door, her heart sore with yearning for Sam. How could she bear it if she were to lose not only her son, but Sam too?

CHAPTER 24

The days of waiting to hear from Sam were some of the most painful Adela could remember. She was still beset with anxious thoughts about John Wesley's fate, though she tried hard to put them from her mind. This mental struggle – and desperate worry over Sam – left her in turmoil. Josey and Tilly tried to distract her with a trip to the theatre and a game of tennis with Mungo and some of his university friends. But Adela found the only relief came from working hard in the café and distracting her mind from thoughts of her collapsing marriage.

It was Lexy who she confided in the most about her innermost feelings, dear Lexy who had been her anchor in her times of trouble. And it was while talking to Lexy, late one evening after work, that Adela began to formulate a plan.

At the end of the week, Tilly took a call from Sam to say that he was back in Cullercoats and wished to speak to Adela. Rather than ringing him back, Adela sent a note asking him to meet her at the café after closing on Saturday evening.

With Doreen and Freda's help, and Lexy giving out instructions from a chair, Adela prepared a mutton curry and set a table behind a screen of potted plants with a fresh tablecloth and sweet peas from the allotment. Adela carried down the old gramophone player from Lexy's flat and borrowed a selection of Josey's records with songs that her old trio, the Toodle Pips, had once sung. Then Adela changed into a red evening dress that she'd bought in Calcutta and applied rouge to her sallow cheeks and lipstick to her pale lips.

She paced anxiously around the café, checking the clock, unable to sit still.

'What if he doesn't come?' she fretted.

'He'll come,' said Lexy. 'Sit down before you wear out the floor.'

But Adela couldn't settle. Only when Doreen dashed in from the kitchen to say he was coming across the backyard did Adela go behind the screen.

She heard Sam talking to Doreen in the kitchen, a note of surprise in his voice.

'Just go in the café, Mr Jackman,' Doreen urged.

The door swung open. Adela could see Sam in profile from her half-hidden position behind the plants. Heart hammering, she wound up the gramophone and lifted the needle on to the record. The jaunty song that had been the Toodle Pips' signature tune, 'Don't Sit Under the Apple Tree', began to play.

'Here you are, bonny lad,' said Lexy, rising stiffly to her feet and pointing to a jug of homemade juice. 'Help yourself to Nimby-pimby or whatever daft name you give lemonade in India.'

'*Nimbu pani*,' said Adela, stepping out from the corner with a nervous smile.

Sam stared at her, his mouth dropping open in astonishment. He was dressed in an old cricket shirt and grey flannel trousers with no jacket. His head was bare of his usual hat and his hair looked unkempt. With a pang of guilt, she noticed how gaunt his face was, his hazel eyes smudged with fatigue.

'I-I didn't realise . . .' he began but his words petered out.

As Lexy hobbled from the room, Adela went forward and poured them both glasses of the iced drink. She handed him one with a shaking hand.

'I want to say sorry, Sam,' she said quickly. 'Truly sorry for the way I've been treating you – for making you so unhappy.'

'Adela—'

'Don't say anything yet,' she stopped him. 'I know you're planning to go abroad without me. I don't blame you. But I want us to try and patch things up – have a meal together – and then talk things over. Please, can we do that?'

Sam nodded. She could see the tension in his jaw and the muscle working in his cheek as he struggled with some emotion. Was it anger or regret that it was all too late? She gulped down her drink and led him over to the table set for dinner. As Doreen emerged with a tray laden with plates of curry and potato, Adela put on another record: 'A Nightingale Sang in Berkeley Square'.

'We'll be off now,' Doreen said with a nod to Sam and a swift encouraging smile to Adela.

'Thank you,' Adela replied with a grateful look.

Adela sat down at the table opposite Sam. Her stomach was so churned up she didn't think she could eat a mouthful.

'Do you remember when I sang this at the army base in Imphal?' she asked.

He gave her a wistful smile. 'Of course I do.'

'And then I sang "You'll Never Know How Much I Love You"?'

He nodded, holding her look. He hadn't touched his food either.

'I sang that especially for you, Sam,' she said. 'I thought I might never get the chance to say how I felt about you, so I sang it in that song.'

Sam gave her a baffled look. 'Adela, tell me what's going on here. Are you buttering me up for something? Are you about to tell me you've found your son?'

Adela winced. How could he distrust her so much?

'No, Sam,' she said, 'I'm trying to show you that I still love you. You're right – I've been obsessed with finding John Wesley to the exclusion of all else – I've pushed you away and hurt you when I never meant to. I *have* found out more about my baby but it took Tilly and Josey to make me see sense. Sam, it's you I want to be with – you're the person I love most in the world – and I can't bear the thought that you might leave me . . .'

Adela's words caught in her throat. Tears flooded her eyes. She looked away, overcome.

In an instant, Sam was out of his chair and raising her to her feet. He held her at arm's length.

'Do you mean that?' he demanded, searching her face.

'Yes,' she croaked, 'every word.'

Sam pulled her into his arms and squeezed her tight. 'Oh, my darling, I thought I'd never hear you say those words again. I thought you didn't love me – that I was only a poor second best to Sanjay . . .'

Adela shuddered. 'Please don't say that. That man doesn't even come close to you in my estimation – I have no affection for him even though he fathered my son.'

Sam buried his face in her hair with a sigh of relief. 'I'm sorry for doubting you.'

'I'm sorry I gave you cause to doubt me,' said Adela. They looked at each other for a long silent moment and then she leant up and kissed him tenderly on the lips.

He gazed into her eyes. 'I never wanted to leave you, Adela, but I thought I was making you unhappy – I was at a loss as to how to make things better.'

'It was a mistake making you come back to England,' she said, 'at least for the reason I did. I felt terrible when your mother told me you'd gone to Edinburgh to fix up a job as a tea planter in Ceylon. It made me realise just how far apart we had become.'

Sam stroked her hair. 'I wasn't quite honest with my mother,' he admitted. 'I did have an appointment to meet a tea planter but there was another reason I went to Edinburgh.'

'Oh?' Adela felt calmed by his touch on her hair and the tenderness of the gesture.

'I wanted to see where my blood family came from – the Logans and Andersons. Sophie had told me with such affection about her time with Aunt Amy Anderson, I needed to see the city for myself. I went to Clerk Street and saw the flat where Sophie grew up, in sight of Salisbury Crags. I met Sophie's old employer, Miss Gorrie, who said how fond she was of my sister and told me anecdotes about their time together.'

Sam gave Adela a sheepish look. 'I didn't want Mam to know that was my main reason for visiting Edinburgh, even though she would probably understand.'

'I'm sure she would,' Adela replied. 'All she wants is for you to be happy – even if it means you leaving her and going abroad again.'

'She said that?'

'Yes,' said Adela. She touched his face. 'Is that what you want to do, Sam?'

'I don't know,' he admitted. 'I realise it will take time to feel I belong here – but even going to Edinburgh where my real family are from, I didn't feel it was home. But I'll make Britain home if that's where you want to be. It depends on you and whether you want to stay and carry on looking for . . .'

'No,' Adela said, steeling herself. 'I'm not going to keep searching for John Wesley. It was a selfish dream. Tilly said it was making me ill and she was right. I just have to come to terms with never knowing what's happened to him – and hope that good people are taking care of him. I have to accept I will never be his mother . . .' Her voice faltered.

'Darling!' Sam clutched her to him.

Adela swallowed hard. 'But,' she said, 'I want to be a mother to a child of our own. I want us to try for a baby.'

He cupped her face in his hands, scrutinising her.

'Are you sure?'

'Yes,' she said, on the verge of tears again. 'If you still do.'

'Of course I do!' Sam cried. He leant and kissed her firmly on the mouth.

Adela felt the ball of tension inside ease a little. A flood of affection washed through her. She held on to him and kissed him back.

'What do we do now?' he asked.

Adela felt her pulse begin to quicken at the look he was giving her. For the first time in weeks, she felt a stirring of desire.

'We can eat the curry before it gets cold,' she said softly, 'or we can go upstairs.'

He gave her a questioning look.

'Lexy and Doreen have leant me the flat for the night,' she explained.

His eyes widened. 'They have?'

'Yes,' said Adela with a smile. 'So I can seduce you.'

Sam laughed in delighted surprise. 'I can eat curry cold if you can.'

Hand in hand, they left the tearoom and headed upstairs to the empty flat.

❧ ❧

Hours later, after bouts of love-making and lying in each other's arms talking, Sam and Adela retrieved the plates of cold curry and carried them upstairs. Adela, dressed in an old dressing gown of Lexy's, reheated the food while Sam stood close, fondling her hair.

'You look very sexy in that,' he murmured, stooping to kiss the back of her neck.

Adela laughed. 'I wouldn't have bothered with the expensive red dress if I'd known that brown worsted drove you wild.'

Sam slid his arms around her waist and pulled her to him. 'I find you irresistible whatever you wear.'

She swivelled around and kissed him. 'Oh, Sam, I've missed our silly conversations. I love you so much.'

He answered her with another long lingering kiss.

They wolfed down the curry. Adela realised she hadn't eaten a proper meal for days. It left her feeling warm and contented – and stirred her desire again.

Sam must have been feeling the same because, as she stood to clear the plates, he stopped her, saying, 'Let's leave those till the morning.'

He pulled at the cord of her dressing gown so that the garment fell open. He pushed it from her shoulders and, scooping her up in his arms, carried her back to bed.

At some point during the night they fell asleep. When Adela woke, she saw Sam propped on an elbow gazing at her in the dawn light. They smiled at each other and Adela was filled with tenderness for Sam as well as relief that they still loved one another.

He brought them cups of tea and lit cigarettes. Adela leant against his chest and they talked again about their future and the possibility of leaving Newcastle.

'I've been thinking of writing to my cousin Jane Brewis to see if she might be interested in taking over the café again,' she said.

'Your Aunt Olive's daughter?' Sam said. 'The one who used to run the café before the War?'

'Yes. She was very good at it but she was called up and joined the ATS – ended up in Yorkshire and married a man she met when driving for the catering corps.'

'But isn't she settled where she is?'

'I'm not sure,' said Adela. 'That's why I thought I'd write. We used to correspond with each other a lot but got out of the habit. I know she's always been a home-bird. Aunt Olive relied on her greatly and I know she'd love it if Jane came back to the area.' Adela looked at Sam. 'If you're really serious about wanting to go back to India, then this would be a way of keeping the café running but handing over responsibility.'

'Is that what you want?' Sam pressed.

'I find the café a real chore,' Adela admitted. 'And I do miss India. But would it be foolhardy going back when most of the British are leaving?'

'Your mother and brother are there,' said Sam, 'and so are Sophie and Rafi. James and Libby may stay on too – and your cousin George. There will always be opportunities for those who are committed to make a go of it.'

Adela felt excitement quicken inside. 'It would be wonderful to be at Belgooree again – I've missed it far more than I thought I would.'

'I wouldn't want your mother to feel she had to give me a job though,' Sam said cautiously. 'We might have to go elsewhere.'

'Would you want to carry on with your photography?' Adela asked.

'I'm not sure,' Sam said. 'I do enjoy being behind a camera – but I also like working outdoors.' He stroked her hair. 'But it's your choice too. I want you to have the chance to enjoy the things you like. Since coming back to Newcastle you've done none of those things – acting and singing and having fun.'

Adela laced her fingers in his. 'That's been my fault for becoming so fixated on finding . . .' She swallowed, unable to mention her son again. 'But I can find society wherever we go. I just want you to be happy and us to be together.'

He squeezed her hand and kissed the top of her head. 'I want the same for you.'

Adela felt a fresh surge of affection for her easy-going husband.

'And what about your mother?' she asked.

'She'll understand,' Sam said. 'My future is with you, my darling.'

Adela's heart lifted with optimism. 'Then why don't we start at Belgooree?' she suggested. 'You could learn more about tea – my mother could teach you so much – if you really are interested in that. Or if you decide you'd rather carry on with your photography, we could go back to Calcutta. We have friends and contacts there. Perhaps Ghulam Khan could give you an introduction to his newspaper?'

'Yes,' said Sam, 'I like both those ideas.'

Adela saw the enthusiasm in his eyes. 'Good.' She smiled. 'I'll write to Jane today. But I'll not mention anything to Mother until things are more certain.'

Sam nodded. 'What about Tilly and the others here?'

Adela grimaced. 'It's going to be hard telling Tilly.'

'She'll not want you to go,' said Sam.

'No, so we won't say anything yet,' said Adela. 'Except to tell her that we've kissed and made up. She'll be happy about that.'

Sam grinned. 'There's no hurry to rush back to South Gosforth just yet. How about a bit more kissing and making up?'

Adela smiled, pushing him back on to the pillow and kissing him eagerly on the mouth in answer.

It was lunchtime before Adela and Sam returned to Tilly's, hand in hand and grinning foolishly at each other. Adela felt heady from their recent intimacy and Sam's demonstrative love for her. She hated to think how close she had come to losing him. Tilly had been right; it was when life became tough that true love was put to the test.

She had blamed Sam for not understanding her huge need to find her son but it was she who hadn't been honest with him about her deep sense of guilt and desperate hope. He had tried to support her but she had kept him at a distance, thinking only of her own feelings. From now on, she would not shut Sam out from anything. They had agreed they would have no secrets from each other.

'Hello! *Koi hai!*' Adela called as they entered the house. 'We're back! Anyone at home?'

After a pause, Josey shouted. 'In the sitting room. Sam with you?'

Adela and Sam exchanged bashful looks.

'Yes,' shouted Sam, taking Adela firmly by the hand and pulling her into the sitting room.

Tilly, Josey and Mungo were sitting down, their faces turned expectantly towards the door. Adela thought at once that Tilly had been crying; her eyes were red-rimmed and glistening. Josey looked flushed from several sherries.

'Is everything all right?' Adela asked in alarm.

'Perfectly,' Tilly said with a teary smile. 'I'm so glad to see you both together again.'

'I hope that means you'll be moving back in?' said Josey with a wink.

'Yes, for the time being,' said Sam. 'Until Adela and I find our own place.'

'Great,' Mungo said with a grin, 'someone to talk to about cricket for once and not theatre costumes or outings with the Mothers' Union.'

'You know I can talk just as knowledgeably about cricket as Sam can,' Josey said with her deep-throated laugh. 'Can I pour you lovebirds a sherry?'

Adela felt a familiar urge for a drink. She remembered how Sam thought she was drinking too much.

'No, thanks,' she said, 'I'll go and make some tea.'

'I'll come and help you,' said Sam, squeezing her hand.

'Before you do,' said Mungo, springing to his feet, 'we've got some news to tell you from India. Haven't we, Ma?'

'India?' said Adela, feeling sudden alarm as Tilly pressed a handkerchief to her mouth. 'Not bad news, I hope?'

'No,' said Mungo, 'it's great news. Though Ma is being all silly and emotional about it, aren't you?' He leant towards Tilly and gave her shoulder a pat.

Adela looked at them expectantly. Tilly looked suddenly too overcome to speak.

Josey said, 'A telegram came late yesterday – from James.'

Mungo smiled broadly. 'Dad's coming back. He's booked a flight. He'll be home by the end of the month.'

'That's wonderful!' cried Adela. 'Home for a visit or for good?'

'For good,' said Mungo.

'I'm so pleased,' said Adela.

'So am I,' said Sam.

Tilly looked up and gave them a teary smile. 'Yes, it's marvellous news.' Then her face crumpled and Tilly dissolved into tears.

'Oh, Ma!' Mungo chided in amusement. 'You're so sentimental.'

Adela and Sam exchanged glances. Adela knew her husband was wondering the same thing; was Tilly weeping for joy or out of unhappiness that her long-absent husband was returning to her after all these years apart?

CHAPTER 25

Belgooree, late July

A week after the emotional goodbye at Cheviot View, James's flight home was arranged. In six days' time he would fly from Calcutta. Libby was to accompany him to the city but was adamantly refusing to return back to Newcastle so soon. Her plan was to stay with the Watsons again but a letter from her Uncle Johnny explained that they were in the process of packing up and returning home too. They could put her up for a few days but would be gone before the fifteenth of August.

'I can't believe they're leaving India!' Libby cried. 'What about poor old Colonel Swinson? He's never known anywhere else.'

'Well, at least Tilly will be pleased to have her brother back,' said Clarrie. 'Where are they going to live?'

'Uncle Johnny's buying a house in St Abbs,' Libby replied. 'So he'll be near Auntie Mona in Dunbar – as well as Mother in Newcastle.'

'Good fishing in the Scottish Borders,' James said in approval. 'I must say I'm glad to hear Johnny will be around – he's a very decent chap.'

Libby found her father's preparations for leaving – and now the news about the Watsons – unsettling. Perhaps Clarrie sensed it, for on the day before departure, she encouraged Libby and Sophie to go riding to the waterfall and take a picnic. The jungle was dense and the waterfall thundering from the recent rain. They picnicked on a tarpaulin.

Sophie seemed preoccupied and a little subdued. Her appetite had deserted her.

'You must be missing Rafi,' said Libby.

Sophie gave an apologetic smile. 'Sorry, I'm not much fun at the moment; I do worry about him.' She picked up a boiled egg and started peeling the shell. 'It's lovely to be here with you – I'm really glad you came back to visit, lassie. Rafi and I have missed all you Robsons so much. It's a shame Tilly and the boys didn't come with you but I suppose they've settled into life at home and don't feel the pull of India like we do.'

'No, they don't,' agreed Libby. 'My brothers are happy where they are. I think Mungo might have considered a career in India once his degree is finished but there won't be the opportunities now . . .'

'Not in the civil service,' said Sophie, 'but maybe in tea planting or business.'

'Perhaps.' Libby shrugged. 'But Mother won't encourage it. She wants to keep her sons close by.'

'Well, Tilly's always been a mother-hen.'

'It's strange,' said Libby, 'but coming back out here has made me understand Mother a bit better. I can see how unsuited she probably was to life on a tea plantation. She loves the city and culture, not the outdoors – a picnic at St Abbs is about as adventurous as she gets.'

'She tried very hard to make a go of it here,' said Sophie. 'Cheviot View was always a very welcoming place.'

'Yes,' agreed Libby, 'that's how I remember it.'

'And she adored you all,' said Sophie.

'I don't think she ever adored me,' Libby said with a pained smile.

'Oh, but she did,' Sophie insisted. 'She missed you terribly when you were sent off to school. I think that's why she mollycoddled Mungo, because she was so upset at losing you and Jamie.'

Libby had a pang of pity for the young Tilly having to make the long sea voyage home three times to surrender her children to the care of strangers in boarding schools. Unexpectedly, it came back to Libby how her mother had written letters to her on a weekly basis and how much she had craved the news from home. Surely they had been practical proof of her mother's affection? Tilly had written far more than James had. Yet Libby had blamed her mother for abandoning her and had railed against the injustice of it for years. She had hated most of her school life and had made sure Tilly felt guilty for it. She had never thought of it from her mother's point of view – the sense of bereavement Tilly must have felt returning to remote Cheviot View without them – and for the first time realised it was not her mother's fault.

It was the practice of the British in India to send their children home to be schooled. Ghulam had once been scathing about girls like Libby being given a privileged education on the profits made by overworked tea pickers. Tilly could hardly have stood against the social pressure to send her children away. Only a forceful woman like Clarrie could ignore such convention and have her children educated in India.

'And what about you, Libby?' Sophie scrutinised her with large brown eyes. 'What do you want?'

Libby had been agonising over this very question for days.

'In the long term,' she answered, 'I know I have to go back to Newcastle. I don't have a home here any more – and perhaps I can help Dad settle back into life in Britain. He's going to find it so hard after a lifetime out here.'

'I'm afraid he probably will. I'm almost as fond of your father as I am of Tilly,' said Sophie, her look reflective. 'After my own parents died, your father was the one who rescued me and sent me to my dear Aunt Amy in Edinburgh. He arranged for the Oxford to pay for my schooling – he couldn't have been more caring.'

'I'm glad to hear that,' said Libby.

After a moment of silence, Sophie asked, 'And in the short-term? What will you do?'

'I want to celebrate Independence Day with you at Belgooree.' Libby smiled. 'But before that I really want to see Ghulam again in Calcutta.'

Sophie gave her an affectionate pat on the arm. 'Och, those Khan boys and their irresistible charm!'

Libby grinned. 'I know, who would have thought it? I didn't take to him straight away – and we got off on quite the wrong foot – but I fell in love with him over large slices of cake and a lot of political talk.'

Sophie laughed. 'That sounds just like Ghulam.'

'The thing is,' said Libby, 'since we've started writing to each other I feel like I know him better than anyone. Yet the last time we met he made it quite clear that nothing could come of our friendship. Despite his newsy letters, I'm still not sure that he sees me as anything more than a penfriend.'

'Well, there's only one way of finding out,' said Sophie, 'and that's seeing him again in person.'

'So you think I should?'

'If you care for him, then, yes, I do. Rafi was brave enough to come looking for me in the hopes that I felt the same way as he did. I've given thanks every day since that he did.'

Libby leant towards Sophie and squeezed her shoulder. 'Rafi will look after himself. He's not going to do anything rash – he adores you too much to put himself in danger.'

'Thank you, dearie,' said Sophie.

Libby had hoped they might plunge into one of the more tranquil pools but Sophie was restless. She didn't want to linger by the waterfall and her nervousness put Libby on edge too. They packed up after half an hour and rode home.

To Libby's surprise, Clarrie wasn't at work. She and James were sitting on the veranda playing backgammon while Harry practised tennis shots against the godown wall. Libby's insides clenched at the scene of domesticity. Maybe Clarrie had organised the picnic trip so that she and Harry could have James to themselves for one last day. Libby felt like an intruder. On an impulse, she stopped Sophie on the path to the house.

'Would you take me to see your Ayah Mimi?'

Sophie looked at her in surprise.

Libby went on hastily. 'I know she's a holy woman now and has removed herself from the world but I remember her from my childhood and I'd love to see her before I go. Do you think she would see me?'

After a moment's hesitation, Sophie nodded.

'Ayah Mimi was always very fond of you Robson children,' Sophie said, 'especially you, Libby.'

'Why me?'

'Because you weren't afraid of an old woman,' said Sophie. 'Let me speak to her first and ask.'

They diverted round the bungalow and the servants' compound to the furthest part of the garden where Ayah Mimi's hut was almost obscured by creepers and overhanging trees. Sophie entered the hut alone to see her old nurse. Libby stood outside wondering what had prompted her sudden urge to see the old *sadhvi*. It was not just to avoid Clarrie and her father. Ayah Mimi was one of the special threads that bound Libby to her early childhood in India, a lowly woman servant who, in later life, had chosen a life of independence and self-reliance by becoming a holy woman.

According to Sophie, the old nurse had saved baby Sam from his deranged father and then, having been forced to hand Sam over, had spent years looking for him. In later times, both Sophie and Sam had been reunited with their former ayah, here at Belgooree. Libby had to admit that once again, it was big-hearted Clarrie who had cared for the old woman and given her a home.

Sophie reappeared with a tiny, hunched figure in a white sari leaning on her arm. Her hair was snow-white and her leathery face was daubed with yellow and white lines. Ayah Mimi blinked in the light and when she caught sight of Libby, her dark eyes lit up and she gave a wide toothless smile.

Libby felt a lump in her throat. '*Mataji*,' she greeted the old woman respectfully.

Ayah Mimi lifted up a hand and beckoned Libby closer. As Libby bent towards her, the *sadhvi* touched her cheek with scrawny fingers.

'Sit, sit, my daughter,' she said, lowering herself on to the rush mat that Sophie had brought outside with them. Libby and Sophie sat either side of her and she held on to their hands.

Ayah Mimi asked about Libby's family and Libby told her of the long time away from India and what her brothers were doing now. Eventually, the *sadhvi* said, 'I'm glad your family are well but something is troubling you?'

Libby's insides tensed. 'I'm worried about my father – whether he will cope back in England – but also because something is causing him mental pain and I don't know what it is. He won't talk about it.'

Ayah Mimi gazed at her with eyes full of compassion. She let silence fall about them. Libby thought she wasn't going to say anything in reply and then she reached out her hand and laid it on Libby's head.

The old woman closed her eyes and began to murmur. Libby didn't understand the words but her head felt suddenly hot where the *sadhvi*'s hand rested. She became acutely aware of the twitter of birds in the trees above. Suddenly, the knot in her stomach that had been there since leaving Cheviot View dissolved and a new feeling of calm spread through her. Libby felt tears running down her cheeks and into her mouth.

Sophie handed her a handkerchief with a kind smile. Ayah Mimi opened her eyes and, without another word, climbed to her feet. When Sophie and Libby tried to help her indoors, she waved off their attempts and disappeared back inside her hut.

Libby was too overwhelmed to speak. Sophie slipped an arm through hers as they walked slowly back towards the house. Libby wasn't sure quite what she had just experienced – a blessing of sorts perhaps – but it gave her courage to face the uncertain days ahead. She hoped it might help her father too in some way – though she doubted his demons would be put to rest by the fluttering of a *sadhvi's* hand.

⁂

Early the next morning, Daleep stood waiting by the car, ready to drive Libby and her father to the railway station at Gowhatty. Once in Calcutta, they were to stay with the Watsons. After James's flight and the Watsons' departure, Libby had arranged that she would stay on in New House for a week or so while the house was made ready for sale, and then return to Belgooree for a final visit.

A sleepy Harry emerged yawning and tousle-haired to say goodbye. Libby said quick farewells to Clarrie, Sophie and Harry, hugging them and promising to be back in time for the August celebrations. She was eager to be on her way. Turning at the top of the veranda steps, she saw her father struggling to speak.

James stuck out his hand to Harry. 'Look after your mother,' he rasped.

Harry's eyes filled with sudden tears. To Libby's astonishment, the tall youth ignored the handshake and flung his arms around James.

'I'll miss you,' Harry mumbled.

James clutched him hard for a moment and then, with a pat on the back, pushed him away. Sophie stepped forward.

'Give my love to Tilly,' she said with a fond smile. 'And thank you for all you've done for me ever since I was a child. I would never have survived or thrived without your help. You've been like a guardian angel.'

'Nonsense,' James pooh-poohed.

'It's true,' said Sophie. 'And I hope one day, when everything is settled, that you will visit me and Rafi.'

'I'd like that,' James said with a bashful smile.

She gave James a swift hug and a peck on the cheek and stood back.

Clarrie had been standing very still since hugging Libby goodbye. She and James looked at each other. Libby could see her father swallowing hard. Then Clarrie reached out her hands to him. He grasped them like a lifeline. For a long moment they stood, their faces etched with sorrow. James cleared his throat to speak but Clarrie spoke first.

'Thank you for being my friend during the dark days after I lost Wesley.'

'You don't have to thank me,' he said hoarsely. 'It's me who owes you the greater debt. I shall miss Belgooree.'

'I know you will,' she said gently.

Libby suspected they were really saying how much they would miss each other.

'Goodbye, James.' Clarrie leant up to kiss his cheek.

In one swift movement, James cupped his hands around her face and kissed her on the lips. It was a fleeting but intimate gesture. Abruptly, James turned away and strode to the steps, his eyes swimming with tears.

Hastily, Libby descended the stairs ahead of him, her heart thumping. The stolen kiss had upset her but she wasn't sure if it was shock at her father being over-familiar with Clarrie or sadness on their behalf.

Just at that moment, Breckon came tearing round the corner of the house, barking and leaping up at James. Libby's father let the dog lick him and then briefly buried his face in Breckon's neck. Pulling away, he called to Harry to take the dog. Harry jumped down the steps and held Breckon by his collar, giving pats of reassurance, while James hurried to the car.

Moments later, Libby was sitting beside her father in the back of the car as they trundled down the drive. James craned round for a final view of the white weathered bungalow festooned in flowering creepers. A sob caught in his throat. In that moment Libby realised that her father saw this moment as the real farewell to India – not Cheviot View or the Oxford – but Belgooree which had been a haven to them all. It also struck her how James had not only been a companion to Clarrie but also a father figure to young Harry. They would probably miss him as much as he would miss them.

She covered his hand with hers and squeezed it, hoping to comfort him in some small way. They passed the factory buildings where the office staff had come out to wave them away, including a beaming Nitin to whom Libby had lent her typewriter until her return.

'What a nice gesture,' said Libby. But James was too overcome to shout a farewell. Her father didn't speak again until Belgooree and its tea gardens were long out of sight.

CHAPTER 26

Calcutta

Both Johnny and Helena came to pick them up from Sealdah railway station. Libby was aghast at the number of families camped out on the platforms under makeshift awnings.

'Terrible business,' sighed her uncle.

'They really should move them on,' said Helena.

'Nowhere for them to go,' said Johnny.

Then it hit Libby. 'Are they all refugees?'

'Yes, from East Bengal,' he answered. 'They've been arriving in Calcutta for weeks now.'

'We at the Girl Guides have been trying to feed and clothe some of them,' said Helena, 'but it's an impossible task. Come quickly, or you'll have dozens pestering you, I'm afraid.'

Libby looked on in anguish at the pathetic sight of scores of people sitting listlessly around a few possessions – cooking pots and bed rolls – looking utterly exhausted. Were these some of the people that Ghulam and Fatima had rescued from further east? Minutes later they were in the safety of the Watsons' car, being driven away to Alipore.

'James, I really think Libby should be getting out before Partition becomes a reality,' said Helena. 'Couldn't you get her on your flight?'

They were sitting on the veranda having a nightcap with their hosts; Colonel Swinson was fast asleep in his chair.

'I don't want to go yet,' said Libby. 'I want to see in the new India.'

'I can understand that,' said Johnny.

'I can't,' Helena protested. 'Calcutta is not a safe place to be. They're preparing for more trouble. God forbid it's as bad as last summer – the slaughter—'

'That's enough, dearest,' Johnny said with a warning look.

'Libby is old enough to make her own decisions,' said James, surprising Libby. She gave him a grateful look. 'I shall miss her but I hope she will follow me shortly.'

Her eyes prickled at his sudden tenderness and she nodded in agreement.

'Now we've made the decision to go,' said Helena, 'I can't wait to get on that boat from Bombay. With the house half packed up, it doesn't feel like home any more. And I'm looking forward to seeing St Abbs. Johnny's talked about it so much – I'm expecting nothing less than Shangri-La.'

'Well, Shangri-La in a cold climate,' said Libby, exchanging amused looks with her uncle.

'It'll be good to have you living close by,' said James. 'And Tilly will be over the moon.'

Helena put a hand on his arm. 'I'm so pleased to hear you are going back to dear Tilly.'

James, looking embarrassed, swigged the remains of his whisky and stood up. 'Long day's travel tomorrow. Bed beckons. Thank you for having us both to stay, Helena.'

Libby watched her father go. He had been preoccupied since leaving Belgooree, as if his thoughts had already turned to home and his family back in Britain. She stayed sitting on the veranda after the others had retired to bed and listened to the night creatures in the garden and the restless sounds of the city beyond. She felt a kick of excitement to think that Ghulam was living close by and that soon she would have the chance to see him again. She had written to say she was coming to Calcutta but he hadn't had time to reply before she'd left Assam. Breathing in the scent of lilies, Libby gave thanks that it wasn't she who was flying away from India in a few hours' time.

'Don't come to the airport,' James told Libby the next morning. 'We'll be seeing each other again soon, won't we?' It was more a plea than a question.

'Yes, we will,' Libby agreed, kissing her father on the cheek, gripped by a sudden sadness that they were being parted again so soon. They were standing in the garden listening to a cacophony of birds as the dawn light filtered through the trees.

Since the news of Partition and her father's decision to go home, Libby had felt a new closeness growing between them. Only they had shared the sorrowful farewell to Cheviot View and together they had experienced the heightened emotion of the past few days at Belgooree. It made her think of the kiss her dad had given Clarrie; she couldn't get the image out of her mind. Would he be greeting Tilly with the same tenderness in three days' time? She felt a pang of anxiety for him. As an adult, she was just beginning to know her father and he struck her as a much more complex and vulnerable man than the one she had remembered.

She slipped her arm through his and laid her head against his shoulder.

'Give Mother and the boys my love, won't you?' she added.

James nodded and kissed the top of her head – a gesture Libby recalled from childhood. He said almost to himself, 'This is the way

I will always remember India – at daybreak with all the promise of a new day.'

For a moment her father's face looked serene, wiped of his habitual frown and haunted look. Libby thought how much younger he looked – more like the man she remembered, with the strong chin and vital blue eyes. Her eyes stung at the bittersweet thought that she had found her father again just at the moment his time in India was coming to an end.

In the distance they heard a call to prayer. Then the gong went for breakfast and, with a sigh, James straightened his broad shoulders and turned back to the house. Libby walked by his side, still holding on to his arm.

❧ ❧

The day her father left Calcutta, Libby had planned to help the Watsons with sorting out their possessions for packing. But the scenes she had witnessed at the railway station were too disturbing. With the two weeks she had before returning to Belgooree, she knew she had to spend them helping the refugees in any way she could.

A distracted Helena offered to put her in touch with the Guide commissioner.

'Thanks,' said Libby, 'but I'm going to find Fatima at the hospital and see if I can help her women's charity.'

'That sounds far too dangerous,' said Helena, frowning.

'It's really not,' Libby assured her. 'They're just distributing food and clothing.'

'Well, our driver Kiran will take you over there,' Helena insisted.

That afternoon, when Libby was dropped off at the Eden hospital, she told Kiran she would ring the house if she needed collecting.

After half an hour of trying to track down Fatima, she was told that the doctor was not at the hospital. She was running a mobile clinic downriver. Libby recalled that Ghulam had written about his sister's work there and how refugees were arriving on overcrowded country boats from East Bengal almost daily.

Libby got the administrator to write down the name of the clinic and draw a map. Returning to the street, she hailed a taxi.

'Chowringhee Square, please,' she instructed. 'The *Statesman* offices.'

In the lobby of the newspaper office, Libby asked to see Ghulam. While a message was sent upstairs, she retreated to a seat by the wall, her insides churning. Libby saw Ghulam before he saw her. Her heart thumped at the sight of his handsome face and unruly dark hair as he clattered down the stairs, shirtsleeves rolled up over muscled hairy arms, searching the hallway for her. She got up and hurried towards him.

'Libby!' The smile he gave her made her legs go weak. 'What are you doing here?'

She felt breathless as she replied in a gush. 'Dad left today. I was looking for Fatima at the hospital. I want to help. I saw so many refugees at the station. I thought you might be able to take me . . . to the clinic, I mean . . .' Her words dried up as he scrutinised her with his vivid green eyes.

'It's good to see you,' he said.

'And you too,' she said huskily. 'I've really enjoyed your letters – and writing to you.'

'So have I.' He held her look for a moment before glancing round distractedly. 'Listen, I'm sorry but I have to report on a meeting now. Fatima will be back home this evening. Why don't you call on her tomorrow at the hospital and tell her you'd like to help?'

Libby felt a pang of disappointment. 'I could call round this evening.'

'It's not safe to be out after dark,' he said. 'Things are very tense in certain parts of the city. Tomorrow would be better. I'll let Fatima know you'll be coming.'

Libby nodded. 'Tomorrow then.'

He touched her arm briefly. 'I'll walk you to the tram.'

As they stepped into the sweltering heat, Libby tried to think of things to say to keep him beside her as long as possible. But most of her news she had already told in her letters. Now that they were together, face-to-face, they were strangely bashful.

As they reached the tram stand, Ghulam asked, 'So you decided not to go home with your father? Does that mean you're staying on in India?'

Libby's insides twisted. 'Only temporarily. I promised Sophie I'd spend Independence Day with her at Belgooree as she doesn't think she'll be able to join Rafi before then. And then I've agreed with Dad that I'll go back to Britain to be with the family.'

Ghulam nodded. She couldn't read his expression.

'But I've got two weeks in Calcutta before all that,' Libby added hastily.

'Two weeks,' he echoed, giving a half-smile. 'We'll have to make the most of them then, won't we?'

Libby's heart raced at his words. 'Yes,' she agreed, smiling back.

Yet too soon, she found herself waving Ghulam goodbye and clambering on to the tram for Alipore. Frustration overwhelmed her at seeing him so briefly.

The following day, Libby tracked down Fatima at the busy women's hospital. The doctor seemed pleased at Libby's offer of support.

'Can you use your British contacts to drum up help?' Fatima asked.

'What sort of help?' asked Libby.

'Donations. Second-hand clothes – cooking pots – tents – anything they might be throwing out rather than taking back to Britain with them.'

Libby's stomach knotted. Fatima was already assuming that Libby and her British family and friends would be leaving Calcutta.

'Of course,' she answered. 'I'll ask Aunt Helena.'

'Ghulam's going to be driving a truckload downriver in two days' time,' said Fatima, 'so whatever you can lay your hands on by then would be very helpful.'

'I'll see what I can do,' Libby said. 'In the meantime, can I help out here?'

Fatima gave her a direct look. 'That's kind of you to offer but you have no nursing training. The best way you can help us is to gather as much kit as you can for the homeless.' She gave a brief smile. 'Your powers of persuasion are what we need the most.'

Libby, seeing how busy and preoccupied Fatima was, left her to get on with her job. She had hoped for an invitation to visit Amelia Buildings but the doctor did not offer one. Libby knew that Fatima would be working late and the last thing on her mind would be spending an evening socialising or entertaining. It was selfish of her to expect it. Libby resisted the desire to track down Ghulam again – he too would be busy – and made her way back to Alipore, her heart heavy with longing.

On the eve of the Watsons' departure, it took little persuasion to get Helena to part with a godown-ful of old camping equipment; pre-Great War tents, camp beds, chairs and canvas washstands that had belonged to Colonel Swinson and not been used in years. Libby, with a bit of cajoling, got her aunt to relinquish a trunkful of old sheets and linen hand towels too, along with boxes of chipped crockery and dented pots and pans.

'Libby is doing us a favour, darling,' Johnny encouraged. 'We're taking far too much stuff as it is – and the shipping costs are more than most of it is worth.'

'I suppose so,' sighed Helena. 'And if it's helpful . . .'

'Oh, it is,' Libby assured her.

She lost no time in sending a message round to the Khans about the donation. To her delight, Ghulam sent a message by return to say he would come round with a van to collect the goods the next day.

Libby, along with her uncle, went round to various British clubs and to the Duff Church and left notices asking for donations to be left at the Eden Hospital for the attention of Dr Fatima Khan.

That evening Libby had a final meal on the veranda with the Watsons and the Colonel: just a simple supper of steamed fish and boiled potatoes followed by bananas in custard – the Colonel's favourite. The next day the Watsons would be embarking from Howrah railway station for the long overland train journey to Bombay.

'Are you sure about staying on here on your own?' Helena fretted. 'Is it what your parents would want? I know Muriel and Reggie would put you up in a jiffy if I asked them. Muriel would do anything for a daughter of James Robson's.'

'That's kind,' said Libby, 'but a room here is all I need – and Dad approved.'

Libby knew that was an exaggeration; her father hadn't given an opinion either way. He had been too distracted by his imminent journey home.

'After all,' Libby added, 'it's only for ten days, then I'll be returning to Belgooree.'

That night Libby couldn't sleep. She lay awake thinking about how her time in India was slipping away but how she would be seeing Ghulam again in a few short hours. Her stomach churned with a mix of dread and excitement. What was he thinking at this very moment? Was she in his thoughts as much as he was in hers? She felt sick with wanting.

With the dawn she rose, washed, and dressed in slacks and a shirt that she pulled from a small suitcase, which was all she needed now to hold her reduced possessions. She had sold off her prim Calcutta outfits at a shop on Park Street and would be giving the proceeds to Fatima's charity. The one luxury she kept was the second-hand green satin dress which would always bring back memories of dancing with Ghulam under a tropical night sky.

She found Colonel Swinson sitting on the veranda in shorts and singlet, having done his morning exercises. With shaking hands he beckoned her over.

'Got something for you, girl,' he said, fumbling in his shorts pocket. He pulled out a brown paper bag and handed it to Libby.

She looked inside and gasped. It was stuffed with rupee notes. 'Colonel Swinson! I don't need money.'

'Not for you,' he replied. 'It's for . . .' He waved a veined hand at her. 'That thing you've been talking to Helena about. Bengalis. Homeless.'

'The refugee centre?'

'Yes, that's it.'

Libby was touched; she hadn't realised that the old man had understood what was going on.

'That's very kind of you, thank you.'

'No use to me in Scotland,' he said.

'Still, it's very generous,' said Libby.

He sucked his lips as he ruminated. 'Would like to have done more. But it's too late, isn't it?'

Libby wasn't sure if he meant too late for him personally or for India. Either way, she saw the tears swimming in his rheumy eyes and knew the day he had dreaded was finally here – the day he must leave Calcutta and start for exile in a Britain he didn't know.

Libby could think of nothing to say that would lessen the old man's sorrow. Instead, she leant towards him and kissed him tenderly on the cheek.

Hardly able to touch her breakfast, Libby leapt up at the sound of a lorry's engine at the gates of New House. She rushed down the short drive and was overjoyed to see Ghulam jump down from the cab.

Libby's insides flipped at the sight of his ruggedly handsome face. The two grinned at each other. They said little as Ghulam organised the fetching and carrying of the donated equipment, Libby almost too breathless to speak.

With the lorry loaded, Johnny offered Ghulam *chota hazri*.

Ghulam declined. 'Thank you, but I've got a busy day ahead – and I know you have too.' He put out his hand. 'Good luck, Dr Watson, and a safe journey home.'

'Thank you,' said Johnny, shaking his hand in farewell. 'And I wish you all the best in the future . . .'

Libby could see that her uncle was suddenly struggling to speak. She chose that moment to make her move.

'Ghulam's kindly agreed to give me a lift round to the Dunlops' flat so I can have a catch-up with Flowers,' she said quickly. 'I don't want any more drawn-out goodbyes, Uncle Johnny. We'll see each other soon enough in St Abbs.'

She shot Ghulam a look; he was trying to mask his surprise at her sudden announcement. He nodded in agreement.

Johnny put up no resistance. Libby dashed on to the veranda and gave swift hugs to the Colonel and to Aunt Helena, who was hovering at the breakfast table, and then to Johnny. Then she picked up a small canvas bag with a change of clothes and hurried back down the drive to a waiting Ghulam.

Climbing into the cab of the lorry, Libby said, 'Sorry to spring that on you but I couldn't bear any more protracted goodbyes. It feels like I'm saying nothing else at the moment.'

'I'm happy to oblige,' said Ghulam, settling into the driver's seat, 'though this isn't the most comfortable of taxis. It's an old lorry we communists used for electioneering.'

'It's perfect,' said Libby with a breathless laugh.

'Remind me where the Dunlops live?' he asked. 'It's Sudder Street, isn't it?'

Libby held his look. 'I'm not going there – I'm afraid that was just an excuse. I want you to take me with you to the refugee centre so I can help. And don't tell me it's too dangerous – I'm prepared to do anything that you and Fatima are. So please let me come.'

His face creased in a familiar lopsided smile that made her stomach flutter. 'I was hoping you'd say that.'

'Really?'

'Yes, really. Together we can be useful.'

Libby felt a flicker of disappointment. 'Yes, of course. Useful . . .'

His look was suddenly intense. 'And if your days here are numbered then I want to spend them with you, Libby.'

Her heart began to thud. In that moment she knew that he wanted her too.

'So do I,' she answered.

Briefly, he put his hand over hers and squeezed it. Then he leant away and started the engine. With a belch of smoke they trundled away from New House and headed out of Calcutta.

CHAPTER 27

East of Calcutta, end of July

L ibby had never seen such squalor. All along the railway tracks makeshift shelters had been planted between pools of rainwater. Everything was caked in mud. The lucky ones were camped under the canopies of the station platforms. Flies buzzed. The stench of human effluent was only partially masked by the oily smell of cooking. Children splashed in puddles while their parents looked on with anxious faces. Elderly men and women sat looking worn out and resigned. Yet everywhere there was quiet industry: people fixing up shelters with flimsy materials trying to create privacy, while others rolled and cooked chapattis.

Fatima's charity had commandeered a derelict mansion house not far from the station for its clinic and the distribution of aid. Libby spent the day there parcelling out rations of rice and flour, and helping distribute bedding to the refugees who were camped out in the grounds. Every available inch of garden was occupied. Inside the house, the grand old reception rooms had also been given over to homeless families.

Only the top floor was reserved for the charity workers: a mix of medical staff, students and well-off Hindus, with a handful of middle-aged Europeans. Libby was the only young British woman there that day.

Libby hardly saw Ghulam all day, until the evening when the work-ers came together for a communal meal on the roof. Libby felt sweaty and exhausted, her hair stuck to her cheeks where it had escaped from her ponytail. Yet the smile Ghulam gave her made all the hard work worthwhile.

The volunteers sat around on bedrolls and shared a simple meal of dahl, vegetables and rice. Below, fires flickered among the dark trees and the hubbub of voices mingled with the sound of crickets. The Bengalis spoke English to Libby and made her feel welcome. She was surprised by their light-hearted humour despite the grimness of the situation and sensed their optimism for the future.

Libby recognised one of them from the ill-tempered political meet-ing where she had gone to hear Ghulam speak. He was called Sanjeev and seemed to be a good friend of Ghulam's. With a wave of his hand, Sanjeev said, 'This is just temporary. Once Independence comes, people will feel safe to go back to their homes – or they will find new ones. It's just the uncertainty that is causing such panic.'

They talked about the news that Gandhi might once more be com-ing to the city to calm tensions in the lead-up to Independence Day – now just two weeks away.

Ghulam's eyes lit up. 'The rumour is that he is going to live in one of the *bustees* where there has been so much of the trouble – and he's insisting that Suhrawardy share it with him.'

'Suhrawardy?' Libby exclaimed.

'Yes, the Muslim leader of the city council.'

'I know who he is,' said Libby, 'but he's a playboy – he won't want to slum it with Gandhi.'

'He won't,' Sanjeev agreed, 'but it's symbolic – a Hindu and Muslim living side by side together, showing how it should be done. If a man like Suhrawardy can do it, then that will send out a powerful message to others.'

'Do you think it will work?' asked Libby.

'It has to,' said Ghulam, his expression turning grim. 'The city is like a tinderbox.'

'All will be well, my friend,' said Sanjeev, with a pat on Ghulam's back.

Libby yearned to have Ghulam to herself but they could manage no more than a few personal words in front of the others.

'Will Fatima come down again soon?' Libby asked.

'She hopes to come by the end of the week,' said Ghulam.

'How long can you stay?' she asked, holding his gaze.

'I must be back at work the day after tomorrow.'

Soon afterwards, the women went below to sleep in a room with crumbling walls while the men stayed on the roof, smoking and chatting until the rain came on again. Libby, tired out, fell asleep quickly.

During the next day, Ghulam sought out Libby.

'There's talk of fresh boatloads of people coming in downriver,' he said. 'I'm going to take the truck and bring them supplies. Want to come and help?'

Libby was quick to agree. They rattled out of the compound, loaded up with rice, blankets and tarpaulin. They chatted generally about the charity work and Ghulam told her more about the other volunteers. Sanjeev was an old comrade from the Communist Party who had switched allegiance to the Congress Party during the War.

'He's one of the few from the old days who didn't turn his back on me for supporting the anti-fascist war effort,' said Ghulam.

Despite his sardonic smile, Libby saw the pain in his eyes when he glanced at her.

'I like Sanjeev,' said Libby, touching his arm, 'he's so optimistic.'

Briefly, Ghulam covered her hand with his own and her pulse began to race. She wanted to ask him about that other former comrade – the woman who had been special to him – who had hurt him with her accusations of treachery. Was he still in love with her? Or in touch with her? But they were soon at the riverside and pulling up near an overcrowded *ghat*.

All afternoon, they helped hand out rations and guide people to shore from small, crammed country boats. The river was a swollen, sluggish brown. Libby knew from Ghulam that it was particularly hazardous for Bengalis arriving by boat as so few of them knew how to swim.

By late afternoon, the rain was starting again and people sought what shelter they could under rude tents of tarpaulin and bamboo.

The sky was leaden and darkness was falling quickly.

'We need to get back up the road before nightfall,' said Ghulam. 'It's not safe to stay longer.'

Just as they were making for the truck, they heard a scream from the water's edge. Libby spun round. It seemed to be coming from a boat bobbing low in the water close to the bank. Then in the twilight she saw a woman scrabbling along a plank of bamboo that linked the boat to the land. She was wailing in distress. At once, Libby doubled back. She slithered in the mud towards the woman, holding out her hand, thinking she was too terrified to climb ashore from the boat.

But the woman resisted, screaming and pointing at the dark water below. Then Libby saw it: a child's head bobbing in the flooded reeds. An instant later it was submerged. Pausing only to kick off her shoes, Libby waded into the brackish water and struck out for where she had seen the child disappear.

The water swirled about her, ripping her away from the bank. Suddenly she caught sight of the child's thrashing arms and long hair: a small girl. Libby swam towards the drowning infant and – just as the girl disappeared again – grabbed at her hair. Libby pulled her into her hold; the girl spluttered and choked. With forceful kicks, Libby kept their heads above water, as she attempted to swim back to shore. But they had already been carried downstream out of view of the mother on the plank. In the weak light and the rain, Libby was disorientated. There seemed to be a myriad of creeks and waterways, while a strong undercurrent tried to suck them away into midstream.

She stemmed the panic that rose in her throat. Anchoring the distraught, struggling girl to her body with one arm, Libby struck out with the other. She could hear shouts from the bank and thrashed towards the voices. Sudden darkness enveloped her like a light being switched off. All at once, she grabbed a handful of reeds and knew she must be near land. But when she tried to stand, she sank into mud and tendrils of swampy vegetation wrapped around her legs.

'Help!' she cried out. 'Please help me!'

Pain shot through her arms at the strain of holding on to the girl and trying not to go under. Her mouth filled with putrid water. She gagged and coughed. She was going to die. She couldn't hold on much longer. Her futile attempt to save the unknown girl was going to end in death for them both. For an instant, Libby thought of her parents being reunited in Newcastle and how she wished she could be with them. And then she was thinking of Ghulam and how much she regretted that she would never get a chance to be with him.

'Libby?' a man bellowed through the drumming rain. 'Libby!'

Libby was galvanised by the voice – Ghulam's precious voice. She was damn well not going to die in a mango swamp!

'Here!' she called out breathlessly. 'Over here.'

With the last of her waning strength, she struggled to rid herself of the tangle of weeds. She felt her legs break free. She kicked for the bank. At that moment, a flaming torch illuminated the undergrowth overhead and she saw a host of anxious faces peering down. People shouted encouragement as arms stretched out towards her.

'Take . . . the . . . girl,' Libby panted.

The child was plucked to safety. Libby heard a coughing of water and a querulous wail. The girl was still alive.

Moments later, strong arms were reaching down and pulling her out of the river.

'My God, Libby,' Ghulam said, gripping her. 'I thought I'd lost you . . .'

Libby was too exhausted to stand; her legs were like jelly. She could hardly breathe. But Ghulam held on to her, clutching her to him in relief. They stood clasping each other in the pounding rain as mud splattered their legs. Libby didn't care. All that mattered was that she was alive and Ghulam was holding her as if he would never let her go.

Then, people were pressing around them. The woman who had screamed for her child now came with a man who carried the girl wrapped in a blanket. They began gabbling at Libby. The woman held out a brass bangle of turquoise stones.

'They're thanking you for saving their daughter,' said Ghulam, still with an arm about her. 'They want you to have this gift.'

Libby shook her head. She hardly had the strength to speak. 'No . . . I can't . . . girl should keep it . . .'

When Ghulam explained Libby's words, they grew agitated.

Ghulam said to Libby. 'You should accept it. Nothing is more important than a child's life.'

Libby felt her eyes sting with tears as she took the brass bangle, nodding her thanks while she still clung on to Ghulam. The people were trying to lead Libby to a fireside and give her their rice but Ghulam said something to them and steered her away towards the truck. There he wrapped a blanket around her sodden body. He was as wet as she was but she was shaking uncontrollably with a mix of euphoria and shock. It could only have been minutes since their first attempt to leave but Libby felt it had been an age. She was utterly drained.

As the lorry swayed along the dark road, she was lulled into a half-sleep, her head nodding against Ghulam's shoulder. They hardly spoke. Libby dozed off. She was vaguely aware of them stopping close to the derelict mansion and two of the helpers jumping down from the truck but when she tried to stir herself, Ghulam told her to rest. When she next awoke, she realised they were on the outskirts of Calcutta again.

'Aren't we going back to the centre?' she asked groggily.

Ghulam shook his head. 'The others will explain what's happened. I'm not going to be responsible for you catching your death sleeping on the floor of a leaky room. Fatima can lend you some dry clothes. You can stay with us tonight.' He glanced at her. 'If that's okay with you?'

Libby smiled. 'Of course it is. Thank you.'

'Did you leave anything behind?' he asked.

'Just a knapsack with a change of clothes,' she said.

'I'll get Sanjeev to bring it over,' said Ghulam.

'No need,' said Libby. 'I'll get it when I go back to help again.'

He gave her a look of disbelief. 'You won't be going back.'

'Of course I'll go back,' she insisted, though she felt weak at the thought.

'Libby,' he protested, 'you nearly drowned.'

'I don't intend jumping into the river again in a hurry,' she said, 'but I still want to help out.'

He let go an impatient sigh. 'Why does that not surprise me?'

He reached out and pushed a tendril of hair behind her ear. 'Oh, Libby, I should never have taken you . . .'

'It was my choice,' she said with a wan smile, 'and I'd do it again if I had to.'

***

It took all Libby's efforts to climb the stairs of Amelia Buildings to the fourth floor. She felt unwell; she was breathless and ached all over. Fatima was full of concern and fussed around Libby, scolding her for being so impetuous and Ghulam for letting her take such risks.

'It's not Ghulam's fault,' said Libby, 'it was just a split-second decision.'

'My brother should never have taken you down to the *ghat* in the first place,' Fatima chided, but Libby could see the admiration in her eyes.

Even though the air was oppressively warm, she couldn't stop shivering. None of Fatima's clothing was big enough for Libby so she resorted to putting on a cotton shirt of Ghulam's and drawstring trousers that were too long and needed rolling up at the ankle. They were loose, comfortable and fresh-smelling and Libby was comforted by the feel of them against her skin. Fatima wrapped her in a soft woollen shawl.

They ate a supper of curried mutton and potatoes. Ghulam and Fatima talked about the growing migration crisis and the rumour that Gandhi might once more be coming to the city to calm tensions in the lead-up to Independence Day. Libby hardly had the strength to eat and struggled to stay awake, even though she wanted to know more about this talk of Gandhi. She felt utterly spent.

'Sorry, Libby,' Fatima said, catching her yawning, 'you must go to bed. You can take mine and I'll sleep on a bedroll.'

'No,' said Ghulam. 'There's no need for that. Libby will have my room and I'll sleep here – or on the roof.'

Fatima frowned. 'I don't think—'

'Libby should have her own room tonight after what she's been through,' said Ghulam firmly.

'Sorry, of course she must,' said Fatima.

'Thank you,' Libby said. 'You've both been so kind.'

Libby could hardly believe she was lying in Ghulam's bed; it smelt of his musky soap. The room was small but high-ceilinged and equipped only with a narrow iron-framed bed, a wooden chair, a bedside table and a cupboard for clothes. Her head swam. Despite the room being warm, she felt chilled in the eddying breeze from the un-shuttered window. Libby wrapped herself in Fatima's shawl and tried to get warm.

Sleep wouldn't come. The hours dragged. She wanted nothing more than to have Ghulam wrap his arms around her and keep her safe. Every time she closed her eyes she was back in the dark, swirling water struggling for breath. The taste of the rank water lingered in her mouth. Her pulse raced to think how close she had come to drowning. If Ghulam hadn't hauled her from the water . . .

Libby clenched her teeth, biting back the panic rising in her throat. She was going to be sick. She scrambled out of bed and dashed for the door. In the dark corridor she stumbled towards the water closet, a hand clamped over her mouth. She reached it just in time and vomited into the thunderbox. Libby was sick until her stomach felt hollow and her throat raw. Then she crouched on the floor and let the tears come. She tried to stifle her sobs but relief came with weeping. She was alive – even though she felt terrible.

Emerging from the closet, weak-kneed and shivering, Libby gasped to see a dark figure looming out of the shadows.

'Libby,' Ghulam whispered, 'are you all right?'

'I've just been sick,' she whispered back. 'I feel a bit wobbly.'

He was bare-chested and his hair tousled. He reached out and took her by the hand, guiding her along to the sitting room. The room was bathed in lamplight. A rumpled bedroll on the floor and a discarded book showed that Ghulam had not been sleeping either.

He sat her on one of the comfortable chairs and fetched a glass of soda water along with a dish of aniseed and mint to freshen her mouth. She drank the soda with shaking hands and chewed on the aniseed.

'I can't stop thinking . . .' she said, her eyes flooding with fresh tears.

'You've had a shock,' said Ghulam, covering her hand with his. It felt warm and comforting. 'But you saved a girl's life. Libby, that was one of the most foolhardy acts I've ever seen – and one of the bravest. You are a remarkable woman.'

'There's nothing remarkable about me,' Libby said, emotion catching in her throat at his kindness.

'To me there is.' He squeezed her hand. 'You care so much about everyone and everything – nothing daunts you – and when I'm with you anything seems possible. You don't let prejudice stand in your way. You went into the river after that unknown girl as if she was your own sister. That is remarkable, Libby.' His vivid eyes were full of admiration. 'And you are beautiful too.'

His words made Libby dissolve into tears. She reached out for him. Libby gulped. 'I was so afraid I would never see you again.'

In an instant, Ghulam was pulling her to her feet and wrapping his arms around her, caressing her hair and murmuring reassurance.

'You're safe now. I won't let any harm come to you.'

Libby cried into his shoulder. She was acutely aware of being pressed to his naked chest, as covered in dark hairs as she had imagined. At that moment she didn't care about the future. All that mattered was being in Ghulam's arms and knowing that he had feelings for her. They stood clinging to each other while her crying subsided. Then Libby looked into his compassionate face.

'I don't want to be alone tonight,' she whispered.

Ghulam fixed her with a questioning look. She could feel the sudden tension in his body. Her heart began to thud.

'What *do* you want, Libby?' he asked.

'I want to be with you,' she said softly, 'to lie with you.'

'Are you sure?' he asked, his voice gravelly.

'Yes, but only if you want it too.'

'Oh, Libby, you must know I do. But you are going home soon. There's no future for us. And if your own people ever found out, you'd be cast out—'

'I don't care what other people think of me,' she interrupted. 'You must know that by now. And I know the future is uncertain for all of us. I'm not expecting you to offer me anything more than this moment together. But tonight I want to feel alive – I want to be with *you*, Ghulam, even if it's only this once. Tomorrow can take care of itself.'

He squeezed her to him and she could feel the drum of his quickening heartbeat. He looked deep into her eyes and she could see the passion in his.

'And I want to be with you, Libby,' he said, bending to brush her lips with a kiss.

Libby felt desire flare in her belly. 'Then take me to your bed,' she said, 'and make love to me.'

They said nothing further as they padded back to Ghulam's small bedroom and closed the door. Ghulam wedged a chair against it to stop Fatima or Sitara coming in unexpectedly. It was almost pitch black in the room at first but as their eyes adjusted they could see each other outlined in weak light from the mosquito-netted window.

They quickly cast off their clothes and stood naked together. Libby ran her fingers across his broad chest, feeling the hairs. She kissed and nibbled his shoulder.

'I've dreamt of touching you for so long,' she whispered. 'Kissing you—'

She felt his arousal at once. Ghulam pulled her closer, his mouth seeking hers. He enveloped her lips in a hungry embrace. His hands caressed her body as he murmured his passion for her. Then they were tumbling towards the bed in their haste to make love.

He covered her body in kisses, making her arch and squirm in ecstasy. She clung to him and tried not to cry out, though she wanted to scream out her love for this man.

They writhed on the bed with suppressed sighs and groans, trying not to be heard. Ghulam's lovemaking was both tender and vigorous, and Libby found herself weeping with emotion.

Afterwards, they lay entwined on the narrow bed, their heartbeats still rapid. Ghulam twisted a strand of her hair in his fingers and kissed her gently on the lips.

'You are truly remarkable,' he said.

'And you are even more remarkable in bed than I ever hoped you'd be,' she replied, with a dreamy smile.

He gave a soft exclamation. 'You make it sound like you've been expecting us to fall into bed together.'

'Hoping rather than expecting,' she said, tracing a finger across his stubbled chin and pushing back the lick of hair from his eyes – something she'd been longing to do for months.

'I've been hoping for it too,' Ghulam admitted, kissing her nose.

'I've daydreamed of this since we sat and ate cake on that day you took me out for lunch,' said Libby. 'Food can be such an aphrodisiac.'

He chuckled quietly. 'For me it was seeing you standing in that green satin dress with your hair loose, looking like a starlet.'

'Really? At the party?'

'Yes,' he said. 'I tried to deny it to myself but I couldn't get you out of my thoughts after that.'

Libby was astonished. She hadn't been at all sure of Ghulam's feelings for her at that point, only that her own had been racing out of control. 'I'm nothing like a starlet though,' she said. 'Not like my pretty cousin Adela.'

'You are more desirable than a film star,' he said, pushing hair away from her face and kissing her throat. 'You are like one of those voluptuous erotic statues on Hindu temples – a goddess.'

Libby stifled a laugh.

'It's true.' He smiled and began to stroke her body again.

Instantly, Libby went weak with longing. She closed her eyes and gave herself up to Ghulam's lovemaking once more.

CHAPTER 28

Just before dawn Ghulam rose from the bed, kissed a sleepy Libby on the lips and crept back to the sitting room. She fell asleep again, sated by their energetic sex and no longer afraid. When she awoke, the sun was high and the street below hummed with noise. It took a few moments to remember where she was and a hot wave of pleasure washed through her at the memory of what she and Ghulam had done in the night.

She got up, feeling light-headed, and pulled on the clothes she had discarded in her haste to make love a few hours previously. Her stomach felt hollow; her appetite had returned.

In daylight, she noticed that there were two pictures hanging on the wall beyond the simple cupboard. One was a photograph of some people at a religious festival – or perhaps a political rally – and Libby peered at it more closely. At the forefront was an attractive woman in uniform, wearing a dark beret and helping Ghulam hold up a banner. Libby's insides clenched. Could this be the woman that Fatima had told her about, the only woman Ghulam had really loved and whose photograph he still kept?

She turned away from it, uncomfortable with the thought, and looked at the other picture. It was a sketch attached to the wall with drawing pins. On closer inspection, Libby blushed to see it was her cartoon of Ghulam as a grumpy tiger. She laughed out loud that he had not only kept it but displayed it on his bedroom wall.

Libby went to the water closet and then padded along to the sitting room, hoping to find Ghulam. The room was empty and the bedroll gone from the floor. The clock on the desk showed it was already late morning. A note on the table bore her name. She unfolded it.

Dear Goddess
Both of us have gone to work. Take the day to rest and recover from your ordeal. Fatima doesn't want you to put yourself at any more risk – and I have to agree with her. We'll talk tonight. Make yourself at home.
Ghulam

Libby grinned at the reference to goddess; it was the only hint at their lovers' conversation of the previous night. Otherwise the note was friendly but not over-familiar, no doubt not wanting to draw Fatima's suspicion. She felt a renewed yearning in the pit of her stomach. The day would drag until she saw him again.

A moment later Sitara appeared with a breakfast tray of tea, fruit and boiled eggs. Libby smiled and thanked her, frustrated that her lack of Hindustani would not allow for more than a few basic words. Her childhood fluency in the language had long been forgotten. She eyed the servant, wondering if she could have heard anything in the night. But Sitara didn't linger and Libby was left alone to eat.

She was ravenous and devoured all the food on the tray. She glanced through the books on the bookcase and chose one at random. It was about the archaeology of Taxila by some nineteenth-century traveller. She wondered whether it was Ghulam or Fatima who was interested in the ancient site near Rawalpindi; she decided it must be Fatima.

Ghulam had no patience for the past; he was a man firmly anchored in the present but always hankering after a better future for the world.

Later, as the temperature climbed again, Libby went for a wash. Returning to Ghulam's bedroom, she found her river-soaked clothes of the day before on the chair. They had been washed, pressed and neatly folded. She blushed to think that Sitara probably missed nothing that went on in the Khan household.

Libby dressed in her own clothes, brushed out her wet hair and settled back in the sitting room to read. Sitara brought her more food and drink, which made her sleepy. She went and lay down on Ghulam's bed and was soon fast asleep.

Libby woke with a start. There was shouting in the street below. Someone was screaming. She scrambled out of bed and ran to the window, throwing open the shutters. It was already dark outside. How long had she been asleep? She couldn't see anything distinctly – a few shadowy figures, people running, a woman in a luminous sari bending over – but she could hear the commotion. The woman was wailing in distress. In the distance she heard the sound of a bell – perhaps from a police van – and more yelling.

Libby's heart pounded. Then lamplight spilled out from an opening door below and she could see more clearly. A man was trying to pull the woman away, remonstrating with her. As they did so, Libby saw a person crumpled on the ground at the woman's feet, his white clothing stained with what looked like blood. Had he been attacked? Was he dead? Something terrible had happened. They needed help. She ran to the door and then stopped. Panic caught in her throat. What if it was dangerous? What could she do? There might be a gang of *goondas*. They might turn on her. They wouldn't see in the dark that she was British . . .

Libby leant against the door gasping for breath. She couldn't move. She stood like that for what seemed an age, paralysed by fear. And yet she wasn't even down in the street. What was happening to the distraught woman? Who was lying on the ground? What if it was Ghulam?

Hot shame at her cowardice flooded through her. With shaking hands, Libby threw open the door and lurched up the corridor. The sitting room was empty; neither Fatima nor Ghulam were back from work. Her heart thumped in alarm. As she fumbled with putting on shoes, she heard the pounding of footsteps on the stairway beyond the flat.

The door flew open. Ghulam's anxious face caught sight of her.

'Are you all right?' he demanded.

She felt dizzy with relief to see him.

'Yes. What's happened? I heard the noise. Has someone been hurt?'

'There's been a stabbing, right on our doorstep,' he said. 'I was frightened the attackers might have been in the building too.'

She rose and went to him, throwing her arms around him and bursting into tears. Ghulam clasped her tightly and stroked her hair.

'Is he dead?' she whimpered.

He swallowed. 'I think so. They were carrying him away just as I arrived.'

'I was so afraid it was you,' she sobbed. 'I was going to see . . .'

'You were going out there?' he asked, horrified.

'I should have gone sooner but I was too afraid.'

'Thank God you didn't, Libby.'

'But I should have.'

He grasped her by the shoulders and frowned. 'My God, woman! How am I supposed to keep you safe if you keep rushing straight towards trouble?'

'But what about that poor woman?'

'She's being looked after,' said Ghulam.

'Was she his wife?'

'I don't know,' he said distractedly. 'She was Hindu like him, so probably.'

'So was it a Muslim gang who did this?'

He gave her a bleak look. 'It could have been a quarrel between neighbours – but whether it was or not, the Hindus will seek revenge.'

'Oh, Ghulam!' she cried, holding on to him.

'That's why I came straight here to make sure you and Fatima were safe.'

'But your sister isn't home yet,' Libby gasped. 'What if she gets caught up . . . ?'

Ghulam looked around him, for the first time seeming to notice that his sister was not there.

'I must go and look for her,' he said at once, dropping his hold and turning for the door.

'Then I'm coming with you,' Libby insisted.

'Certainly not!' he ordered. 'You'll stay here and keep the door bolted.'

'Ghulam, please—'

He rounded on her in exasperation, his expression grim. 'Stay out of this, Libby. It's not your fight and I've got enough to worry about.'

She recoiled from his words and the hard look in his eyes. She watched him go.

'Lock the door behind me.' Those were the last words he said to her before he disappeared back into the dark stairwell and clattered away out of sight.

Libby, heart hammering, retreated into the flat and did as he said.

***

The waiting was interminable. Sitara appeared and Libby gestured for the old widow to stay and sit with her. The clock on the desk ticked on into the evening and no one came. Libby's mind was filled with every horror she could imagine: Fatima had been caught up in the fracas, dragged off into a dark side alley and violated; or Ghulam had been ambushed by vengeful Hindus and was now lying mutilated and dying, his blood seeping into the gutter . . .

Libby was nauseated by her thoughts. She couldn't sit still and kept pacing to the door and back. Sitara tried to calm her with soothing words that she didn't understand and pressed her to drink tea.

'I know you're trying to be kind,' said Libby, knowing that the woman probably didn't understand her either, 'and you must be as worried as I am – but I'm going out of my mind. What's happened to them? Why hasn't Ghulam returned by now?'

She thought of going up on to the roof to try and see if she could spot them returning, or find out what was happening below. But that would mean leaving the door unlocked and Sitara vulnerable. Ghulam would be furious with her for disobeying him.

'Oh, Ghulam! Where are you?' she cried aloud.

Then doubts beset her. The words he'd flung at her came back to taunt her. *Stay out of this, Libby. It's not your fight.* How it wounded her to be told that despite all she had been through in the past couple of days, Ghulam still did not see her as one of his kind. This was a matter for real Indians not the Indian-born British like her. She was already an irrelevance in this land.

Not only that, she was a burden to the Khans. To them, the violence in Calcutta was a real and ever-present danger. They were Muslims – albeit non-practising ones – who would be in a vulnerable minority should the city be parcelled off to West Bengal and India after Independence. It struck Libby how brave they were, carrying on their work amid the ferment of a divided city, as well as volunteering to help refugees from the opposing community. Not that either Ghulam or Fatima saw the fleeing East Bengali Hindus as their opponents. They were simply fellow Indians in extremis who needed their help.

Libby sat down and buried her face in her hands. In contrast, she had done so little for ordinary Indians since returning to the land of her birth. For all her talk about freedom for India and anti-colonialism, what had she done that had been of any practical use? At best she had dabbled in playing the bountiful memsahib – a couple of days volunteering in a canteen and doling out blankets. Her Aunt Helena had done far more in her role as a Girl Guide leader and yet Libby had been scornful of her aunt, not prepared to see beyond the bossy memsahib exterior.

Libby dug her nails into her palms as she was beset with self-criticism. What was she doing here? Her obsession with Ghulam had controlled her every thought and action. She had pursued him for her own gratification, not stopping to think what effect it might have on his life. She wanted him so much that she didn't care if it was short-term, that she might soon be leaving for England, never to see him again. She felt a stab of pain at the thought. But that was the reality. She had her family in Newcastle waiting for her to join them; the future might look dull and colourless after India but it would be safe and secure.

Whereas Ghulam faced a future fraught with danger and uncertainty. As a Muslim, would he keep his job after Independence? Would he stay in Calcutta or be forced to flee to East Bengal, where the new East Pakistan was being created? What about Rafi and the rest of the Khan family cut off in the part of the Punjab that was shortly to become West Pakistan? Would they be safe and would Ghulam ever see them again?

In the light of such turmoil, no wonder Ghulam had rounded on her. Daily, he must feel anxiety in the pit of his stomach, worrying about his sister and the days ahead. Libby was only adding to his worry. Only now did it dawn on her how selfish was her desire to be with him. His instincts had warned him to resist becoming involved with her emotionally – Fatima had also cautioned her against a relationship with Ghulam – but Libby had ignored the advice and gone after him. She was the one who had pressed him to come to her party, had encouraged a correspondence between them and had urged him to go to bed with her. She had turned his world upside down.

He had shown last night that he enjoyed intimacy with her – relished it even – but it could only be a temporary affair. They both knew that they lived in very different worlds and that once she left Calcutta they were unlikely to see each other again. Libby felt winded by the thought. However much it would devastate her to be parted from Ghulam, she couldn't stay here; it wasn't fair on Ghulam and it was probably causing Fatima embarrassment. The doctor was liberal-minded about many things but Libby suspected she was a prude when it came to sex outside of marriage, let alone between people of different races.

Please just let them be all right! Libby began to pray in her head. *Let them be safe, please, God! Then I promise I will leave them alone.*

A few minutes after the clock chimed ten, Libby heard footsteps outside and a knock on the door. She leapt up, heart hammering.

'Libby, it's me.' Ghulam called. 'Open up.'

Libby scrabbled with the bolts and unlocked the door. To her relief, Ghulam stood there with an exhausted-looking Fatima. Libby flung her arms around the doctor, who almost lost her footing in surprise.

'Thank goodness you're both safe!' Libby cried. 'I've been so worried.'

'I'm fine,' said Fatima, gently disengaging herself. 'Just tired.'

As Ghulam locked the door behind them, he said, 'I found her at the hospital working late.'

'There's been a string of attacks across the city,' Fatima said, her look harrowed. 'Knife wounds mainly. Even children.'

'Oh, how horrendous!' exclaimed Libby.

She wanted to ask more but the warning look Ghulam gave silenced her. Fatima sank into a chair and closed her eyes. Sitara hurried back into the room with fresh tea and hot samosas.

They ate without speaking. Eventually Libby couldn't bear the silence any longer.

'What is happening out there? Why the sudden increase in violence?'

When Fatima said nothing, Ghulam answered. 'It may be because of the news that Gandhiji is about to arrive in the city. Gangs are settling their scores before he comes. But who knows? There seems to be no rhyme or reason to the killing.'

'What will you do?' asked Libby. 'Is it safe for you to stay here? Perhaps I could arrange for you to take rooms in New House. Alipore is safe.'

Ghulam gave her a sad smile – the first tender look since he'd returned – and said, 'That's kind of you but it doesn't really solve anything. We still have to go to work in the city and it would be a longer journey home after dark.'

'So are you going to just carry on as if nothing happened outside here tonight?' she asked.

Ghulam glanced at his sister and she nodded for him to speak.

'No we are not. Fatima is going to live in at the hospital for the next few weeks until things settle down,' he said. 'It'll be safer there.'

'And you?' Libby pressed him.

'I'll stay here,' he said. 'If things get worse I know I will be welcome at Sanjeev's or with another of my Hindu friends.'

'Can't I do anything to help?' she asked, hating the feeling of helplessness.

Fatima spoke up. 'You have done more than enough,' she said. 'You saved a little girl's life and we'll never forget that. But you're not safe staying here, Libby. We can't look after you and guarantee no harm comes to you when we are struggling to do that for ourselves.'

'I understand that,' Libby replied. 'I'll go back to Alipore.'

Ghulam frowned. 'I don't think you should stay in Calcutta on your own. I think you should go to Belgooree as soon as you can.'

Libby felt pained by his haste to see her gone.

'I agree,' said Fatima. 'You'll be safer in the Khasia Hills away from the violence. Ghulam says that you've promised Sophie you'll be there for the celebrations on the fifteenth. I'm so glad you'll be able to keep her company while Rafi's away in the Punjab – it'll help keep her spirits up.'

'Yes, I'll try.' Libby nodded, feeling a lump form in her throat.

'Is there anyone you can travel with?' Fatima asked. 'I'd be concerned about you making the journey alone.'

'I can stick to the first-class memsahibs' carriage,' Libby said with a mock smile. 'The only danger there is the blocks of ice running out.'

They didn't laugh at her feeble joke.

'Perhaps Flowers would travel with you again?' suggested Ghulam.

'I don't think she'll be rushing back to the hills in a hurry,' said Libby. 'She found up-country life very dull.' On the spur of the moment she added, 'Maybe Clarrie Robson's nephew, George Brewis, might want a trip up to Belgooree. He hasn't been to see his aunt yet.'

She saw Ghulam's jaw darken. He flashed her a look. Libby glanced away. Perhaps it was best if he thought she was still in touch with George; it would make it easier for him to banish her from his thoughts.

'That would be a good idea,' said Fatima with a smile of approval. 'Now I think we should all get some sleep. It sounded like you had a disturbed one last night.'

Libby flushed. She didn't dare look at Ghulam. 'I was a little bit sick.'

Fatima frowned in concern. 'You should have come and told me.'

'I didn't want to bother you,' said Libby. 'And I felt better soon after.' Libby stood up and glanced at Ghulam. 'I don't want to turf you out of your room for a second night,' she said. 'I'll sleep in here.'

Ghulam gave her a perplexed look. 'I don't mind . . .'

'But I do,' said Libby. She couldn't bear to lie sleepless and alone in a bed where she had known such ecstasy just a few hours ago – or have to look again at that photo of the beautiful revolutionary that Ghulam kept on his wall. He clearly wanted her gone as soon as possible.

'Very well,' he said, his expression tightening. He left the room to fetch the spare bedroll.

Fatima said softly, 'I'm sorry it has to be this way – I know you are fond of my brother – but I think it's for the best.'

Ghulam returned before Libby had time to question Fatima on what she meant was for the best. Probably that Libby went quickly and got out of her brother's life. In her heart she knew that the doctor saw no future for Libby with Ghulam.

After a night of fitful sleep in which Libby had to restrain herself from creeping along the corridor to Ghulam's bedroom, she rose early. Tidying away the bedroll, she scribbled a note of thanks and left as dawn broke.

The city, awash with pearly light, was waking to a chorus of birds, calls to prayer and the stirrings of shopkeepers opening up their stalls. It was as if the violence in the night had been a bad dream. Yet as Libby stepped out into the lane, she saw where someone had attempted to wash away blood from where the stricken man had lain. Nauseated, she thought pityingly of the distraught widow and prayed fervently that there would be no repercussions.

Libby returned to her digs in Alipore, bathed and changed into a summer frock. Feeling refreshed, she braced herself to make a telephone call to the chummery in Harrington Street. George had already gone to the office, she was told. She left a message for him to call her back. Next she took a taxi to Sealdah railway station and booked herself a ticket for two days' time. Now that she had made the decision to go early to Belgooree – or rather the Khans had – she was keen to be gone. Perhaps putting distance between her and Ghulam would help ease the leaden feeling inside. She forced herself to stop trying to imagine what he was thinking in the wake of their one-night affair and its unexpectedly abrupt ending.

She sent a telegram to Belgooree to say when she would be arriving in Shillong, hoping they might send Daleep to collect her. By mid-afternoon she was making her way by tram back into the city; she would call on Flowers and explain what she was doing. If the nurse wasn't there, she would leave a message with her parents.

Libby was welcomed warmly by the Dunlops; she had forgotten quite how hospitable they were until Winnie Dunlop began plying her with sandwiches and cake and endless cups of tea. They wanted to hear all about her time away in Assam.

'Flowers told us very little,' said Danny Dunlop.

'Except to say what a jolly good time she had,' chipped in Winnie.

'Found out nothing about my family,' complained Flower's father. 'Didn't even go to Shillong in the end, did you?'

'I'm sorry, we didn't,' said Libby, feeling a guilty pang. 'My father wasn't very well so we took him straight to Belgooree.'

'See, Danny,' his wife reproved, 'the poor man was ill. Of course he wouldn't want to go chasing about your old school.'

'Sorry,' he said with a sheepish look at Libby, 'I didn't mean to be critical of your father. How is he?'

'Back in Britain,' said Libby, suddenly realising that she was missing him. 'I haven't heard much except a telegram to say he got safely home and that it's raining and cold.'

'Wonderful!' said Danny with an envious smile. 'Do you hear that, Winnie. Cold and wet. Not like this infernal soup that passes for air in Calcutta.'

Winnie rolled her eyes. 'Give me hot soup over icy rain any day,' she said cheerfully.

'I would like to have met your father,' Danny said with a sigh of regret, 'and talked about his life on the tea plantations. Pity he never knew anything about the Dunlops.'

Libby's guilt increased that she hadn't made more effort on Mr Dunlop's behalf. 'I'll write to him and ask again. He has an old planter friend in Newcastle – a Mr Fairfax – who might help. He's very old now. I remember meeting him at one of Mother's fundraisers during the War. If anyone knew of any Dunlops in Assam it would be him.'

Danny's face brightened. 'Would you do that?'

'Of course.' Libby smiled. 'I'll send Dad the details Flowers gave me so he can pass them on to Mr Fairfax.'

'That would be splendid!' Danny beamed. 'You see, if we're ever to go home to Britain, I need to prove my British blood. I won't get a passport otherwise.'

Winnie rolled her eyes at Libby but didn't contradict her husband. Libby suspected that Flowers and her mother thought the best way to deal with Danny's preoccupation with leaving India was to ignore it.

Just as Libby was thinking of going, Flowers arrived. They hugged affectionately.

'Come and tell me all your news while I change out of my uniform,' said Flowers, ushering her out of the sitting room. In the bedroom, she closed the door and said, 'Now you can tell me how things really are. How is your father?'

While Flowers discarded her work clothes, Libby told her everything that had happened in the intervening weeks – about her father's decision to retire and go back to England, Sophie coming to stay at Belgooree and Libby's plan to visit one last time before returning to Newcastle to re-join her family.

'I assume Dad's settling down okay as he hasn't had time to write – unless there's a letter waiting at Belgooree.'

'So you're definitely going home after Independence?' asked Flowers.

'I promised Dad I would. There's no home in Assam any more.' Libby tried to sound more positive than she felt. 'Anyway, it'll be good to see all the family back together again.'

'And Ghulam?' Flowers said. 'Have you seen him since you came back to Calcutta?'

Libby nodded, her eyes stinging.

'Didn't it go well?' Flowers scrutinised her.

Libby said, 'At first, yes. Your idea of writing to him was wonderful. We wrote to each other almost daily. I fell in love with him completely.'

'So what happened when you met up again?'

Libby told her about the happenings of the past few days, from the trip to the refugee centre and rescuing the girl, to staying with the Khans and the appalling murder on their doorstep. Flowers was horrified.

'Right outside Amelia Buildings?' she gasped. 'How simply ghastly.'

'Ghulam just wants me gone now,' Libby said unhappily, 'and I can't blame him. I'm just someone else he has to worry about if I stay. And he knows I'm leaving India soon, so there can't be any future in our relationship. But the thing is, I think about him constantly. I . . . Two nights ago we . . .'

Flowers, in her slip, sat down on the bed next to Libby and put a hand on her arm. 'You what?' she asked, looking alarmed.

'We made love,' Libby admitted.

'Oh, Libby!' Flowers's eyes widened in shock. 'And now he's had his fun he's sending you away?'

'It's not like that,' Libby said, stung by Flower's comment. 'He's thinking of my safety. It was me who pushed him into going to bed. He's not a womaniser like George.'

Flowers flushed. 'George has calmed down since his divorce came through.'

Libby looked at Flowers in surprise. 'Have you two been dating?'

Flowers gave her a bashful smile. 'We still go dancing now and again. I sometimes think . . .'

'Think what?'

Flowers sighed. 'Oh, nothing.' She stood up and continued changing into a slim-fitting flowery silk dress.

'I was thinking of asking George if he wanted to visit Belgooree with me,' said Libby. 'His Aunt Clarrie would love to see him and it might make the celebrations on the fifteenth more jolly. I've left a message for him to contact me at Alipore but it's not giving him much notice.'

Flowers gave her a direct look. 'Well, you can ask him in an hour or so.'

Libby glanced at her questioningly.

'He's coming here,' said Flowers.

'He's taking you out this evening?' Libby exclaimed.

'Yes.' She smiled shyly. 'To Firpo's. Come with us.'

'And be your wallflower?' Libby said with a dry smile.

'There will be others too,' said Flowers. 'Eddy and the gang.'

'I've nothing to wear.'

'That dress will be fine,' Flowers replied. 'I insist. Looks like you could do with a good night out before you head off into the *mofussil*. Stop you pining over that troublesome lover of yours. Then you can stay the night here. I don't like to think of you being on your own, rattling around that big flat in Alipore.'

Libby gave her a grateful smile. 'Thanks, I'd like that.'

'Good, that's settled then. You can borrow anything of mine tonight and go and fetch your belongings tomorrow.'

Libby watched Flowers continue to prepare for the evening out.

'Doesn't the situation in Calcutta worry you?' Libby asked. 'You're right in the heart of it here in Grey Town.'

'We just have to be careful to be chaperoned after dark,' said Flowers. 'But we Anglo-Indians are okay. It's not our fight, is it?'

Libby was struck again by the phrase *not our fight*. It was the one Ghulam had used when he'd lost his patience with her. She shivered with foreboding. As the British raced towards a hasty handover and exit from India, she wondered just how much division and violence they would leave in their wake.

CHAPTER 29

L ibby enjoyed the evening out far more than she had anticipated. Firpo's was only half-full with diners and dancers – there was still a jittery atmosphere despite Flowers's nonchalance – but Libby found George's bonhomie just the tonic she needed.

'We've missed you at our socials, lass,' he said with a wink.

Later, when they took to the dance floor, he said, 'Flowers tells me you've been a right little Florence Nightingale with your dad. Glad to hear he's on the mend and back home with the family. You following on shortly?'

'Yes,' said Libby. 'Later in August most likely – depending what flights I can get.'

'Better book early,' said George. 'There'll be a stampede to leave once the handover comes.'

'Will you be part of it?' Libby asked.

'Not likely.' He grinned. 'I'm having too much fun here. And the job's good.'

'So no regrets about leaving England?' Libby pressed him.

'Not one,' he insisted. 'There's nothing to go back for, is there? Joan's getting wed again and Bonnie's getting a new dad, so everybody's happy.'

'And you, George? What would make you happy?'

'Having the next dance with you, bonny lass,' he quipped.

Libby laughed. But it didn't escape her notice how much George's attention was taken up with keeping an eye on whom Flowers was dancing with. Libby didn't mind. She had long ceased to have any romantic interest in George and she knew that Flowers was more than capable of keeping an amorous George at arm's length – if that's what she wanted.

George prevaricated about a possible trip to Belgooree. He had plans to celebrate on the fifteenth in Calcutta.

'There's a dinner-dance at the Palm Court in the Grand Hotel,' he'd enthused, 'and there'll be fireworks. Don't want to miss the biggest night out in Calcutta since before the War.'

It was left that he might combine a work trip with a visit to his Aunt Clarrie later in the month, before Libby left Belgooree.

On her last day in Calcutta, Libby retrieved her case from New House where Ranjan, Colonel Swinson's bearer, had been keeping it safe. While Flowers was at work, Libby went for a final walk around the Maidan in the late afternoon, as the worst of the heat dissipated. Using an umbrella lent by the Dunlops to shelter her from the hazy glare of the afternoon sun, she wandered through Eden Gardens and past the solid fortifications of Fort William. Soon exhausted by walking in the humid air, she hailed a rickshaw to take her up Chowringhee Street, thinking to take tea in an air-conditioned tearoom.

On the spur of the moment, she directed the driver to take her to Nahoum's in Hogg's Market, where she bought some fudgy sweetmeats. She would go and eat them on the steps of the Duff Church as a way of saying farewell to Calcutta and her affair with Ghulam. Tomorrow she would be on her way to Belgooree to spend her final days in India.

But on reaching the church and seeing the shaded spot where she had first fallen in love with Ghulam, she couldn't bear to stay there. Dismissing the rickshaw driver, Libby found herself walking in the direction of Hamilton Road. Fifteen minutes later she was standing outside Amelia Buildings. It seemed incredible that only two days ago a man had been butchered here in this ordinary street.

Shivering with the horror of it, she hesitated and then went inside. She had no idea if anyone would be at the flat. The *chowkidar* nodded for her to go up. She would leave the fudge with Sitara for Ghulam, who probably wouldn't be back from work until nightfall.

Libby got a shock when Ghulam answered the door himself. He was barefoot and wearing the old cotton kurta and pyjama trousers that he had lent her to wear. He looked just as surprised to see her. They gaped at each other and then spoke at the same time.

'I didn't expect—'

'I was just going to leave this—'

They stopped. He regarded her warily. He wasn't going to invite her in. Libby stepped away.

'I leave tomorrow,' she said. 'I went to Nahoum's and bought fudge.' She held out the package of sweets. 'I wanted to say goodbye, that's all.'

His look softened. 'Wait.' He stretched out a hand to stop her going. 'I can't eat this all by myself.'

'I'm sure you can,' she answered wryly.

He gave a twitch of a smile. After a moment's hesitation, he said, 'Let's go up on the roof and share it.'

Without giving her the chance to decline, Ghulam closed the door behind him and steered her towards the steps that led up to the roof. There was a balustrade around the rooftop that was just the right height to lean on and view the streets below. One corner of the roof was shaded by an awning of bamboo leaves and another was strewn with someone's drying washing, but the place was deserted.

Already the sun was beginning to slide towards the horizon, the early evening light turning golden. Libby hadn't realised how late it was. Ghulam opened the packet and offered it to her first. She took one and started chewing, even though her stomach was knotting at their proximity. Ghulam popped two in his mouth at the same time and gave a sigh of satisfaction.

Libby gazed out at the view of rooftops and trees and the glimpse of busy riverside in the far distance.

'Listen,' said Ghulam, pausing in his eating. 'What do you hear?'

Libby gave him a questioning look.

'Close your eyes and listen,' he ordered.

Libby did so. 'I can hear rickshaw bells,' she said, 'and dogs barking.'

'What else?' he asked.

'Umm, that sounds like a call to prayer in the distance? Traffic. Some sort of horn – a tug boat?'

She opened her eyes. Ghulam was watching her intently. Her heart thumped as she looked into his green eyes. His face glowed in the golden light, his skin bronzed against the white of his open shirt. He looked unbearably handsome.

'What am I supposed to be hearing?' she asked, trying to keep her voice even as her heart began to pound. 'It all sounds normal to me.'

'Exactly,' he said, breaking into a smile. 'No drumming – no sounds of the *goondas* gathering – no ambulance bells.'

'Which means?' said Libby.

'Which means,' echoed Ghulam, 'that Gandhiji is spinning his magic in the *bustee*. Long may it continue.' He held out the bag to Libby, grinning. 'Let's celebrate with more fudge.'

She grinned back and took another sweet, even though her teeth were already aching with the sweetness in her mouth. Ghulam took another two and turned back to the view while he munched.

'Are you more optimistic now Gandhi has come here?' Libby asked him.

He nodded. 'Yes. If he can calm Calcutta then that might help pacify other areas – Punjab in particular.'

'I do hope you are right,' she said. 'Flowers doesn't seem as worried as you are about how things will turn out. Neither does George.'

He shot her a look. She explained. 'I'm staying with the Dunlops until tomorrow when I go to Belgooree. George took Flowers dancing last night and I went along. I think he's sweet on her.'

Ghulam made a dismissive noise. 'We won't get rid of the Raj overnight. Enjoy your dinner-dances while you can.'

Libby felt hurt that he bracketed her with the likes of the pleasure-seeking George Brewis, though she wondered if he was jealous too. She bit back her suggestion that if peace was coming to Calcutta there was no reason for her to rush away to the hills. But what would be the point? She had promised to go to Belgooree and Ghulam was certainly not urging her to stay.

They stood side by side as the sunset spread across the sky and birds rose squawking and resettled in the trees. Libby thought back to her first evening in Calcutta, arriving by aeroplane and being overawed by the sight of the sun like a ball of fire rolling into the Hooghly River. How could she have foreseen that her return to India would be so short-lived, that her father would choose to go home to Britain – or that she would lose her heart to a man across the cultural and social divide that the British had created?

The pain in her heart grew stronger. She shouldn't have come. Seeing Ghulam again was like tearing the dressing off a fresh wound.

'I should go,' she said, trying to keep her voice steady. 'The Dunlops will be expecting me for supper. Winnie's having a cake made – not that I'll have any appetite to eat it after all this fudge.'

'You've hardly eaten any of it,' said Ghulam. 'Are you all right?'

Libby's eyes swam with sudden tears. She couldn't bear it if she broke down now.

'I'll be fine,' she said. She faced him and held his look. 'I just want you to know that I don't regret anything that's happened between us, Ghulam.'

'Neither do I,' he said. 'In other circumstances, perhaps . . .' His eyes were full of sadness.

Libby touched his face. 'No other man,' she said, her voice shaking, 'has made me feel the way you do.'

He caught her hand and kissed the palm. Tears trickled down her cheeks.

'Oh, darling Libby,' he said, seeing her distress. He pulled her into his arms and hugged her tightly.

The sky was blood red as he cupped his hands about her face and kissed her on the lips. She opened her mouth and instantly they were kissing fiercely. Seeing the desire in each other's eyes, they hurried under the awning. Ghulam pulled off his shirt. He laid it down for her to lie on. In moments, they were making frantic love, Libby crying out as they did so, overcome with longing and filled with sorrow that this was their parting.

In minutes they were dressing again, almost bashful with each other at the passion that had seized them. Someone could have walked on to the roof at any moment. What they had just done was madness. He was like a summer fever in her veins.

'I'll see you back to Sudder Street,' he said.

'Thank you,' she murmured.

Downstairs, Ghulam hailed a rickshaw. They sat in silence as it bumped along Park Street and Chowringhee Street, before turning into Sudder Street. As the vehicle swayed and jostled them together on the short journey, Libby was acutely aware of their arms and thighs touching for the last time and savoured every last painfully sweet moment. It was over all too soon. As Libby dismounted, she felt misery claw at her insides.

'Will you write to me?' she asked.

He nodded. 'If you'd like me to.'

'Yes, very much.'

The street was still busy. People were glancing at them in curiosity.

They stood for a moment, gazing at each other with regret. Libby thought she would always remember the tender look he gave her. He took her hand and held it, squeezing it in encouragement.

'Take care of yourself, Libby,' he said.

'And you,' she answered, swallowing down tears.

He disengaged his hand and clambered back into the rickshaw but waited to see her walk safely into the building where the Dunlops lived. Libby smiled and waved and turned away, forcing herself to walk into the building and not look back. She failed. As she glanced round to give one more wave, the rickshaw driver was already pulling away. All she could see was the back of Ghulam's dark head as the rickshaw vanished into the sultry night.

CHAPTER 30

Belgooree, August

Sitting out on the veranda after dinner on her first night in the hills, Libby caught up with Clarrie's and Sophie's news.

Libby had been surprised and delighted to find her childhood friend Manzur was now living on the Belgooree estate. Clarrie, hearing from Libby about his ambition to be a teacher, had swiftly offered him a position as a schoolmaster in the plantation school.

'I know that the schooling here has always been rudimentary,' Clarrie admitted, 'and that it's high time the education for the pickers' children was improved.'

'I'm sure Manzur will be just the man for the job,' Libby enthused.

'Oh, he's already making a difference,' said Clarrie. 'The children love him and he's so full of energy. I really can't thank you enough for tipping me off about him wanting to leave the Oxford.'

'I'm glad it's working out,' said Libby. 'Though Dad will probably tell me off for interfering.'

'Not a bit of it,' Clarrie had replied. 'Your father is pleased that Manzur is doing a job he loves.'

'So you've heard from Dad since he's been back in Newcastle?' Libby exclaimed.

'Yes, an airmail came a couple of days ago.'

Libby flushed. She was longing to hear how the reunion between her parents was going. 'I haven't heard a thing – except to say he arrived safely. I know he's not the world's greatest letter writer.'

'I'm sure he'll have written to you too. Perhaps it's just missed you in Calcutta. James wouldn't have known that you were staying at Flowers's flat, would he?'

'No,' Libby conceded. 'So how is he? What does he say? Is he getting on all right with Mother?'

'Yes, I'm sure he is. They've been looking at houses together,' said Clarrie.

'To buy?'

'To rent to start with,' said Clarrie. 'They can't agree on town or country, so they're going to do both for a short while. James is keen to rent a house on the Willowburn Estate up the Tyne Valley.'

'He'll want somewhere he can keep horses and dogs,' said Sophie.

'Why does the Willowburn Estate sound familiar?' asked Libby.

'According to Adela,' said Clarrie, 'it's where Joan Brewis and her daughter Bonnie have gone to live.'

'That's right!' Libby remembered. 'Joan's new husband runs the stables there. George told me. That sounds just the sort of place Dad would be happy.'

Libby caught a look pass between Clarrie and Sophie.

'What?' she asked.

'Apparently he still has to persuade Tilly,' said Sophie.

'That's why renting is such a good idea,' said Clarrie with an optimistic smile. 'Give them both a chance to see if it's a suitable family home.'

'Well, Tilly should just be happy she's got her husband back and can start afresh on married life,' said Sophie. 'I can't wait to be with Rafi again.'

'Is that likely to be soon?' asked Libby.

Sophie smiled. 'I'm hoping so. He's more or less certain he's going to be offered a job in the Rawalpindi Forest Office. Rafi's old friend Boz is staying on in the new Pakistan too – they trained together in Edinburgh – and Boz has already been guaranteed a post in 'Pindi. It would be grand if they could both be foresters together again.'

'I'm so pleased,' said Libby, quelling a familiar pang of longing for Ghulam. Rafi was a different man; he had always put his love for Sophie first rather than his ideals. At heart he was a romantic. And Libby had always admired Sophie for being brave enough to break ranks with the British and marry her beloved Rafi. She felt a stab of envy that the pair of them had had years of happiness together, whereas her bittersweet affair with Ghulam had been so short-lived. 'Does Rafi say what the situation is like in the Punjab?'

Sophie shook her head. 'He doesn't mention the bad things that we hear about in the newspapers. I don't think he wants to worry me. But he won't let me travel there yet – not until he's got the job in the bag and has found somewhere for us to live.'

'That's sensible,' said Clarrie. 'And I'm sure you won't have to wait long.'

'And what about Ghulam?' Sophie asked Libby. 'Did you manage to see him in Calcutta?'

Libby felt herself go hot at the question. 'Yes, I did. I helped out for a couple of days with Fatima's rescue charity – Ghulam took me.'

'And?' Sophie probed.

Libby's insides clenched. 'I care a lot for him,' she admitted, 'and I know he likes me but he was adamant I should leave Calcutta and go to the hills. I fear for him and Fatima.'

Libby told them about the murder outside Amelia Buildings. The women were aghast.

'Do you think they will stay in India or go to Pakistan?' Sophie asked.

'Ghulam will never leave India,' Libby said. 'I'm certain of that.'

Sophie sighed. 'Yes, he's always been far more stubborn than Rafi.'

'It's not a question of being stubborn,' Libby said. 'Ghulam is Indian to the core – to leave would be turning his back on everything he believes in.'

'Rafi didn't want to leave either,' Sophie retorted, her tone sharp, 'but he's more or less been forced out of Gulgat. He knows it's not safe for us to stay there because we're Muslim. Ghulam shouldn't be staying if his life is in danger.'

'Both men are right in their own way,' said Clarrie swiftly. 'Rafi is doing what he thinks is best for the both of you – and Ghulam is sticking to his principles. Men like him will be needed in an independent India – the country has always thrived on being a mix of races and religions. It would be a great tragedy if people are driven out because of their beliefs – that's not what Nehru and the Congress Party want, as far as I can see.'

'You're right as ever, Clarrie,' said Sophie. She stretched out and squeezed Libby's hand. 'I'm sorry if I snapped at you, lassie. My nerves are a little frayed at the moment worrying about my husband.'

'I'm sorry too,' said Libby quickly. 'I didn't mean any criticism of Rafi.'

'Of course you didn't,' said Clarrie with a smile. 'Now tell me what my nephew George has been up to. Is he ever going to come and visit his old aunt or are we too boring in the *mofussil*? I do wish he would. I've always been tremendously fond of George.'

'He's just as charming and irrepressible as ever.' Libby laughed. 'And he hasn't admitted it but I think he's smitten with Flowers Dunlop.'

CHAPTER 31

Newcastle, August

J ust come with me to see it,' James pleaded with Tilly.
She was brushing her hair in front of the dressing-table mirror,
her back to him. He tried to catch her look in the mirror but she
was studiously avoiding eye contact. It was almost impossible to have
a private conversation with his wife as there was always someone else
with her in the house or she was dashing out to one of her numerous
commitments, leaving him with long hours on his hands. If he didn't
have his trips to Willowburn Estate up the Tyne valley to go riding,
James knew he would not be able to endure his retirement.

It was kind Adela who had come to his rescue and contacted
Tommy, the stable master there, who had introduced James to the genial
Major and his nice family. James relished his twice-weekly rides around
the estate and talking about tea and India to Major Gibson, who had
once been a young subaltern in Burma. When the Major had offered
to rent James a house on the estate, he had jumped at the chance. He
knew that, given time, he and Tilly could recreate the loving home they
had once shared in Assam.

So he curbed his irritation and said to Tilly's back, 'The house is
big enough for you to do your entertaining and you can furnish it any

way you want. You'll make it into just as comfortable a home as Cheviot View. And the grounds are spectacular—'

'Cheviot View!' Tilly exclaimed. 'God forbid. I don't see why we have to live so far from Newcastle.'

'It's not far and I thought we'd agreed to give it a try?' James said in exasperation. 'I've more or less promised Gus Gibson that we'll take it. And he has the most charming young American wife, Martha – she'll be company for you.'

'I've got the company I want here in Newcastle,' she replied.

'But the Major has been most accommodating . . .'

'You shouldn't have made promises before I've had a chance to see it,' said Tilly, her hair brushing becoming more vigorous.

'I'm giving you the chance now,' James cried. 'A trip out. The fresh air will do you good.'

'Fresh air is overrated. Unless it's sea air.'

She carried on brushing the same wavy piece of hair, though there were no knots left in it. James noticed how it had lost its reddish sheen and was peppered with grey at the roots.

'Tilly! When I suggested St Abbs to be near Johnny, you said you didn't want to move to the seaside. I wouldn't mind that – somewhere near the River Tweed for fishing.'

'No, I don't want to live in St Abbs either,' said Tilly in agitation. 'Visiting Johnny is one thing – but hearty Helena would drive me mad as my neighbour.'

'Then what do you want?' James demanded.

She paused in her brushing and turned to face him. 'You know what I want – to stay in the city.'

'But this house is too small,' James pointed out. 'Especially with all the extra lodgers you seem to have acquired.'

Tilly gave him a sharp look. 'They're not lodgers. Adela and Sam are family – and Josey is like a sister to me.'

'I'm sorry,' James relented. 'I didn't mean that I don't want Adela and Sam living with us.' Privately, he could quite happily see the back of the chain-smoking Josey and her droll waspish remarks.

Tilly said, 'Poor things haven't found settling back here very easy so the last thing Adela and Sam need is for us to throw them out.'

'I don't want to throw anyone out,' protested James.

In fact, life in the house would be intolerable without Adela and her affable husband. Years ago, he had misjudged Sam as a rootless dreamer who would never stick long at any job, and had resented him for being critical of how workers were treated on the Oxford Estates. But since returning to Newcastle James had quickly grown fond of Sam: he was hardworking and a devoted husband to Clarrie's daughter. With Sam he could reminisce about India, and the younger man understood how he missed his old home in Assam.

'If we move to the countryside,' said Tilly, 'that's exactly what will happen. Adela and Sam can't possibly carry on the café if they're stuck out at Willowburn.'

'They have a van,' said James. 'It's not a long drive.'

'It is with petrol still rationed. They wouldn't manage. You have no idea how hard life has been in Britain.'

James sighed in frustration. His wife never tired of telling him of all the deprivation those on the Home Front had suffered during the War. When he had alluded to how dangerous Assam had become under imminent threat from a Japanese invasion, Tilly had said that it just made her all the more thankful that she hadn't returned to India with the children.

'Tilly,' James said, trying to stay calm, 'I just want us to have a proper family home – big enough to accommodate us all – so that Jamie can stay whenever he wants and Libby will have her own room when she returns.'

Tilly seized on this. 'I can't believe you let her stay on alone in India,' she chided.

'She's not alone – she'll be at Belgooree with Clarrie by now.' James broke off, reddening. Tilly didn't like him talking about Belgooree or Clarrie or 'harping on about India' as she called it.

'We've no idea what that girl is up to,' said Tilly. 'You obviously had as little influence over her as I did. I told you what a handful she could be. She just does whatever she wants without thinking about the consequences.'

'That's not fair,' James said. 'Libby is a fine young woman. She's made a lot of friends in India and is passionate about the country, so I wasn't going to stop her having a couple of extra weeks there. Besides, she's a grown woman and we can no longer order her to do what we want.'

'We never could,' Tilly sighed.

'Anyway,' said James, 'stop trying to use Libby to divert our conversation. What are we going to do about where we live?'

Tilly put down the hairbrush. She gave him a contrite look.

'I'm sorry, James; I don't want us to argue like this. I know it's difficult for you,' she said, 'but I'm finding this hard too. Perhaps we could compromise on where we live?'

'How?' he asked.

'What about if we spend part of the week at Willowburn – and the rest in town? We could see if it suits us and I could still do my voluntary work – I don't want to let people down.'

'You mean keep on two houses?'

'Yes, just for a few months,' Tilly said, turning back to the mirror while she clipped on earrings – silver and jade ones that Libby had helped James choose before he left Calcutta.

James felt a tightening in his chest at the thought of his lively, cheerful daughter. He missed her. Several times he had sat down to write to her but hadn't known what to say. He knew she worried about him but he didn't want to fill a letter full of lying platitudes that everything in Newcastle was fine. He knew how much she hoped for a perfect family reunion. Anyway, she would be joining them any day soon. His spirits lifted at the thought.

He watched while Tilly sprayed on perfume. For an instant the scent reminded him of long ago when he'd courted her – the young, garrulous, blushing, plumply pretty Tilly – and he felt a stirring of affection. He wanted to recapture their early days. If only he could have Tilly to himself more often, he was sure they could rekindle their early passion.

'But that doesn't get around the fact that we're crammed in here like chickens in a coop,' said James, trying to lighten the mood.

He put a hand on her shoulder and felt her stiffen. She shifted away from him, leaning forward to apply lipstick. He never remembered her wearing make-up in India.

'Well,' said Tilly, pressing her lips on a handkerchief and sitting up straight. 'I've been having a look around and there's a house in Jesmond which would fit the bill perfectly.' She turned and gave him a tentative smile. 'It's got five bedrooms and a large garden and it's just a stone's throw from the Dene so you can take the dogs for a walk – when we get dogs – and I can walk to church easily from there.'

James gaped at her. Her hazel eyes lit up as she talked about the house in the prosperous suburb where she had grown up.

'And all the bedrooms are a good size. The boys can share the largest one so that Libby and Josey can have their own rooms – and we'd still have a spare room for Adela and Sam if they needed it. You and I could have the one with the view over the Dene and all the trees – just like being at Cheviot View or Belgooree.'

She gave a small nervous laugh. James was dismayed.

'Have you already been to see it?' he asked.

'Yes, I took Josey to have a look last week.' Tilly's look turned defiant. 'It's for rent or sale, so if we like it we can buy it. Mungo likes it too.'

'Mungo's been to see it?' James exclaimed.

'Just from the outside,' said Tilly, rising from her stool and adjusting her sack-like dress over ample hips. James wondered fleetingly when Tilly had begun to wear such matronly clothes. Perhaps she always had but he had never noticed.

Tilly gave him a smile of encouragement. 'I'll come and see the house at Willowburn if you agree to look at the Jesmond property. What do you say?'

James hid his despondency. It sounded as if the family was already lining up to support Tilly on the matter – just as they deferred to her on all the petty daily decisions that had been taken since his return. He felt bewildered. His sons made topical jokes and hooted with laughter over radio comedy that left James baffled. Jamie was a kind young man but was diffident with his father and as he worked long hours in a hospital in Sunderland, he was rarely at home. Mungo was friendly and talked to James about sport but was far more at ease with Tilly, although he teased his mother mercilessly. Neither son seemed remotely interested in his stories about India; nor did they want to reminisce about their childhood there in the way that Libby had done.

It was James who felt like a lodger in his own home. Except this wasn't his home; it was the house Tilly had rented for her and the children during the War. It was full of their possessions – his were still in transit at sea – and it was like staying in a boarding house where nothing was familiar. At least if they went to Jesmond they would be starting again afresh together.

'Okay, I agree,' James said, stifling a sigh. 'I'll view the house in Jesmond.'

'Good,' said Tilly, beaming. She crossed the bedroom swiftly. 'Breakfast then,' she said as she disappeared into the corridor.

James surveyed the room. His spirits plummeted at the sight of the twin beds. Tilly refused to sleep in a double bed, saying she had got used to a single bed and remembered how James was far too restless and always pulled off the covers. Hers was neatly made; his was a crumple of sheets and blankets. They had had sex once since his return but it had not been a success. He'd climbed into her bed but she'd lain tense and with her face turned away while he'd tried to arouse her. Ten minutes later he was back in the other bed, staring at the ceiling, engulfed by loneliness.

Neither of them had talked about the unsatisfactory copulation and after that Tilly was always in bed first with her bedside lamp switched off pretending to be asleep. Would his wife agree to buy a double bed in their next house? Could he demand such a concession from her? If only they could lie next to each other and fall asleep in each other's arms like they used to, then surely they could reignite a healthy sex life.

James yearned for physical contact but Tilly shied away from it. She didn't even appear to want to be kissed by him. Whenever he touched her, she froze or slipped past him saying she had a dozen things to do. The most he got from her was a peck on the cheek – he suspected more for appearance's sake in front of the others – and a distracted wave as she hurried away from him.

James closed his eyes in despair. He clung on to the one positive element of their lonely sleeping arrangements: he'd hardly had any bad dreams since his return. He was sure Tilly would have complained at once if he'd woken her up with his shouts and babbling.

James pulled back his shoulders and raised his chin. He'd go riding today, come what may. That was the only way he could bear this strange dislocated life he found himself living.

CHAPTER 32

Belgooree, mid-August

On the fifteenth of August, Clarrie gave the servants the day off. Libby and Harry decorated the veranda with streamers in the colours of the new India flag, while Sophie helped Clarrie cook a lunch of omelettes, jacket potatoes, salads and curried lentils. This was followed by rice pudding, fruit salad and a ginger cake that Mohammed Din had ordered to be made the day before.

Clarrie's old friend Dr Hemmings – who had delivered both her children – came from Shillong to share the meal and a celebratory bottle of champagne that had languished in Wesley's wine cellar for over a decade. The tea garden managers, Banu and Daleep, were invited along with their extended families. Harry was happy that Manzur had decided to stay for the holiday and not journey to Bengal to spend it with his parents.

In the afternoon, Sophie and Harry organised a tennis tournament on the newly rolled lawn, with Libby and Manzur helping some of the local children to wield tennis rackets and hit balls over the makeshift net. Nitin and his brothers took to the game enthusiastically. Libby was pleased to hear from Nitin that he was enjoying his new position as under-*mohurer* in the factory office. She had bought spare typewriter ribbon in Calcutta for him.

In the evening, the women of the house, along with Harry and Manzur, went down to the village to watch the celebrations. There had been drumming from early morning and now the lanes were lit with the flares of fireworks and noisy with the sound of firecrackers. A fire-eater was performing on the riverbank and there was much singing, music and merriment.

Clarrie led them to a compound in the village. 'This is where Ama, my old nurse, used to live – she was Banu's grandmother and the most important woman in the village in her day. Her daughter Shimti is the headwoman now. I'd like to call on her.'

Libby was fascinated to see inside the compound and the circle of huts that made up the simple homestead. The air was thick with the smoke of cooking fires and the chatter of people who were sitting around eating, drinking and smoking. She was in awe of Clarrie's ease with the local people and her quick chatter in their language.

Clarrie handed over presents of tobacco and a woollen shawl to the toothless old woman who sat on a mat by the fire. Shimti's thin arms shimmered with silver bangles which tinkled when she raised her hands in an expressive gesture of thanks.

She commanded that they sit with her and chew paan while some of her great-grandchildren danced in their honour. After a while Libby's head began to buzz with the music and the narcotic; she felt a sudden euphoria and optimism for the future. This was the first day of a new India and she was there to witness it.

'I'm so glad I didn't go home with Dad,' Libby babbled to Clarrie. 'I wouldn't have missed this for anything. You are so loved by the people here, Clarrie. I think you are an amazing person and I'm sorry if I was jealous of you before for spending so much time with Dad – I know it wasn't your fault, it was Dad not wanting to go home. But everything's going to be all right. Dad and Mother. I'm really looking forward to seeing them – but I wanted to be here for Independence – Dad understood that. This is all so wonderful.'

Libby was baffled as to why she was in tears. 'I'm happy, really I am. Except I miss Ghulam. That's the only thing I'm really sad about.'

Libby had only a hazy recollection of Manzur and Harry steering her out of the compound and back up the drive to the bungalow. She thought she probably kissed them and told them that she loved them like brothers. She had a memory of insisting on lying on a veranda rug so she could gaze at the stars. Her head was spinning – and then she remembered nothing more.

Libby woke with a pounding head. She was lying in bed but couldn't remember how she had got there. She had only the vaguest recollection of how the night had ended. What on earth had old Shimti put in her paan? Or was it the bowl of potent rice beer that she'd been encouraged to drink that had made her so intoxicated?

By the time she emerged, breakfast was already over and only Harry was in the house.

'Mum's gone to the factory and Sophie's out riding with Banu,' he told her. 'Would you like to play tennis with me and Manzur? He's coming round soon.'

Libby pressed fingers to her throbbing forehead. 'Think I might just sit in the shade for a bit – write some letters.'

'Got a headache?' Harry grinned. 'You were very funny last night, Libby.'

Libby groaned. 'Was I?'

'Yes. You were singing at the top of your voice all the way home – silly songs like "Daddy Wouldn't Buy Me a Bow-Wow". And you told me I was as handsome as my father and you kissed Manzur on the nose and told him he had perfect ears.'

'Stop!' Libby cried. 'This is too embarrassing. I don't know how I got so drunk.'

'It wasn't the drink,' said Harry, 'it was the bhang that Shimti mixes in the paan on special occasions. It's very strong.'

'How do you know about such things?' she asked in surprise.

'It's made from ground-up hemp leaves – Nitin told me,' said Harry nonchalantly, 'and I've seen how merry people get.'

Libby gave a weak laugh. 'You are having an amazing upbringing, Harry. At your age I was stuck in boarding school trying to earn toffees by doing the other girls' prep.'

'I'd rather have toffee than paan any day,' Harry said with a smile. Then he was swinging down the veranda steps and rushing off with Breckon barking at his heels.

Libby felt a pang of emotion at the sight of her father's old dog. How was her dad really coping back in Newcastle? She wished he would write and tell her. A letter had come from Tilly but it was full of her usual breezy chatter about the family and her busy life, with hardly a mention of James, except to say that he was spending his time riding with Major Gibson and talking of buying a dog. Neither did it tell her how her brothers were coping with having their absent father back in their lives. Surely they would be happy at that? Perhaps everything was fine and she was worrying unnecessarily. She would find out for herself soon enough.

Libby went to fetch paper and a pen; she would write to him anyway. She described the celebrations at Belgooree and her time in Calcutta, mentioning how she had helped out at the refugee centre with the Khans as well as staying with the Dunlops and socialising with Flowers and George. But she didn't tell him about nearly drowning or the murder outside the Khans' apartment block.

Libby enclosed the envelope from Flowers containing details about Danny Dunlop.

> . . . *Please can you see if old Mr Fairfax remembers any-*
> *thing about Mr Dunlop's family? He's so keen to find out*
> *about them and whether he has relations in Britain. I*

think he has a dream of settling in Britain – even though Mrs Dunlop is against the idea. I'm not sure what Flowers wants – she keeps her cards close to her chest on personal matters. But I don't think she wants to leave India either, although she's not sure what life is going to be like for Anglo-Indians from now on.

Oh, Dad, I'm going to find it so hard to leave this place – not just Belgooree but Assam and Calcutta too. I've grown to appreciate India as a grown-up and not just relying on my childhood memories (which I must admit were a little rose-tinted!). I love so much about India and I've made some good friends – I will find it all very hard to leave behind. I can't imagine how hard it must have been for you after a lifetime of living here.

But I'm going to be positive. I'm looking forward to being with you and Mother and the boys – all of us together after so long! We'll be a family again. Have you managed to rent the house on the Willowburn Estate? Can we go out riding together in the early mornings? Just like old times!

Please write soon and tell me all the home news. I'll probably stay on here another couple of weeks – until Sophie travels to the Punjab (or West Pakistan as I suppose we now call it). Flowers says I can stay with them while I arrange my flight home.

Could I ask a favour? Would you send out a tin of toffee for me to give to a good friend?

Heaps and heaps of love,
Your adoring daughter,
Libby xxx

CHAPTER 33

Newcastle, mid-August

On Friday the fifteenth of August, Adela and Sam returned from the café with half a dozen leftover fairy cakes decorated with yellow, white and green colouring. They found Tilly, James and Mungo finishing afternoon tea in the sitting room. Josey was nowhere to be seen. In the past couple of weeks, Adela had noticed how Tilly's companion had been keeping out of the way, not wanting to be caught in the middle of Tilly and James's bickering.

'Cake!' Mungo grinned, helping himself to one straight away. 'What are we celebrating?'

'It's India's Independence Day,' said Sam, with a look of astonishment. 'Surely you knew that?'

'Oh, yes, so it is,' said Mungo. 'Should we really be celebrating it?'

'Libby will be,' said James.

'Well, we're marking the occasion if not exactly celebrating,' Adela said with a smile.

At this, Tilly got up quickly. 'I'll leave you to it. I've got to get ready for a committee meeting. I'll see you all at supper.'

As Tilly hurried away, Adela offered James a cake. She thought how haggard he appeared. He was perched awkwardly on a dainty upholstered chair that was too small for his wide frame, looking forlorn.

He took one with a grateful expression. 'Thank you, Adela. Nice to know someone else has been thinking of India today. I wonder what will be going on at Belgooree.'

Adela heard the longing in his voice and knew, like her, he would rather be there on such a day.

'If Libby and Sophie are there with Mother,' said Adela, smiling, 'then definitely a party.'

Mungo picked a second cake from the plate as he sauntered towards the door. 'Tell Freda these are very good,' he said through a mouthful of cake.

'Where are you going?' James asked.

'Tennis club,' he answered. 'Doubles match. Don't include me in supper.'

'Tell your mother before she goes out,' James told him.

'She knows,' Mungo called over his shoulder and disappeared.

James sighed. 'I always seem to be the last to know what's going on around here.'

Adela sat down on the sofa and patted the space next to her for James to join her. 'Have you been up to Willowburn today?'

'Yes,' James said, as he sat beside her, his face brightening. 'I've signed the lease on the house for six months. Will you come up and take a look soon?'

'Of course,' said Adela. 'We'd love that, wouldn't we, Sam?'

Sam nodded, occupying the chair that Mungo had just left and stretching out his long legs. 'Do you think we could spend an afternoon riding up there too?' Sam asked.

'I'm sure that could be arranged,' James said with a nod of enthusiasm. 'You'll like the Major and his nice young wife – second wife. Gus was widowed young in Burma. New wife's American. I've tried to get Tilly to meet her but I think she's already decided not to like her just because I do.'

'Aren't you being a little unfair?' said Adela. 'Tilly's very broad-minded about people – she's probably just been too busy.'

'You're right,' said James. 'I'm just so afraid of putting my foot in it where Tilly's concerned. I can't seem to say or do the right thing.'

Adela felt a surge of sympathy for the unhappy man. 'Just give it time,' she said. 'You've got to get to know each other all over again.'

'Yes,' James said, putting on a brave face. 'I'm so glad that you and Sam are here – you two know what it's like trying to adapt. Sometimes I wake up wondering where on earth I am. And I find myself calling out for Breckon. Ridiculous, isn't it?'

'Not ridiculous,' said Sam. 'You're bound to miss things about your old life – it would be odd if you didn't.'

'Mother says that Harry is missing you,' said Adela. 'She lets Breckon sleep in his room because it comforts him.'

James's eyes shone with sudden emotion. 'Does it?'

'Yes.' Adela smiled. 'Mother was very grateful for you taking an interest in my brother after Dad died.'

'He's a fine boy,' said James, 'and a credit to your mother – to both your parents.' He looked at her with glistening eyes. 'How is Clarrie? I've written to her but heard nothing back since her brief message telling me about Manzur becoming a teacher. Maybe she thinks she shouldn't . . .'

Adela said gently, 'She's well. In her most recent letter, she said she and Sophie were looking forward to Libby joining them.'

'Good,' said James, his voice sounding hoarse. 'I can't wait to hear all Libby's news. I hope she'll be home in time for our September visit to St Abbs to stay with Johnny and Helena.'

'Yes,' said Adela, 'it'll be good to see her before . . .' She stopped herself.

'Before what?' asked James.

Adela exchanged looks with Sam. She hadn't meant to let slip their plans; they had agreed not to say anything until everything was certain.

They hadn't wanted to distract James and Tilly from their decisions about their own future, though both were pressing ahead regardless with renting the places they wanted most: James at Willowburn and Tilly in Jesmond. Adela worried about them both – James most of all – but didn't feel she should intervene. She was hardly in a position to pontificate on marriage, given that she had almost ruined her own. She hoped that Tilly and James would work things out in their own time, like she and Sam had.

James was looking at her in alarm. 'Tell me what you were going to say. Are you thinking of moving out? I wouldn't blame you.'

'Not just moving out, Cousin James,' said Adela, 'but moving away.'

He looked at them in confusion. 'Where to?'

Sam spoke up, seeing Adela's reticence. 'We're planning to go back to India – Belgooree to start with – then we'll see what happens.'

'When?' James gasped. Adela could hardly bear the shattered look on his face.

'It all depends when my cousin Jane Brewis – or Latimer as she is now – can take on the café.'

'You're giving up Herbert's?'

'Yes,' said Adela, 'I never wanted to run it long-term. Jane's keen to come back to Newcastle and her husband supports her. Jane's father is due to retire and isn't in the best of health – and she's worried about her mother sinking back into depression now that Joan and Bonnie have gone to live at Willowburn. My Aunt Olive doted on Bonnie.'

James nodded. 'She's an engaging child. I see her at the stables with her new step-father – she's a chatterbox just like Libby used to be.'

'I'm glad the girl is taking well to her new life in the country,' said Adela. 'We all miss Bonnie at the café – even if we don't miss Joan quite as much.' She threw Sam a droll look. 'Still, I really hope she's happy at Willowburn.'

'She seems to be,' said James. 'Joan is already good friends with Martha Gibson – they take their children on picnics together – and the Gibson boy is teaching Joan to play croquet.'

'Joan will love that,' said Adela with a roll of her eyes. 'Hobnobbing with the gentry.'

'Adela,' said Sam, wagging his finger, 'don't be unkind. I bet Joan is lively company for Mrs Gibson.'

'Yes, she will be,' Adela conceded.

'But why go now?' asked James, still struggling to take in their shock news. 'I thought you were building up a good photography business, Sam?'

'I can do the same in India,' Sam answered. 'But I'm hoping Adela's mother is going to teach me about tea production so I can be of use at Belgooree.'

James flinched. 'You're going to work with Clarrie at Belgooree?'

Sam smiled. 'Well, I'm hoping to.'

'I've written to Mother,' said Adela, 'and expect to hear back soon. I know she will say yes. She'll be glad of Sam's help.'

'I envy you, Sam,' James blurted out. Adela gave him a surprised look. He swallowed hard. 'I mean I envy you being young enough to start out on a career in the tea gardens. It can be a wonderful life.'

Adela felt a wave of pity. 'Please don't tell the others yet until things are finalised. I hadn't meant to say anything this soon.'

James let out a shuddering sigh. 'Of course I won't. But Tilly is going to be so upset. She is tremendously fond of you Adela – of both of you.'

'She'll have Libby coming home soon,' said Adela, 'so that will be something for her to look forward to.'

James shook his head. 'Well, I'm not going to be the one who tells Tilly,' he said. 'You'll have to do that.'

Suddenly Tilly was standing in the open doorway, in the middle of pinning on her hat. She must have been in the hallway and heard her name mentioned. Her round face was creased in concern.

'Tells me what?' she asked.

CHAPTER 34

Belgooree, August

It was several days before news came through about the final geographical plans for severing Pakistan from India: Partition. The women pored over maps printed in a copy of *The Statesman* that Manzur brought them.

'Calcutta stays in India,' said Libby.

'Srimangal is in East Pakistan now,' Clarrie pointed out. 'That's where Flowers grew up – her father was stationmaster there: a tea-growing area. It's so strange to think it's no longer part of Assam.'

'Look at the Punjab,' said Sophie in dismay. 'The border runs right between Lahore and Amritsar – the Sikhs will be hardest hit. Rafi says they have land and businesses all over what is now Pakistan.'

'It's not really a surprise,' said Libby. 'They've been fighting over it for months. It just confirms their worst fears.'

'Poor Sundar Singh,' Sophie said, her eyes glinting with tears.

'Rafi's army friend?' Libby queried.

Sophie nodded. 'I hope he managed to get his son safely away to Delhi. That's where Rafi says he's setting up home.'

'But he has so many friends like Rafi in Pakistan,' said Libby. 'Surely it will be safe for him to stay there?'

Sophie looked at her sorrowfully. 'You've read about the violence as much as I have. The Sikhs and Muslims have been burning each other out of their homes – especially in Lahore.'

'Let's hope,' said Clarrie, 'that now Independence has come, each country will settle down with their neighbours whatever their religion.'

But the news over the following week grew ever grimmer. Far from calming fears, Partition appeared to be fuelling the fire of violence. Tens of thousands of people had fled across the new borders and the exodus showed no signs of slowing down. Rumours reached the remote tea garden of terrible savagery in the Punjab – mass murder, abductions, rape and mutilation – with neighbours turning on each other and marauding gangs of men on the lookout for revenge killings.

Sophie lost her usual sunny outlook and could settle to nothing. She would stand on the veranda, tensely smoking and staring out through the monsoon rain, waiting in vain for word that Rafi was safe.

Clarrie refused to let her travel. 'You're not leaving for the Punjab until we know it's safe for you to go.'

Libby continued to worry for Ghulam and Fatima, yet the news from Calcutta was heartening. There had been no repeat of last August's bloodletting and the city appeared calm. The newsmen put it down to Gandhi's presence and the calming effect of his peaceful co-existence with Suhrawardy, the city's Muslim leader, as they prayed and fasted together.

Libby longed to hear from Ghulam – he had promised to write to her – but maybe he now thought better of it. With distance between them, perhaps he had decided that it was better not to prolong their relationship. She was soon to return to Britain and he would be concentrating his thoughts and efforts on helping forge the future of the newly liberated country.

She forced herself not to write first. She didn't want to appear demanding or reproachful, so would let him write if he wanted to and not because of any sense of obligation.

As the monsoon kept them marooned indoors or at the factory, Libby turned her thoughts to home and wondered yet again how her father was coping. Had the bad dreams and black moods been banished by his move back to Britain? Had he found peace of mind? Was he happy? Somehow she just couldn't picture him living in the terraced house in Newcastle, hemmed in by streets and traffic. Yet she could imagine him riding at Willowburn and striding down country lanes with a new retriever at his heels. She hoped he had managed to persuade her mother to spend some time in the countryside. She tried to conjure up an image of her parents going for picnics together but failed. Tilly hated sitting on a rug and eating off her lap, and always complained about flies.

A couple of days later, while Libby was in the factory office helping Nitin overhaul his typewriter, Clarrie came in waving letters, beaming.

'Dak from home.'

'Good news?' Libby asked.

'Yes,' Clarrie said, unable to stop smiling. 'Wonderful news.'

'Tell me,' Libby encouraged her.

Clarrie beckoned her to follow. Outside, Clarrie said quietly, 'I don't want to say anything in front of the staff – not until I've told Harry.'

'Can you tell me?' asked Libby.

'Walk back up to the house with me,' said Clarrie, linking arms with Libby. When they were out of earshot of the office staff, Clarrie stopped and faced her, hardly able to contain her excitement. 'Adela and Sam are coming back to Belgooree.'

'For a visit?'

'No, to *live*,' cried Clarrie. 'Sam wants to be a tea planter. They haven't really settled in England.'

Libby's spirits plunged. She had been looking forward to having Adela and Sam living in Newcastle on her return. It would make it easier to adapt once again to life in Britain. She could talk to them about India and the people they knew without being told she was being a bore. But she could see how thrilled Clarrie was at the thought of her daughter and son-in-law returning. She tried to be cheerful.

'I'm so glad for you – and for Harry. When are they planning to come back?'

'Possibly as early as the end of September,' said Clarrie. 'It's a matter of getting the café transferred back into my niece Jane's hands.'

'So – so Adela is as keen on the idea as Sam?' Libby asked.

Clarrie met her look. 'Yes, why shouldn't she be?'

Libby said, 'You see, I know why Adela was so set on returning to Newcastle. I know about her baby – the whole story.'

Clarrie flushed. 'Oh, did Adela . . . ? She told you that . . . ?'

'Yes, before I left Newcastle,' said Libby. 'I was at Lexy's flat when Adela got upset and Lexy told her she might as well tell me why.'

Clarrie's eyes welled with tears. She glanced away. Libby saw her struggling to speak and felt guilty for causing her pain.

'I'm sorry, I shouldn't have said . . .'

'No, Libby, don't be sorry. I'm glad Adela had you to confide in.' Clarrie took a deep breath. 'She's decided to stop looking for the boy. I think both she and Sam want to make a new start and in time – if they are blessed – have their own children.'

Libby squeezed Clarrie's arm in comfort. 'Perhaps that's all for the best. Sam adores Adela but it must put a strain on things if she's been looking for another man's child all this time, don't you think?'

Clarrie nodded. She put a hand to Libby's cheek. 'Where do you get such wisdom from at your age?'

Libby looked rueful. 'It's easy being wise about other people's business – I'm continually making a hash of my own.'

Clarrie said abruptly, 'I'm so sorry, Libby, I quite forgot: there's a letter for you in the dak. With Adela's news, it slipped my mind.'

Libby felt her pulse begin to race as Clarrie flicked through the pile of post.

'Is it from Calcutta?' she asked eagerly.

Clarrie gave her a look of pity. 'Sorry, no. It's from home. It looks like your mother's writing.'

Libby stifled her disappointment and took the letter. 'Thanks anyway.'

They walked back to the bungalow in silence as Libby read Tilly's letter. It was full of news of her usual activities and social engagements, of Jamie's job and Mungo's sport-filled summer holiday. Her younger brother was spending every day playing cricket or tennis. There was no mention of Mungo going riding with their father or spending time with him; in fact, there was precious little mention of James at all until the end.

> . . . *Your father is being very tiresome about where we live. The house I've found in Jesmond is absolutely perfect, with heaps of space and a lovely garden and overlooking the Dene – darling, you will love it! But he is persisting in his idea of making us all de-camp to the country and live in a draughty cottage like some bucolic peasants in a Shakespearean play.*
>
> *It's high time you came home, Libby, and talked some sense into him. When are you coming back? I don't see why you have to stay on at Belgooree. What on earth is there for you to do there? Besides, you mustn't outstay your welcome with Clarrie – she's really been far too kind to waif-and-stray Robsons. Come home, darling – we're all missing you. If you're running short of money, your father will*

*wire some out to you so you can buy air flights home. Don't
attempt to go to Bombay and get a passage – it sounds far
too risky and I imagine the ships will be chock-a-block
with troops and civilians trying to get back to Britain.*

*What news of Sophie and Rafi? I do worry for them.
If Sophie is still there, give her my love – and Clarrie too.*

Love

Mother x

'Does she mention anything about Adela and Sam?' Clarrie asked
her as they reached the house.

Libby shook her head. 'Here, you can read it. She thinks I'm outstaying my welcome.' She handed Clarrie the letter. 'And Dad is obviously driving her mad.'

'Oh dear, poor Tilly,' said Clarrie, 'and poor James.' She laid a hand
affectionately on Libby's head and smiled. 'But you are certainly not
outstaying your welcome. I love having you here and you can stay as
long as you want.'

⚜

September came but there was no news from Rafi. Libby knew she
should be making arrangements to fly home but didn't want to leave
Belgooree without Sophie. Given the turmoil in the wider country, they
had agreed to travel together. Then one morning, as the women and
Harry were finishing breakfast, two letters arrived: one for Libby from
James and one for Sophie from Rafi.

Sophie almost snatched hers from the hand of the *chaprassy* and
tore it open. As Harry excused himself and ran off with Breckon at his
side, Libby and Clarrie waited in anticipation for Rafi's news.

Sophie's face lit up. 'He's got the 'Pindi job! It's definitely his.'

'That's great news,' said Clarrie.

'Well done, Rafi,' said Libby.

'And he's got a house,' Sophie continued in excitement. 'Oh dear, it's one that used to belong to an engineer with the Public Works department – a Sikh.' Sophie glanced up with a guilty look. 'Do you think that's happening a lot? Abandoned houses being requisitioned?'

'I'm afraid it's all too likely,' Clarrie said, sighing.

'But Rafi shouldn't feel guilty,' said Libby. 'He hasn't chased anyone out of anywhere.'

Sophie carried on reading. Libby waited to open her own letter in case Sophie had more news of the Khans. Suddenly, Sophie was gasping and sinking into a chair.

'What's the matter?' Libby asked.

Sophie gave a cry of dismay. 'Oh, no! Rafi's father is very ill. Rafi's going to Lahore. I wish he wasn't . . .'

'How ill?' Libby demanded. 'What's wrong with him?'

Sophie read the letter again. 'Heart attack. He's at home. The hospitals are too overwhelmed with casualties. That's what Rafi says: too overwhelmed.' Sophie screwed up her eyes.

Libby and Clarrie both hurried to put their arms about her shoulders.

'I should be with him,' Sophie exclaimed. 'Rafi shouldn't have to face all this on his own. He hasn't seen his family in years. And Lahore! It's so dangerous.'

'What does he say about you joining him?' asked Clarrie.

'He says I mustn't yet,' Sophie admitted. 'But how can I stay here knowing how much he needs me? Clarrie, what should I do?'

'Stay here,' said Clarrie firmly. 'I know it's hard and all your instincts are to go rushing to Lahore. But if something happened to you on the way, how would that be helping him?'

'The trains aren't safe,' said Libby. 'People are being butchered on the Delhi to Lahore line – there are stories in the newspaper every day.'

'I know!' Sophie cried. 'But I could get to Calcutta and fly.'

Clarrie squeezed her hand. 'Don't do anything just yet,' she advised. 'Write to Rafi and suggest it but please don't go rushing off into danger before things are clearer. Perhaps his father has already recovered or . . .'

Clarrie and Libby exchanged looks. Libby knew she was thinking the same thing: perhaps Rafi's father was already dead and rushing there would prove to be futile.

Sophie let out a long sigh. 'You're right. I mustn't do anything to cause Rafi any more worry.'

Libby asked, 'Does he say whether Ghulam and Fatima know about their father being so ill?'

Sophie shook her head. 'No, he doesn't.'

Libby's insides twisted. 'Do you think I should write and let them know?'

'Surely Rafi will have done that?' said Clarrie.

Sophie shrugged. 'His father may not want him to. Mr Khan hasn't spoken to Ghulam since he banished him from home as a youth – and he wiped his hands of Fatima too when she refused to get married. He's not the type to forgive and forget.'

'But they have a right to know,' insisted Libby. 'Ghulam might pretend he doesn't care but I know he's troubled by his estrangement from his father. He encouraged me to go and see Dad when he was recuperating here and not to let a rift open between us. I think Ghulam would want to send his father a message before it's too late.'

'Then write to him,' said Clarrie. 'He and Fatima ought to know.'

Libby started a letter to Ghulam several times but the right words wouldn't come. They either sounded too formal, as if she were an official passing on information about his father, or they were too alarmist, as if he ought to rush at once to his father's bedside. She didn't want him to do that – was strongly against him going in person – given the carnage going on in the Punjab. Yet she knew he would want to know. What if his father should die before he had a chance to make his peace with him? How terrible would it be for Ghulam to find out later that she had known and yet made no attempt to tell him?

The trouble was that Libby wanted to pour out her heart to Ghulam but didn't want to do so in such a letter. Should she write two separate ones? In exasperation with herself, she abandoned her writing pad and lay back on her bed re-reading her father's letter.

It was unexpectedly affectionate; he told her that he was missing her. He was also surprisingly candid: he was surrounded by dear family but felt very alone. No one wanted to hear him talk about Assam or the tea gardens – indeed he found it difficult to talk to her brothers about anything very much. James made no criticism of her mother and his opinion on the house move was fatalistic.

> *. . . I realise I am going to have to fall in with your mother's plan to set up home in Jesmond. She has her heart set on it and who am I to deny her after all these years of coping on her own? Still, I'm determined to rent the house at Willowburn until the winter so that I can take advantage of the riding. I'm enjoying the company of Major Gibson very much. He's ten years my junior but we seem to share the same outlook on life and he indulges me in my India tales, dear man! You and I, Libby, will spend the autumn riding around the Tyne Valley pretending we are after snipe and blackbuck before returning for a* chota hazri *of kedgeree and Assam tea. How does that sound?*
>
> *Write and tell me about life at Belgooree. How are dear Clarrie and Harry? Is Breckon behaving himself? Is Manzur well? And Sophie – is she still with you? I think about them all such a lot. In some ways Belgooree is more real to me than my life in Newcastle. I miss the early*

morning rides with Clarrie and talking to Harry about fishing – your brothers aren't in the least bit interested. What would I give for one day at Belgooree! Inspecting the gardens with Clarrie, Breckon barking at my side, and finishing off the day with a chota peg *as the sun's going down and a decent curry to look forward to!*

Goodness, what a ramble this must sound. I'm sorry but I haven't done anything about finding the information that Danny Dunlop wants. I promise I will do soon. I'll go and see Fairfax. At least we can have a chinwag about our koi hai *days – and it's possible he might remember something I don't.*

Write soon, dearest daughter – or better still come home! Your mother expects you back in time for the annual trip to St Abbs in mid-September.

Your loving father

Libby sighed and pushed the letter under her pillow. She got up and went to look for the others. Clarrie and Sophie were picking fruit in the garden. For a moment, Libby stood watching them working side by side, Sophie reaching to pick gooseberries with gloved hands while Clarrie held out the basket. Such a tranquil domestic task. It was almost impossible to imagine that elsewhere in the country, women were being dragged from their homes and violated or hacked to death. She felt nauseated, her stomach clenching. What did the future hold for any of them?

Unease gripped her. How safe was Clarrie staying on here with only thirteen-year-old Harry and her staff to protect her until Adela and Sam returned? Would they be any safer then? Clarrie kept insisting she had nothing to fear among the Khasi, though she had offered to pay for her *khansama*, Mohammed Din, and his family to travel back to their home in Kashmir if they had any concerns. They had chosen not to do so,

Mohammed Din declaring he would never desert Robson memsahib while there was breath in his body.

Clarrie caught sight of Libby and waved her over. 'Finding it hard to write that letter?' she asked.

Libby pulled a rueful face. 'How did you know?'

Clarrie gave her a sympathetic smile but didn't answer.

'Let me help,' said Libby.

For a few minutes the three women picked fruit in silence. Then Clarrie spoke. 'Did your father mention about Adela and Sam leaving?'

'No,' said Libby. 'But it was written nearly two weeks ago.'

'Is James all right?' Clarrie asked.

Libby shook her head. 'No, I don't think he is. He sounds unhappy and homesick.'

'Homesick for Cheviot View?' asked Sophie.

Libby glanced at Clarrie. 'No, for Belgooree.'

She saw Clarrie and Sophie exchange looks.

'Dad misses Breckon and Harry and riding round the gardens and even curry,' said Libby. 'He asks after both of you. But especially you, Clarrie. He misses you the most.'

Clarrie turned red under her sunhat. 'Does he say that?'

'Not in so many words,' said Libby, 'but it's obvious he does. He keeps mentioning you and wanting news.'

'I told you he would,' Sophie murmured.

Clarrie bowed her head. 'What am I supposed to do about it?' she said, her voice full of sadness.

Sophie put a hand on her shoulder. 'Nothing. He's gone back to Tilly and you just have to let them get on with it.'

Libby was shocked. It sounded as if they had discussed her father before – as if Clarrie had feelings for him.

She blurted out, 'Are you in love with my father?'

Clarrie met Libby's look. 'Not in love,' she said softly, 'but I care for your father a great deal. If you'd asked me ten years ago, I would have said we didn't particularly like one another. He was a typical hard-drinking planter who thought women should stay at home and certainly not criticise fellow planters like I did.' Clarrie gave a wry laugh. 'I thought James pompous and he thought me opinionated. But all that changed after Wesley died and the War came. We've been a support to each other.' Clarrie's look was reflective. 'I've grown very fond of your father. If he's missing me then I miss him too – more than I realised I would.'

Libby felt her insides knotting. She had suspected all along that Clarrie and her father cared deeply for each other. It had been so obvious to her. She waited for the surge of jealousy on her mother's behalf to come, but it didn't. She just felt deeply sad for all three of them. None of them were particularly happy; all of them just trying to carry on as best they could.

'I think Dad loves you more than he loves Mother,' Libby said. 'And you've been a lot kinder to him.'

She saw tears brimming in Clarrie's eyes.

'I hope that's not true,' said Clarrie. 'Please, whatever you do, don't ever tell James what I've just said about him. It won't help matters.'

Abruptly their conversation was interrupted by the sound of a motor engine chugging up the drive. They exchanged glances.

'It couldn't be Rafi, could it?' Sophie cried, seized with sudden hope.

She took off at a sprint across the garden and round the side of the bungalow. Libby and Clarrie hurried after her.

Libby didn't recognise the man who climbed out of an old Chevrolet. He was middle-aged and tallish with a slight stoop, dressed smartly in a white uniform and clutching an old-fashioned topee. He was already shaking Sophie by the hand.

As Libby and Clarrie caught up, Libby heard Sophie asking anxiously, 'But how did you know I was here?'

'An educated guess,' he answered, 'that you would take refuge with friends.'

Sophie introduced him. 'This is Mr Robert Stourton, the Agent from Gulgat,' she said, tension in her voice.

'Ex-Agent,' he said with a stiff smile. 'As of two weeks ago, I'm officially retired from government duties.' He shook hands with Clarrie. 'I was acquainted with your late husband. A good man. Terrible business.'

'Yes it was,' said Clarrie, keeping her composure. 'I believe you were on that tiger hunt too, Mr Stourton.'

He shot her a look of alarm. 'Y-yes, I was as a matter of fact. We did what we could. I'm awfully sorry.'

'Please don't be,' said Clarrie. 'No one could have saved Wesley. It was a tragic accident.' She turned to lead the way. 'Please come inside and have some refreshment – then you can tell us what brings you to Belgooree.'

While slaking his thirst with several cups of tea, the British official told them of the volatile situation in Gulgat.

'Unrest continues,' he said. 'There have been protests in the capital – they have been dealt with by the Rajah's police but . . .'

'What sort of protests?' asked Clarrie.

'Anti-Mohammedan,' said Stourton. 'The Rajah wanted me to warn you and Rafi in case you were still in the area.'

'Sanjay sent you to warn us?' Sophie asked, agitated. 'I find that hard to believe. He did nothing to keep us safe while we were still there.'

Stourton gave her a sour look. 'If you had confided in him more – or come to me with your concerns,' he chided, 'then we could have protected you.'

'Rafi tried his hardest to get Sanjay to take seriously the attacks on Muslims,' Sophie protested, 'but he wouldn't listen. And you, Robert, have always tended to side with the old Rani and the palace. Once

Rajah Kishan died and Rita left, we felt we had no friends at court. Rafi didn't want to leave but we could see the trouble building.'

'Making a run for it hasn't helped,' said Stourton. 'In the eyes of the Rani and the courtiers it just confirms that your husband couldn't be trusted.'

'Mr Stourton,' said Clarrie indignantly, 'that is most unfair.'

'It's not what I think, Mrs Robson,' he said, 'but it plays right into the Rani's hands. She is whipping up hatred against the Mohammedans in Gulgat – she sees it as her way of reasserting her authority in a state that is now part of India.'

'And is Sanjay just prepared to go along with that?' Sophie said with disdain.

'The *Rajah*, as he now is,' said Stourton pointedly, 'has sent me to warn you that feelings are running high and not to return to Gulgat any time soon.'

'He has nothing to fear on that score,' said Sophie. 'We shan't ever be returning to Gulgat.'

'Good,' he said, looking relieved. 'I don't want any harm to come to either of you; I hope you believe that?'

'I'm sure she does,' said Clarrie swiftly.

'So where is Rafi?' he asked.

The women exchanged looks.

'You can trust me,' Stourton insisted. 'I'm not returning to Gulgat either. I'm booked on a passage out of Calcutta in a week's time.'

'He's in the Punjab,' said Sophie. 'He's secured a job with the Pakistan Forest Service – I'm shortly to join him.'

Stourton's eyes widened in surprise. 'I thought you would be returning to Scotland.'

'And we thought we'd be seeing out our days in Gulgat,' said Sophie, her eyes clouding with sadness, 'but that's not to be.'

He nodded. 'I saw myself staying there a lot longer too. I'm glad Rafi has found a new position. I'm just . . .'

'Just what?' Clarrie asked.

He hesitated and then said, 'I'm concerned to still find you in the area, Sophie. I was hoping you would both be long gone.'

Libby felt her insides tighten. 'Why would that be, Mr Stourton?' she asked.

'There are gangs from Gulgat causing trouble,' he said. 'I've seen them on the road. I fear Sophie might be in danger here – and you might be at risk for harbouring her.'

'Harbouring her?' Clarrie exclaimed. 'She's no fugitive! She's a British woman and nobody here would harm her.'

'She's the wife of a prominent Mohammedan – and one herself. Just the sort of scapegoat that the ultra-nationalists, whipped up by the Rani, are looking for.'

'Surely not?' Libby gasped. 'And anyway, Gulgat is miles away from here.'

'It took me just half a day to drive here,' said Stourton. 'These gangs are armed and someone is providing them with trucks.'

Libby's heart began to thump in alarm. Sophie was turning ashen.

Clarrie said calmly, 'No one is at risk here – the people of Belgooree are loyal and will defend us from any troublemakers.'

Stourton shook his head. 'I admire your courage, Mrs Robson, and your trust in these people. But we British can never really understand the Indian or what passions prompt him to do what he does.'

'Utter nonsense!' cried Libby. 'You sound like a Victorian imperialist.'

He gave her a contemptuous look and turned to Sophie.

'Despite the bravado of your friends, I urge you to go and join your husband sooner rather than later. You will be safer in the new Mohammedan state.'

The agent didn't linger. There were stilted goodbyes. The women stood at the veranda rail watching his car retreat down the drive and out of view. After he was out of sight Sophie said, 'I've never warmed to Robert. He was always too quick to curry favour with the palace and he'll hate giving up his luxurious lifestyle, but perhaps this time he's right. His talk of gangs on the road really scares me – I've already seen how Muslims in Gulgat have been attacked. I think I should go. My being here is putting you all in danger.'

Clarrie put a hand on her shoulder. 'That man doesn't know the Khasi like I do. You're safe among them. I promised Rafi I'd look after you here.'

'Clarrie's right,' said Libby. 'You can't go to Pakistan yet. It would be more risky to travel if there are men out on the road seeking to do harm.' She shuddered at the thought.

'Besides,' said Clarrie, 'who's going to know you are here? We'll keep our heads down but carry on as usual till we hear from Rafi. What do you say?'

Sophie smiled, encouraged by their support. 'Thank you, Clarrie,' she said. 'And you, lassie.' She gave Libby a hug.

The agent's visit left Libby feeling on edge; she hadn't liked Stourton. Perhaps it was because of what Adela had once told her about the terrible day of the tiger hunt in Gulgat. As Adela had crouched in the car beside her wounded father, her last sight of the camp had been Stourton supervising the skinning of the tiger he had shot. What sort of selfish, unfeeling man would turn his back and do that while a fellow huntsman was being rushed mortally wounded in a car to the mission hospital?

But it had the effect of galvanising Libby into writing to Ghulam to tell him about his father's grave condition. None of them knew what the next day might bring. Just in the way he had encouraged her to rekindle her relationship with her own father, she wanted Ghulam to have the chance to send his father a message before it was too late.

She kept the letter brief and ended it with a loving message.

> . . . *you are always in my thoughts and I want you to know – if it hasn't been obvious to you for months – that I love you with all my heart, Ghulam, and I always will.*

I realise there is little I – or you – can do about it. I'm not asking you to. But I couldn't leave India without you knowing how I felt. I have memories of us together that I'll treasure for the rest of my life.

Please take good care of yourself, my darling prodigal – and Fatima too.

My love forever,

Libby xxx

In the days that followed – after the letter was sent – Libby kept dwelling on Stourton's sudden appearance. Why had he come at all? If he had been so worried about Sophie's safety, then why hadn't he offered to drive her away from Belgooree himself that very day? She didn't voice her unease to the others but it nagged at her whenever she thought of the enigmatic official in the white suit. Something else bothered her about him. Why, if he had left Gulgat and was on his way home to Britain, was he travelling in an open-topped car in which he appeared to have no luggage?

Each day, as they waited for news and sweltered in the monsoon humidity, Libby was aware of a sense of foreboding gathering about them like the inky clouds of a tropical storm.

CHAPTER 35

Newcastle, early September

James was glad of the excuse to get out of the house. Tilly and Josey were engaged in a frenzy of packing and Mungo had gone ahead a week early to St Abbs to stay with his Uncle Johnny and go sailing. Since Tilly had discovered that Adela and Sam were leaving Newcastle, she had been all the more determined to press ahead quickly with the move to Jesmond, as if she feared he might have a change of heart too. In some unfathomable way, James felt his wife was blaming him for the young couple's decision to return to India. 'If you hadn't kept going on about Belgooree . . . !' Tilly had accused him.

James was just as sad as Tilly that Adela and Sam were soon to be going – they had a passage booked from Marseilles at the end of the month and were talking about a few days in Paris on the way – but he had to keep stopping himself from reminiscing about Belgooree in front of his wife. That had been easier since Adela and Sam had moved out. Rather than go to the Robsons' new home, they had arranged to spend the last few weeks living with Sam's mother in Cullercoats. He envied the young couple their closeness and ease with each other – the way Adela's eyes lit up when Sam came into the room – and wondered if it would ever be like that with Tilly again. Perhaps it never had been; it certainly wasn't now. Tilly continued to look at him as if he were a tiresome guest who kept getting in the way – that's when she looked at him at all.

So on the days leading up to the move to Jesmond, James kept out of the way. He'd been up to Willowburn twice that week and was finally going to visit his former fellow planter, Fairfax – now well into his nineties – in his nursing home at Tynemouth.

The place had a pervasive smell of urine and boiled vegetables. He found the old man in his room, sitting in an armchair by the window dozing. James peered around before waking him. The room was a shrine to Fairfax's time in India. The bed and chairs were covered in faded Kashmir woollen blankets and the room was cluttered with Indian tables displaying sports trophies, brass bowls and ivory ornaments. The walls were hung with framed photographs of Assam: hunting trips with men standing in front of tents or with their feet proudly on the animals they had just killed. There was one of a polo team. With a start, James recognised both himself and his cousin Wesley in the photograph.

Wesley had been a superior horseman to James and had taken quickly to the game of polo. In fact, Wesley had embraced the tea planting life with gusto the minute he had arrived in Assam. James had a stab of grief for his younger cousin. Often they had clashed over business, as well as over his marriage to Clarrie, which James had thought would be a disaster. But latterly, he had enjoyed Wesley's company more and more, and come to realise that his cousin had the perfect life in India with his attractive, spirited wife and his family around him. Poor, dear man!

'That you, Ali?'

James swung round to see his old mentor awake and peering myopically at him. His head was sparsely covered in a few wisps of white hair and his jowly face sagged like a bloodhound's. But he still sported a bushy tobacco-stained moustache below his beaky nose.

'No, sir; it's Robson.' He crossed the room. 'James Robson.'

He held out his hand.

Fairfax frowned in confusion. 'Robson?' he queried.

'From the Oxford Estates,' James prompted. 'We worked together before the Great War – and you were my best man here in Newcastle, remember?'

The old man's faded brown eyes lit with recognition. 'Young Robson!' He took James's hand in a surprisingly firm handshake. 'How very good to see you!'

'And you, sir.' James thought it incongruous to be called young at the age of seventy but he had slipped straight back into his junior role in calling his old bachelor friend sir.

'What brings you here, Robson? Home on furlough? How is the old place? I don't get to hear from anyone these days. All my contemporaries are long in the ground.' Fairfax waved a scrawny hand. 'Pull up a chair, Robson. Sit close and speak up – hearing's not tip-top these days.'

James sat on the chair opposite. 'I've retired too,' he said. 'Been back in Newcastle since July.'

'Not long then,' said Fairfax.

'No, I suppose not; though it feels like it.'

Fairfax snorted. 'Give it ten years and you'll feel part of the furniture. I still dream about the place though . . .' The old man looked reflective.

James felt a familiar tension in his gut. His frighteningly vivid dreams of the plantation had hardly plagued him since returning to England. For that reason alone, he would stick it out in Newcastle with Tilly. He could cope with her aloofness towards him as long as he had peace of mind. Physical closeness would return given time.

'That nice wife of yours,' said Fairfax, 'came to visit me while you were away. Cheery sort, Polly.'

'Tilly,' James corrected.

'What?'

'Tilly is my wife's name.'

439

'Yes, kind of her. You can count the number of visitors I get on one hand – or two thumbs!' He broke into wheezy laughter.

James felt guilty for not coming sooner. It wasn't that he hadn't wanted to but somehow he had kept putting it off. Was it his reluctance to talk about Danny Dunlop's parentage and where such questions might lead? Ironically, it was Tilly who had suggested the visit, no doubt to get James out from under her feet while she organised the house move.

'Let's have a *chota peg*,' suggested Fairfax. 'Glasses and bottle are hidden in that bedside cabinet. Nurse doesn't let me touch it before tiffin but this is a special occasion, eh what?'

Once James had poured them both a generous whisky, they fell to reminiscing about long-ago days on the tea plantation. An hour passed and the old man began to tire. His head was drooping and he was beginning to lose the thread of their conversation. James realised that if he didn't ask about the Dunlops now then the chance would be gone.

Bracing himself, he pulled out the envelope from his inner jacket pocket. It was crumpled from being carried around for so long, but still unopened.

'Just one thing before I go,' said James. 'I've been asked by an acquaintance to see if you remember any tea planters in your day called Dunlop.'

'Dunlop?' Fairfax frowned.

'I have the details here,' said James. 'This man is keen to establish his British credentials – but I worry it will just stir up a hornet's nest. He's Anglo-Indian, you see.'

'Anglo-Indian,' Fairfax echoed.

'Yes, what in our day we called Eurasian,' said James.

'Ah,' said the old man, nodding in understanding. 'There was a lot of that went on in the old days. Quite wrong, of course. Not fair on the children. What to do with them – always the problem.'

James felt his heart begin to beat erratically. 'Yes, quite so.'

'Well, read it to me,' said Fairfax. 'Can't think of a Dunlop in Assam, mind you.'

James reached for an ivory letter opener on the table in the window, slit open the envelope and put on his reading glasses. His breath stopped. He stared at the neat list of facts about Danny Dunlop. It wasn't possible! He felt winded with shock.

'Not a tea planter anyway,' Fairfax said, still searching his memory. 'Though I did know of a Reverend Dunlop in Shillong. Or was he a doctor?'

James closed his eyes but he could still see the name seared behind his lids. Aidan Dunlop: born circa 1896, orphan of a Scottish planter in Assam, admitted to the Convent of the Sisters of the Holy Cross by Sister Placid.

Sweat broke out on his brow. His heart raced. The one thing that he had clung on to was that Danny stood for Daniel. But Danny clearly stood for Aidan, the name he had given the Logan boy. It could be no other child. Perhaps kind Sister Placid had given him the Scottish surname to give him a veneer of respectability.

'Are you feeling all right, old boy?' asked Fairfax, peering at him in concern.

James crumpled the letter. 'No – yes – I . . .' He tried to order his thoughts. 'It doesn't really tell us anything more. School in Shillong – ended up on the railways.'

The whisky curdled in his stomach. James thought he might be sick.

'There you go,' said Fairfax. 'Dr Dunlop in Shillong – probably related.'

'Yes,' James said, balling the letter in his pocket as he stood up. 'Well, I better be off. Tilly has got me moving house so I should get back to supervise.'

'Dunlop, Dunlop . . .' Fairfax had resumed a faraway look; he was lost in the past.

James regretted bringing up the subject. Why on earth hadn't he opened the letter before now? Deep down he knew why: he had feared that digging into the past might raise long-buried ghosts. Suddenly he couldn't wait to be gone from the stuffy tobacco-smelling room with its myriad reminders of the Oxford tea gardens.

He shook Fairfax by the hand. 'Don't get up, sir; I'll see myself out. Good to see you.'

'I've enjoyed our chin-wag about the old days, Robson.' The old man smiled. 'You will come again and see me, won't you? No one in here has the foggiest idea about Assam.'

'Yes, of course I will,' James promised, making hastily for the door.

'What a life we had, eh?' Fairfax continued as James left. 'Work hard, play harder . . . !'

James felt the bile rise in his throat at the words. A memory of the hateful Bill Logan saying just the same thing forced its way into his mind. He clattered out of the nursing home as fast as he could.

꧁ ꧂

The night-terrors began again. James so alarmed Tilly that he offered to move into the room vacated by the Jackmans.

'I don't want to disturb you,' he'd said when Tilly had asked him what was causing the nightmares.

'Is it the house move?' she asked in concern one night, following him into the spare bedroom. 'If you're that unhappy about it . . . ? Am I being too selfish?'

'No, it's nothing to do with that,' said James. 'It's probably too many nightcaps before bed – or cheese or something.'

'James,' Tilly said, hovering in the doorway. Her expression softened. 'Is this what it was like . . . ? Were you like this when you had your . . . exhaustion . . . when you went to Clarrie's?'

James reddened. He was about to rebuff the suggestion and then decided to be honest. 'Yes.' He glanced away. 'I couldn't sleep and when I did I had these terrible dreams that were so real I thought I was experiencing them.'

Tilly came and sat down on the bed beside him. 'Libby wrote and told me. I'm afraid I thought she was being over-dramatic as usual.' She placed her hand over his – lightly, briefly. 'I'm sorry. I shouldn't have dismissed her worries.'

'I wanted to confide in Libby,' James admitted. 'She's so mature in many ways. But it didn't seem fair to burden her . . .'

'Burden her with what?' Tilly asked gently. 'James, we've been apart so long, I've no real idea what it's been like for you. Is there something we can do?'

James felt a pang of affection for his wife and this glimpse of the old Tilly, the one who had fussed over and cared for him. Here she was, wrapped in a threadbare silk dressing gown that had once belonged to him, her hair loose about her shoulders, concerned about him once more. She looked almost girlish in the lamplight. How he missed their former companionship! Years ago, one of the things that had attracted him to Tilly was that he had found her so easy to talk to – her warmth of personality and ability to listen.

He took a deep breath. 'I'm haunted by the past, Tilly,' he confided. 'I can't get it out of my head.'

'The War?' Tilly guessed.

James shook his head. 'Much longer ago – before I met you.'

'Ancient history then,' Tilly said with a wry look.

James gave her a fleeting smile. 'Yes, when I was a young man at the Oxford.'

'This isn't to do with Sophie's father, is it?'

James flinched. 'How could you possibly know—?'

'Darling, I was the one who unearthed it all, remember? Poking my nose into why the Logans were staying at Belgooree when Sam was born and Sophie was a little girl.'

James let out a sigh. 'No, Tilly, it's not about that. But it does involve Logan – before he was married. God, how I wish I had never worked for that wicked man!'

'James!' Tilly admonished. 'You mustn't say that. He was ill when he did that terrible thing.'

'You mean murdered his wife and then committed suicide?' James said angrily. 'No, Logan wasn't ill; he was a vicious, jealous, drunken bastard who mistreated his wife and was notorious for taking advantage of the tea pickers.'

Tilly gaped at him in shock. James felt himself shaking. All the old hatred for Logan and disgust at himself for doing his bidding surged through him. He waited for Tilly to defend Sophie's father with excuses; his wife rarely saw fault in anyone – apart from in him and Libby.

'Tell me,' said Tilly softly. 'I promise I'll say nothing to Sam or Sophie.'

James felt his eyes sting with tears. Swallowing hard, he began to tell Tilly the secrets that he had buried for decades but which would no longer leave him in peace.

***

Adela was encouraged by the thawing of frosty relations between Tilly and James. Since they had moved into the Jesmond house a few days ago, they appeared to be getting on better.

Josey cautioned, 'It's not all sweetness and light, but at least they've stopped snapping at each other in front of others.'

'Well, it's a start,' said Adela. 'And I'm glad they've settled on the Jesmond house. I'm sure Major Gibson will let James go riding at Willowburn any time he wants – and follow the hunt.'

'Tally-ho and all that,' said Josey with a wink.

'And what about you, Josey?' Adela asked. 'Are you happy to stay on living in the Robson household now that James is back?'

Josey paused. 'I'm not a great fan of James,' she admitted. 'But I feel sorry for the man. He's like a fish out of water in Newcastle . . . and I know he has nightmares – heard him shouting in the night on more than one occasion.'

'Really?' Adela asked in concern.

'Yes. Tilly says it's something to do with an incident at the plantation years ago but she won't say what. She's being kinder to him as a result. So I've decided to stay on with them and help Tilly. She and the children – well, they're my family too. I feel more affection for them than I ever did for my own. I don't want to go anywhere else – and Tilly has insisted that I stay.'

Adela smiled. 'I'm not surprised; you've been a wonderful friend to her.'

Josey gave a droll look. 'Having said that, I'm looking forward to a week on my own, looking after the house while the family are at St Abbs. Would you and Sam like to come round for supper one evening?'

'Thanks, we'd love that.'

'I'll have a go at making you a curry, shall I?' Josey suggested. 'Or at least throw some curry powder into a fish pie.'

Adela grimaced. 'Actually, I'm off—' Abruptly she stopped herself. But Josey was immediately suspicious. Her eyes narrowed.

'Off curry? Tell me, are you . . . ?'

Adela flushed.

'You're pregnant!' Josey cried in glee.

Adela grinned and shushed her. 'I think so. But don't say anything. I haven't told Sam yet and he hasn't guessed. I want to be sure.'

Josey darted at Adela and threw her arms around her in a jubilant hug. 'That's the most wonderful news!'

Adela's eyes welled with tears as she laughed and spluttered, 'I know, isn't it?'

Josey broke away and fished out her cigarettes. 'Celebratory smoke?'

Adela pulled a face. 'No thanks; I've lost the taste for those too.'

Josey chuckled. 'Sweetie, it's not going to take Sam long to work out why. Tell him.'

'I will soon,' said Adela. 'When we get a quiet moment alone. We're so busy. Jane's only been back a week and the café business is already picking up.'

'Leave her to it,' said Josey. 'You need to start putting your feet up.'

'Not yet,' said Adela. 'And Joan's gracing us with her presence this weekend. I said we'd have an early fourth birthday party for Bonnie at the café. I want to see the girl before we go – and we won't be here in October for her birthday. Jane's doing most of the organising but I want to help. Jane's excited to see her niece again and determined that she's going to keep in touch with George's daughter.'

Josey gave a wry chuckle. 'Except us two know that Bonnie is no more George's daughter than she is the King's.'

Adela gave her a warning look. 'Which neither of us is ever going to tell.'

'My lips are sealed, sweetie,' said Josey with an earthy laugh, as smoke escaped from her nostrils.

***

With each day, Adela's impatience to be travelling back to India grew. She knew that many people thought her and Sam mad for heading back to a country that Britain was so quickly disengaging from and where there was an upsurge in violence since Partition, but to her and Sam, India would always be home. Deep down, she also knew that she needed to get away from Newcastle and put the pain of her failure to find John Wesley behind her. Perhaps distance would help her come to terms with the past more quickly.

Now that she was almost certain that she was pregnant again, Adela was filled with a new excitement and urgency to get back to her mother and Belgooree. It would be a fresh start for her and Sam – how pleased he would be to be a father at last – and this time she would enjoy her pregnancy. There would be no shameful hiding of her pregnant state or cruel separation from her baby. This one would be loved unconditionally. Her emotions see-sawed between tearfulness and euphoria as she contemplated the future.

Adela's plan to hand over the café to Jane was going smoothly and it was an added joy to discover that Jane was still the caring, slightly reserved but unflappable woman that Adela remembered.

They had fallen immediately into their old friendship, though this time Jane was more ready to tease Adela back. Her cousin had grown in confidence since living away. Sam said he was struck by the family resemblance between Adela and her dark-haired cousin.

'Mother says that we both take after our Grandmama Jane who married our grandfather, Jock Belhaven,' Adela had told him. 'He was the first tea planter at Belgooree. Mother has a photograph of her parents and my cousin looks very like our grandmother – more than I do.'

Adela also liked Jane's cheerful, red-cheeked husband with his bluff Yorkshire humour. Charlie Latimer had a knack of cajoling the staff into doing Jane's bidding in the kitchen while entertaining them with lurid catering stories from his time in the army. He had twice the patience that Adela did. She wrote to Clarrie full of confidence that the café would not only survive under its new management, but also thrive.

As Adela's thoughts turned increasingly to India and Belgooree, she hungered for news, but her mother had not written since shortly after the Independence celebrations. Sam was reassuring.

'Your mother will be run off her feet in the gardens at this time of year,' he said. 'The factory will be at full production.'

Adela put her hands around his face and kissed him in affection. 'You sound like a tea planter already,' she teased.

He caught her round the waist and tugged her closer. 'I can't wait.' He grinned and kissed her robustly back.

On the afternoon of Bonnie's birthday party, Adela felt even more queasy than usual. She had been busy all morning helping to decorate the café and had hardly stopped to eat or drink.

'Sit down for a minute,' Jane ordered, 'and have a sandwich. You've lost all your colour. I hope you're not sickening for something?'

'Thanks.' Adela didn't argue. 'Just five minutes' rest will do it.'

They had partitioned off half the café for the birthday tea and a space had been cleared for games, which Sam was going to organise while Charlie Latimer bashed out tunes on the old piano. Adela had hoped her Aunt Olive would be persuaded out of her house but Jane had shaken her head.

'Mam won't come. You know how she hates crowds. I'll get Joan to stop off with Bonnie and see her before they go back to Willowburn.'

Soon the café was filling with children and their mothers: friends and relations of Joan's. Adela had to admit that George's ex-wife was popular and she felt guilty for resenting her. It wasn't just because of loyalty to her cousin George whom Adela felt had been wronged by Joan's infidelity. Adela had to admit that she still harboured a residual jealousy towards Joan for another reason. While Adela had been hiding in disgrace for being pregnant and had had to give up her baby, Joan had got away with her affair. George had gallantly married her and taken on another man's child. Adela swallowed down resentment as she watched an excited Bonnie arrive, dressed in flounces of pink right down to her ankles and clutching Joan's hand. Bonnie slipped Joan's hold and skipped across to her Auntie Jane, who immediately began making a fuss of her niece.

Abruptly, Adela was seized by a yearning for John Wesley so acute that she thought she would pass out. She gripped her stomach and tried to hide her distress. It would pass; it always did. She just had to endure it for a moment or two. She never knew when the sense of loss would take hold of her. Little things triggered it: the sight of a baby being pushed in a pram or a boy kicking a football in a back lane. But the bouts of grief had lessened since her decision to give up the search.

It was probably being pregnant that was making her feel suddenly teary. The thought that she was carrying her and Sam's baby gave her immediate comfort. Adela stood up and went to join her husband, slipping a hand into his. He gave her a quizzical smile, squeezed her hand and turned to deal with a couple of small boys who were already fighting over a balloon.

As Charlie started to play 'Three Blind Mice', Adela put on a smile and greeted Joan and her new husband Tommy. She liked Major Gibson's head groom, though they had only met briefly on a couple of occasions. Joan was enjoying showing him off and playing the country lady. She was dressed in a smart tweed jacket over a linen dress, her blonde hair neatly coiffured and with only the slightest hint of make-up.

'Joany tells me you're going back to India,' said Tommy.

'Yes,' Adela replied. 'We'll be joining my family and helping on the tea garden.'

'That's grand,' he said, 'isn't it Joany?'

Joan was beaming at Adela with that look that Adela had always found so disconcerting: half assessing, half vacant, as if she was only partially listening.

'Grand, yes,' she agreed.

'You must come up to the stables before you go,' Tommy said. 'Mr Robson says how you and Mr Jackman like to ride. You'd both be welcome. Wouldn't they, Joany?'

'Thank you,' said Adela. 'We've been meaning to but haven't found the time.'

'I'm learning to ride,' said Joan, putting a possessive hand on her husband's arm. 'Tommy's teaching me so I can accompany Martha Gibson.'

Adela looked at her in surprise. She thought Joan's boasting about being friends with the major's wife had been exaggerated.

'You can ride with me and Martha if you like,' Joan said, smiling.

Adela smiled back. 'I'd like that. James has told me about her. She sounds a nice woman.'

'She is,' said Joan. 'She's not snobbish like the other gentry. Must be 'cause she's American. And generous too. She gave me this dress; it's from New York. Says so on the label.'

'It suits you,' said Adela.

'And I help do her hair,' said Joan. 'She used to have it very old-fashioned.'

'They're best of friends already,' Tommy said proudly. 'And the Gibsons' son thinks the world of Joany too – he follows her around like her shadow.'

'Like my shadow,' Joan repeated.

'Joany's a natural with kiddies,' Tommy said proudly.

Adela felt her nausea returning. 'Help yourself to tea and sandwiches, won't you? I must help Sam with the games.'

'And Mrs Gibson bought the dress Bonnie's wearing,' Joan continued. 'Lovely, isn't it?'

Adela thought it was rather fussy, and the small girl was already tripping on its hem trying to run about.

'Bonnie looks very pretty,' Adela answered as she turned to go and help with the children.

Amid the shrieking and laughter, Sam was pairing up the children to play 'Oranges and Lemons'. Bonnie rushed up to Adela and seized her hand. 'You play with me, Auntie Delly!'

'Love to,' said Adela, kissing her on her matching pink hairband.

They marched round in a chaotic circle, Sam leading the raucous singing. Bonnie squealed with delight when she and Adela were caught in Sam's arms as the music stopped.

'Again! Again!' Bonnie cried.

After that, they played musical bumps and Sam tried to teach them the hokey-cokey. The children ended up running into each other deliberately and an older boy stepped on Bonnie's dress which made her fall over and bang her knee. She burst into tears. Sam scooped her up and declared it was time for birthday cake.

At the sight of Jane carrying in a large iced cake with candles lit, Bonnie's wailing quickly subsided. While Sam sat her at the head of the table and Bonnie blew out her candles, the other children scrambled for seats and were soon tucking into the birthday tea.

Adela tried to quell her queasiness by sipping tea and eating cake. The smell of the paste sandwiches and pork pies was turning her stomach. She watched Sam as he showed the children a trick he did with his hands that made it look like his thumb was falling off. He was so good with the children; he would make a loving father to their child. Adela felt a flood of affection for her husband. She couldn't wait for the party to be over and to have him to herself so she could tell him her news. There was no doubt in her mind now that she was carrying their baby.

Charlie continued at the piano during tea, playing popular tunes. Some of the parents were gathering around him, singing along.

'Get Adela to sing for you,' Sam called out, giving his wife a smile of encouragement.

Lexy, who was sitting beside the piano clapping along to the music, shouted, 'Gan on, hinny; give them a Toodle Pips special.'

Adela took little persuasion: hearing her old favourites being played made her want to get up and dance. Soon she was singing 'Don't Sit Under the Apple Tree', followed by other songs that had proved popular during the recent war. The café rang to the sound of voices joining in the chorus and Charlie's enthusiastic piano playing. Nobody seemed to mind the children racing around the café, jumping off the chairs and playing 'tiggy-on-high' while the adults sang their nostalgic songs.

Eventually, it was time for the café to close and the party to end. Bonnie burst into tears. 'I don't w-want to go home!' she blubbered. 'I w-want to stay with Uncle Sam!'

Joan and Tommy had to coax her away with promises that Sam and Adela would come and visit her very soon. Her Aunt Jane produced a sticky toffee apple which brought a smile back to her face.

With the guests gone, they began to clear up.

'We can finish this,' said Jane, 'if you two want to go. You've earned a rest after the games and sing-song.'

Sam was helping Lexy to her feet. Lexy said, 'Aye, you look done in, hinny. Get yersel' away home.'

Sam gave Adela a concerned look. 'Aren't you feeling well?'

'I'm fine; we'll stay,' said Adela. 'It won't take long if we all give a hand.'

'Come up and see me before you go,' said Lexy, making her way towards the stairs as Adela began to brush crumbs from the tablecloths. Sam and Charlie pulled the tables and chairs back into their usual positions. Charlie stooped to pick something from the floor.

'Must have come off when the children were playing,' he said, holding up a chain to the light. 'Or maybe it belongs to one of the mothers.'

Adela glanced round; she noticed Lexy had stopped too and was staring at the upheld pendant.

'Give it to Jane,' said Sam. 'They'll come back for it when they realise they've dropped it.'

'Doesn't look worth the bother,' said Charlie. 'Just an old pebble of some sort.'

Adela saw the chain glint in the light, a pinkish stone dangling from it. Something about it made her peer closer.

'Let's see,' said Adela.

Charlie held it out to her. 'Is it yours?'

Adela's heart fluttered. She took it from him and laid it on her open palm. Her heart began to pound. She ran a finger and thumb over the smooth pink stone. It was almost heart-shaped. Adela's breath stopped in her throat. The chain was familiar too, with its old-fashioned catch. She sat down quickly. How was this possible? It didn't make sense!

'Darling, are you all right?' Sam asked at once, coming to sit beside her.

Lexy turned back from the stairs. 'Adela?'

Adela stared at the necklace, trying to catch her breath.

'What is it?' Sam asked, putting a hand to Adela's clammy brow. 'Are you going to be sick?'

Adela couldn't speak. Pressure like an iron weight was building up in her chest, smothering her.

'Fetch a glass of water,' Lexy said to Charlie, as she lumbered towards Adela. Charlie rushed off into the kitchen where Jane and Doreen were washing up.

'Let me see,' said Lexy, lifting the necklace from Adela's shaking hand. Lexy scrutinised it and then looked at Adela, her eyes widening in shock.

'It's Clarrie's, isn't it?' she said quietly. 'I remember her wearing it.'

Adela nodded, her throat tightening with emotion.

Sam looked baffled. 'How can that be? Is this yours, Adela? I've never seen you wear it.'

Adela struggled to speak. 'Yes, it's mine,' she croaked. 'Mother gave it to me . . .'

'So when did you lose it?' Sam asked.

'Before the War,' she whispered.

'Surely it hasn't been lying here all this time?' Sam said in astonishment.

'No,' said Adela. She felt herself begin to shake all over. She wasn't sure if she was going to faint or be sick.

Sam's arm went around her. 'Well, at least you've got it back now.'

'Tell him,' said Lexy softly.

'Tell me what?' Sam asked, frowning.

At that moment, Charlie reappeared with a glass of water. Lexy took it from him.

'Just give them a minute, will you?' she asked. Charlie nodded and retreated through the kitchen door which swung behind him.

Adela looked at Lexy, her heart thumping.

'Go on, lass,' her old friend encouraged.

Adela swallowed hard. 'Mother was given this necklace by the swami who lived in the clearing above Belgooree – for good luck and protection. When I came to England in '38 she gave it to me for the same reason.' She struggled with how to tell him the next detail.

'And?' Sam said gently.

Adela met his look. His eyes were so full of compassion that it gave her the courage to tell him the truth. 'The day John Wesley was taken away I – I wrapped the necklace in his blanket and told Maggie to ask the mission women to keep it with him. It was my most important possession and it was all I had to give him. I hoped it would keep him safe . . .'

She tensed, expecting to see his expression change to disappointment or resentment at her mentioning John Wesley again. But Sam laid a hand tenderly on her head and pulled her to him, cradling her against his strong shoulder. Adela's eyes brimmed with tears.

'But how's it got here?' Lexy asked, baffled.

'I don't know,' said Adela tearfully. 'Did you see one of the mothers wearing it?'

'No,' said Lexy with a shake of the head. 'But someone here today must know where it came from.'

Adela's heart began to pound. She tried to recall all of the children who had been at the party. Perhaps one of the girls was a step-sister to John Wesley? Or was one of the women who had been singing around the piano her son's second adoptive mother? But maybe none of them had anything to do with her boy and the necklace had been given away or sold years ago to raise funds for the mission.

Yet something that Tilly had said about the Belgian Segals gave Adela hope that they had kept the swami's stone with her son. When Tilly had rescued the infant from the Anderson shelter after the bombing raid, she said he had been found with a small box of possessions; from what she could remember there were a handful of photographs, keepsakes and a floppy miniature teddy bear.

Adela felt sure the kind Segals would have kept the necklace and that this would have been handed on to whoever had taken on her son next. What if it was someone who had been there that very afternoon? Adela was suddenly overwhelmed by the shock. Bile rose in her throat. She tore herself from Sam's hold and bolted for the kitchen door.

Clamping a hand over her mouth, Adela didn't stop until she was out in the backyard breathing in gulps of air. Her head spun. Her throat watered. Adela doubled over and retched into the gutter. She couldn't stop. She vomited until her insides felt hollow and sore. Even though her eyes were tight shut, she was aware of Sam there beside her, holding her hair away from her face and rubbing her back.

When the spasms finally stopped, Adela felt so weak she would have collapsed if Sam had not been holding her firmly in his arms. He stroked her hair. Adela realised that she was still clutching the necklace tightly in her hand. It pressed into her palm, a painful reminder of all she had lost. Her longing to find John Wesley returned with a new ferocity. Yet would her marriage survive if she started searching again? What on earth did they do now?

'You mustn't upset yourself like this, Adela,' Sam said in gentle reproof.

Adela looked at him with a mixture of tenderness and sorrow.

'Sam, this isn't just because I'm upset,' Adela said, feeling utterly drained. 'It's because I'm pregnant.'

CHAPTER 36

Belgooree, mid-September

After a week of anxious waiting for marauding gangs to appear in the district, nothing had happened. Libby began to hope that Stourton's unsettling visit had been for nothing.

Yet rumours were rife around the tea garden that there had been terrible atrocities in neighbouring Gulgat. Whole villages had been torched and the Muslim minority had been butchered or had fled to East Pakistan. Abandoned houses that were still standing were being given to Hindu refugees escaping in the other direction. There were tales of these Bengalis arriving with horrific wounds and mutilations. Each new wave of displaced, traumatised Hindus appeared to provoke a fresh round of attacks on Gulgat's dwindling minority of Muslims.

Libby sent a telegram home: *Sorry will miss holiday stop still with Sophie at Belgooree stop all well stop love Libby.*

She didn't want to give them any cause for worry about her safety or reveal that they were marooned at Belgooree by fear of the troubles in Gulgat spreading. She would write later when the situation had calmed down. But Sophie no longer went for rides and kept mainly to the house or compound. Libby kept her company, though she insisted on helping Clarrie each morning in the office.

'I have to do something,' she protested. 'And I'm not the target.'

Clarrie had given her a worried look. 'A group of angry men aren't necessarily going to know what the wife of Rafi Khan looks like – only that she's British,' she warned. 'I don't want you going further than the factory either.'

Clarrie had agonised over whether to allow Harry to return for the new school term in Shillong or to keep him at home and let Manzur tutor him again. In the end she had decided that it was best to keep things as normal as possible and the boy had gone back to school, eager to see his friends. It was arranged that he would board there until Christmas. All the women had been sad to see him go. Harry had shrugged off their attempts to hug and kiss him, though he'd hung on to Breckon and shed tears when parted from the dog.

Each day Libby checked the dak for a reply from Ghulam, but none came. She knew with the upheaval of people and the unforeseen chaos of Partition that services had been badly disrupted. In some parts of the country post lay uncollected, trains stood idle awaiting firemen to shovel coal, police forces were depleted and milk went undelivered. Perhaps Ghulam had never received her letter. Or had something happened to him? How she worried about his safety in Calcutta!

Then one sultry afternoon, as Libby and Sophie dozed on the shady veranda, Libby jolted awake to the sound of distant firecrackers. She sat up and listened. In the jungle beyond the compound, birds flew into the air screeching. There was a sound like a rumble of thunder before a downpour but there was no stirring of wind in the trees that normally preceded a monsoon storm.

'What is it?' Sophie asked, sitting up.

'That noise . . .' Libby said.

They both strained to hear.

'Sounds like rifle fire,' said Sophie.

They scrambled to their feet and went to peer over the veranda railing. The glare dazzled Libby's eyes. At first she saw nothing. Then something caught her eye; some movement in the pearly sky. It looked like a cloud. Then she realised what it was.

'Something's burning,' she gasped. 'Over there on the hill.' She pointed.

Sophie stayed calm. 'It could just be charcoal burners.' But she went inside to fetch binoculars.

Returning, Sophie gazed at the distant plume of smoke. 'It's difficult to say what it is.'

'The road to Gulgat is in that direction,' said Libby. 'I'm going to find Clarrie.'

'Send Alok,' said Sophie.

But Libby was already leaping down the veranda steps and running down the garden path. Halfway down the drive she heard gunshot again, nearer this time. She arrived at the factory, breathless. Clarrie was in the tasting room.

'I think there's trouble on the Gulgat road,' Libby panted.

In the short time it took for the women to emerge from the building, word had spread from the village of a disturbance a dozen miles away.

Banu rode up from the gardens. '*Goondas* from Gulgat,' he reported grimly.

Libby's heart thumped in fright. Clarrie calmly began issuing instructions. She told Nitin to ring and alert the police in Shillong. She closed the factory and office and sent the staff home. She issued her managers with firearms. Banu went to call in the tea pickers from the gardens and rally his family, sending Nitin to protect the Robsons. As Clarrie and Libby hurried back with Nitin to the bungalow, Clarrie was ordering the compound to be secured.

They found Sophie watching anxiously from the veranda.

'Banu thinks there are two truckloads,' said Clarrie. 'Maybe a score of troublemakers. It's nothing we can't handle.'

'This is all my fault,' Sophie said in distress. 'I should have gone when Stourton warned me.'

'How is this your fault?' said Clarrie. 'They can't know you're here. They're a paid mob out to make trouble where there's been none.'

They had barely got the iron and mesh gates of the compound shut with Nitin's help when they heard the commotion on the garden road. Men were shouting and yelling. It was no more than half an hour since Libby had awoken to the first sounds of trouble. She was appalled at the speed at which danger had arrived at their door.

Clarrie ordered Mohammed Din to hide his family in the house and then handed him a gun with which to protect them.

'Where's Manzur?' Libby cried.

The women looked at each other in alarm. The garden school lay beyond the compound.

'Banu will be making sure he's safe,' Clarrie said. 'And he's got Breckon with him.'

She handed them both hunting rifles. 'You know how to handle one of these, don't you?' Clarrie asked them.

'Aye,' said Sophie.

'Not really,' said Libby.

Clarrie smiled in reassurance. 'It won't come to that. Here, take Wesley's old revolver – just something to scare them off.'

Libby felt nauseated by fear. It was the same feeling of helplessness that she had experienced in Amelia Buildings, knowing that a man had been brutally and randomly murdered in the street below. What she wouldn't give to be back in Calcutta with Ghulam now! She had never felt more vulnerable.

The commotion grew louder as more men arrived. Looking through the binoculars from the veranda Libby could see them milling around beyond the gates. Most looked young, dressed in grubby *dhotis* and vests. They were wielding lathis and knives, and shouting angrily. One let off a gun. Others seized the mesh of the gate and violently shook it, trying to find a way through.

Libby felt her insides go to jelly. She marvelled at how Clarrie and Sophie kept calm and reached for their rifles.

'Do you recognise any of them?' Clarrie asked Sophie.

Sophie took another look through the binoculars. 'That older man – the one in an army jacket – he's one of the palace police. Name is Sen.' She passed the field glasses to Clarrie.

'He's standing back letting them get out of control,' said Clarrie in disgust.

'But he'll be in charge,' said Sophie.

The demands of the men grew into a chant.

'What are they shouting?' Libby asked.

Clarrie didn't answer as she kept watch from the steps.

Sophie swallowed hard. 'They're shouting for me.'

Libby began to shake. She could hear it now: the shrieks for Khan memsahib. She gaped at Sophie in disbelief.

'Stourton's given you away,' Libby gasped. 'Why would he do that?'

Sophie shook her head. 'He wouldn't have. Word travels easily, that's all. This can't be Robert's doing.'

But Libby saw the doubt on her friend's face.

Just then, a shot cracked the air. 'Stay out of sight,' Clarrie barked at them.

Libby and Sophie dived down behind furniture. Libby heard a shriek of triumph. She peered out. One of the young men, with the help of others, had scrambled up the stone gatepost and was almost over the wall. In horror, she saw Clarrie hurry down the steps, calling to Alok as she went.

'Fetch the old speaking trumpet – the one we use for the garden sports' days.'

'Clarrie don't!' Sophie cried.

Nitin went with Clarrie. As Alok emerged with the loudhailer, Libby grabbed it from him and dashed after them, revolver in her other hand. Clarrie looked at her in alarm.

'They're less likely to shoot at me than Alok,' Libby said.

The young man on the gatepost saw them approaching with guns at the ready and jumped back down to safety. Halfway to the gate, Clarrie stopped and called through the loudhailer in a clear voice.

'I am Robson-mem'. What are you doing on my estate? The police are on their way. Go back to your homes. We are peaceful people. Jai Hind!'

Then she repeated her words in Hindustani.

The noise subsided a little but the assailants continued to chant while battering at the gates.

Clarrie tried again. 'I wish to speak to Sen sahib. Come forward, please, and explain why you are attacking my property.'

After a few moments, the men parted to let their leader step forward. He held up his hand for calm. Clarrie walked towards him.

'We don't wish to harm you, Robson memsahib,' he said, 'but you are hiding a fugitive from my state – the Khan woman – and we demand that you give her up.'

'I don't know what you're talking about,' replied Clarrie. 'There are no runaways here.'

'We know that is not true,' said Sen. 'She has been seen here. She must come back to Gulgat to face charges. The Khans have taken state property – I can see the palace car from here.' He nodded through the gates to Rafi's old Ford that was parked by the godowns.

'That car doesn't belong to Gulgat,' said Clarrie, 'and you have no jurisdiction here. Please take your men away; otherwise it will be you facing charges when the police get here.'

'Better to hand her over now,' Sen threatened, 'or I won't be able to answer for what these men might do. They want to see justice done.'

Libby was suddenly incensed. 'You call terrorising women justice?' she said. Clarrie put a restraining hand on her arm but Libby carried on. 'You have been misinformed about Mrs Khan. She was here but she's long gone.' She saw the doubt cross his face. Despite her drumming heart, Libby continued with as calm a voice as she could manage. 'In fact, it was someone from the palace at Gulgat who came here and told her to leave and never come back, so she took his advice and left. So I'm afraid you've had a wasted journey, Mr Sen.'

He looked at her with dislike. 'I don't believe you – there's another Britisher woman at the house – I saw her just before.' He focused on Clarrie. 'And how else would you know my name, Robson-mem? Please tell Khan memsahib to come with us now and no one else will be harmed.'

'We have nothing more to say to you,' said Clarrie, 'until the police get here.'

He gave a mirthless laugh. 'It will take hours for police to come if at all. We will be long gone by then.'

Clarrie turned away and hissed at Libby and Nitin to follow. They walked back to the bungalow. Libby's chest was so tight she could hardly breathe. At any moment she expected a gun might be fired at them through the gate as they made their retreat.

No sooner had they gained the top of the veranda steps than there was an explosion behind them on the drive. The women grasped each other in shock. A firecracker had been hurled over the perimeter wall. More followed. The clamour beyond the gate started up again. Clarrie tried once more to reason with the unruly gang through the loud hailer to no avail. There was no sign of Sen, who must have retreated to one of the trucks. Mohammed Din wanted to use his gun to warn them off but Clarrie said no.

'Hold your fire,' she ordered, 'I don't want to provoke them further. The police should be here soon.'

But the rabble showed no signs of going away. The shadows began to lengthen across the garden. Libby listened in vain for sounds of rescue but no police came. Sen was right; the police could take hours. Their service was overstretched, their British officers retired and Muslim rank and file transferred to Pakistan. It might be days before anyone came.

Sophie stood up. 'I won't see you all be harmed because of me. Perhaps if I agree to return the car to Gulgat . . .'

'You're going nowhere,' Clarrie declared. 'We'll face whatever's coming together. This is my home and no jumped-up official from Gulgat is going to tell me what to do.'

Just then, Libby heard a change in the chanting. Or was it the sound of something else? Gradually a swell of voices grew louder – not aggressive but melodious.

'What's that?' Libby hissed.

Sophie's anxious expression turned to surprise. 'It's women singing.'

Clarrie grabbed the binoculars from the table. Libby held her breath, looking at her for explanation.

'It's Shimti,' gasped Clarrie. 'She's leading the tea pickers. There's hundreds of them!'

Libby and Sophie rushed to her side. Even without the binoculars, Libby could see women pouring out from the village. They advanced through the trees, a multi-coloured army, ringing bells, banging pots and singing at the top of their voices. Within minutes they were surrounding the trucks and milling around the *goondas*.

Libby watched, stomach knotted and heart pounding, fearful that the men would retaliate with violence. The men were shouting at them, threatening them with their long knives. Shimti faced them clutching nothing but a thick staff and berated them.

Clarrie tensed beside Libby. 'Sophie,' she hissed, 'you must keep out of sight.'

Reluctantly, Sophie withdrew into the shadows. 'Tell me what's happening,' she begged.

'Shimti's putting herself in front of the gates,' Libby said, marvelling. 'The other women are following.'

Still the men shouted and jostled. Some of the women were punched to the ground. The situation was volatile. Libby felt that the violence could erupt into a bloodbath at any minute. The women had no more than pots and sticks with which to protect themselves. The stand-off seemed to last an age.

Suddenly, from the corner of her eye, Libby saw a movement. The garden below was now in complete shadow. But someone was creeping across it.

'Clarrie!' Libby warned.

Clarrie swung her gun around and took aim at the figure emerging on to the path.

'Wait!' Libby gasped. 'It's Ayah Mimi.'

They watched in disbelief as the tiny frail woman made her way determinedly down the drive.

'Mimi!' Sophie cried. She dashed out of the gloom.

Clarrie grabbed her. 'No, Sophie, not you.' Clarrie turned to Nitin. 'Go and stop Mataji.'

Libby struggled to breathe as she watched Nitin hurry down the steps after the old *sadhvi*. She saw him remonstrating with her. Then a moment later, she was leaning on his arm and he was helping her continue down the track.

'What's he doing?' Clarrie exclaimed.

'Mimi's bidding,' Sophie answered.

Appalled, they stood looking on as the old ayah reached the gates. For a moment she stopped, catching her breath, and then Nitin was lifting her on to his shoulders. From there she scrabbled on to one of the gateposts and stood up straight. Libby was astonished at how lithe she still was. Erect in her homespun sari, she looked as serene as a statue.

Libby watched through the binoculars, heart in mouth, as the old woman put her hands together in a prayerful greeting to the people below and then began to speak. She was too far away for them to hear her words but Libby was awestruck at the sight of her lined face, streaked in yellow and white paint, lit up in the dying sun.

The clamour beyond the gates began to subside. Libby was sure she saw fear on the faces of the men – in the fading light they looked even younger than before. Ayah Mimi remained at her post, praying over the crowd as the sky turned green and the sun sank below the tea bushes. Abruptly, the fight went out of the intruders – either fear or shame making them back away.

Next, Sen was ordering them back into the trucks. The women parted to let them through. They climbed aboard and with some shaking of fists retreated in a cloud of exhaust smoke. The sound of the women singing rang out in the sudden dark, chasing them away from Belgooree.

Sophie was the first to run down the drive and help Ayah Mimi down from the gatepost. The old woman collapsed into her arms after the effort, as Sophie wept and thanked her for helping save her. She and Nitin carried the frail *sadhvi* back to her hut in the garden, where she insisted on being taken, asking only for milk and no fuss.

That night, the three British women elected to sleep in the same room, while Nitin, Banu and Mohammed Din took it in turns to patrol and guard the house. Banu explained how Shimti had organised the women's resistance and forbidden him to challenge the Gulgat men with guns. Clarrie gave thanks for the wisdom of the village headwoman and the loyal support of the brave Khasi people. To Libby's great relief, Banu had also brought Manzur safely back into the compound. They went out to greet him.

'Until things are clearer,' Clarrie said, 'I want you to teach the children inside the compound.'

The women got little sleep. They sat up late into the night discussing what should be done.

'They'll come back,' said Sophie. 'A man like Sen won't want to be outwitted by mere women.'

Libby voiced her fear. 'And they might return in larger numbers.'

'We need to get you away from here as quickly as possible,' said Clarrie. 'Both of you.' She eyed Libby. 'You were very brave out there earlier but I won't have you putting yourself in danger a second time.'

'I'm not leaving you on your own,' Libby protested.

'Dear Libby, I'm not on my own,' said Clarrie. 'I'm surrounded by friends here – and soon I will have Sam and Adela too.'

'But what if Sen is lying in wait somewhere along the road?' Libby worried.

'When the police arrive,' said Clarrie, 'I'll get them to escort you down to Shillong.'

'And if they don't come?' Sophie asked quietly.

'They will,' said Clarrie stoutly. 'And if not, then Daleep and Banu will see you safely away from here.'

They lay in the shuttered bedroom, hot and unable to sleep. In the middle of the night, Libby was struck by a thought.

'Why don't we fool them into thinking we're someone else?'

'Meaning?' Clarrie asked.

'Dress up.'

'As who?'

Libby said, 'We could dress Sophie as a man.'

Despite the tenseness of the situation, Sophie giggled with amusement. 'What sort of man?'

'In uniform or something. Didn't Adela leave a trunkful of costumes here from when she finished with ENSA?'

'Yes,' said Clarrie, 'but I think they're mostly dresses and feather boas.'

'Did Sam leave any clothes?'

'Well, yes . . .'

'Let's have a look,' Libby said, swinging out of bed. 'None of us can sleep so we might as well be doing something useful.'

They trooped into Harry's room, where Adela and Sam had left possessions they hadn't needed for Newcastle. The three women spent the next hour rifling through Adela's trunk and Harry's wardrobe, holding up clothes and getting Sophie to try them on. Eventually they settled on a pair of Harry's trousers and a bush shirt and jacket of Sam's. Libby found Adela's military cap that fitted Sophie.

'We'll have to cut your hair even shorter,' said Clarrie, touching Sophie's bobbed hair fondly.

'And dye it,' said Libby. She pulled out a box of stage make-up and rummaged through it. 'And how about this?' She held up a false moustache. 'We have to make you look more manly. And what about an eyepatch?'

Sophie laughed. 'I'll look like a pantomime villain.'

'Okay.' Libby grimaced. 'I'll wear the eyepatch.'

'Who are you going to be?' Sophie asked.

'A tea planter,' said Libby. 'I'll put my hair up in a topee and plump up my stomach with a cushion to hide these.' She pointed at her breasts.

Clarrie disappeared for a minute and returned holding up a jacket of Wesley's. 'This might fit.'

'Don't you mind?' asked Libby. 'I don't want to take it if it's special.'

'It's just a jacket,' said Clarrie brusquely. 'And if it helps disguise you and keep you safe then that's the best use possible.'

After dressing Libby, Clarrie scrutinised them both. 'I have another idea,' she said. 'We'll bandage you both up and pretend you're being rushed to hospital after some riding accident.'

By the time Clarrie had finished with them, Sophie had one eye covered, and Libby had her jaw bandaged and an arm in a sling across her chest.

Shortly before dawn, Libby fell into an exhausted sleep. She was roused by Clarrie – it seemed just minutes later – but the air was full of birdsong and day was breaking.

'It's time to go,' she said softly. 'There's *chota hazri* on the veranda, then we'll get you dressed up.'

Libby looked at her sleepily. 'Have the police come?'

Clarrie shook her head. 'Daleep will drive you to Gowhatty in my car and Banu will go with him, well armed.'

They spent the final hour at Belgooree in an atmosphere of tension as they forced down breakfast and got into their disguises. Clarrie gave them the contact details of friends in Gowhatty they could stay with while they secured onward travel to Calcutta.

'I have old army friends of Rafi's who will put us up once we get to Calcutta,' said Sophie.

'Send me word when you are safely there,' Clarrie said.

Sophie was transformed with her hair shorn and blackened with boot polish, the stage moustache applied and her face obscured in a large eye bandage. Libby was already sweating in her padded outfit, with her hair pinned up under a topee and jaw bound as if it had been dislocated. She could only speak incoherently but she was so nervous and emotional at leaving Clarrie that she could hardly find words adequate to thank her anyway.

When the time came for departure, Clarrie took her in a hug and said, 'Dearest Libby, I shall miss you so much. I can't tell you what a joy it has been to have you here. And thank you for all your help in the office. I shall send on your typewriter.'

Libby shook her head. 'Let Nitin have it,' she mouthed.

Clarrie kissed her cheek and let her go. Libby watched as Sophie embraced her friend and said a tearful farewell. Neither of them knew if or when they would ever see each other again.

'God go with you,' Clarrie said. She didn't let them linger but led them down to the car where their luggage was being loaded into the boot.

At that moment, Manzur appeared, to say goodbye. His eyes widened at sight of Libby. He stared hard and then, as recognition dawned, amusement spread across his face.

'Is that really you, Libby-mem'?'

She nodded and tried to smile but the bandage inhibited her.

'You are a brave Robson,' he said, 'always the bravest.'

Libby's eyes pricked with tears. She murmured goodbye to him.

'Goodbye and good luck,' Manzur answered.

Quickly, Libby and Sophie climbed into the back of the car. The gates were being opened as they set off down the drive. Libby tensed as she scoured the dark track ahead for signs of anyone lying in wait. All seemed peaceful; the early stirrings of jungle birds and creatures were the only sounds. The gates closed swiftly behind them and Libby caught a fleeting last glimpse of the bungalow where Clarrie and Manzur stood waving them away.

Then they were heading off down the garden road. Sophie reached out and took Libby's free hand. She squeezed it tight in encouragement. Libby blinked away tears and returned the comforting gesture.

CHAPTER 37

Newcastle, September

On the day following Bonnie's party, Adela felt so wretched and sick that Sam and his mother confined her to bed. Mrs Jackman was delighted to discover the reason for her daughter-in-law's bouts of nausea.

'My first grandchild! I wish you could stay till after the baby's born,' she said with a pleading look at Sam.

Adela was grateful to hear Sam reply, 'I know you do but our passage is booked and Adela wants to be with her own mother when the time comes. We promise to come back and visit.'

But all Adela could think about was whether anyone had returned to Herbert's Café to claim the necklace. She felt guilty about such thoughts and was hesitant to voice her feelings to Sam and risk provoking old arguments. Sam though was being concerned and attentive towards her, one moment anxious that she rested, the next grinning with happiness at her pregnant state.

After four days in bed, Adela couldn't bear to be confined to the Cullercoats flat a moment longer.

'I'm not ill,' she insisted, 'and I'm feeling much better.'

They returned to the café to help, though it was becoming apparent to Adela that the efficient Jane and extrovert Charlie didn't really need them. Jane had persuaded a former waitress, Nance, to come back and work for her. Nance greeted Adela with cries of delight and they swapped news. Adela remembered her as friendly, competent and mildly flirtatious with the shipyard workers.

'I got engaged twice during the War but they both got away!' said Nance with her infectious giggle. She nodded towards Sam. 'I might have known you'd end up with a bonny-looking lad.'

After a week, when no one had come in for the necklace, Adela had to admit that Charlie was probably right. Whoever had lost it didn't think it worth returning to reclaim it. The stone had only ever been precious to Adela and her mother.

Adela was at the allotment picking green beans, while Sam pulled up onions, when Joan appeared.

'Jane said I'd find you here,' she said, pushing back a strand of blonde hair.

'Hello,' Adela said, putting down her basket of beans and glancing around for Bonnie. 'Have you brought Bonnie for a visit?'

'No, I'm in town on my own doing some shopping,' said Joan. 'Just wanted to come and thank you both for the party.'

Sam leant on his spade, pushing his hat back to wipe his forehead. 'No need for thanks,' he said. 'We enjoyed it too.'

'Bonnie's not stopped talking about it,' said Joan. 'Don't know what we're going to do on her actual birthday. It'll be so dull for her. I don't know many folk up at Willowburn yet.'

'I'm sure Mrs Gibson will make a fuss of Bonnie,' said Adela.

Joan's look darted from Sam to Adela. 'Yes.' She stood there, hesitating. 'You see, that's the other thing.'

'What is?' Adela asked, wondering if Joan was here to extend an invitation to meet her new friend.

'I – er – well,' Joan floundered. 'I sort of borrowed something from Mrs Gibson so Bonnie could wear it at the party. It went with her dress, you see. And Jane said Charlie found it but you have it so I wanted to have it back.'

'The necklace?' Adela gasped. 'Bonnie was wearing it?'

Joan went puce. 'Yes, I know it's just an old trinket but it looked so sweet on her—'

'Whose is it?' Adela demanded, her pulse racing. 'Where did you get it from?'

Joan looked startled by her abrupt questions. 'There's an old box in Mrs Gibson's bedroom,' Joan said. 'I looked in it one time I was doing her hair.'

Adela's heart drummed. 'Tell me about the box: did it have old photos in?'

'Yes,' said Joan, bemused. 'How did you know?'

Adela scrabbled in her pocket and pulled out the swami's necklace. 'Is this what you took from Mrs Gibson's box?'

'That's it,' said Joan in relief, reaching out for it. 'I'll have it back, ta very much.'

Adela held on to it. She was aware of Sam coming to her side. She began to shake. She clamped her teeth together, unable to speak. Sam put a reassuring hand on her back. Alarm flitted across Joan's face.

'Please, Adela,' she said, 'I need to put it back in the box before Mrs Gibson finds out it's gone.'

'You took it without asking?' Sam said in disapproval.

'Yes, but I was always going to put it back after the party,' said Joan, tears springing to her eyes. 'I'm not a thief.'

'Did Mrs Gibson tell you where the box came from?' Sam asked.

Joan shook her head. 'But she keeps it on her dressing table so I know it must be special. She's bound to notice the necklace is gone sooner or later. Please, Sam, make Adela give it back. I don't want to get in any trouble and Mrs Gibson's been so good to me and Bonnie.'

'Her son,' Adela said, her voice shaking. 'How old is he?'

Joan looked baffled. 'What's that got to do with it?'

'Just answer her,' said Sam.

'He's eight, I think.'

Adela felt her knees weaken. Sam gripped her around the waist.

'What's he called?' Sam asked.

'Jack. Except they say it in a funny way.'

Adela let out a soft moan.

'What's the matter?' Joan looked at her in alarm. 'What have I said?'

Adela's teeth began to chatter as if she was freezing, yet the day was mild and warm. Sam hugged her to his side. He didn't speak. He wasn't going to tell her what to do. Adela saw tears trickling down Joan's face and knew she was terrified of being found out and losing the friendship of the well-to-do major's wife.

After a moment's hesitation, Adela held out her arm and opened her clenched fist.

'Take it,' she said in a hoarse voice.

Joan snatched at the necklace in relief. 'Ta very much.' She looked contrite. 'You will come and see us before you go to India, won't you?'

Neither Sam nor Adela answered as Joan turned and hurried away. After she was out of sight, Sam said, 'That was kind of you to give her back the necklace.'

She turned and looked at him in distress. 'It's him, isn't it? The boy they call Jack or Jacques,' she whispered. 'It's John Wesley.'

In a tight voice Sam said, 'It sounds likely.'

'Oh, Sam, what should I do?'

He put his hands around her face and held her look. 'I think you have to go and see for yourself if it's your son. It may not be the right thing to do but I know you will always regret it if you don't.' His eyes were full of sadness. 'I won't try and stop you. It will only come between us if I do.'

Adela gulped down tears. 'Come with me,' she beseeched him. 'Please, Sam. I can't do this without you.'

He let go a sigh and nodded. She put her arms about him and held on tightly.

'Thank you.'

It was Sam who suggested that they ask James to take them up to Willowburn to visit the Gibsons. It meant waiting till James got back from St Abbs, but he swiftly arranged for them to go riding on the following Monday, pleased that they wanted to go with him. Adela was dismayed to see James looking pinch-faced and subdued after his holiday, but his interest was immediately sparked by the suggestion of a ride at Willowburn. She felt embarrassed at his eagerness but couldn't bring herself to tell him about her ulterior motive for wanting to go to the Gibsons' home. She assumed Tilly would never have told him about her having an illegitimate baby, knowing he would disapprove of scandal in the family.

All week, Adela tried to keep herself busy and control her nervous excitement but could hardly settle long to any job. Jane was quick to notice her distraction so Sam kept her away from the café by finding Adela lightweight jobs to do on the allotment. As the day of the visit drew nearer, Adela became beset with doubts. What if it turned out not to be John Wesley after all? There might be some other explanation as to how Mrs Gibson came by the swami's necklace. Then an old anxiety resurfaced: what if she didn't recognise her son?

On the Sunday evening, Sam took her for a late walk along the promenade towards Whitley Bay, knowing she would hardly sleep a wink that coming night. Adela unburdened her greatest worry.

'If it is John Wesley,' she said, 'how will I know it's him? I mean *really* know. He's an eight-year-old boy. He won't look anything like the baby I last saw.'

Sam stopped and regarded her with tired eyes. Adela was suddenly struck by how this waiting and not knowing must be taking its toll on Sam too. She knew all he wanted to do was plan for their future family life back in India, and yet here he was, standing by her once more as she searched for her son.

'Adela, I don't know,' he answered. 'We just have to take things as they come. But we'll face it together.'

Adela felt a grateful pang. She slipped her arms around his waist. 'Thank you, Sam. I don't know what I did to deserve you.'

He encircled her in his arms and laid his chin on her head. 'Oh, Adela,' he sighed, 'I don't want to lose you over this. That is my biggest fear. That's why I'll come with you tomorrow and do what I can to support you.'

She was jolted by his words. 'Oh, darling Sam, you will never lose me – I love you far too much. Whatever happens tomorrow, my future is with you and our baby – I promise you that.'

He squeezed her to him and they stood in silence watching the evening stars prick the darkening sky, expectant and fearful of what the next day would bring.

❧ ⚬ ☙

Adela found James preoccupied as he drove them west up the Tyne Valley. She coaxed him into talking about the family holiday at St Abbs.

'It wasn't altogether a success,' he admitted. 'Tilly was still annoyed at Libby for not coming back in time and just sending a telegram with no explanation. I got it in the neck all week as if I'd somehow been party to her delay. Johnny told her to stop going on about it and that Libby was obviously having a good time up at Belgooree.' James sighed. 'Of course that just made Tilly crosser. But thank goodness Johnny was there. We spent most of the week out fishing. He's got a boat. We caught some cod on the long line. Mungo said it was better sport than sitting with a rod thigh-deep in a river for hours. He's enjoying having his uncle around and Johnny seems to know what to say to Mungo better than I do.'

They passed Corbridge and then turned north and uphill.

'I've left Tilly rearranging furniture for the umpteenth time,' he said glumly. 'And she's acquired a dog – a foolish fluffy thing that will need washing after every walk and be absolutely no use to me as a gun dog.'

Adela gave distracted replies, thankful that she was sitting in the back while Sam kept up the conversation in the front of the car. By the time they drove through the gates to the Willowburn Estate, Adela was sick with nerves. She feared she might be unable to control her emotions in front of the Gibsons; she seemed to succumb to tears so easily since becoming pregnant again.

Up the drive lay a Gothic mansion with battlements and towers which, according to James, had been built by a Victorian who had made his money in iron production and shipbuilding. James drove past the main entrance and carried on under an archway bearing a clock tower and parked up in the stables' courtyard.

A small, slim woman with permed pale-fair hair, dressed in riding jodhpurs and jacket and wearing dark glasses against the bright late-summer sun, met them with a wave and a 'Hey!' James introduced them to Martha Gibson. The woman pushed her sunglasses on to her head and gave them a gleaming smile. So this was John Wesley's adoptive mother! Adela's heart drummed and she couldn't stop staring. The American had pretty grey eyes, Adela noticed.

'So nice to meet you,' Martha said, shaking Sam and Adela by the hand. 'Can I call you Adela?' she asked. Adela nodded, too tongue-tied to answer. 'And you must call me Martha. We don't stand on ceremony here. Gus won't be riding with us I'm afraid – he has a meeting with the land agent or some such. But we'll catch him later. You will stay for tea after our ride, won't you?'

Martha turned from Adela and slipped an arm through James's. Adela tried to slow her rapid breathing. 'And James,' said Martha, 'I want to hear all about St Abbs and the fishing. Did you catch anything big? And did you dive off the harbour wall with the youngsters?'

James laughed. 'I'm afraid my days of swimming in the North Sea are long over.'

'James!' she admonished. 'You've become such a softie since living overseas. I thought a man of your vigour would be bathing in the sea before breakfast every day.'

Adela saw him flush with pleasure at her teasing. No wonder her cousin enjoyed coming to Willowburn, being flattered by the attractive American. Martha seemed friendly and extrovert, but was she kind and loving? Sam seemed charmed by her too. Within minutes, she had him telling her all about his time with the mission in the Himalayan foothills and his planting of apple orchards.

'Some of the saplings came from America,' he told her, as if she was personally to be thanked.

'Well, isn't that wonderful?' she cried. 'I know missionaries in India too: the Hakings. Now where is it they live? Madras, I think. Have you heard of them?'

Adela couldn't stop herself saying, 'India is a very big country.'

'Of course, how stupid of me,' said Martha with a laugh.

Sam flashed Adela a look before smiling at Martha and saying, 'No, I don't know them but tell me more. Have they been in India long?'

Adela took a deep breath to calm herself. She wanted to like this woman: if she was John Wesley's adoptive mother then it was important that she liked her. The American woman was unstuffy – just as Joan had indicated – yet there was something mildly irritating about her over-familiar manner. She was so self-assured, while Adela now found herself completely at a loss for words and unable to make any small talk. But what was Martha like with her son? Adela kept looking about for any signs of the Gibson boy but there were none.

Tommy greeted them cheerfully and supervised the stable boys readying the horses. Joan, it appeared, had gone into Hexham for the day with Bonnie. Adela wondered if Joan was deliberately keeping out of their way, still too embarrassed by the incident with the necklace.

They rode out of the grounds, James and Martha leading, and headed up on to the high ground to the north. Adela's anxiety began to subside as they rode further, enjoying being on horseback for the first time since they had left Belgooree in January. She filled her lungs with the clear air and emptied her mind of everything but the sound of skylarks and bleating sheep.

As they skirted a copse of wind-blasted trees, Adela allowed herself to ponder a future where she and Sam didn't return so soon to India. Perhaps she could help him with his photography business on the sales side, promoting his work and making new contacts. They could come regularly to Willowburn to ride and she would have the chance to see her son growing up, even though she could never be more to him than a friend of his American mother's . . .

Adela looked at Sam riding ahead of her, easy in the saddle, his long lean back and muscled legs at one with the animal that he rode. Would Sam be able to keep up the charade of them being an 'uncle' and 'aunt' to Sanjay's son? Adela felt heavy-hearted at the thought of the tension that might arise between her and her husband over John Wesley and where the boy would fit – if at all – into their future life together. How soon would Sam grow to resent her abandoning a future back in India and plans for him to become a tea planter?

'Sam tells me that you were a Toodle Pip.'

Adela was so lost in thought that she hadn't been aware of Martha falling into step beside her as they emerged below the wood.

She blushed and dragged her thoughts from her son. 'Yes, during the War I sang with ENSA – that was the Entertainments wing of the Services.'

'Yes, I know,' said Martha. 'I saw the Toodle Pips perform in Newcastle. You were terrific. I remember one with a great voice – dark-haired – so it was probably you.'

Adela gaped at her in astonishment and laughed. 'Did you really?'

She smiled. 'Yes, Gus used to give me a night off once in a while and I would high-tail it into town to see a show.'

'A night off from what?' Adela asked.

'From the kids.'

Adela's stomach flipped. 'You have more than one child? I know from Joan that you have a son.'

Martha shook her head. 'No, I mean the evacuees. Gus and I took in dozens of children during the War – and a few of their moms. Gus was like the Pied Piper, leading them all over the estate picking mush-rooms and giving piggy-backs and showing them how to climb trees. My husband is just a big kid himself at heart.'

Adela had a sudden vision of the major carrying a young John Wesley on his back and the boy giggling in delight. Her pulse raced as she asked, 'How did your son Jack get on with the other children? Wasn't he a bit jealous?'

Martha didn't reply straight away. Adela couldn't read her expres-sion behind her dark glasses. Her tone became less jocular and more confiding.

'Jacques was one of the evacuees too,' she said quietly. 'His parents were killed in a raid over Tyneside. We felt so sorry for him. He cried and wet the bed for a long time – even after being potty trained – but he has such a sunny nature that he became a favourite with the other kids and the moms. We couldn't bear to see him go; we'd come to love Jacques the best of them all. So Gus and I adopted him. I can't have children, you see. He knows we're not his blood parents – we've been upfront about that. I don't believe in keeping secrets like that from a child, however young.'

Adela gripped the reins; she was shaking so hard that she feared she would faint and fall. She managed to ask, 'S-so there was no extended family on Tyneside who could take him?'

'No.' Martha sighed. 'All we were able to discover were that his parents were from Belgium and they were called Segal. Jacques has a box of mementoes that his parents had collected. I'm keeping it safe until he's older.'

Adela had to bite the inside of her cheek to stop herself crying. This was the proof she needed: Jacques Gibson was her long-lost son. Now was the moment to tell Martha about the boy's true parentage. Adela's proof lay in the Segals' box; an Indian stone on a gold chain that she had gifted at birth. She would tell Martha everything; Martha, being an open-minded woman, would believe Adela. The American's sense of fairness would allow Adela to reclaim her son; Martha would be sad to see him go but if the major's wife loved Jacques as much as she claimed she did, she would give him up. Adela felt heady as she pictured the future: she and Sam bringing up John Wesley with their child-to-be. The boy would be a half-brother to their baby – and he would have a brother or sister and not have to grow up as an only child. Sam would grow to love him just as much as their other child, because John Wesley was sunny-natured and easy to love. Her family would be complete and her life full of joy.

Adela looked away and blinked back tears. She was deluding herself! If Martha was the woman she thought she was, she would fight like a tigress to keep her Jacques. There was strength beneath the outward show of bonhomie. If Adela confided in her now, Martha might be so alarmed that she would refuse to let her even meet John Wesley. Martha might send her away and tell her never to come near Willowburn again. Adela knew that she could not bear to leave this place without having set eyes on her son.

She cleared her throat and asked as calmly as she could, 'Where is Jacques today? Is he keeping the major company?'

'No,' said Martha with a fond smile, 'he's at school.'

Adela's heart sank. Of course he would be on a Monday. Why had she not thought of that? Would she have to wait now until the weekend to make an excuse to return? Or perhaps he was at boarding school and would be away all term. The thought of leaving for India without ever seeing him was unbearable.

'Boarding school?' Adela asked in a breathless voice.

'Good heavens, certainly not!' Martha exclaimed. 'I told Gus that no son of mine was going to be sent away from me for weeks on end. It might be your British way but I simply couldn't bear it. No, Jacques is at prep school near Hexham. He'll be home at tea time.'

A sob rose up in Adela's throat that she had to disguise as a cough. After that, she was incapable of speech and slowed her pony to a walk so that Martha went ahead and was soon chatting to James again. Sam dropped back to keep her company. He could tell by the look on her face that something had happened.

'Tell me,' he murmured.

With Martha out of earshot, Adela told Sam all she had discovered. She couldn't stop the tears rolling down her cheeks; they dried in the wind, making her skin feel tight and her eyes gritty.

'So you haven't said anything?' Sam asked gently.

Adela shook her head. Sam nodded and put out a hand to squeeze her shoulder. 'Are you going to manage this?' he asked. 'You mustn't break down in front of the boy. It wouldn't be fair on him, Adela.'

Adela gulped back tears. 'I know,' she rasped, 'but I *have* to see him.'

Major Gibson, smiling broadly, strode towards them as they emerged from the stable yard. He reminded Adela of a younger James, his physique stocky and complexion ruddy. His handshake was bone-crushing and his laugh loud. He apologised for missing the ride.

'Martha, I've ordered tea on the terrace,' he boomed. 'It's far too nice to be sitting indoors on such a day.'

'I quite agree, darling,' she said, pecking him on the cheek. 'Let our guests freshen up first.'

The men were shown into a downstairs cloakroom, while Martha led Adela to a bathroom on the first floor. 'Come downstairs when you're ready,' she said and left her.

Adela splashed her face with cold water and dried it on a worn linen hand towel. Some of the bathroom tiles were cracked and the plumbing clanked. There was an air of faded grandeur about the place; it was more scuffed and homely than she had imagined it would be. It didn't fit the cliché that all Americans who married British gentry were heiresses with lots of money. From what she had seen and heard about the Gibsons, their marriage was definitely a love match.

Adela emerged on to the landing feeling faint and nauseated. She craved something sweet to eat – preferably with ginger in it – to keep her sickness at bay. Just then, she heard a door slam somewhere behind her and footsteps came thumping along the passage. She turned to see a young boy running towards her in grey shorts and a grey shirt that had come untucked. He stopped breathless in front of her.

'Hello, I'm Jacques. Are you the lady who's been riding with Mummy?'

Adela froze on the spot. She stared down at him. It was like looking at her brother Harry a few years ago. He had dark unruly hair and thick eyebrows. The eyes that gazed back at her in curiosity were the same green as hers. That startled her. She had remembered John Wesley as having Sanjay's dark, almost inky black eyes.

'Hello, Jacques,' Adela said, her voice hoarse with emotion, 'I've been looking forward to meeting you.'

He grinned. 'Have you?'

She reached out to hug him. Confusion crossed his face and he stuck out his hand. Adela stopped herself just in time and shook his hand instead. Her heart twisted to feel the boy's warm hand in hers, the fingers bony – fragile yet dextrous – and the skin the colour of hers.

'My name's Adela,' she said.

'Am I not supposed to call you Mrs-something?' he asked, his brow furrowed with a faint frown, the way Harry's did when he was thinking.

Adela laughed. 'I suppose you are. I'm Mrs Jackman, if you prefer.'

His hand wriggled out of hers. 'Oh, are you related to Mr Jackman downstairs?'

Adela nodded. 'He's my husband.'

'Daddy says he's a war hero who flew aeroplanes and beat the Japs,' Jacques said in excitement. 'I want to be a pilot when I grow up. Does Mr Jackman have his own plane?'

'Not any more,' said Adela, 'but I'm sure he'd talk to you about them.'

The boy asked, 'Does he play cricket?'

'Yes, Sam loves cricket.'

'Oh, good.' He grinned. 'Do you think he might play with me after tea?'

'I'm sure he would.'

The way he was scrutinising her made Adela breathless. 'Have you been crying?' he asked.

Adela swallowed. 'It's just the wind on the ride,' she answered. 'It made my eyes water.'

'Oh, that's all right then,' he said.

Suddenly Martha shouted from below. 'Adela, are you lost?'

Her stomach clenched. 'No,' she called back, 'I was just meeting Jacques.'

'Coming, Mummy!' the boy shouted.

Adela put a hand briefly on her son's head as he moved past her. 'Will you show me the way to the terrace, Jacques?'

'Come on, Mrs Jackman,' he said brightly. 'Follow me.'

As she did so, Adela was hit by the thought that Jacques sounded just like Major Gibson.

Adela was not sure how she got through teatime. She see-sawed between wanting to rush away to vomit and staying put so that she didn't miss a second of watching John Wesley. He chattered non-stop about school and games and about a pet squirrel called Bunty. He asked Sam dozens of questions about cricket and aeroplanes. His parents looked on indulgently and laughed at his observations; they were completely devoid of the old-fashioned attitude that children should be seen and not heard when in adult company.

As tea drew to an end and James made the comment that they probably ought to be leaving, Adela felt panic grip her.

Jacques protested. 'But Mrs Jackman said Mr Jackman would play cricket with me.'

'I'm afraid there isn't time for that,' said James. 'Perhaps another time.'

'Well, can I show Mr Jackman my treehouse before you go? *Please*, Mr Robson; it won't take a minute.'

'I suppose we can delay a little bit longer,' James relented, with a smile.

Adela breathed in relief. James was probably in no great hurry to get back to Tilly and her fussing over the new house and dog.

Jacques clapped his hands and sprang off his chair.

'Wait a minute, you little scamp,' said Martha. 'What have you forgotten to say?'

Jacques sat back down quickly. 'Please may I get down from the table?'

'You may,' said Martha with a wink.

Jacques scrambled off his chair again. 'Come on, Mr Jackman.'

'Can I come too?' Adela asked, holding her breath.

Jacques squinted at her in the late sun. 'Of course. As long as you aren't scared of heights like Mummy is.'

Adela laughed. 'I used to climb trees all the time as a girl in India.'

Jacques's eyes widened. 'Gosh, really? Were they as big as houses? Did monkeys and tigers live in them?'

Sam and Adela exchanged amused glances. 'Monkeys, yes,' said Adela.

They quickly said their thanks for tea and followed Jacques, who bombarded Adela with fresh questions about wild animals in India. Her heart swelled with love to see his animated face and hear his quick-talking voice. He was so bright and inquisitive. She searched for traces of Sanjay in her son. Perhaps the shape of his eyes and the straightness of his nose – certainly the beige tone of his skin – but there was no doubting that he was a Robson.

Sam abruptly said, 'I'll race you to the tree.'

Jacques laughed in excitement as they sprinted the last few yards and Sam made a pretence of almost getting to the treehouse first but slowing up to allow the boy to win. Adela hurried to catch up. Each climbed the ladder into the treehouse, a platform built at the level of the lower branches with a protective wall and no roof. They sat cross-legged, catching their breath. Adela noticed Sam's camera hanging round his neck; she hadn't seen him pick it up.

'This is where Bunty lives,' Jacques told them. 'Soon she'll be collecting nuts and putting them in her nest for winter. Do they have squirrels in India, Mrs Jackman?'

'Yes,' said Adela, 'we have palm squirrels in our garden at home.'

'What do they look like?' he asked. 'Are they sort of red like ours?'

'No, they have brown and white stripes,' she said, 'and make a noise a bit like a rattle.'

He gazed at her in wonder. 'Golly gosh! I wish I could see them.'

Adela glanced at Sam, her eyes stinging. 'So do I,' she murmured.

Sam's look was full of compassion. He said, 'Perhaps one day you'll come out to India and visit us?'

Jacques gave a broad smile. 'Do you think I could? That would be swell.'

Adela felt her insides twist at the Americanism. Jacques picked up his enthusiastic phrases from both his parents.

'Yes,' said Sam, 'it would be.'

'Can you show me how your camera works, Mr Jackman?' Jacques asked.

'Of course.' Sam slipped it over his head and put the strap around the boy's neck, taking off the case. Sam showed him where to look and which button to press, helping Jacques keep it steady.

After a couple of shots Jacques said, 'Say cheese, Mrs Jackman!'

Adela laughed and did so. Then Sam took back the camera and said, 'I'll take one of you and Adela, shall I?'

'All right,' Jacques agreed.

He shuffled up to Adela and she put her arm about his narrow shoulders. She leant close, breathing in his boy smell of unwashed hair and jam on his chin. She resisted the urge to lick her finger and wipe it off as her mother used to do with her and Harry. For one brief idyllic moment, as they grinned at Sam for the camera, Adela was a mother again, sitting with her son tucked in the crook of her arm.

It was over in an instant as Jacques wriggled out of her hold and began telling them about how he'd made a pin camera at school.

Too soon, Major Gibson was calling for his son. 'Jacques, old boy, time to let our guests go home.'

Adela's heart weighed like a stone as she climbed back down the ladder. Sam held out his hand to her as she reached the bottom. Jacques was already dashing ahead, waving a shiny horse-chestnut that he'd found on the ground. 'Look, Daddy, my first conker! Can we put it on a string?'

Sam gripped Adela's hand in his all the way back to the house, only letting go so that they could shake their hosts by the hand in farewell.

'I've so enjoyed today,' Adela said to Martha, fighting back tears.

Martha smiled, giving her a quizzical look. 'It's so nice to meet you. You'll visit again before you leave for India, I hope? Jacques has quite taken to you and Sam.'

Adela forced herself to say, 'We may not have time to come again, but thank you.'

She turned away quickly and braced herself to say goodbye to Jacques.

'Thank you for showing us your treehouse. Would you like me to send you a photograph of a palm squirrel when I get back to India? Sam could take one with his camera.'

Jacques grinned. 'Yes please, Mrs Jackman. Then I can take it into school and show my friends.'

'Good,' said Adela, putting on a brave smile.

She gazed at her son, trying to memorise every little detail about him to store away and think about later. She had to restrain herself from grabbing him and pulling him to her in a fierce hug. How she longed to kiss him and tell him that she loved him – always had and always would. Instead she briefly put out her hand and touched his head – the soft, silky dark tufts of hair that grew in the same haphazard way that her father Wesley's had and her brother Harry's did.

Then Adela turned from him and Sam was taking her arm and guiding her towards the car. Moments later, she was sitting in the back of the car with Sam beside her. James didn't question why Sam didn't sit in front as before.

As the car pulled away from the house, Adela stared out of the window, drinking in the sight of her son waving and smiling. Before they were halfway down the drive, Jacques's interest had been caught by something else and the boy was dashing off across the terrace and out of view.

As they journeyed rapidly further away from Willowburn and her son, Adela sat back, engulfed in sorrow. Sam held her hand tightly in his. She looked into his face and saw that his eyes were brimming with tears too.

'He's a fine boy,' Sam murmured.

'He's happy,' whispered Adela, though it broke her heart to think that another woman would be bringing him up as her own. But she had seen how completely the Gibsons loved John Wesley and she knew that in time, the knowledge of how much they cared for the boy would come to be some consolation to her aching heart.

Sam put his arm around her shoulders and pulled her close. He whispered into her hair. 'He looks just like you, Adela.'

She smiled through her tears. 'Yes he does, doesn't he?'

She wondered if Martha had seen the similarity and whether she pondered how that could be.

Adela closed her eyes. Today she had found the son for whom she had been searching and the questions that had tortured her for so long had finally been answered. She had always known that to find out the truth was likely to bring as much pain as it did relief; having to tear herself away from John Wesley had been almost intolerable. But at least now she knew what had happened to him and that he was secure in a loving home. She had to cling on to that thought. She would do anything for her son – and the biggest sacrifice of all was to let him go into the hands of others. Adela knew that that was what her love for John Wesley demanded of her. For the first time, she had it in her heart to forgive her eighteen-year-old self her immaturity. She couldn't change the past but – however painful – she would find a way to accept and bear it.

Crushed by her sense of loss, there was another emotion that gave balm to her raw feelings – gratitude to Sam. Her husband had supported her today, although it must have been difficult for him too. More than that: Sam had liked John Wesley and been kind to the boy.

In other circumstances, she knew that generous-hearted Sam would have taken on her illegitimate child without hesitation.

Adela reached up and kissed Sam on the lips and then laid her head on his shoulder. They didn't need to say anything more. Both knew what the other was thinking and how much they loved one another. James, perhaps sensing their sadness, drove on without any prying questions. They travelled back to Newcastle in silence.

CHAPTER 38

Calcutta, late September

T wo weeks after leaving Belgooree, Libby and Sophie arrived back in Calcutta. They had discarded their disguises soon after Shillong, euphoric at having safely avoided capture by Sen's gang, though it had taken several days before Sophie had managed to wash all the boot-black from her hair. She still looked boyish with her severe haircut but she didn't seem to care.

'It'll grow back soon enough,' she said. 'I'm just thankful we never met any trouble on the road.'

Libby had been convinced that Stourton had betrayed Sophie for financial gain, probably salving his conscience that he had given Sophie some warning of trouble, even though he must have known she was in no position to join Rafi in the Punjab. But she kept her suspicions to herself. Libby and Sophie had stayed with Clarrie's contact in Gowhatty, an old planter friend of Wesley's whom the women remembered meeting at Wesley's funeral. Eventually they had taken a train to Siliguri and on into West Bengal, the old steamer route south being too hazardous with the new partition border.

They arrived into Calcutta exhausted but elated – until they saw the encampments of refugees at Sealdah Station. Libby was aghast. If she had thought the camps wretched before Independence, the situation now looked even grimmer. There were squatters as far as the eye could see; every platform was occupied and makeshift shelters lined the tracks. They looked like some shattered, defeated army. Was Ghulam still trying his best to help the displaced families? Had word reached him about the plight of his own father and had he ever read her letter? She longed to know where he was and how he was doing.

Sophie, who hadn't been to the city since the end of the War, was speechless with horror. She couldn't utter a word until they were almost at Ballyganj and the home of Rafi's retired army colleague, Captain Ranajit Roy, and his wife, Bijal.

As they sat round the dinner table that night, sharing gloomy news, the captain said, 'I don't know when it will stop. Each day, more and more people are crowding into the city.'

'They're setting up camps on the outskirts,' said Bijal, 'but it's quite inadequate.'

'Is there still a refugee centre run by the doctors from Eden Hospital?' Libby asked.

Bijal shrugged. 'I wouldn't know. Many people are trying to help but the numbers are overwhelming.'

Exhausted from long days of travel, Libby and Sophie retired early to bed. It was nearly two months since Libby had last been here, yet it seemed longer. The all-pervasive mineral smell of food being cooked on coal fires was sweetly familiar but she fell asleep with a heavy heart to think how much misery lay beyond the walls of the Roys' gated home.

Libby was gripped by a strange lethargy. For two days she could do nothing more than sit in the Roys' garden, dozing and reading the newspapers to try and glean news of Ghulam. But there were no articles which bore his name. Sophie managed to put through a telephone call to the office at Belgooree to assure Clarrie that they were safe and well in Calcutta. To Sophie and Libby's relief, Clarrie told them that there had been no more disturbances at the tea garden. Libby had snatched a few words.

'Is there any post for me?' she asked in hope.

'Sorry, no,' Clarrie answered. The line crackled so much that any further conversation was futile. 'Write to me when you get home,' Clarrie said, and then, 'Tell James—' But the line went dead before she could say what Libby should tell her father.

Sophie wrote to Rafi, explaining that she was now in Calcutta and eager to join him. She sent the letter to their new address in Rawalpindi, hoping that her husband was safely there and not still in Lahore. Impatient to go, she began to make arrangements to fly to Karachi in West Pakistan via Delhi and then to make her way onward to Rawalpindi.

'Libby,' Sophie said, as they sat in the shaded garden, 'isn't it time you made arrangements too?'

Libby's insides knotted. 'You mean to go back to Britain?'

'Aye, lassie,' said Sophie. 'I know the Roys would have you to stay as long as you wanted but I imagine your parents are anxious to have you home.'

Libby nodded. Now that the danger of their escape and living for the moment was past, she felt a strange anticlimax. She was weighed down with the thought that her Indian adventure was over. Now she had no excuse not to return home. Worst of all, she was going to have to face up to the fact that her relationship with Ghulam was also at an end.

Yet the realisation that time was indeed running out galvanised Libby into seeking out her friends to say goodbye. Ghulam was her priority; she had to know if he was safe and well. She took the tram along Park Street, alighting close to Hamilton Road. In the middle of the day, Libby found herself once more outside Amelia Buildings, heart pounding.

She was struck at once by the number of people crowded in the hallway. Gone was the *chowkidar* at the desk. A family of squatters had taken up residence under the stairwell. People stared at her. Libby hesitated and almost turned to go. Then she chided herself for being cowardly. If she didn't make this last visit to see Ghulam then she would probably never have the chance of seeing him again. She strode purposefully towards the stairs.

As she climbed up to the Khans' flat, doubts beset her. Fatima might still be living at the hospital and Ghulam would be at work. But at least she could leave a message with Sitara. She arrived, heart thumping, at the Khans' door. She could hear voices beyond and her hopes soared.

A woman she had never seen before, dressed in a sari, answered her knocking. She looked out through the half-open door, her expression wary.

Libby stared back in confusion, wondering for a second if she was at the wrong door.

'Hello,' said Libby, 'is Dr Khan or her brother at home?'

The woman shook her head and answered in what Libby thought might be Bengali.

'I'm sorry,' Libby said, feeling embarrassed, 'but I don't understand.'

The woman called over her shoulder, speaking rapidly to someone else out of view. A moment later, a tall man with greying hair and dressed in ill-fitting Western clothes appeared.

'Can I help you?' he asked, his look guarded.

'I'm a friend of the Khans,' Libby explained. 'I've come to say goodbye. I'm leaving India. I just wanted to know that they were all right.'

'I'm sorry but there is no one here of that name,' said the man a little frostily.

'But this flat belongs to them,' said Libby.

'That is not the case,' said the man, growing agitated. 'We have been renting it for a month. We have no knowledge of this Dr Khan or his brother.'

'*Her* brother,' said Libby. 'Dr Khan is a woman.'

'We do not know them,' he insisted. 'I'm sorry but we cannot help.' With that he closed the door on her.

Libby stood there reeling from the encounter. What did this mean? Had Ghulam's landlord thrown him out? From the noise coming from the flat, it sounded as if several families were now sharing it. Perhaps they were migrants from East Bengal and the landlord was packing them in, making as much money out of them as he could. She turned away feeling disheartened and nagged by worry for her friends.

Libby made her way to the Eden Hospital. The place was even busier than when she had last visited. She waited ages before a harassed-looking Fatima emerged into the hallway from one of the wards. She caught sight of Libby and rushed forward.

'Libby!' she exclaimed. 'They didn't tell me it was you. I didn't think you'd still be in India. How are you?' She clutched Libby's hands and Libby felt a tug of gratitude that Fatima looked pleased to see her.

'I'm fine,' Libby answered. 'But what about you? I went to the flat and found strangers in your home. What's happened?'

Fatima looked about nervously. 'Let's go on to the terrace for a minute while I explain.'

Outside, under the porticoed veranda, Fatima swiftly told her.

'I've been living at the hospital since I last saw you. After that poor man was murdered, the landlord put up the rent of all the Muslims in the building – Ghulam said it was extortion and refused to pay so he was told to go.'

'Where to?' Libby asked, her stomach clenching.

'He was living with Sanjeev,' said Fatima.

'Was?' Libby questioned.

'Until we heard from Rafi about my father's heart attack,' said Fatima, sorrow clouding her face.

'From Rafi?'

Fatima nodded, her eyes glimmering with emotion. 'He sent a telegram to me at the hospital. I wrote to my father but Ghulam got it into his head to try and get to Lahore and see him before . . .' She broke off, pressing a hand to her lips.

'Ghulam's gone to Lahore?' Libby asked, aghast. 'Is he safe? Is your father okay?'

Fatima shook her head and gulped. 'My father is dead.'

Libby squeezed her friend's arm. 'I'm so sorry. Was Ghulam too late?'

Fatima let out a sob. Libby's heart lurched.

'What is it?' she asked in fright. 'Has something happened to Ghulam?'

Fatima struggled to control her voice. 'I don't know,' she croaked. 'He promised he would let me know when he arrived in Lahore but for three weeks I've heard nothing from him.'

'Have you heard from Rafi or your family?'

'Just a telegram telling me about my father just after Ghulam left,' said Fatima. 'I've sent messages to my father's house asking and I've tried to ring but never got through. Everything is so chaotic. I don't even know if Rafi is still there.'

'So even if Ghulam had arrived, he would have been too late to see his father?' said Libby.

Fatima nodded in distress. 'I begged him not to go but he wouldn't listen. He said he had to make his peace with his father and his family before it was too late.'

Libby's stomach churned; she hardly dared ask. 'Did he go by train?'

'Train to Delhi, yes,' said Fatima. 'But he promised me he would fly from there to Lahore and not risk crossing the border by train.'

Libby felt nauseated at the thought that Ghulam could have risked going on one of the notorious trains of death between Delhi and Lahore. Surely he would not be so reckless when his aim was to reach his father before he died? She saw how agitated Fatima was over the subject. The doctor looked worn out, her face gaunt and eyes smudged with exhaustion. Libby searched for words of comfort.

'He's probably in Lahore but unable to get a message to you,' she said. 'As you said, things are so chaotic. You'll hear something soon.'

Fatima's frown of anxiety eased a fraction. 'Yes, I'm sure you're right.'

Libby didn't like to voice her worry that even if Ghulam was in Lahore, how would he get safely back to Calcutta? Or would he decide to stay in the city of his birth and help his family and fellow Punjabis who were suffering so greatly?

Fatima said, 'I must return to the ward but perhaps we can meet before you leave? I haven't even asked you about your time at Belgooree.'

'I'd like that,' said Libby. She told the doctor where she was staying. 'You must come for a meal – the Roys would make you very welcome and you could see Sophie before she leaves for Pakistan.'

They walked back to the entrance together. As Fatima turned to go, Libby asked, 'So Ghulam wouldn't have got my letter?'

Fatima gave her a look of pity. 'I'm sorry, Libby, but if you sent it to Amelia Buildings then I doubt it.'

Libby's heart ached to think he hadn't read it – might never get to read it. She had to face the truth that her relationship with Ghulam was fated never to be more than a transient affair. Standing watching Fatima walk away through the entrance, Libby was engulfed by regret. How she had longed for so much more!

She turned away, anxiety for Ghulam twisting inside. Where was he? She would find no peace of mind until she knew what had happened to her lover.

Libby couldn't sleep. She spent the long humid night worrying over Ghulam, trying to keep at bay the spectre of him being dragged off a train and butchered. Had he been attacked before he even reached Delhi? If he'd got to Delhi and flown to Lahore then he would have arrived at his family's house over two weeks ago. Perhaps he had heard about his father's death and had decided to go no further. He might still be in Delhi.

Libby was hit by an uncomfortable thought. Ghulam's former lover had come from Delhi. What if he had taken the opportunity to go and see her, repair their friendship? What if the spark between them had been rekindled and Ghulam had decided to stay in India's capital? She imagined him helping to build a just, egalitarian India with the woman he had loved so strongly and whose ideals he had shared in their days of struggle against the British.

Libby felt desolate at the thought. But she would rather that Ghulam was alive and safe, even if it meant he had returned to this woman. She would put up with the pain of never seeing Ghulam again just as long as no harm had come to him.

Restless and tossing under the mosquito net, Libby realised all of her speculation was fruitless. Earlier in the day, Sophie had been horrified to learn that Ghulam had attempted the hazardous journey but she had calmed Libby with her rational words.

'There's no point thinking the worst,' she had said, 'when it's quite possible that Ghulam arrived in Lahore and is with his family. You said Fatima hadn't actually been able to get through to them, so we have to be optimistic.' She had squeezed Libby's hand. 'I'll write at once to Rafi in 'Pindi, assuming he's now back there. I'll ask him to ring me here at the Roys'.'

Libby held on to that encouraging thought, that word would soon come from Rafi that Ghulam was at the Khans' home in Lahore. She determined that she would make no travel plans until she knew about Ghulam. She couldn't possibly leave India until she did.

The next day, Libby sent a message to the Dunlops to say that she was once again in Calcutta and a chit came back from Flowers inviting her round for afternoon tea the following day when she would be off work.

Libby was welcomed enthusiastically by Danny and Winnie Dunlop, who apologised that Flowers would be a little late. Libby was surprised to find them in such good spirits; after her last visit they had been so anxious about looming Independence. Libby relished being once more in their cluttered, fussily decorated sitting room with Winnie plying her with sandwiches and cake, while Danny demanded to hear every detail of her time at Belgooree. Libby told him about their Independence Day party but avoided any mention of the traumatic siege by the Gulgat men or her daring escape with Sophie.

'Tell me about the plantation,' Danny said eagerly, 'before Flowers gets here. She ticks me off for badgering you about the tea planting life. I don't suppose your father has been able to discover more about the Dunlops?'

Libby felt pity at his hopeful look. 'I'm sorry, Mr Dunlop, I don't think he has. I did send on the details and he promised he was going to see his old planter friend, Mr Fairfax, and ask him. I'm sure he will have tried.'

Danny looked dashed but tried to put on a brave face. 'I know your father will have done his best. It doesn't really matter, I suppose. Not now that—'

'Danny!' Winnie cut him off with a cry of warning. 'It's not your news to tell.'

Before Libby could ask what she meant, the door swung open and, with a waft of perfume, in walked Flowers. Libby stood to greet her and then saw with delight that she was followed by George.

Libby smiled. 'How lovely; I didn't think I'd get to see you both.'

The women kissed cheeks and then Flowers held up her left hand for inspection. An emerald and diamond ring glinted in the electric light.

Libby gasped. 'You're engaged to be married?'

Flowers's pretty face creased in a broad smile as she slipped her arm through George's. 'Meet my fiancé.'

'That's wonderful news!' Libby cried.

She gave George a peck on the cheek; he was grinning foolishly.

'It is, isn't it?' he said. 'I still can't believe this gorgeous lass said yes.'

Libby had a pang of misgiving. Not so long ago, Flowers had been warning her off about getting involved with George because of his philandering. But as they settled down to chat, Libby's doubts faded. They both looked so happy and Libby knew that Flowers was too sensible to have accepted marriage on a whim.

'We're getting married in a month's time,' said Flowers. 'It was going to be sooner but when we heard that Adela and Sam were coming back, we decided to wait so they can be our witnesses.'

Libby wondered if Flowers and her parents were disappointed that she couldn't have a church wedding because of George's previous marriage. But the Dunlops seemed delighted with the match. When Libby rose to go, Flowers and George offered to walk with her to the tram.

It was then that she was able to tell them about the trouble at Belgooree and her escape with Sophie.

'That's awful!' George said in shock. 'I should have come to visit – I should have been there to protect Auntie Clarrie.'

'She's all right,' Libby assured him. 'There's no one as strong or determined as Clarrie. You couldn't have done any more than she did to keep us all safe.'

'She's an amazing woman,' said Flowers. 'Does Adela know what happened?'

'She might do by now,' said Libby. 'Clarrie was going to explain in a letter after we'd got safely away. She didn't want Sam worrying about his sister when he was too far away to help.'

'So what are your plans, Libby?' Flowers asked. 'You were a bit vague when Daddy asked.'

Libby felt tears sting her eyes. She unburdened her fears over Ghulam. She could hardly bear the look of pity Flowers gave her; her friend had been critical of Ghulam having a casual affair with her and then packing her off to Belgooree. George looked embarrassed by talk of the Indian – he'd been disapproving of Ghulam too – and Libby wondered how much Flowers had told him about the affair. But Libby knew that George had never been in love with her and she was glad that her girlish crush on him had long since vanished. She felt nothing for George except mild affection.

'I'm sorry,' Flowers said. 'I hope you get news of him soon.'

'If you're still in India at the end of October,' said George, 'promise you will come to our wedding.'

Libby smiled. 'Thank you, I'd love to.'

CHAPTER 39

South of France, early October

Adela sat on their hotel balcony in the mellow autumn sunshine, gazing out over the busy port of Marseilles. The aromatic whiff of French tobacco wafted up from the café below, masking the pungent smells of the docks. Sam had gone to make final arrangements for their passage east and supervise the loading of their luggage. Before taking the train south, they had enjoyed four days in Paris. The city still bore the scars of Nazi occupation but the atmosphere was one of optimism and joie de vivre. In the south of France they had been struck by the plentiful supplies of food and the mouth-watering array of cakes in the many bakeries.

'No sugar rationing here,' Sam had said with a wry look, as he'd wolfed down a strawberry tart.

Soon they would be embarking on their voyage across the Mediterranean. Adela had no idea when she would next be back in Europe. Breathing in the salty, oily tang of the port, Adela felt a kick of excitement. She had no regrets about the decision Sam and she had taken to return to India; she relished the prospect of a married life there and of starting their family together at Belgooree. Her pregnancy sickness was abating and there was now a small swelling where the baby

was growing; Sam liked to put his hand over it and talk excitedly about
how he would teach their child – girl or boy – to fish and play cricket.

Only one thing marred her happiness: leaving John Wesley behind.
Adela felt the familiar ache inside when she thought of him. He was
no longer just a memory of a downy-haired baby; John Wesley was a
bright-eyed, chattering, inquisitive boy with a heart-melting grin, who
found it hard to stay still for a minute.

Adela fished out the photograph that Sam had taken of her with her
son. Just to see him grinning at the camera made her smile. They looked
so natural together, so alike. Her eyes stung with tears. She kissed the
photo and slipped it back into the book she was reading. She carried
it everywhere.

She stared out at the busy scene below. Soon Sam would be back
and they would be leaving the hotel for a last meal on French soil before
boarding the ship. Time was running out. Adela came to a decision. She
went into their bedroom and retrieved her attaché case from their hand
luggage. Pulling out some writing paper and her fountain pen, Adela
went back to sit at the balcony table.

> *Dear Martha*
>
> *I wanted to thank you once again for your kindness to
> Sam and me when you took us riding and gave us tea.
> I'm sorry that we didn't get to see you all before we left
> but when I explain why not, I think you will understand.*
>
> *Meeting you and your husband – and even more so,
> your dear son Jacques – was a very important moment
> for me. You told me that you didn't think it right to keep
> secrets about Jacques's parentage from him, so that is why
> I'm writing to you now.*
>
> *You see, Martha, I am Jacques's mother by birth. He
> was born on the 17th of February 1939 in Cullercoats.
> I was only eighteen and unmarried. Jacques's father was*

Indian and knew nothing about the pregnancy, as I had returned to Newcastle before I discovered I was carrying his baby. I named him John Wesley (after my grandfather and father) and gave him up for adoption. I bitterly regret having done so but at the time I saw no other option. I left a keepsake with him – a pink stone on a gold chain that was given to my mother by a holy man – and I hope that Jacques still has it.

I came back to England with Sam to search for my son (Sam knows everything) and discovered that he had been adopted by the Segals. Now he is in your care. Forgive me for visiting your home under the false pretence of a riding expedition. What I really wanted more than anything in the world was to see John Wesley with my own eyes – to discover if he really was my boy. He looks very like his grandfather Wesley and my younger brother Harry – I have no doubt that he is the son that I gave up.

I am sorry if this all comes as a horrible shock to you – although perhaps you too saw the family resemblance? I am not seeking to make trouble or upset anyone. I must admit that I used to daydream of finding John Wesley and rescuing him from some orphanage or unhappy home, believing that he could only really be happy with me, his blood mother.

But now I know that is not true. I have seen how much he is loved by you and Major Gibson – how very happy he is too. Jacques is a delightful boy and that is because of you. I know he will be cherished and nurtured and guided by you and your husband. That makes me able to bear being parted from him.

If I may ask anything of you, then it is this. When Jacques comes of age, will you tell him what I have told you? I know you have been frank with him about the Segals, thinking that they were his real parents, but I see no point in confusing or upsetting Jacques by telling him of his true origins until he is old enough to understand. When he is a grown man, I would love him to have the chance to seek me out and meet his family in India – the Robsons.

Until then, I hope you will allow Sam and myself to send him the occasional letter – Jacques was very keen that we send him a photograph of a palm squirrel! I understand if you would rather we didn't but it would be a great kindness if you would let me stay in contact.

Whatever you decide, Martha, I wish to thank you for loving Jacques the way you do. It means the world to me.

Kind regards,
Adela Jackman

Adela enclosed it with details of her address at Belgooree in the hopes that Martha would reply, and sealed the envelope. She would post it before they embarked.

'Ahoy there!' a voice called jauntily from below.

Adela leant over the railing and saw Sam grinning up at her. He had bought himself a new hat – a brown Trilby – which was perched on the back of his head. Her heart swelled with affection. Sam seemed incapable of wearing a hat at the proper angle and she loved him for it.

'Ready for *le déjeuner*, Madame?' he asked.

Adela's heart skipped a beat. '*Oui*, Monsieur! Coming.'

She tucked the letter in her pocket and hurried down to meet her husband.

CHAPTER 40

Newcastle

James sat out of the way in a back pew while Tilly bustled around with Mrs Marshall, the vicar's wife, arranging flowers for the Sunday service. Autumn light filtered in through high stained-glass windows, throwing coloured light on to the cold flagstones. Adela and Sam would have boarded their ship back to India by now. They would be sailing past Malta, towards Egypt and the Suez Canal. By next week they would be at Aden and turning east across the Arabian Sea . . .

James felt his stomach clench with longing and he forced his thoughts back to the chilly church. Tilly had been surprised at his suggestion he accompany her and then a little alarmed that he wanted to attend the service with her the following day too.

'Are you sure?' she'd questioned.

'Yes,' James had said with more conviction than he'd felt. 'I think it's time I did more with you, Tilly. Perhaps meet some of your friends.'

What he couldn't bring himself to tell her was that he was increasingly desperate to fill up the void inside him that leaving India had created. Adela's departure – the thought of her and Sam returning to Belgooree – had only worsened his feelings of emptiness and uselessness.

Tilly had given him a baffled smile and nodded in agreement. So here he was, sitting in the shadows waiting to be called upon to do something useful, such as lift heavy vases or move tables. The women, though, appeared to be managing without him. That's why his mind kept drifting back to Adela and Sam and their journey to India.

His thoughts slid to Belgooree and Clarrie. Why was it that he longed to be with Clarrie and her family more than with his own? Clarrie and Harry were more real to him – he could imagine what they were doing and thinking at every stage of the day – whereas his own wife and children were so distant with him, their former closeness ruptured by the long years apart. Except for Libby. Oh, Libby: how he missed her too!

James stood up. It wasn't healthy to think of India. It was safer to shut the past from his mind as best he could. The more he forced himself to do things with Tilly, the less he would be plagued by his guilt over Aidan Dunlop and the traumatic events of his early life on the Oxford plantation. Since unburdening himself to his wife, the nightmares had lessened a little – he was grateful to her for that – but they hadn't vanished completely.

'Can I do anything to help?' he called out. His voice echoed off the pillars.

Tilly looked round startled as if she'd forgotten he was there.

'I don't think so, dear,' she said.

'Well, perhaps you could take out the dead flowers and put them on the compost heap?' Mrs Marshall suggested.

'Of course,' James agreed, crossing quickly to the vestry where he'd seen them taking the wilting flowers.

He took his time outside, spinning out the task, hoping Tilly would be ready to go home soon. Perhaps they could take Fluff for a walk in the dene together before it got dark. As he re-entered the church, he heard music, hymn tunes. The organist must be practising for the next day. James hovered in the nave listening while Tilly readjusted a display of chrysanthemums. There was a break in the playing and then the church was filling with a different sound – a slow dignified air – that struck James as deeply familiar.

The music began to gather momentum and the notes sored into the air, resonating in the dark space above. James felt his chest tighten. Pachelbel. It had been played at their wedding. He turned towards Tilly. She had stopped fussing over the flowers and was looking round. They caught each other's look. James felt his vision blur. He groped for a nearby pew. A sob rose up from the pit of his stomach. Tilly came rushing towards him.

'James, don't upset yourself!'

It was too late. Abruptly, James began to howl in distress, tears coursing down his craggy face. He couldn't understand why but there was no way of stopping. Tilly steered him past an astonished Mrs Marshall.

'Is there anything I can . . . ?' she asked.

'No, thank you,' said Tilly. 'He needs fresh air, that's all.'

James would have laughed at his wife's robust reply if he hadn't been weeping so helplessly. He felt distress and shame in equal measure.

Tilly guided him towards the back wall of the surrounding churchyard.

'Sit, darling,' she said, coaxing him on to a damp weather-beaten bench.

James did as he was told. Finally, after several more minutes of sobbing and blowing his nose into a handkerchief, he regained control of his emotions.

'I'm so s-sorry,' he apologised. 'I don't know what came over me. The music . . .'

'James,' Tilly said gently. 'This isn't about the music, is it? You've never got sentimental over Pachelbel before.'

'It made me think of our wedding,' said James, 'of how happy we used to be.'

'Yes.' Tilly sighed. 'I think we were once, weren't we?' She took his hand and held it between her plump ones. 'The music might have opened the floodgates, James, but I don't think you were crying for us.

Why won't you consider seeing a doctor? I know Jamie worries about you—'

'No! I couldn't possibly burden our son with my problems,' James said.

'Johnny then?' Tilly suggested. 'Couldn't you speak to him? He understands about India. Tell him what you told me about the Danny Dunlop affair. He might be able to treat you.'

'Treat me?' James said, aghast. 'I don't need treating.'

'Well, I think you do,' said Tilly more brusquely.

'I just have to be a man and bear it,' James said, his jaw tightening. 'And I really don't want to talk to my brother-in-law about it – much as I like Johnny. I shouldn't have burdened you with it all either.'

'But you have done,' Tilly pointed out. 'And I'm glad you did. I want to help you have peace of mind but I'm no expert. Praying for you doesn't seem to have helped.'

James was touched by her concern. He knew she no longer loved him as she had once done. The moment they had looked at each other in the church as the music overwhelmed him, he had known it for sure. And the desolation he had felt told him that he no longer loved his wife. Yet she was prepared to put up with him and try to help him recover from his dark thoughts.

'It's just these ghastly dreams,' he confided.

She gripped his hand. 'Then do something about them,' she urged.

'What can I possibly do?' he asked in bewilderment.

Tilly glanced away. He knew she was turning something over in her mind but dreaded what it might be. He waited for her to speak. After a long pause, she turned back and held his look.

'If you refuse to go and see a doctor,' said Tilly, 'then I only see one other option.'

James tried to unclench his jaw. 'What's that?'

'You have to confess to Danny Dunlop all that you know. Until you do,' said Tilly, her hazel eyes filling with pity, 'you will never be rid of your nightmares.'

CHAPTER 41

Calcutta, early October

L ibby and Sophie were taking tea on the Roys' veranda when a telephone call came through for Sophie from Rawalpindi. Libby's heart
lurched as she watched her dash indoors. Her pulse raced until she
felt faint. She wanted to follow. The wait was interminable. Kind Bijal
Roy tried to distract her with conversation.

'You mentioned how you were teaching typing at Belgooree,' she
said. 'Well, I have a friend whose niece is looking for a clerical job but
she needs typing skills. I know it's a bit of an imposition to ask but . . .'

'Of course,' said Libby at once, 'I'd be pleased to help. I can't promise for how long but while I'm still in Calcutta I'd be happy to teach
her – and if you don't mind me staying longer?'

'We like having you here, Libby. It's so quiet now that our own
daughters are married and living elsewhere.' Bijal smiled. 'You don't
have to go when Sophie goes.'

Libby felt a wave of gratitude. 'There's one problem though,' she
said. 'I left my typewriter in Belgooree so I'd have to buy a new one.'

'Let us do that,' Bijal insisted.

Libby was about to protest, when Sophie reappeared. It was impossible to read the expression on her face. Her cheeks were flushed and her

eyes glinting as if she'd been crying. But were they tears of happiness or upset?

'How is Rafi?' Libby asked, rising to her feet.

'He's well,' Sophie said, relief flitting across her face. 'He's been in the new job a week. He got my letter.'

'And?' Libby's heart pounded.

'Walk with me,' Sophie said, holding out her hand as if to a child.

Libby hurried over. Sophie slipped her arm through Libby's and led her into the garden. Out of earshot, she turned to Libby and cleared her throat.

Quietly she said, 'Rafi says Ghulam never arrived in Lahore. They didn't even know he was on his way – no messages had got through. The first Rafi knew about it was from my letter. He drove straight back down to Lahore to see if Ghulam was there but he's not. No one has seen or heard from him. Rafi's very upset. He's blaming himself for telling Ghulam about his father's heart attack, never thinking for one moment that Ghulam would attempt to see the old man.'

Libby thought she would be sick. All her worst imaginings assaulted her anew.

'That doesn't mean that Ghulam's . . .' Sophie let her words trail off.

Libby looked at her in distress. 'Ghulam wouldn't have let Fatima worry about him all this time. He would have got a message to her. It can only mean that something dreadful has happened.'

Sophie put her arms about Libby's shoulders and hugged her. 'I'm so sorry, lassie,' she whispered. 'I know how much you care for him.'

Libby's resolve to be brave dissolved at Sophie's tender gesture and words. She buried her face in Sophie's shoulder and let out a sob. Sophie held her and rubbed her back while Libby wept. After a moment, Libby tried to compose herself. She pulled away and wiped her eyes.

'Oh, Sophie,' she said, her heart leaden, 'how am I going to tell Fatima?'

In the end, both Sophie and Libby went to break the bleak news to Fatima about Ghulam's failure to turn up in Lahore. Fatima collapsed in shock. Libby berated herself for blurting out the news so quickly but Sophie said there was no other way. Fatima had reached complete exhaustion, driving herself relentlessly at work and carrying the burden of grief over her estranged father, as well as worry about Ghulam.

The Roys insisted that Fatima be brought to their house to rest and recuperate. Libby kept a close watch over the doctor, keeping her company when she wanted it and leaving her in peace when she slept. As for herself, Libby only slept fitfully, remaining awake for long hours of the night thinking about Ghulam. She was filled with desolation. She believed something terrible had happened to her lover. She was haunted by the memory of the Gulgat mob, baying for Sophie's blood and ready to lynch her for being a Muslim. Had Ghulam been caught and butchered by a similarly vengeful gang? Libby had to stuff her tearstained handkerchief into her mouth to gag her sobs. With daybreak, relief came in getting up and keeping busy, and pushing the horror of her thoughts to the back of her mind till night-time came again.

Gradually Fatima's strength began to return and with it her dogged belief that her beloved brother might still be alive.

'He could be helping in some refugee camp,' she suggested. 'That would be just like him. He used to disappear for months without a word in his campaigning days.'

Libby wanted to believe her. But the grim reality of the weeks following Partition were that tens of thousands of people were missing and unaccounted for because they had been slaughtered in the bloodbath of forced migration. It was far more likely that Ghulam had perished like countless others. She admired Fatima for her optimism but her heart was leaden with sorrow. Deep down, she knew that Ghulam was lost to her. She knew she couldn't stay indefinitely at the Roys' or in India but she couldn't think of leaving India just yet – not while Fatima needed her and she could be of use to others – and while there was still a glimmer of hope of discovering what had happened to Ghulam.

Libby coped with the strain of Ghulam's disappearance by keeping as busy as possible. She had started teaching the niece of the Roys' friend to type. Eighteen-year-old Parvati came to the house in Ballyganj each morning for lessons and, with Libby's encouragement, was soon competent and increasing her speed.

On Sundays Libby resumed attendance at the Duff Presbyterian Church, where her Uncle Johnny had taken her in the early days of her return to India. There had been an exodus of British members of the congregation but several of the Anglo-Indian and Gurkha families who had befriended her in the cold season welcomed her back.

At the end of each service, when Libby stood on the steps in the sunshine listening to people chatting, she would have a pang of longing for the time she had sat there with Ghulam eating cake. It made her feel closer to him for a few precious, bittersweet moments.

After a couple of weeks, Fatima revived and was determined to resume her duties at the hospital. Libby hid her reluctance to see the doctor go. More than with anyone else, being with Fatima made Libby feel Ghulam's presence strongly. They would talk about him and Libby would encourage Fatima to reminisce and tell her stories about her brother. Occasionally they would laugh as some small incident was recalled – his voracious toffee-eating or the way he swung his arm in bowling practice without ever realising he was doing it.

'I'm sorry now that I discouraged your friendship with my brother,' Fatima confessed to Libby. 'I didn't realise how very much he meant to you.' She squeezed Libby's hand. 'Thank you for looking after me and being my friend. We will keep each other strong until he comes back to us.'

Libby wished with all her heart that this would come true. With Fatima around she could almost believe that Ghulam might return. She had to force herself not to beg Fatima to stay on at the Roys'. Libby berated herself for her dark thoughts. If brave Fatima refused to give up hope that Ghulam was still alive, then so should she.

Once Fatima had moved back to the hospital, Sophie, who had delayed joining Rafi while his sister was ill, made swift plans to go to Rawalpindi. Libby had to brace herself to say goodbye to the Scotswoman – one of the few people who really understood about her love for Ghulam and who, unlike most others, had encouraged her relationship with Rafi's brother.

On Sophie's final evening she asked Libby, 'What will you do?'

Libby answered, 'I'm going to stay till after Flowers gets married. Apart from being at the wedding, I want to see Adela and Sam before I go home. I can't deny that I'm sad they won't be in England when I return.'

'I long to see them too,' said Sophie. 'But with all that's happened, I just want to be with Rafi as soon as possible.'

'Sam will understand,' Libby assured her.

'You know you are welcome any time to stay with me and Rafi,' said Sophie. 'It's so hard to say goodbye to you, lassie. We've been through such a lot together in a short time.'

'I know,' said Libby, growing teary. 'I'll miss you so very much too.'

Sophie said, 'Don't give up hope of finding Ghulam. Fatima hasn't. We'll keep making enquiries in the Punjab in case he made it that far. Someday we'll find out what's happened to him.'

Libby could only nod in agreement; her heart was too full and her throat too constricted to speak.

After Sophie left, Libby renewed her determination to fill her every hour. Putting the word around that she was teaching typing, Libby gained another couple of students from among the congregation at the Duff Church: young Anglo-Indian women who were eager to find good jobs in the city. Although the Roys said they were happy for her to use their home for teaching, Libby preferred to visit her new pupils at home. That way she quickly learnt more about them and their needs. They were willing students and when two of them swiftly secured jobs, word soon spread about Libby's success and her number of pupils grew.

As October wore on, Libby got caught up in the excitement of Flowers's impending marriage. She had resumed the occasional evening out with Flowers and George and their circle of young friends, though not as often as they asked her. Libby went with Flowers and her mother on shopping trips to buy her wedding trousseau. The gown was being made by a dressmaker friend of the Dunlops, but Flowers wanted clothes for her honeymoon.

'I'm not supposed to know,' Flowers said, 'but I overheard George telling Eddy that it's Ceylon. George was stationed there during the War and I know he wants to go back and see it properly.'

Libby knew that George had been posted to Ceylon during his time in the Fleet Air Arm. Yet it was only as an adult that Libby had discovered that during this time George's sweetheart Joan had had a fling and become pregnant. It was while on leave from Ceylon that George had done the decent thing and swiftly married Joan. Seeing how happy Flowers was – and how besotted George was about his new love – Libby had to admit that she may have judged George too harshly over his behaviour in the past year.

He had never truly loved Joan and never had the chance to form an attachment with baby Bonnie, who wasn't his own. Freed from his obligations to wife and child, George had been almost frantic in his attempts to make up for lost time and enjoy himself. Perhaps he had been more hurt by Joan's infidelity than Libby had realised. George was naturally gregarious and flirtatious – but apart from the one enthusiastic kiss in the Botanical Gardens he had never led Libby to expect anything more than friendship.

When she thought back to six months ago and the various dances and dinners she had attended, it struck her that it was always the attractive, independently minded nurse that George was trying to pursue. He danced with Flowers more than anyone and made sure she was the last to be dropped off home. Flowers had been wary of George, not wanting either herself or Libby to catch him on the rebound after his divorce. Somehow George had finally convinced Flowers how serious he was about her.

Perhaps the upheaval and uncertainty of Independence had concentrated Flowers's mind on what she wanted out of life – and she had chosen George. No doubt the Dunlop parents were relieved to see their only daughter settled, and with a young Englishman too. If George ever decided to return to live and work in Britain with his new wife, then the Dunlops would be able to follow. Danny Dunlop no longer needed his unproven connections to some tea planter; he was soon to have a son-in-law with a British passport.

While Libby buried her grief over Ghulam with as much activity as possible, she could not avoid the signs of distress on the streets around her. Even in the main shopping thoroughfares, the numbers of homeless and destitute people begging seemed to grow weekly. At night they would huddle in doorways and scavenge what was left in the gutters from street stalls. Libby's spirits weighed heavily at the sight of them but what could she do that would make the slightest difference? The numbers were too overwhelming. Then she would think of Ghulam and how he would have chided her for her defeatist attitude.

It prompted Libby to ask Fatima where Sanjeev lived. Of all Ghulam's comrades, the cheerful Sanjeev had always been the most optimistic. She wondered if he still was. Perhaps he would have some suggestion as to how she could help. Libby knew he could shed no light on Ghulam's whereabouts as he had been the first person Fatima had contacted when she had heard no word of Ghulam arriving in Pakistan and had begun to grow worried.

A few days before Flowers's wedding, Libby tracked down Sanjeev to a flat behind Hogg's Market in Lindsay Street, close to where the Dunlops lived. Sanjeev welcomed her in, not showing as much surprise to see her as Libby had expected. The tiny spartan flat had little furniture, save for an old desk piled with books and a *charpoy* in the corner. It reminded Libby of Ghulam's bedroom in Amelia Buildings. The thought brought her pain.

Sanjeev brewed up tea and they sat on rugs, swapping news and discussing everything that had happened since they had last met at the refugee centre outside Calcutta. She told him about her teaching young women to type but that she was seeking to do more to help the destitute too.

Finally, Libby asked, 'Tell me about when Ghulam lived here.' They had been skirting the subject of their mutual friend, apart from Sanjeev's initial words of sorrow about Ghulam's disappearance. 'Was he in good spirits or depressed about what was happening after Partition?'

'He was full of hope that things would get better,' said Sanjeev, rubbing his temples. 'We both were. Despite the hostility of some towards him, Ghulam was going to stand for the city council for the Communist Party and he was working on a series of articles about how Calcutta could be improved.'

'Had he given up working for *The Statesman*?' asked Libby. 'I hadn't seen anything by him for a while.'

'No, he was still there part-time. His editor was very good about giving him as much leave as he needed to travel to Lahore to see his father. In fact, he gave Ghulam enough for the airfare from Delhi and told him not to take the train.'

Libby's insides twisted. Ghulam had so much to live for. She forced herself to ask what she had been unable to ask Fatima.

'Do you think he might have got as far as Delhi and then stayed for some reason? For some person . . . ?'

Libby glanced up and saw Sanjeev regarding her intently. She reddened.

'Why do you think that?'

With burning cheeks, Libby said, 'I know the big love of his life was a woman who came from Delhi. Perhaps he took the opportunity to find her and that's why he never made it to Lahore.'

'Cordelia?' Sanjeev said in astonishment.

'I suppose so – I never knew her name – just that she was very special to him but she rejected him for his stance over the War.'

Sanjeev retorted, 'She gave him the run-around, that's for certain. Ghulam was in love with her once, but that was a long time ago.'

'Fatima seemed to think . . . She warned me that Ghulam couldn't commit to another.'

'Fatima, like all sisters, was being protective of her brother. She had seen him get badly hurt. But she didn't know Ghulam's true feelings.'

'So how are you so sure that he no longer cared for this Cordelia?'

'Because he told me so,' said Sanjeev. 'We talked about it before he left for Lahore.'

'Did you? What did he say?' Libby held her breath.

Sanjeev didn't answer immediately. He got up and crossed the room, opened a desk drawer and rummaged inside. He came back holding an envelope.

'Before Ghulam went, he gave me this letter. He said if he didn't make it back safely and you ever came to look for him, I was to give you this.' He held it out.

Libby's heart punched in her chest. 'For me?'

'Yes,' said Sanjeev, 'take it.'

Libby reached for it with trembling fingers. At the sight of the familiar handwriting she almost broke down. For a moment she couldn't speak.

Sanjeev said gently, 'I know he wouldn't have gone to find Cordelia because he confessed to me how he was in love with you, Libby. He said he had to tell someone. He knew what a hazardous journey he was undertaking. The last night he was here, he sat up writing that. Whatever it says, it was from the heart. I thought about sending it to you but he was very insistent that I should only give it to you if you came to seek him out.'

Libby tucked it into her trouser pocket. 'Thank you, Sanjeev,' she said, her voice hoarse with emotion.

She got up quickly to go. She wanted to be alone to read Ghulam's words. At the door she hesitated. 'Did he get a letter from me before he left? I wrote from Belgooree and told him about his father.'

Sanjeev shook his head. 'I'm sure he would have mentioned it if he had.'

Libby nodded, heartbroken that Ghulam had never read her declaration of love. As she went she said, 'If I can be of any help to the refugees you are helping – perhaps free typing lessons or arithmetic – then please let me know.'

'I will,' Sanjeev agreed. 'Thank you.'

It was only a short walk from Hogg's Market to the Duff Church. Libby retraced the steps that she had taken with Ghulam the day she had realised she was falling in love with him. On the steps of the church she pulled out the letter and with shaking hands tore open the flimsy envelope.

> *My darling Goddess*
> *Tomorrow I set off for Lahore to see my ill father. I suspect*
> *I might already be too late to find him conscious and*
> *make my peace with him, but I must try. Tonight I will*

get no sleep for I have decided to fill the dark hours think-
ing of all the people who are most dear to me.

My special sister Fatima – she has kept me strong
through so much. Rafi and his faithful Sophie – I wish
I'd got to know her better. My good comrade Sanjeev who
keeps my spirits up on the bad days. Kind Sitara who has
cared for Fatima and me so well and continues to serve
my sister at the hospital. Other good and true friends at
the newspaper and in the Party. But there is one person
who keeps barging her way into my thoughts and won't let
me sleep. She has been the cause of many sleepless nights
and not just this last one in Calcutta. You must know
that it is you, Libby – my goddess in the green satin dress.

I love you with all my body and my whole heart –
every part of me yearns for you just now. I wish that you
were lying here beside me, loving me with that intensity
that we shared so briefly but so utterly. I still think of those
two occasions that we lay together and made love. I never
felt so alive. I will always cherish those moments.

But more than that, Libby, you have been a true
friend. I think, given time, we could have gone on to do
good things together in this world. Perhaps I could have
started a newspaper and you could have done the satirical
cartoons! Or maybe we could have set up a school here
in Calcutta where there is so much injustice and need –
the streets are full of lost or abandoned children. I could
teach them to read and write and you their sums and
times tables.

Since you left me for Belgooree I have often dreamt
of what a future together might have been. I imagine by
now you have returned to Britain. I half hoped you might
write before you did so – or turn up at my door. I know

I promised to write to you, but it seemed unfair to do so when you had decided to go home.

I don't imagine you will ever get to read this letter. I write it more for myself – a way to pour out my heart in the depths of night. But I shall leave it with Sanjeev just in case you ever try to find me – or him. For if you have done so and are reading this, then it means that you have decided to stay in Calcutta at least for a while – and that means that India is still important to you and not just a place of nostalgia that existed only in your memory of childhood.

But it also probably means that I have not succeeded in returning safely to Calcutta. I know there are risks ahead but I am so much luckier than many of my fellow Indians. The senseless killings of the past weeks make me almost give up in despair.

Yet I will not allow myself to give up – not while there are people of passion like you and Sanjeev and Fatima in the world who get up every new morning intent on making this a better place.

My darling Libby, the dawn is beginning to creep in at the window. I must get ready for the journey ahead. Wherever you are – and wherever you go in the future – enjoy your life, Libby. Please know that I treasured our friendship and that you were dearly beloved by me.

Ghulam x

Libby sat on the steps, with tears streaming down her face, reread-ing the letter over and over again. His words of love – the depth of his feelings for her – took her breath away. If only he had been able to express them when they had been together! She might never have left him in Calcutta or gone to Belgooree. She would have opened her heart to him too, instead of waiting to put her true feelings in a letter that he had never received.

It grieved her beyond words that Ghulam would never read her love letter to him. Yet there was comfort in her sore heart to know that he had written such tender words without any prompting from her or feeling of obligation that he should respond in kind. His passionate message had come from his heart. She was in no doubt now that Ghulam Khan had loved her, loved her deeply and completely.

Libby stood up on shaky legs, shattered and comforted in equal measure by what she had read and now knew of Ghulam's feelings. She kissed the letter and slipped it into her blouse so it could lie close to her heart. Then Libby walked away from the shade of the palm trees and into the late October sunshine.

CHAPTER 42

Flowers and George were married on a balmy day at the end of October, two days after Adela and Sam arrived in Calcutta. Delayed in Bombay disembarking, the couple almost didn't make it in time for the wedding. Sophie, before leaving, had arranged with the hospitable Roys for her brother and his wife to stay a few nights with them at Ballyganj.

The reception was a lunch held at Firpo's, where George had done much of his courting of Flowers and where he had proposed over an intimate dinner and finally persuaded her to marry him.

Libby was greatly cheered to see Adela and Sam again. When the wedding was over, and the happy couple had been waved away in a taxi to the airport, bound for Colombo in Ceylon, Libby and her friends went back to the Roys' and spent the evening sitting in the garden catching up on each other's news.

An emotional Adela told Libby all about her search for John Wesley and the shock at finding him living at Willowburn when she had given up looking.

'In the end we decided that it would be cruel to uproot him from his new home,' she said tearfully. 'He's so happy with the Gibsons. But

I live in hope that one day Martha Gibson will tell him who I really am and maybe he will want to know me better . . .'

Sam held her hand. 'Tell Libby your other news,' he said with a tender smile.

Adela wiped away her tears and smiled at her husband. 'You tell her – it's as much your news as mine.'

Sam grinned. 'Adela's expecting. I'm going to be a father.'

Libby's eyes stung to see the pride and happiness in his face. 'That's wonderful!' she cried. 'I'm so very pleased for you both. I can't imagine a couple more suited to being parents. Sophie and Rafi will be overjoyed to hear your news too.'

Adela beamed. 'Thank you, Libby.'

Sam said, 'I wish Sophie had hung on a couple more weeks to see us but I understand how she must have been impatient to be with Rafi after their time apart.'

'And after the awful incident at Belgooree,' said Adela. 'We were deeply shocked by Mother's letter, though she made light of it. Tell us what really happened.'

Libby told them about the Gulgat troubles, the attempt to snatch Sophie from Belgooree, their escape and how their relief at being back in Calcutta had been overshadowed by the terrible news of Ghulam's disappearance. Adela and Sam sat in silence, stunned by the news. Libby had held back from telling them so as not to spoil Flowers's wedding day. But now she poured out her story: of how she and Ghulam had grown very close, of how much she missed him and of the letter she treasured that he had written to her on the eve of his journey.

'It's six weeks since he was last heard of,' Libby said in distress. 'Fatima won't give up hope that he's still alive but I don't believe it. I know there are literally millions of people on the move but I'm certain that Ghulam would have got a message to his family by now if he was okay.'

Adela stood up and went to Libby, putting her arms around her. 'I'm so very sorry,' she said. 'My heart breaks for you.'

Libby hugged her tight, her pain easing a fraction for having confided in her friends. Adela had been the person she had felt closest to while growing up in Newcastle and the one who had confided in Libby as an adult about her own deeply personal loss of her baby. But more than that – both Adela and Sam had liked and admired Ghulam. Libby wept into Adela's shoulder while her cousin stroked her hair and tried to comfort her.

Two days later Adela and Sam left, impatient to be back at Belgooree and reunited with Clarrie. Libby gave them Wesley's old coat to return with a message of thanks to Adela's courageous mother. That day, after giving typing lessons, Libby went to the centre where Sanjeev doled out food and began teaching sums to a roomful of children of all ages. Libby almost gagged at the rank smell in the airless, fetid room. But the look of trust and expectation on the children's faces spurred her on. They were mostly boys and, from what Sanjeev told her, were refugees from the countryside, quite unused to the city.

Libby, with the help of the Roys, was picking up a smattering of Bengali, but she taught numbers to her ragged pupils in English and with a lot of gesticulation. There were no jotters and pencils, or even slates for the children. But when the Roys discovered Libby was improvising with drawing numbers in sand with a stick, they provided a board and chalk.

She thought of Ghulam's pipe dream of them setting up a school together for the impoverished of Calcutta. She knew by heart the words in his letter: *the streets are full of lost or abandoned children – I could teach them to read and write and you their sums and times tables.* She felt hollow inside to think she was doing it alone, but Ghulam's vision gave her the courage to carry on helping the children as best she could.

After an exhausting week of teaching typing and giving arithmetic lessons, Libby returned home to hear the Roys entertaining on their veranda. Halfway up the garden path, Libby stopped in astonishment at the sound of a familiar voice. It boomed out of the shadows. But it wasn't possible!

Libby hurried forward. 'Dad?' she called out, running on to the veranda.

To her incredulity, her father rose from a rattan chair clutching a tumbler of whisky.

'How . . . ? When . . . ?' Libby gaped at him. Then she was seized by sudden dread. 'Has something happened to Mother or one of the boys?'

'No, nothing to worry about,' James quickly reassured her. He put down his drink and held out his arms. 'I have business in Calcutta, that's all. And your mother wanted me to check up on you too.'

Libby rushed to hug him, her eyes smarting with tears. Her father felt solid and comforting and dearly familiar. She clung on to him until he patted her and said 'well, well', which she knew meant that that was enough show of affection.

She sat down next to him, still hardly able to believe he was there, while he talked about his flights and the weather en route.

'Your father flew in this morning,' said Ranajit.

'He was going to book into a hotel,' said Bijal, 'but we insisted he must stay with us so he can see you properly.'

'I can see why you don't want to go home, Libby,' James said with a smile, 'when you are treated like a princess by these kind people.'

'It's no more than she deserves,' Bijal said, 'after she works so hard all day.'

'The Roys have been telling me all about your charity work,' said James.

'Not just charity,' Libby answered. 'I'm beginning to make a living from the typing lessons.'

She waited for him to chide her for delaying in Calcutta when she should have been back in Newcastle weeks ago. But he didn't. He took up the conversation with the captain that she had interrupted, asking him about his war work. Sanajit talked about timber supply and how innovative Rafi had been in trying out goran wood from the Sundarbans when their supply of teak from Burma had been stopped. This led on to James reminiscing about his part in the war effort on the Burmese Front.

Libby watched her father, still perplexed. What on earth had made him come all this way? Was it tea interests? Perhaps he had been asked by the board of the Oxford Estates to carry out some business on their behalf. Her father might have seized on the chance to visit India again so soon. She longed to get him alone and ask him; he was obviously reluctant to talk about it in front of the Roys.

They went inside for dinner and then James, looking tired out, retired to bed.

'We'll talk more in the morning,' he told Libby, dropping a kiss on her forehead.

Libby was up at dawn. James was already shaved, dressed and drinking tea on the veranda. His face was grey and drawn as if he hadn't slept.

'Walk with me in the garden, Libby,' he said.

For a few minutes he talked about the family at home, the new house in Jesmond and the holiday she had missed in St Abbs. Libby listened to this chit-chat and curbed her impatience to know the real purpose of his visit.

Eventually she asked, 'Are you really here on business or is this just to make sure I come home?'

He stopped and looked at her. 'Are you coming home?'

Libby struggled with her thoughts. Part of her felt she was just biding her time till the right moment came to leave India. She had been filling every waking moment with activity, putting off that moment. But standing in the dawn light with the sounds of the city stirring beyond the garden wall, the answer seemed simple.

'No, Dad, I'm not,' she said quietly. 'I'm sorry. I know I said I would. I've disappointed you both again. But I don't think of Newcastle as home. To me, this is home now – Calcutta.'

He asked gently, 'Is this because of your Indian friend – Rafi's brother? The Roys have told me what's been going on. I know I was dismissive of your friendship with him but I'm very sorry to hear he's missing.'

Libby felt her heart ache with sadness. There was hardly a moment of each waking day when she didn't think about Ghulam.

'No, it's not because of Ghulam.' She tried to explain her feelings. 'I miss him terribly – I was very much in love with him – and he with me. But I don't hold out hope that he's still alive.' She gulped back tears. 'I want to stay in India anyway. I feel I can be more useful here. What would I do in Newcastle? The thought of going back to the bank or being at the beck and call of some boss would be too depressing. I don't fit in there like my brothers do.'

At that James gave her a wry smile. 'Oh, Libby, you are so like me. No wonder your mother despairs of us.'

Libby wanted to ask him what it was really like for him at home. From the little he had said about the house in Jesmond, he seemed to be making an effort to be reconciled with her mother. But his next question surprised her.

'Libby, can you take me to meet Danny Dunlop?'

She stared at him. 'Yes, but why? Do you have information for him?'

James nodded.

'So Mr Fairfax remembered the family?' Libby asked.

James gave out a long sigh. 'In a way, yes. But it is I who must do the explaining.'

Libby was baffled. 'What do you mean?'

'Something that's been preying on my mind,' he replied, 'that I should have faced up to a long time ago . . .' His expression was tense. 'That's why I've come back.'

Libby guessed that it must have something to do with her father's previous fragile state of mind but she thought it better not to press him further. If he wanted to tell her, he would in his own time.

'Of course I'll take you,' said Libby. 'Mr Dunlop has been keen to meet you – he'll be delighted.'

James gave her a strange wistful look but said nothing. She put her arm through his and together they returned to the house.

⁂

An invitation to Sudder Street came back by return. The following day Libby took her father to meet the Dunlops.

'Flowers won't be back from honeymoon yet,' she said, 'so it will just be the parents. Do you want me to stay or meet you afterwards?'

'Stay,' said James firmly. 'You've had to deal with my erratic behaviour – you have a right to know what I have to say.'

Libby felt nervous at his words but he was treating her as an adult and she would give him whatever support he needed.

The Dunlops welcomed them enthusiastically with broad smiles and a lavish afternoon tea. Danny attempted to stand to greet his important guest.

'It's an honour to have you here, sir,' Danny said.

Libby thought how much happier and more invigorated he looked since his daughter's engagement and marriage.

'Please, there's no need,' James said, embarrassed by the younger man's deference.

'And so jolly kind of you to entertain our daughter at your home in Assam,' added Winnie.

As they took tea, Danny asked a string of questions about life in Newcastle.

'We hope one day to visit with our new son-in-law George,' said Danny. 'Don't we, dear?'

Winnie nodded. 'He is such a nice boy. We are very pleased for Flowers. I'm sorry you've missed her. Are you staying long in Calcutta?'

'No,' said James, 'not long.'

'Pity,' said Danny.

Libby could tell her father was trying to summon the courage to say what he had come to say. She could hardly bear to hear what it was but feared that he might leave without unburdening what weighed so heavily on his mind.

'Dad,' she coaxed, 'don't you have something to tell Mr Dunlop about Mr Fairfax?'

James shot her a look of alarm. Danny's face lit up in expectation.

'You've discovered something about my tea planting father?' he asked.

James pulled out a handkerchief and mopped his brow; he was the only one perspiring.

'I— I have something to tell you,' he began hesitantly. 'I'm not sure you will thank me – it's not what you might want . . . but when I saw the details, I realised . . .'

Libby, who was sitting next to her father, put a hand on his in encouragement. 'You mean the details in Flowers's letter about Mr Dunlop?'

He looked at her and for a moment she saw the fear in his eyes.

'So you remembered something?' she prompted.

James nodded. He took a deep breath and turned his gaze on Danny.

'Do you remember anything about your early childhood?' James asked.

Danny stroked his moustache. 'Very little. I'm sure I remember tea bushes though – and playing on a wide veranda – sitting next to the *punkah-wallah*.' He gave a half-laugh. 'I don't remember the names of my parents but I remember his; isn't that strange? Sunil Ram.'

Libby gasped and looked at her father. That was the name he had cried out in his nightmares at Cheviot View.

'I knew you as a boy,' said James, his voice trembling, 'until you were about three years old.'

Danny looked at him in astonishment. 'Really? Where was that?'

'At the Oxford Estates. That's where you were born.'

'Good heavens!' cried Danny. 'Did you work with my father?'

'Yes,' said James. Libby could see fresh beads of sweat pricking his brow.

'Fancy that!' Danny gave a puzzled smile. 'I thought you didn't know any Dunlops?'

'Your father wasn't called Dunlop,' said James, ploughing on. 'He was called Logan, Bill Logan. He was my boss in the 1890s when I first went to Assam.'

Libby stifled her astonishment. Bill Logan was Sophie and Sam's father.

'Logan had a . . .' James hesitated. 'Before he was married he had a relationship with your mother. She was a beautiful hill girl – a tea picker called Aruna.'

Libby saw Danny flush pink. 'No, I don't think that's right – my parents were both British – that's what I was told.'

'I'm sorry, but that's not true. Your father decided that you must be sent away before he brought his newly married wife to the plantation. You looked too like him and he thought it would be awkward.'

'You're mistaken,' said Danny, red with indignation. 'Mixing me up with another boy.'

'No,' James insisted. 'There's no mistake. I was the man tasked with taking you to the orphanage in Shillong. I handed you over to Sister Placid at the Convent of the Sisters of the Holy Cross. I even gave you your name, Aidan. I chose it at random – named you after a local saint from my home county of Northumberland – because you never had a Christian name up till then. Sister Placid must have given you your surname. There were never any Dunlops working on the plantations in Assam in those days.'

Danny stared at James as if trying to recall a distant memory. 'There was a big man who led me into the convent . . . ?'

'That was me. I think you remember me, don't you?' James said. 'I certainly never forgot you.'

Danny looked stunned. He was speechless.

Winnie said in agitation, 'Why are you telling my husband this? Why come all this way to upset him? I was right; nothing good comes of digging up the past. Let sleeping dogs lie; that's what I say.'

Danny held up his hand to ward off her criticism. 'What was my father like?'

James hesitated. 'Tea planting was a hard life and Logan was a hard man. Work hard, play harder, was his motto. But he was fond of you. If Logan loved anyone in his life then it would have been you, Aidan. He certainly liked you more than the children from his marriage.'

Libby winced at his bluntness. She was as shocked as Danny was at the revelation; the man sitting opposite her – Flowers's father – was Sophie and Sam's illegitimate half-brother.

Abruptly Danny put his face in his hands and let out a sob. Winnie rushed to comfort him.

'I f-feel s-such a f-fool!' Danny cried. 'Thinking I was B-British to the core. I feel s-so ashamed.'

Winnie gave James a despairing look. 'I think it best if you go. I don't want you to see my husband like this.'

Libby stood up but James leant across the table and gripped Danny's arm. 'You shouldn't feel ashamed! It was Logan who was in the wrong, not your mother and not you. You were a lively, happy boy – a loving boy – always singing and playing around the burra bungalow, helping Sunil Ram with the *punkah* and following your father like his shadow.'

Libby could see the effect of her father's words on the distraught man; tears were coursing down his cheeks.

'Dad,' she cautioned.

James's voice grew urgent. 'I'm not telling you all this just to unburden myself of the guilt I have felt all these years for doing Logan's dirty work – though God knows I've been plagued by it. It's because you have a right to know and the not-knowing has been haunting you all your life too, I'm sure of that. The worst thing is to bottle up secrets and let them fester. That's what I've done and it's poisoned my life. I can no longer live with such destructive secrets.'

He hung on to Danny's arm. 'So I want to tell you this: you may have had a flawed man as your father but your mother was a good woman. She loved you dearly – would have done anything to protect you. I have never seen a mother adore a child as much as she did you, Aidan.'

Danny looked at him in disbelief. 'But she didn't protect me, did she? She let me go.'

'She tried to keep you,' James insisted, 'hid you in the lines, hoping Logan would forget to banish you, but you kept returning to the burra bungalow. I was ordered to take you away. Your brave mother ran after us, shouting for you, distraught at losing you.'

'She did?' Danny questioned.

James nodded, suddenly overcome, sinking back into his chair. Libby was alarmed to see he looked on the verge of tears too.

'I remember riding high above the tea bushes,' Danny whispered. 'There was a kind man holding me so I didn't fall.'

'Aslam,' James croaked, 'my bearer.'

Libby felt tears flood her own eyes at the mention of Manzur's father. James cleared his throat.

'Your mother couldn't live without you, Aidan. She never got over you being taken away – never understood why the sahibs were being so cruel. While Logan was away fetching his new bride, Aruna took her own life. That is how much she loved you.'

Danny bowed his head and broke down weeping. Winnie put her head next to his and murmured soothingly. 'It's over, Danny. Now you know. There's nothing left to worry about. You knew a mother's love. You always said you had a vague memory of a kind ayah. It must have been your mother, Danny – your mother.'

James stood up, patted Danny's shoulder and turned to go. Libby followed. As they reached the door Winnie said, 'Mr Robson?'

James paused, holding the door for Libby.

'Thank you for coming and telling Danny the truth,' she said.

James nodded as Libby led the way out.

⁂

That evening, after the Roys had retired to bed, James told Libby the full story of the Logan affair over a late nightcap. She was still reeling from his revelation about Danny's parentage and his cruel banishment. How could Sophie and Sam's father have been such a callous man?

'It was Sunil Ram who raised the alarm about Aruna,' James recalled. 'I thought everything was under control and the affair could be forgotten. Until he took me to the bungalow.'

'The Lodge?' Libby queried.

'Yes, or Dunsapie Cottage as it was called in those days.' James struggled to describe what he had found. 'She must have slipped past

Sunil Ram. She – she was – Aruna was lying there – there was blood soaking the bed – she'd cut her wrists. Oh, God! The smell of blood!'

Libby thought her father was about to vomit, so vivid was the memory. She fought back her own nausea.

'It was in that room on the left, wasn't it?' she asked.

'Yes,' said James. 'How did you know that?'

'Flowers had a bad feeling in there – she was really shaken up – don't you remember?'

James sighed. 'I was in such a state I don't remember what was real and what I dreamt. I'd got to the stage where I was reliving it all every night – whenever I closed my eyes I couldn't get it out of my head.'

Libby reached out and took his hand. 'Oh, Dad, what a terrible burden to carry all these years. Did you never tell anyone?'

James shook his head. 'I tried to forget. Do you know the worst of it? Logan never even asked about Aruna or the boy again – *never*! He was monstrous.'

Libby shook her head in disgust. 'How could a man like that produce such loving children as Sophie and Sam – and Flowers's father?'

'Perhaps because they had loving mothers,' James answered. 'Not that any of them had their mothers for long, poor things. I feel so very guilty that I couldn't save either of those poor women from Logan. At least with Jessie Anderson I tried to save her – went to see her and begged her to leave Bill Logan – but I let Aruna down so badly.' He gave a tortured sigh. 'Flowers reminded me of her grandmother Aruna – she has the same eyes . . .'

'So that's why you were so ill at ease having Flowers to stay?' Libby guessed. 'It probably triggered off your bad memories again. I'm sorry if I made things difficult for you by bringing her along.'

'No, it wasn't your fault,' James said quickly, 'or Flowers's. She's a delightful young woman. It was me being such a coward and not facing up to what I'd done. I'd spent most of my life trying to pretend Aruna's death never happened.'

Libby sat, absorbing everything her father had confessed. Finally she asked, 'Does Mother know what you've come all this way for?'

James gave her a wistful smile. 'It was Tilly who suggested I do so.'

'Really?' Libby exclaimed.

'After I went to visit Fairfax,' said James, 'the nightmares began again. Your mother kept on asking questions until I told her what was haunting me. Tilly made me realise that I couldn't escape what troubled me by putting thousands of miles between me and the source of my mental anguish. I would solve nothing by running away from my past. She has your tenacity, Libby. And your ability to make people confide their secrets.'

'Good for Mother,' Libby said in admiration. 'She succeeded where I failed. Flowers knew there was something very wrong and that you needed help.' After a moment she added, 'Will you be all right?'

James squeezed her hand. 'You don't need to worry about me.'

'It's good that you and Mother have cleared the air,' said Libby. 'It'll make it easier when you go back.'

James slipped his hand out of hers. He took a swig of his whisky. Quietly he said, 'I'm not going back.'

Libby thought she had misheard. 'What?'

James said, 'Your mother and I are separating. It's amicable. Well, by that I mean there won't be any wrangling over who keeps what.'

'Dad!' Libby cried in dismay. Her stomach knotted.

James held her look. 'You can't pretend it comes as any great shock. Your mother and I haven't seen eye to eye in years. She's happy in Newcastle – very happy – with the new house and her committees, and the boys nearby and Josey as her companion – and a ridiculous new dog called Fluff. She doesn't need me. It's taken me a long time to realise it, but I don't need her either. We had some very happily married years together and we love our children; we still care about each other – but not enough to stay together now.'

Libby's heart drummed at the unsettling news. The thing she had feared ever since war had separated her parents was now coming to fruition: the break-up of their marriage. She had yearned for them to be reconciled – had badgered them both to return to each other – but it hadn't worked. Had she tried hard enough? She should have gone home with her father when he'd wanted her to and maybe she could have helped him settle down better in Newcastle. She could have stuck up for her dad in the face of her mother's criticism.

But maybe that was being unfair to Tilly. By the sounds of it, she had tried to understand James's deep unhappiness – had got him finally to talk about what distressed him – and had encouraged him to face Danny Dunlop with the truth. Her mother had shown greater understanding than she, Libby, had towards her father's mental state – and a good deal of tolerance towards his desire to leave her. Tilly would no doubt set the tongues wagging at home for separating from her husband. She risked censure from her friends at church and colleagues on her charitable committees. Yet rather than try to paper over the cracks in their marriage, Tilly was allowing James to be free to return to India.

Libby attempted to absorb the enormity of what it meant. She swallowed hard, trying to stem the feeling of panic she felt at this sea change in her parents' relationship.

'What will you do?' she asked.

'I'm staying on,' he said with a tired smile, 'like you.'

'In Calcutta?' Libby asked in sudden excitement.

James took another sip of his drink and said, 'I'm thinking of settling in Shillong. The Percy-Barratts have moved up there and I have other old friends in the area.'

Libby slid him a look. 'Such as Clarrie?'

Even on the dimly lit veranda, she could see her father's face redden. 'I suppose Clarrie is nearby too – yes, that's true.'

Libby laughed at his coyness. 'She misses you too, Dad,' she said. 'A lot, as a matter of fact.'

'How the devil would you know?' James blustered.

'Because she told me,' Libby said, smiling. 'She said how fond she had grown of you – and Harry too. He talks to Breckon about you – I've heard him. If you go to Shillong you'll see him a lot, seeing as he's at school there. A lot more than you did your own children.'

James said, 'Do you still resent us for sending you away? I know it was particularly hard for you, Libby. It wasn't your mother's fault – she would have kept you here if she could. I was the one thought it would do you all good. I regret that now.'

Libby felt a pang of sadness. It confirmed her increasing awareness that her mother had not been to blame for her long, isolated years at boarding school. Tilly had suffered just as much being separated from her children – including her. Her mother's regular, affectionate letters were proof of that.

'It's pointless staying resentful,' Libby replied. 'I've come to realise that. And I'm doing what I want now.'

'You'll be welcome in Shillong if you decide you want to do your teaching there,' said James. 'You know you will always have a home with me.'

She felt a wave of affection for him. 'Thanks, Dad. But I'm going to try and make a go of it here. I'll soon have enough put by to rent my own place. There're a couple of Flowers's friends who are looking for a third person to share a flat with, so I won't be a burden to the Roys for much longer.'

James reached out and took her hand, squeezing it in his large one. For a moment he just held on to her but then he cleared his throat.

'I wasn't very kind about your young man,' he said. 'I'm sorry about that now.'

Libby felt a renewed stab of loss. 'Ghulam?'

'Yes, Ghulam.' His eyes shone with pity. 'That's another thing your mother taught me – not to be so judgemental about people – or perhaps that was Clarrie's doing.'

Libby's eyes smarted. 'I think you would have had more in common with Ghulam than either of you realised,' she said reflectively. 'Both single-minded about your work and both loving India with a passion. I wish you had met each other.'

James said gently, 'Is there really no chance that he's still alive?'

Tears flooded the back of Libby's throat. 'It's my greatest wish that he is,' she said hoarsely. 'I will never love anyone else as much as him.'

She expected her father to come out with some comforting platitude that she was still so young and was bound to love again. But he surprised her.

'If you loved him so much, Libby, then he must have been a good man. I too am sorry that I never met him.'

'Thank you,' she whispered.

He squeezed her hand. They sat in silence, each lost in their own thoughts. Libby had never felt closer to her father than in that moment. It wasn't the same as her childish adoration of him; it was a mature feeling of love and mutual understanding.

After a while, James raised his glass in his other hand. 'To you, Libby,' he said with a tender smile. 'To my amazing, intrepid daughter!' He finished off his drink.

Drained by the day's events, they both went swiftly to bed. Despite the shock revelations of the past few hours, Libby slept soundly for the first time in days.

CHAPTER 43

In early November, James left for Shillong. Libby promised she would visit him at Christmas. She had received a letter from Clarrie reassuring her that the situation in Gulgat had calmed down. After her complaints to the police, the Rajah Sanjay had disciplined Sen and promised that there would be no more trouble from the princely state. As an apology, he had sent Clarrie a gift of a Bentley motorcar filled with flowers and fruit.

It's totally impractical on Belgooree roads! Clarrie had written in amusement. *But I can sell it and invest the money in the factory.*

'Perhaps we can get together with Clarrie and the family?' Libby suggested to her father before departure. 'She and Harry will be so happy to have Adela and Sam back home again. And Belgooree is like a second home to me now.'

James looked pleased at the idea. 'Perhaps we could ask ourselves over for a couple of days of *shikar*?'

'Does Clarrie know you're back in India?' Libby asked.

Her father reddened. 'I haven't had time . . . I'll get in touch when I'm settled . . . don't want to be a nuisance.'

After James had gone, Libby wrote to Clarrie and told her about her father's move to Shillong. She didn't want Clarrie to get a shock on seeing James just turn up out of the blue with no explanation or warning. Her father might be cross with her for interfering but that would be nothing new. It would give Clarrie time to absorb the news that James and Tilly had separated, and allow her to work out her own feelings.

Libby also wrote to her mother to say she was sorry about the separation and that she blamed neither parent; it was the long years of being apart and growing apart that had been the cause. Encouraged by her father's sympathy over Ghulam, she confided in her mother too, pouring out her feelings about Ghulam and her huge sense of bereavement. It was a long, affectionate letter also telling Tilly about Flowers's and George's wedding, her typing lessons, how she was moving into a flat in Theatre Road with new friends and that her father had been very courageous in telling Danny Dunlop about his past.

> *. . . What a terrible man Bill Logan was! I don't suppose we should ever say anything to Sophie or Sam about the callous things he did. He caused them enough traumas as it is, without burdening them with more.*
>
> *Dad said that it was you who encouraged him to return to India and tell Mr Dunlop the truth about his parents. That was brave of you too, Mother – to help Dad face up to his past and not just brush things under the carpet – to let Dad go. Even before he left Calcutta, he was looking better – younger – as if a huge weight had been lifted from his shoulders. He sounds happy in Shillong. I hope you are happy too, Mother.*
>
> *As for me, I'm going to stay in Calcutta for the time being. I have interesting work here and I hope to make a difference to the lives of the children I teach, however tiny a contribution that is in the great play of things. Ghulam would have wanted me to do it – and I feel closer to him here in Calcutta, so that brings a bit of comfort too.*

Perhaps next year I'll come back to Newcastle for a visit. Please give my love to the boys and Josey – and dear Lexy if you see her. But most of all, I send my love to you, Mother, and hope you understand why I'm staying on in India.

Your loving daughter,

Libby xxx

Libby resumed her work and kept fully occupied, expanding the number of hours she helped with Sanjeev's free school and taking on more students for typing and bookkeeping. She moved out of the Roys' comfortable home but continued to visit them once a week, knowing how they missed their own daughters who lived hundreds of miles away.

She heard back from Tilly. Her mother's letter was an emotional one: full of thanks for Libby's understanding over the separation and warm words of sympathy about her grief for Ghulam.

. . . of course you miss him! He was the love of your life – and by the sounds of it, you were his. My heart goes out to you, my darling. But there are women in this world who have never known that depth of love for a man, so at least you have had that. Dearest Libby, I can't deny I'm disappointed that you're not coming home but I don't give up hope that you will! Your room is ready and waiting in the new Jesmond house whenever you decide to come. I'm afraid Fluff thinks of it as hers and I often catch her curled up on your bed – it's such a warm room and gets all the south-facing sunshine.

Darling girl! Take care of yourself. Try not to be too sad. Enjoy your time in Calcutta – and keep an eye on

*your father when you can. I want you to know that I do
care what happens to him, even though I don't want to
be with him.*

    Lots of love,

    Mother x

Libby stored away the letter with her most precious possessions – her cherished letters from Ghulam and a photograph of him in cricket whites, grinning and smoking, that Sanjeev had given her.

One November afternoon, as the light was fading and she was rubbing down the chalkboard at the end of the children's lesson, a shadow fell across the doorway. Libby glanced round. It took her a moment to realise that it was Fatima. She looked extremely agitated. Libby's heart jumped in alarm.

'Fatima, what is it?' Libby hurried towards her.

The doctor was shaking and gulping, trying to speak. 'He . . . he's . . .'

Libby felt fear claw her stomach. This was the moment she had dreaded: when she finally discovered Ghulam's fate.

'Tell me,' Libby urged. 'Is it Ghulam? Is he dead? Please tell me!'

Fatima reached out, seizing Libby's hands as if to save herself from falling, and began sobbing. Libby held her, her heart pounding so much she could hardly breathe.

Fatima made a supreme effort to control herself and speak. 'He's alive,' she rasped. 'My brother's alive!'

Libby almost fainted with shock. 'Ghulam's alive?' she gasped.

'Yes!' Fatima cried, half sobbing, half laughing.

Libby was suddenly choked with emotion. Ghulam alive? It wasn't possible! She clutched Fatima.

'How do you know?' Libby demanded. 'Where is he?'

'Come!' Fatima said. 'Come now. He's at Sanjeev's. He's asking for you.' Fatima began pulling her through the door.

The street children crowded around them, peering in astonishment at the crying women. Libby stumbled after Fatima, loosing a torrent of questions in between sobs of emotion.

'How is he? Is he all right? How did he get here? Where's he been?'

'He's very weak,' Fatima said tearfully, hurrying along the street. 'He's had a terrible time. Robbed in Delhi. I've dressed his wounds again.'

'Wounds?' Libby cried in horror.

'But he's alive,' Fatima repeated in triumph. 'I never gave up hoping.'

In minutes they were at Sanjeev's flat. Fatima almost pushed Libby through the door. The room was already lit with a lamp. Libby stared. Half prone on Sanjeev's *charpoy*, propped up on a bolster, was a man resembling Ghulam. He was thinner – his gaunt face bearded – and his hair was long and unkempt. But when he caught sight of her and smiled, Libby's heart swelled with emotion.

'Ghulam!' Quickly she went to him.

'Libby,' he whispered, attempting to sit up. He winced in pain.

'Don't move,' she said, sitting down gently on the edge of the bed and taking his hand. The skin was rough and nicked with cuts. She put it tenderly to her cheek, tears stinging her eyes. 'How is this possible?'

He gazed at her, his green eyes huge in his drawn face. 'You stayed,' he said in wonder. 'I thought you would have left long ago.'

'This is where I belong,' she answered. She kissed the palm of his hand.

She held his look, not wanting to blink and miss a moment of seeing him, proving to her disbelieving eyes that it was her beloved Ghulam and he was really alive.

'What happened to you?' she asked. 'I thought you were d-dead.' She sobbed over the word.

Ghulam took her hand and kissed it in return. 'By rights I should be,' he said, pain passing over his face. 'I was left for dead . . .'

'You don't have to speak of it now,' Libby said hastily. 'It's just enough that you've come back to me – to us.' She looked around but Fatima and Sanjeev had left them alone. She could hear them talking in the corridor.

Libby leant closer to Ghulam and smoothed the hair from his brow.

'Sanjeev gave me your letter,' she said with a tender smile. 'I know it by heart. It's the most precious thing I possess. I missed you so much – I would read it whenever my spirits were low. Just to know that you loved me . . .'

Tears spilled down Libby's face.

'You stayed,' he repeated, brushing at her tears with his roughened fingers. 'Does that mean you won't be going back to Britain?'

'No, I won't be,' said Libby. 'I've made up my mind to live in Calcutta. I have work here and friends – and now I've got you.'

'So you feel the same way?' Ghulam asked, his look searching.

'Of course I do,' Libby replied. 'I wrote you a letter from Belgooree to tell you about your father being ill – but also to say how much I loved you and always would love you. I sent it to Amelia Buildings, thinking you were still there.'

Ghulam smiled his broad uneven smile and Libby's heart melted.

'Then we love each other,' he said simply.

'Yes.' Libby smiled and leant towards him, kissing his cracked lips.

He reached for her and she put her arms about him. Suddenly he flinched and Libby realised he was bandaged under his shirt.

'Sorry.' She pulled back. 'Are you badly hurt?'

'I can bear any pain if you'll stay with me,' Ghulam said with a wincing smile.

She curled up next to him and stroked his face until he fell asleep.

Darkness fell and Fatima left for her hospital digs before it grew too late. Libby rose to go too but Ghulam stirred, fretful.

'Don't leave, Libby,' he murmured.

Sanjeev said, 'I will sleep next door with friends. Knock if you need anything.'

Left alone together with Libby, Ghulam sighed in contentment and fell asleep again.

In the hour before dawn, Ghulam said in a hoarse voice, 'Are you awake?'

Libby, who had hardly slept for watching over him, whispered, 'Yes. Is there something you need? Water?'

He nodded. She helped him sip. Then he began to talk, telling her in hesitant words what had happened to him. He had arrived safely in Delhi but had been appalled at the sight of the huge refugee camps stretching out on the broiling plain. Aghast at the scale of the misery and then the frantic scramble at the aerodrome of families trying to leave India for Pakistan, Ghulam had had second thoughts.

On the point of boarding the aeroplane to Lahore, he had given up his seat to a distraught young woman who feared being separated from her family. It struck him how his desire to see his father one more time was selfish in the face of the panic and terror around him. He was taking up a valuable place on the plane just to indulge his daydream of being reconciled with a long-lost father. In contrast, this woman's life was in the balance as to whether she got safely to Pakistan or was left behind.

'So I gave up my seat. I knew that my father would have approved. We never agreed on much, but he believed strongly in charity and help-ing the stranger.'

'That was a great kindness,' said Libby.

'I wrote a brief letter to my father and family,' Ghulam continued, 'and asked her to deliver it when she got to Lahore. It was only much later that I realised the letter had never reached them. I had asked them to tell Fatima . . .' Ghulam's jaw clenched in anguish. 'I never meant to cause so much distress.'

Libby kissed his cheek. 'She knows that.'

After a moment Ghulam carried on. 'I knew my boss at the newspaper wasn't expecting me back for a month or more, so I decided to stay and help in the camps. It was mostly manual labour – digging latrines and such – but I felt I was of most use speaking to the refugees in their native Punjabi. They were so homesick and traumatised by what they had been through. To protect myself, I pretended to be Christian. I knew enough from school to pass as one. The stories they told . . . unspeakable things . . .'

Ghulam broke off. Libby slipped her arm gently around him and held him close. He swallowed.

'Then, after about six weeks, I decided it was time to return to Calcutta. I had just enough money left to buy a ticket. On the way to buying it, I was knifed and robbed.' His breathing grew rapid as he relived the attack. 'I remember lying in the street, helpless, and then I must have passed out.'

He turned to look at her, his eyes glinting. 'The only reason I'm alive is because a chai-wallah came to my rescue – took me back to the one room he shared with a dozen others and stopped the bleeding. They were a Hindu family. They must have known what I was – they nursed me for a fortnight – but when gangs came round looking for Muslims, not one of them gave me away.'

'How brave and kind of them,' said Libby, feeling immense gratitude towards these people she would never meet.

'Once I could stand and walk again,' said Ghulam, 'I knew I had to go – they had little to spare and I had already taken so much.'

'So how on earth did you get back to Calcutta?' Libby asked. 'You were destitute.'

'I was. I thought of going to beg at the door of an old friend,' he said, his jaw tensing.

'Cordelia's?' Libby questioned.

He started. 'How did you know?'

'I know she came from Delhi,' she said. 'I wouldn't have blamed you.'

'But I didn't,' said Ghulam, 'because something extraordinary happened. I was making my way to her home in New Delhi – I'd stopped to rest in Connaught Circus – when a car drew up beside me and a man in uniform got out. He was Sikh – I recognised his uniform: it was the Lahore Horse – Rafi's old regiment. He stared at me and asked me if I was Ghulam Khan.'

'Who was he?' asked Libby.

'Rafi's old friend Sundar Singh,' said Ghulam. 'Rafi had asked him to search Delhi for me in case I was there and still alive—' Ghulam stifled a sob. 'He had been looking for me for weeks. It was only then that I realised that my family had never got my letter . . .'

'We thought you must have taken the train to Lahore,' Libby said. 'I didn't think you could have survived – you'd been missing too long. But Rafi and Fatima never gave up believing you were out there somewhere.'

'If Rafi hadn't told Sundar to look for me,' Ghulam rasped, 'I might never have got back.'

Suddenly the relief of survival and the knowledge of his brother's love was too overwhelming. Ghulam began to weep. Libby cradled him close until he gained control of his emotions and was able to finish his story.

Sundar had rescued him, given him a hot meal and a change of clothes, and put Ghulam on a train back to Calcutta with enough provisions and money to complete his journey. By now, Rafi would probably have heard from Sundar about his brother's rescue. Libby assured him that, if not, Fatima would get a message through to Rafi and the extended family in Pakistan anyway.

As the dawn light filtered between the shutters, Ghulam turned his face to Libby's with an intent look. His voice turned deep and steady as he spoke.

'I want us never to be parted again,' he said.

Her heart jolted. She cupped his bearded face with her hand. 'I want that too. I can't describe how happy I feel that we're here together. I thought I'd never feel you next to me again.'

Ghulam leant towards her and kissed her mouth. He gazed at her with a loving smile. 'I know this sounds bourgeois, but I want to marry you, Libby.'

She gave him a wry smile. 'Good – 'cause that's what I want too.'

'It is?' He looked at her in delight. 'Are you sure?'

'Ghulam, if it means I can stay with you forever, then yes!' She grinned.

'Oh, my darling goddess!' Ghulam pressed his lips against hers and kissed her as robustly as he could, sealing their pledge.

Libby, her heart bursting with joy, kissed him back. She was filled with a renewed optimism about the future, the plans and dreams that Ghulam had written about in his love letter to her. They would work and live together side by side in the new India, enjoying the good moments and sharing the bad.

She had been prepared to face a future in Calcutta without him – but how much richer her life would be now that Ghulam had come back to her! As Libby kissed him and felt overwhelming love for Ghulam, she knew with an utter certainty that each of them had found their true soulmate.

EPILOGUE

Belgooree, early December

A t dawn Clarrie rode along the path through the jungle up towards the temple clearing. She knew it so well that every tree and bend in the track was familiar. The jungle was alive with birdsong. As she reached the shadowed glade, dew was already glistening on the ferns and grass as the sun spread across it.

She dismounted and went to lay a posy of flowers on one of the stones from the monkey temple that had collapsed into ruins long ago.

'For you, dear Ayah Mimi,' Clarrie murmured.

She gazed at the tumble-down hut where Sophie's old nursemaid had once lived as a holy woman before Clarrie had brought her to live at Belgooree well over twenty years ago. The old woman had never recovered from her exertions on the night of the Gulgat attack. Exhausted, the *sadhvi* had been carried back to her hut. She had never emerged again. Two weeks later, when Clarrie had taken her daily bowl of milk, eager to let Ayah Mimi know that Sophie was safely in Calcutta, she had found the old woman cold and lifeless on her sleeping mat.

The ayah had protected her beloved Sophie right to the end. Perhaps she had felt able to let go of life, knowing that Sophie had got safely away. Clarrie was sure that the *sadhvi* had known without being told.

Clarrie sat down on a damp stone and breathed in the earthy smell of vegetation, watching the sky lighten in the east to a vivid peacock blue.

How long ago it seemed when she had ridden here on her pony, Prince, as an impulsive eighteen-year-old and fallen from the saddle – only to be rescued by the handsome Wesley Robson.

Clarrie smiled wistfully. How infuriating and arrogant he had been that day – yet so attractive and full of life. They had both been so young and foolishly confident, not guessing at all the trials ahead of them – separation and war, loss and heartbreak. Yet Clarrie would have gone through it all again rather than miss a minute of her precious time with Wesley. Sitting here in the place where they had first met, forty-five years later, Clarrie still felt as alive and young at heart as she had then.

How she missed him! She wished he could have known about Adela marrying kind Sam – and that the young couple were expecting a baby. Clarrie felt her heart lift at the thought of a new life being born at Belgooree in the spring. The start of the next generation. She had so much still to be thankful for.

She knew how her passionate daughter grieved for the son she had left behind in Britain. Adela had shown her the precious photograph that Sam had taken of Adela with John Wesley – the likeness to his grandfather Wesley was heartbreaking. Yet Adela had been cheered by a letter from Martha Gibson promising that when Jacques turned twenty-one, he would be told about his true parentage and the origin of the swami's stone. None of them knew how the boy would react to discovering he was John Wesley, the son of an Indian prince and a tea planter's daughter. That was far in the future but she knew how it gave Adela comfort and hope.

Clarrie felt the winter sun warming her face as it strengthened. Harry would be home soon for the Christmas holidays. She felt a familiar fierce tug of love for her dark-haired, lively son. Then there was James . . .

Clarrie had been unnerved by Libby's letter – kind, interfering, generous-hearted Libby – telling her of James's return. She had not been able to settle for days for thinking about this development. What did it mean? Why Shillong? Was it to be near his old tea planting friends for fishing and hunting? Or was it because it was a couple of hours from Belgooree and her?

She would know soon enough. Clarrie had taken Libby's hint that she invite her and James to Belgooree over Christmas. She had replied at once, insisting that Libby and her father must join them on Christmas Eve for the holidays. Just two days ago, she had received a phone call from a joyous Libby telling her excitedly of Ghulam's miraculous return and their swift engagement. At once, Clarrie had invited Ghulam too. How Libby deserved her happiness! Despite the uncertain times, there was so much to be thankful for and celebrate this Christmas. Little had she thought she would be seeing James again so soon – if at all.

Clarrie's stomach fluttered with excitement. She gave a laugh of embarrassment that echoed against the rocky cliff that sheltered the glade. She was behaving like eighteen-year-old Clarrie Belhaven again and not the matron approaching sixty-two that she was! She stood up. She had lingered long enough. There were jobs to be done. The last of the autumn pickings had to be processed before she shut down the machines for the cold season.

Just then she heard a crackling of twigs and the soft thud of hooves. Clarrie turned to see if Adela or Sam had come to join her. The rider appeared on the edge of the clearing, a man in shadow with the light streaming in behind him. Clarrie gasped. For a shocking moment she thought it was Wesley. He sat up in the saddle, a silhouette of wavy hair and broad shoulders. Clarrie pressed her hand to her mouth to stifle a sob.

A deep voice disturbed the quiet. 'Clarrie? Are you all right?'

Clarrie felt a flicker of sadness. Wesley would have called her Clarissa.

It had never struck her quite so strongly as it did in that instant that the Robson cousins were passably alike.

'James,' Clarrie said, suddenly breathless. 'What are you doing here?'

He dismounted and walked into the light. Now she could see that his thick hair was white and his bullish face was not as handsome as Wesley's. Yet the penetrating gaze of his blue eyes was unsettling; it was the look of a much younger man.

'I'm looking for you of course,' he replied. 'Adela told me you'd be here but I'd already guessed.'

'You must have set off very early from Shillong,' she said, trying to slow the thumping of her heart.

'So you know about Shillong?' James asked in surprise.

'Libby wrote and told me,' said Clarrie.

James grunted. 'Of course she would.'

He stood several feet away, as if fearing to come nearer. It struck Clarrie that James was as unsure about her feelings for him as she was about his for her.

'What else did she tell you?' he asked.

'Everything,' said Clarrie. 'At least about you and Tilly. I'm sorry.'

'Don't be,' said James. 'Tilly isn't and neither am I.'

Clarrie felt suddenly awkward. 'Well, then I'm glad to see you back,' she admitted. They stood regarding each other. 'Have you had breakfast? You must be hungry after the journey,' she gabbled. 'You were up so early. Shall we—'

'Clarrie,' James blurted out, 'Libby said you'd confided in her about me – that you missed me – missed me a lot.'

Clarrie blushed. 'She shouldn't have. I said those things in confidence and asked her not to . . .'

'No, she was right to,' James said eagerly. 'Libby is usually right about matters of the heart. She knew I would do nothing unless I had a little encouragement.'

'Do nothing about what?' said Clarrie.

'About telling you how much I care for you,' James said, stepping nearer. 'I know I'm not half the man that Wesley was – can never replace him in your heart – but I love you, Clarrie.' He reached out and took her hands. 'I don't expect anything in return – I just hope you might hold me in a little affection – enough to put up with me coming over to visit now and again and for us to spend some time together.'

Clarrie felt a flood of love towards him. He was so boyishly gauche in her presence. She knew that inside this seventy-year-old man, a young, vigorous James was declaring his passion for her. She moved closer.

'Dear James.' She smiled. 'Of course I want us to spend time together.'

'Do you?' He looked amazed.

'Yes,' she laughed. 'A lot of time.'

She leant up and drew his face towards hers, giving him a lingering kiss on the lips, so that he would be in no doubt about how she felt. She saw the desire light in his eyes. James let out a cry of exultation.

'God, what a lucky man I am!'

He pulled her to him, wrapping strong arms about her slim body, and kissed her roundly. Clarrie felt suddenly light-headed. She had never thought to feel such a physical response again for a man. Strange that it should happen in this same romantic glade where she had first fallen in love so long ago. She gave thanks for second chances and for the spell that this magical place cast over the young at heart. She gave thanks too for Belgooree, her beloved Belgooree.

They broke apart, but she held on to his hands as she gazed at him lovingly.

'I want to share this place with you,' said Clarrie, 'if you want to. There's no other man alive who understands what Belgooree means to me as much as you do, James.'

She saw his eyes shimmer. 'Share it with me? What are you saying?'

'Come and live here with me,' Clarrie urged. 'I don't want to be alone any more.'

When he replied, his voice was full of emotion. 'Oh, my darling, nothing would give me greater joy. If you're sure that's what you want?'

Suddenly Clarrie was very sure. She loved James – not with the deep passion she had felt for Wesley, but with a tenderness that had grown out of strong friendship. They had gone through so much together and she knew they would make each other happy. Clarrie was also certain that her family would welcome this dear man into their home too – Harry would be ecstatic at the news.

Clarrie gave him a broad smile. 'Yes, James, that's what I want more than anything.' She leant up and kissed him again.

James laughed in delight and, like a man half his age, swept her up into his arms and carried her towards her pony.

The sun was filling the whole glade and warming their backs as Clarrie and James made their way down the jungle path towards the tea garden and the Belgooree bungalow – towards home.

Birth announcement:

A daughter, Samantha Clarissa Robson Jackman, was born on April 21st, 1948, at Belgooree Tea Estate, Assam, to Mrs Adela and Mr Samuel Jackman. Mother and baby are doing well.

GLOSSARY

bidis	cheap Indian cigarettes
bhang	ground up cannabis buds and leaves
burra	big, most important
bustee	slum
chaprassy	messenger, deliverer of post
chota	small, young
chota hazri	breakfast
chota peg	small alcoholic drink/sundowner
chowkidar	watchman, gatekeeper, doorman
chummery	living quarters for bachelors
dak	post, mail
dak bungalow	travellers' rest house
dhoti	loincloth/loosely wrapped trousers
ghat	quayside/wharf
godown	storage shed
goondas	hired thugs
Hindu Mahasabha	right wing nationalist party
jaldi!	Quickly!
khansama	male cook/house steward
khitmutgar	table servant/under butler

koi hai!	Anyone there! (greeting/command)
(old) koi hai	veteran of service in India
lathi	long stick/truncheon
lungi	sarong
mali	gardener
mofussil	countryside
mohurer	bookkeeper
nimbu pani	lemon drink
paan	stimulant made of betel leaf and areca nut
punkah	a cloth fan that worked by pulling a rope
punkah-wallah	man who worked the *punkah*
sadhvi	Hindu holy woman
sahib-log	British in India
shikar	hunting
swami	Hindu holy man/teacher
swaraj	freedom
syce	groom/stable boy
topee	sunhat

AUTHOR'S NOTE

My grandfather, Robert Maclagan Gorrie (known as Bob, or sometimes a touch disparagingly by the 'heaven-born' in India as Jungli-Gorrie), served in the India Forest Service from 1922 until Independence in 1947. He was a forest officer in the Punjab, beginning in Lahore, Changa Manga and Rawalpindi, and then in Simla and Bashahr Province (in the Himalayan foothills) with secondments to Dehra Dun as lecturer in the Forest Institute and 'foreign service' in independent Mandi State in the 1930s. He became an expert on soil erosion and conservation but the big promotions eluded him in the British Raj, perhaps because as a forthright Scot he spoke his mind in ways that weren't always diplomatic. While acknowledging his huge enthusiasm, energy and initiative – calling him 'a tiger for work' – his superiors noted that 'in his early years he was considered to have rather too high an opinion of himself and to require suppressing' and was 'apt to ignore procedure and financial implications'.

My grandmother, Sydney Easterbrook, was equally intrepid, travelling out from Edinburgh to Lahore to marry in 1923 and live the itinerant life of a forester's wife. She defied one of Bob's bosses by insisting on going into camp with her husband for months at a time rather than being left behind to fill in the endless hours of cantonment life with other British wives. When my mother Sheila was born, they took her with them and she was carried into the mountains along with the camping equipment!

In other respects they enjoyed the social life typical of the British ex-pats; both were keen tennis players and were very sociable with a wide circle of friends and their letters and diaries mention numerous fancy-dress parties and dinners, especially around Christmas and New Year. Looking back, my Uncle Duncan (their second child) thought that his parents were probably unusual in that they had Indian friends at a time when Raj society was rigidly segregated. They appear to have had the most diverse friendships in Lahore, which was a cosmopolitan city with a rich heritage and mix of people.

During the Second World War Bob was seconded to the Army to help with timber supply and products. Based in Jubbulpore, his job took him all over India. My grandmother, who had gone back to Edinburgh in the summer of 1939 to see her ailing parents, was separated from Bob for the duration of the War. She remained in Scotland doing voluntary work and providing a home for the children when they were home from boarding school. After the War Bob returned to the Punjab as Deputy Conservator of Forests in charge of the Silvicultural Research Division. With Independence approaching, Bob (unlike many of the British) was determined to try and secure a job in the new India. With his expertise in the Punjab, it was the newly formed state of Pakistan who offered him a position. On the 15th of August 1947 my grandfather was in his new post and attending the Independence Day celebrations in Rawalpindi 'in a heavy shower of rain'.

While Sydney chose to remain in Edinburgh, Bob continued to work for the Pakistan Government until the end of 1949. In mid-December eighty people attended his leaving dinner. The following day Bob left with a handshake to all the staff, a lump in his throat and clutching a shield bearing the names of twenty-three colleagues and an inscription thanking him for his years of service:

To R Maclagan Gorrie, D Sc., F.R.S.E., I.F.S.
Pioneer of Soil Conservation
in the Indo-Pakistan Sub-Continent
From
His Pakistani Colleagues
as a mark of
Esteem and Love
on his retirement from Pakistan
17th Dec. 1949

The India Tea Series, though not directly based on my grandparents' story, draws some of its inspiration from their experiences of being British in India, their observations, their daily lives, the Indian background and settings – and the emotional hold that the Subcontinent continued to exert over them long after they had retired back to Scotland.

(You can read more about my child's eye view of Bob and Sydney in Edinburgh in my childhood memoirs *Beatles & Chiefs*.)

ACKNOWLEDGMENTS

The India Tea Series would not have been possible without the rich archive of my grandparents' diaries, letters and cine films that survived all the upheavals of the twentieth century. For that – and the oral stories that my mother, Sheila, shared with me – I am immensely grateful.

I would also like to thank my wonderful editors at Lake Union: Sammia Hamer for commissioning the fourth tea novel and Victoria Pepe for guiding it to publication. Also, many thanks to Sophie Wilson for her wise and helpful comments, to Jill Sawyer for her careful copy-editing, Elizabeth Cochrane for eagle-eyed proofreading, and to Bekah Graham for her continued amazing author-support. Altogether a remarkable team!

I would like to acknowledge the National Archives as the source for the quotes from Mountbatten's speech about Partition, which was broadcast in June 1947 and reported in *The Times* (CAB 21/2038).

ABOUT THE AUTHOR

 Janet MacLeod Trotter is the author of numerous bestselling and acclaimed novels, including *The Hungry Hills*, which was nominated for the Sunday Times Young Writer of the Year Award, and *The Tea Planter's Daughter*, which was nominated for the Romantic Novelists' Association Novel of the Year Award. Much informed by her own experiences, MacLeod Trotter was raised in the north-east of England by Scottish parents and travelled in India as a young woman. She recently discovered diaries and letters belonging to her grandparents, who married in Lahore and lived and worked in the Punjab for nearly thirty years, which served as her inspiration for the India Tea Series. She now divides her time between Northumberland and the Isle of Skye. Find out more about the author and her novels at www.janetmacleodtrotter.com.